PRAISE FOR THE ART OF TAKING SECOND CHANCES

"Full of drama, angst, and multifaceted characters, *The Art of taking Second Chances* by Varsha Chitnis cogently explores first love, heartbreak, and forgiveness against the backdrop of familial obligation with adroit prose."

— INDIEREADER BOOK REVIEW

"Amazing debut novel by a conscientious and smart writer."

— DR. AMANDA LEWIS-NANG'EA

"Highly recommend this delightful romance. The characters are well drawn, with strong interactions."

— DR. SKYLAR BRE'Z

PRAISE FOR THE RULES OF PLAYING WITH FIRE

"Varsha Chitnis doesn't just tell you a story, she takes you on an immersive journey through the lives of her characters. *The Rules of Playing with Fire* is visceral, honest and powerful on every page....Grab your emotional support ice cream and cancel your other plans, Sona and Mihir need your full focus."

— ANNA P., AUTHOR OF LOVE IN WILDES SERIES

"Clever, compelling, and impossible to put down, *The Rules of Playing with Fire* brings the heat—and the heart."

— ALLIE OLEANDER, AUTHOR OF WILLING PREY

THE ART OF TAKING SECOND CHANCES

THE ART OF TAKING SECOND CHANCES

THE DALLAS CONNECTION SERIES
BOOK ONE

VARSHA CHITNIS

Editor: Sherri Shackelford
Cover Artist: Zuchal Rosyidin

To Aadi,
my greatest champion,

and Himika,
who believed from the start that
this is exactly what I'm supposed to do in life.

A NOTE ON CONTENT

Dear Reader,

Thank you for choosing The Art of Taking Second Chances. This book leans heavy on dramatic elements and I want my readers to be aware of the issues included in the book.

First and foremost, the central thread running through this story is infidelity. The two main characters DO NOT cheat on each other, but both leads have to contend with issues of cheating and betrayal.

A secondary character struggles with and succumbs to cancer, and there are related discussions about the loss of a parent. There is also a mention of alcoholism and loss of pregnancy.

Please prioritize your well-being if any of these are triggering factors for you. I have tried to be sensitive to both my characters and my readers, and I hope I have done justice to both.

With much love,
Varsha

TARA

$\mathcal{T}$he idea of a self-made person is absurd, a myth, but that's exactly how people described me.

As I walked from my office to the contemporary art gallery of the museum, the muted click of my heels echoed in the silent hallways. This sound of broken stillness ruffled my already unsettled mind.

No one could be truly self-made. There were forces supporting you, rooting for you. Of course, I had worked hard and tirelessly to get here, but nothing I had accomplished would've been possible without the support of people who loved me, believed in me. Parents, teachers, friends, lovers. A sibling now estranged. Sometimes, it was luck. Sometimes, a staunch mentor.

I saw Dr. Hadden waiting by my painting in the East Wing. The slight smile gracing her ageless face, the fleeting gleam of admiration in her eyes, were high praise if you knew her.

"Thank you," I said, standing beside her. It was all I needed to say.

She patted my shoulder. "This is momentous, Tara. I hope

you're proud of yourself," she said, touching the plaque with my name on it in yet another validation of my achievement.

Very soon, the makeshift cardboard would be replaced with a metal plate, engraved with my name and the title of the work, *Love and Loss*, a title I now regretted. Almost as much as I regretted selling it the way I did: for a covetable five-figure sum, but to the one person who shouldn't own it. The one person who actually knew what I had captured on the bold linen canvas. *Own*, such a crass word for an emotion so beautiful. I sighed silently, clutching my clammy hands into fists.

"Susan will bring him in." I heard Dr. Hadden's voice again and I unclenched my jaw. Susan was her executive assistant. "I hope you don't mind. He insisted on meeting you here."

Of course he had. He loved a grand entrance, and he never had trouble getting everyone and everything to bend to his will.

"Do you know him?" I asked with curiosity.

She nodded. "He's been a generous donor for the past few years. A well-connected man. A decent one, I've heard. His patronage can put you in the right limelight, Tara."

I knew that limelight. I had blinked in its glare once before. I managed a gracious nod, but Dr. Hadden read my face with the same quick, discerning eye that had made her the director of this art museum in Dallas, and of numerous others before that.

"Make good use of this connection." She delivered the curt advice in her heavy voice, at once commanding and kind.

Her short hair was not completely silver yet, but she had always given me a fairy godmother vibe. Not that I would ever dare say it to her face. She'd swat off that moniker with the same haste she would a princess-aspirant. We had our generational differences when it came to ideas of femininity, but she'd had my back since she'd realized, years ago, that I was more than a brown, immigrant, pretty-face.

I was a brown, immigrant pretty-face who was talented, hardworking, and knew her shit. And I had continued to live up to her high standards. On the plus side, her headstrong feminism meant she didn't mind my cursing in her presence, which I often did when I was happy, displeased, or neither. With another reassuring pat on my arm, she walked away, her slender frame carrying all its power in those firm shoulders and that straight back.

I attempted to recreate the pride I had seen on Dr. Hadden's face as I appraised my own work on the wall. My eyes drifted to the plaque. *Tara Kadam*. The name carried some weight in the art world. If you were inclined to believe social media, I boasted of a small but fanatical following. Not as an artist but as a technical expert in oil paintings, consulted by galleries, museums, and private collectors alike. I had temporarily shelved the dream of having my own work displayed in galleries and museums while I authenticated and appraised masterpieces that sold for a fortune.

This job at the Dallas Museum was a rare chance, offering me the best of both worlds. The museum had hired me to appraise a collection of oil paintings bequeathed by the family of a local tycoon and curate a body of art for the new wing they had donated. But the cherry on top of this particular parfait was their invitation to showcase my work at an upcoming exhibition alongside other emerging artists. This break, in no small part, was on account of Dr. Hadden's faith in me and the power she wielded in the art community.

The wooden door behind me closed with a faint thud, and I heard two distinct pairs of footwear treading in my direction. My heart began to race, ramming against my chest cavity. I should've turned, it was only polite, but I stood frozen. It had been thirteen years since I had last seen Sameer. Unlucky thirteen, my friend Sona would've reminded me, but thirteen had nothing on the pain and humiliation Sameer had dealt me. Thirteen needed to up its game if it wanted to compete with this man.

"Here she is!" Susan's exuberant voice eventually compelled me to turn around.

It was easy to focus on her wide smile, but my eyes inevitably moved to Sameer, and the world around me came to a standstill. He was no longer the twenty-year-old I once knew. The boyish face had sculpted into tough, albeit familiar, features. He wore his hair shorter and sported a smart stubble on his strong jaw. He was more handsome now, more confident. In a formal suit but no tie, he looked every bit the rich, powerful man he probably was. The only thing that hadn't changed were his soft brown eyes and the look of open adoration I found in them. My stomach dipped as he beheld me with blatant desire. I took a reluctant step forward and he strode toward me with Susan trotting beside him.

"Mr. Rehani, the inimitable Tara Kadam. I suppose she needs no introduction," Susan gushed.

I smiled at her, grateful that she had pronounced my name with the dental T like I do, and not Tay-Raa but Taa-Raa.

"Tara, this is Mr. Sameer Rehani. He just told me he's your biggest fan."

Despite the professional setting, Susan allowed herself a chuckle. And despite my resentment for Sameer, I couldn't help but respond with a pleased smile.

Quickly dabbing my palm on my pants, I extended it and spotted a tiny smirk at the corners of his mouth.

"We were briefly acquainted," he said as she shook my hand, and an errant spark zipped through my body. "She was just as brilliant then. I've been a fan ever since."

I promptly retracted my hand and scoffed silently. Briefly acquainted? He'd had his dick inside me every night for almost a year. But sure, *briefly acquainted*, let's go with that.

"Good to see you again, *Mr. Rehani*," I said, trying to put distance between us while nerves and anger pumped blood into my ears.

"Nice to see you, *Tara*." He swatted off the distance promptly. His penchant for power games was alive and kicking.

Susan's face had frozen into a smile at our awkward exchange, her golden bob rocking against her perfectly contoured cheeks as she looked between us. The tension in the room was heavy and palpable.

"Well, I'll let you get reacquainted then," she said politely.

"Thank you, Susan." I offered her a sincere smile.

She gave me a graceful nod and swayed out of view on her enviable heels. I could never pull off high heels that elegantly, especially because I wasn't allowed to wear them growing up. I was always tall for my age, and my mother insisted that they were as impractical as they were unnecessary.

I stepped away from Sameer and sat on a bench facing the wall. In the large, vacant hall, currently closed to the public, I heard the echoes of his shoes striding toward me.

"Sweaty palms? I thought you'd be angry, not nervous," he said, sitting beside me. I clenched my jaw, determined not to give him what he sought: another fight. I allowed the silence between us to draw out and turn into a buzz in my ears before I heard him again. "Meeting you like this cost me a lot of money, you know. That painting wasn't cheap."

"It was never up for sale," I responded in a perfectly calm voice, much to my own surprise. "You lured my agent into the deal and blackmailed me into selling it."

"Blackmail! Such a harsh word," he said with a crooked smile. "I'd never known you to be this dramatic."

It was just like him to use an accusatory tone and push my buttons, to elicit my anger so he could justify his flippant behavior. Had he forgotten that well I knew him, too?

"You paid seven times your initial offer until I had no choice but to sell. I call that blackmail," I said, still managing a calm voice.

"Are you actually accusing me of forcing you to sell me the piece you made *for* me?"

"It wasn't *for* you. It's *about* you, but I never intended for you to have it."

"Same difference." He got up and paced the gallery. "And you call it *Love and Loss*?"

There he was again, with his games. But I wasn't inclined to concede. "Creative license," I replied. "I stretched the truth."

"Of course you did." With hands locked behind his back, he resumed his scrutiny of the paintings on the wall, then stopped mid-stride and turned to me. "Why did you insist on meeting me?"

I avoided his gaze. "I always insist on meeting the buyer."

"But this time you knew it was me."

When I glared at him in response, he returned to analyzing the sparse exhibits.

My curiosity was not piqued. "Why did you insist on buying it anonymously?"

"Because if you knew it was me, you wouldn't have agreed to sell," he responded matter-of-factly.

He'd got that right.

Resuming his his leisurely trek, he studied the exhibits as if looking at the displays was more interesting than holding a steady conversation with me.

"You're doing it again," I blurted, stunned that I had said it aloud. His expensive shoe yelped a light squeak on the polished floor as he made that quick turn to me, his eyebrows raised in question. "This bravado," I said, pointing with my index finger. "The squared shoulders, the display of nonchalance. Are you this person again?"

His face darkened, and his jaw clenched, but he quickly composed himself. I had caught him red-handed in the act when no one was supposed to recognize it as a pretense. I could've flashed a triumphant grin, but I wasn't interested in playing his games.

Instead, I returned his smoldering gaze with the ferocity I felt in my heart. But when my eyes inadvertently slipped to the shapely mouth under his short mustache, my lips parted at a memory I thought I had crushed a long time ago. A shiver swept across my body. He stepped over and sat so close, I felt the touch of his fresh, woodsy cologne.

"What do you want?" I demanded with some anger.

My mother always worried that my inability to back out of a confrontation would land me into trouble one day. But until today, it had only helped me survive.

"You wanted to see me. You tell me. What do you want, Tara?"

"I wanted to meet the fool who spent an outlandish amount on an unknown artist."

"You know better than to take me for a fool. I know exactly what you've captured on that canvas."

Synchronously, our eyes drifted to the frame on the wall. He had recognized the peculiar use of light against the soft black palette as the night we walked together to his apartment. The way the darkness gently blended into a rosy hue represented our first time together. He also saw the smudge where my brush had slipped, and instead of rectifying it, I had chosen to amplify it with a flash of crimson on my knife. That was the pain he had caused. I knew he saw it all.

"You *think* you do," I retorted and allowed my annoyance to creep into my voice, but was met with a soft smile.

His détente smile.

"How are you?"

But I wasn't interested in playing. "No." I shook my head and turned away. "You lost the right to ask me that when you sent me that text."

I heard his startled inhale.

"What do you want, Sameer?" I asked again.

"When I saw the painting, I had to see you again. I needed to. *Love and Loss*, that's not just you. That's us." His words came hurtling at me like a swarm of locusts, stinging, biting, bringing devastation in their wake.

My body bubbled with rage, and I jumped to my feet. "It's mine," I said, barely managing a steady tone. "The painting is mine, the pain is mine, the labor is mine. You own it only because I was foolish enough to let it go."

"It's mine now." No smug smiles or power moves accompanied that statement, just a calm, steady gaze into my eyes.

"Well, enjoy it. It'll be delivered after the exhibit closes."

I turned on my heel, but he came around swiftly to block my way.

"Tara—"

"Look, I only agreed to this meeting out of respect for Dr. Hadden. I knew it was you the moment you overrode my refusal to sell. I was inclined to cancel it, but Dr. Hadden thought it would be unprofessional. She isn't aware of our history. I'm here as an artist. You're my patron. Nothing more."

It took a moment, but a nasty sneer came to rest on his face. He pulled himself upright into his tall figure and thrust his left hand into his trouser pocket. "All right, if that's how you want to play it, tell me about this painting I bought, Ms. Kadam."

I wanted to scream with frustration, but I had to concede. He had won this round. He had always been clever, but I felt compelled to add *cunning* to the list. That didn't mean I was giving in easily. "Didn't you just say you knew exactly what it was about?"

"Don't be a smartass, Ms. Kadam. My twenty-five thousand dollars have bought me at least the privilege of having the artist explain her work to me."

Another completely expected googly rubbing his wealth in my face. I was tempted to roll my eyes as I walked away from him and toward the wall.

"*Love and Loss*," I began dispassionately. "Created in the post-impressionist tradition, it flirts with colors and contrast, darkness and light to—"

"I can see that. I've studied art," he interrupted with blatant condescension. "What does it mean to you?"

"Meaning is a private relationship between the viewer and the piece. It's not my place to—"

"Yes, reception theory. I don't need you to recite Stuart Hall to me, Ms. Kadam. What emotions have *you* tried to capture?"

"Sameer..." I hated myself for pleading this way.

"Yes, Ms. Kadam. I'm waiting."

I quickly added *cruel* to my running list and zeroed in on his eyes, searching for a glimmer of compassion. "This painting represents a time when my life changed completely. In an instant, everything good, everything I valued was taken. I lost a dear friend. I almost lost my father. It depicts my grief as much as it captures my joy. This painting is a prayer. It's my way of seeking forgiveness and redemption."

An eerie silence engulfed us as I continued to look into the eyes that I had once loved. Light brown with tiny specks of amber and chocolate. Right now, they reflected the sorrow I felt in my heart.

"I'm sorry about your father." His soft voice broke our trance.

"No, you've lost that right too. You left without a word. Without an explanation. Without a thought of what it would do to me. I meant nothing to you. Disposable, replaceable. Who did you replace me with, Sameer? How quickly?"

He closed the distance between us and held my shoulders. "You think I saw you as replaceable?"

Behind the dilated black pupils, his eyes were brown and familiar.

"I was never enough for you. Not rich enough, not sophisticated enough, not socially acceptable. Was it the realization of my caste status that finally drove it home for you? Or was it my class position? Or was I just a body you used until you were bored?"

His eyes widened with horror. "How can you use such vile words? You know what you meant to me."

"Oh, I'm sorry! See, I'm not as cultured and classy as you. I wouldn't know if this is more vile than ghosting someone you've been with for a year, then responding to their frantic phone calls with a text, *Stop calling. We are D-O-N-E*, all caps."

"I was twenty. I was a fool."

"Yes, I was twenty and a fool for thinking I meant more to you. You've no idea what I've been through."

"You've no idea what I've been through either."

"But you are the one that left. What you did was cruel and unfair, and it hurt."

He regarded me with sorrowful eyes. "And you're still hurting."

"Yes, I'm hurting. And I'm angry and humiliated." I stared defiantly into his face. "But don't let my changed appearance and polished accent fool you. We still remain worlds apart."

"We were worlds apart when we met."

"And yet I let myself fall for you. I regret it every single day," I said and tried to mean it, but my voice gave me away—or maybe it was my eyes, because he smiled into them.

"No, you don't. You still have feelings for me."

I should've denied it, but I clammed up, almost handing him the confirmation rolled up nicely and adorned with a bright, cheery ribbon. I knew I couldn't lie to him. He'd see right through it.

"Then here's something you should know. Not a day has

passed in the last thirteen years when I haven't thought of you. Not one."

He took a small step back from me and looked down at the floor, resting one hand gently on his brows. Lifting his head with a deep inhale, he said, "Thank you for your time, Ms. Kadam. I will see you again, I promise."

He turned around and walked away. But his scent lingered on, holding me in a warm embrace.

I slumped down on the bench behind me. *What had I done?* The man had a propensity to feed off people's weaknesses, and I had just handed him mine on a silver platter. My weakness? *Him.* Now he knew it.

With a deep breath, I pulled myself up and walked back to the beautiful office the museum had assigned me with its huge windows overlooking a lush garden. This time, the rhythmic clicking of my heels didn't annoy me. Instead, it reminded me of the way I lay on his chest, listening to our hearts beating in tandem after we had made love.

SAMEER

I returned home feeling defeated. Dropping my suit jacket on the recliner, I flopped onto the couch as Tara's words played on repeat in my head. The sorrow in her eyes and the pain in her voice filled me with guilt and regret. I had to come to terms with the hurt I had caused and find a way to heal her broken heart.

And I had to get her back—a goal that seemed slated for failure no matter how I considered it. All I wanted was to stay in and drown myself in Tara's memories, but today wasn't a day I could indulge myself. There was never time for that. My father had planned a small gathering at their house, and my presence was required.

Thirteen years ago in India, my father took everything he had built with my mother and burned it to the ground. To save face, I moved us from Delhi to Dallas, where we made a fresh start. Since then, it had become my burden to restore my family's name. I made connections and increased my worth through relentless hard work, trying to rebuild the life we knew.

Success demanded persistence and diligence, and I wasn't

hesitant to put in whatever it took. Determined to leave no stone unturned, I even deferred to my father's whims and ended up on the arm of a beautiful socialite who would make me a household name in Dallas. People called me a savvy businessman and I considered myself a smart, rational decision-maker. But now I felt like I had lost control of the steering wheel.

For years, I had followed Tara's life from afar, reading her blogs, perusing her website, tracing her move from Baroda to the U.S., where she got her master's degree, to Rome for another master's, and back to the East Coast, where she had set up her career. But I never imagined she had held on to us. Now that I knew, I found myself grappling with a strange feeling. Something I hadn't encountered in a long time. For the first time in thirteen years, I felt happy. I felt like myself.

After a quick shower, I stood before my spacious wardrobe, trying to figure out what to wear. If I showed up in casual clothing or chose the wrong jacket, I'd never hear the end of it. After all, appearances were everything. I had learned early on how to sink beneath the skin of a chameleon, knowing when and how to change my colors to blend in. How to adapt to any situation, to speak effectively across the lines. How to appear disarming before launching that final, deadly attack.

Adaptation was *the* key to survival in the animal kingdom. If you failed to adapt and change, you perished. You became the prey. It wasn't by sheer luck that I had acquired three firms over the last six years. Tough decisions required shrewdness and dispassion. My friend Mihir had drilled both traits into me over the years, along with a certain degree of cruelty. I wasn't quite the ruthless bastard he was, but I was aggressive enough to lead the fourth largest financial conglomerate in the Southwest.

My wedding to my girlfriend Aarti was all that stood between me and becoming the most powerful South Asian in the region.

Only now, life had shoved a giant Tara-shaped wrench into the well-oiled machinery I had crafted over the last decade.

The powder blue shirt I chose paired perfectly with the textured navy and grey blazer and my favorite tan brogues. I styled my hair with the meticulousness I had acquired from Mihir. Finally, I spritzed the very expensive cologne that Aarti had gifted me last week. The notes of patchouli didn't meld with my skin or flatter my personality, but she wanted me to try it anyway. It had only cost a few hundred bucks, after all. She'd asked me to discard it if I didn't like it. After throwing a change of clothes into my small holdall, I pulled out of the garage and merged into the Friday night traffic.

When we moved to the U.S., I had made it clear I wouldn't live under the same roof as my father. It was the only way I could interact with him again. I needed to breathe without his shadow bogging me down. It was bad enough the specter of our past hovered over me every moment, I could do with a little distance from him.

Mom was a different story. I missed having her around, but she refused to live apart from her husband. It wasn't the proper thing to do, she said. My buying a place in uptown Dallas, instead of the lush green suburb where they lived was part rebellion, part spite. I didn't want to be within driving distance of my father. I wanted it to be an effort for me to visit them and for them to see me. It worked. Dad despised city traffic and seldom came over.

Pulling off the highway, I turned and drove to an affluent neighborhood, where well-groomed topiaries ran along perfectly manicured lawns. I parked my humble Mercedes at the tail end of a line of luxury cars in their driveway, each screaming for attention, vying for style and status. I noted a couple of Teslas in the mix, although in certain circles, the Tesla was seen as a choice of the nouveau riche. It was the difference between toting an LV bag and carrying a discrete Hermès, Aarti had explained. Although her brand-new Audi R8 wasn't intended as a snub at the electric car, she just loved her Audis. These social events were occasions to project one's wealth, to establish one's status in the hierarchy, and my simple car notwithstanding, I was about to land at the top of the food chain.

"Hi Durgaben," I said fondly and reverently to my parents' housekeeper when she answered the door.

A sprightly, middle-aged woman, she sported an easy, playful smile that pulled you in with love and kindness. And she had a personality to match. Durgaben had been with my parents since we moved here and meticulously managed their massive house.

"Hello," she said in her heavy accent. "They are in the backyard. Everyone is waiting for you."

"How bad is he?"

She shrugged. "Just regular annoyed." We shared a short, hearty chuckle before she patted my arm. "Go now. Your pretty girlfriend is waiting."

Out of habit, I squared my shoulders before stepping over the threshold into the sprawling backyard. The place was festooned with lights that stayed up all year to bring cheer to soulless lives. About ten families were scattered in groups. Under the pergola, on a set of plush outdoor sofas, sat the women, chatting and laughing in their rich clothes and subtle, expensive jewelry.

Their eyes scanned me as I walked in. I responded with a cordial wave and smiled at Mom. The younger kids were probably somewhere in the house, busy on their devices. The older ones had gathered around the outdoor bar, from which short bouts of laughter erupted periodically. Mihir was perched on a barstool, silently observing the youthful conversations around him.

I walked up and whispered, "I need to talk to you."

He responded with his signature single nod and trademark stoic face, then sipped the scotch in his hand.

My father held court at his usual spot on the woven sectional.

He loved the attention. He needed it, and he had no trouble getting it. Just like me. Tonight he sported a laidback blazer that was easily more expensive than anything anyone around him was wearing. His thick mane, not quite gray yet, lied about his age. A handsome face concealed the cold blood running through his veins. Only his eyes gave away his viciousness, but he knew how to mask them too. He had a terrifying combination of charm and intimidation that pulled you in effortlessly and held you in awe, despite him. Only Mom knew how to peel away that mask, but he had managed to fool her too that one time.

"Here he is now." The deliberately loud voice was my father's passive-aggressive way of announcing I was late. With a grand hand gesture, he beckoned me as if I was a prince being shown off to commoners. "Come, come, my son."

"Hello," I said to his companions just as Aarti glided toward me.

"Hey," I said to her, my voice soft and perfectly measured for the occasion.

"Hey yourself," she replied as she hugged me and whispered, "I missed you."

"Sorry. Work, you know."

"As always," she chided with a smile, then inhaled me. "You're wearing the cologne I got you."

"I knew you'd notice if I didn't."

"That's true," she said with a playful hand on my chest. "You smell amazing. Do you like it?"

"I like it if you do." That earned me her brilliant smile.

"Come here, you two." I heard my father again. "Sit with us. You have all night to mingle. Why, Bhatia sahab, isn't that right?" he said, roping Aarti's father into the conversation.

My insides cringed at his pathetic attempt to tease us.

But Mr. Bhatia smiled. "Yes, how's work, Sameer?"

"Hectic."

He laughed. "That means it's going well."

Reluctantly, I followed Aarti, who had already settled herself between our fathers. I stole a glance at Mom. If she could've rolled her eyes amid company, she would've. We shared a knowing glance before I took a seat beside Aarti.

Aarti, beautiful and delicate, was my girlfriend via an arranged relationship. She was an heiress to her father's real estate empire, so the underlying instruction to me was *make it work*. Not that there was anything wrong with her. She fell far from the stereotype of the vacuous heiress. Intelligent, accomplished, and erudite, she single-handedly managed her father's expansive businesses. She was also slender, gorgeous, and always elegantly dressed.

This evening, she looked radiant in a salwar-kurta. The light pink and gold of the ankle-length kurta brought out the brown in her eyes. Her hair was styled into effortless, flowing curls. Her makeup was flawless, complete with false eyelashes, pink-hued lips, and matching nails. She was perfect.

But she wasn't Tara.

My stomach twisted in a knot, as if by admiring my girlfriend, I had somehow strayed. I had lost the feeling in my limbs when I saw Tara that evening. She was always attractive, but she had grown into a beautiful woman, her bronze skin still perfectly smooth and lustrous. She had never used makeup when I knew her in college, not even lip gloss. Now her makeup was immaculate and flattering. Thin liner and light mascara amplified her big, almond eyes without adding drama. The hair that was once thick, black, and wrapped around my hand most nights was now a glossy, deep brown. The carefully styled waves fell straight down her back, drawing attention to her shapely waist. Her slender form had filled into gorgeous curves. A scar above her left eye, a remnant of a childhood injury, cut into a perfectly shaped brow.

Like the dark spot on the moon, the scar defined her. It made her special, more beautiful. I had touched it, kissed it; she had let me.

Her diction had evolved from routinely mispronouncing English words to a suitably upper-class British. Although she effortlessly slipped into a discernible American accent in her Rs. But what caught my eye that evening were her full lips, colored in a reddish shade of brown. Seductive but not vulgar. Powerful but playful. It screamed artist. It screamed Tara. Tara...

"...so what do you think?" Aarti's hand on my thigh yanked me away from Tara.

I gaped at her. "I...I'm sorry. I was someplace else."

"He's always preoccupied. Even in his off time." Her sweet criticism was followed by an exaggerated shake of the head, but she was cute enough to get away with a gesture so frivolous.

Pulling myself upright, I took her hand and smiled. "Sorry, tell me again?"

"I was saying, we should go away for a week or two, somewhere fun. Uncle suggests the Italian coast. Dad says Tahiti or Bora Bora. What do you think?"

My chest constricted. I couldn't leave now, not with Tara in Dallas. I couldn't afford to miss a single day of being in the same city as her.

"What's wrong?" Aarti asked. "Your hands are cold."

I faked a smile. "Nothing, I've had a really long day."

"You need to unwind. You work too hard," my father interjected, and every cell in my body reacted with rage.

"Please excuse me a moment."

I stepped away to pour myself a drink. Two shots of whisky did little to calm my jumpy nerves. I caught Mihir eyeing me with concern as I swigged another gulp, but my mouth was still dry, and the pit of my stomach felt hollow. I couldn't get Tara off my mind. She was so close, within reach.

I poured more whisky in a glass, dropped in two ice cubes, and rejoined Aarti. Appearances were everything.

I took her hand and smiled at her father before turning to her. "A vacation is a great idea, but the crowds are brutal this time of year. Let's wait a bit. That way, I'll be more relaxed at work too." I kissed her hand.

It was a lie, but I was an expert liar now. It had become second nature, as if it would somehow shield me from pain and hurt.

"That reminds me." My father dropped his voice. "You should start thinking seriously about a date for your engagement. What you think, Bhatia sahab?"

"Oh, yes, absolutely. The sooner we formalize this relationship, the better."

Aarti gave me a shy smile, and I gulped down my drink.

"Of course," I said, unflinching at another lie. "We'll talk about it?"

She nodded and squeezed my hand.

The hot, humid day had become a cool, pleasant Dallas night, and yet, I couldn't breathe.

It was past midnight when I kissed Aarti goodbye and watched her car roar out of the driveway. When I returned inside, I found my father lounging in the living room with a drink in his hand. He had already had quite a few. Mom sat across from him on the couch, but they might as well have been on different continents.

"I'll head home now," I announced, retrieving the car keys from my pocket.

"Don't even think about it," Mom warned. "You're drunk, and you're not going anywhere. Durga has made up your room."

I wasn't drunk, but I didn't argue. Sharing Saturday morning breakfast with Mom used to be the highlight of my weekends. Usually, she made my favorite, paneer paratha. I dropped down beside her and sank into the couch.

"It was a good party," my father began softly. When neither of us responded, he jabbed a finger at me. "I don't need to remind you how important this relationship with the Bhatias is for us." I continued to ignore him. "You better set a date soon. That girl likes you."

He scoffed in disbelief at the thought and swilled his drink. This time I was ready with a scowl, but Mom placed her hand on my clenched fist. *Let it go.*

"And you know what's at stake here. With their money in our family, no one in the coming seven generations will need to work." He beamed as he delivered the cliché in Hindi. "And she likes you," he repeated as if it were the most unbelievable thing in the world. "I did well. If it wasn't for my charm and connections, you two wouldn't be together. You have much to thank me for, boy."

"Go to bed, Pavan," Mom said sharply before I could respond.

He looked at her, stood up, and hauled himself toward the bedroom.

"What's wrong?" she asked when we were alone.

"Nothing."

"Is it about the engagement?"

"I don't love her, Ma."

I undid the top button on my shirt in an effort to ease the stiffness in my chest. If only it were that easy.

She patted my hand. "I won't push you into doing anything you don't want to." I looked at her. "But make sure you know what you want. Such relationships don't come by every day. Aarti is smart and determined. And she loves you. I hate myself for thinking like your father, but he's right. You'll be taken care of for life."

"Is that all there is to life?"

She sank onto the couch. We reclined side by side as I reflected on the events that had brought us here.

I dropped my face to hers. "How does Dad still have the nerve after everything he did?"

She shook her head and roused herself. "Well, I'm off to bed." But two steps out, she stopped and put her hand on my shoulder. "Beta, whatever you decide, make sure you're faithful to her." Then she walked away, tall and proud, the pallu of her beautiful saree trailing behind her.

TARA

A month ago, I was excited about the opportunity. Now I was exhausted, and it had only been two weeks. With a dramatic sigh, I crashed onto the couch in my rented, furnished uptown apartment and pulled out my cell phone to call Sona.

Sona Thomas, my closest friend, was a geographer by training and an Assistant Professor of Feminist Studies at a college in Brooklyn. And that told you everything you needed to know about her. Brilliant, wise, street-smart, with a generous side of sass, she was gifted with the patience and impulse control that I lacked.

We shared the kind of bond that women without sisters tend to form, but we had more in common than the mere absence of a female sibling. We shared the same mother tongue, Marathi, although, on account of her father, Sona was also fluent in Malayalam. We had both migrated from Western India, having grown up in the neighboring states of Gujarat and Maharashtra. With so many overlaps in food, language, and culture, we could put a Venn diagram to shame.

So it was a no-brainer that we connected. But it was our

uncanny ability to understand and read each other that had brought us closer over the past five years.

"Hey." Her sweet voice jingled over the phone. "How's it going there?"

"Okay, considering. I miss home."

"Already?"

"Don't ask."

"Was it him?"

"I'll tell you. But first, how's Aai? I called her twice today. She didn't answer and hasn't called me back. Just wanted to check with you before I begin to panic."

Her amused laughter spilled over the phone. "Your mom is fine. I stopped by to see her on my way back from campus. She didn't want to bother you at work, so my guess is she'll be calling you later tonight."

"Thank goodness!"

"Oh, and your knight in shining armor was there too." That would be my boyfriend, Sujit. "He'd also come to check on her."

"Stop calling him that. It makes me sound like a damsel in distress." I slid down the couch.

"As if," she said with a snort. "Tell me, was it Sameer who bought the painting?"

"Yup, and I saw him. In the flesh."

"Hmm, so can I start bashing him now, so you feel better?"

I laughed. "We're way past that age, Sona."

"Never. We'll bash our exes when we're in our nineties and in a retirement home together."

I laughed again, grateful for her endearing self.

"What did he say?"

"A lot of things, but it's what I said that bothers me. Or rather what I didn't say."

I recapped the encounter for her.

"Tara?" she asked in her gentle, beautiful voice. "Do you

really have feelings for him? I mean, I know you do, but they're in the abstract, right? You're in love with a certain image of Sameer, your first boyfriend, who knew you better than anyone. It's a memory you've built and carried through your life. We all do that. But that's not the real Sameer, is it?"

"Then why couldn't I say it to him, Sona? Why couldn't I tell him to his face that he meant nothing to me anymore?"

"Because you have a history, but it's time to move on. You have a solid relationship with Sujit. Don't waste your time and energy chasing an imaginary one. You gave me the same advice once, remember?"

"I know, I know!" I cried. "It's just that being so close to him again stirred up a lot of buried emotions, but Sameer's in the past. Plus, Sujit has helped me so much with Aai's situation. I can never be ungrateful to him."

"Hey," Sona said. "I know you feel obligated to Sujit for his help. But I hope that's not the only thread binding you to him. Is it?"

"No! I didn't mean it that way. I care about him the way he does about me."

Thankfully, my phone buzzed in my hand.

"Aai's calling, Sona. Talk to you later?"

"Sure, but we'll talk about this."

"I promise," I said and ended the call.

"Hi, Aai, I called. Twice," I teased my mother in Marathi.

"Aga, I was at yoga class, then Shaila called me over for tea. How are you?"

"I'm okay. Tired. Had a long day at work."

"Do you have any home-cooked food, or are you going out to eat?"

I smiled. "I have some leftovers. How are you doing? Are you bored yet?"

"I get bored sometimes, but I go for a walk. It's getting hotter now. Sujit came over today. He's such a kind boy."

Sujit was my age, but anyone my age was a child in her eyes.

"Yes, Sona told me. I just talked to her."

"She came over too. I'm so glad you have such good people in your life."

"Yes, Aai, they're both gems. But it's a big city. Don't trust everyone around you, okay? I'm worried about leaving you alone there. You should've come here with me. Maybe you would've made new friends here."

"I'll come for a visit when you've settled in. But this is a good routine for me. I have my phone, and I don't travel too far from the apartment."

"Okay. I worry about you, that's all."

"Don't worry. Get your work done quickly and come back. It does get lonely without you."

"I know. There's no one to bug you all the time," I teased, visualizing a warm smile on her gentle face. "Okay, I'll hang up now. I'll eat something then call Sujit."

"Bara," she said and disconnected.

Aai had refused to move from Brooklyn to Dallas, to relocate again. Despite my worry for her living on her own, I had to applaud her grit and feel grateful that she could express herself freely now. She didn't have many chances to do that in the past.

In our rather conservative community in a small town on the outskirts of Baroda in western India, women were seen as less worthy than men. But my father had dreamed of raising an educated, independent daughter.

"Be famous. Be powerful. Don't live and die in obscurity," he'd tell me.

People ridiculed him for sending me to an English school alongside my brother. Daughters are strangers, they said. Daughters get married and become part of another family, so give them just enough education to land them a good husband. Any more, and it was money down the drain, an investment that would never pay off. But my father defied all norms and expectations to give me everything he couldn't afford. An ardent supporter, a true champion, he stretched himself thin trying to give me all the right opportunities. He raised me to be strong-willed, self-reliant, and outspoken, but didn't extend the same rights to his wife. He expected her unquestioned obedience while rejoicing in all the ways that I challenged him.

It wasn't that Aai couldn't speak to him or contradict him. But there were things she could talk about and things she couldn't. They often bickered about the right amount of money to gift a certain relative or how to budget the household, but always within the privacy of the home and never in front of a non-family member. The rising prices of meat and vegetables, inching steadily toward unaffordability, were a recurring theme in our home, but the discussions never touched the sacred parameters of politics or economics. Women didn't understand these things. Well, women of Aai's generation didn't, my father held. And if they did, they should keep their opinions to themselves. Such was the paradox of a man who fought against his family and his community to hold all doors open for his daughter.

But Aai had always been smart and industrious, and within two months of being in the U.S., she had become unprecedentedly independent. When she first arrived, she felt stifled by her tenuous grasp of English. But I took her everywhere, waiting patiently while she spoke in her broken language, until she found her confidence. She realized that despite the erroneous tenses and misplaced pronouns, most people understood her if they made an effort. Those who had no patience for her, she ignored. I loved her for that.

Last month, before I left Brooklyn, Sona helped me persuade her to join us at the local salon. Its owner, a fellow Indian immigrant, had mastered the secret art of coaxing recalcitrant women of my mother's age to agree to eyebrow threading and a facial massage. Aai had never looked better, and I'd felt a deep sense of contentment. I was finally at a place where I didn't need to worry about her.

I reheated the previous night's leftovers for a light dinner. A sad situation for a Friday evening, but I didn't have the energy or the motivation to explore the city solo. Then there was the other thing consuming my thoughts. Seeing Sameer again had muddled my head and confused my heart in ways I had not anticipated.

To stop myself from dwelling on the past, I placed a video call to Sujit. It rang for a while before he answered with dripping hair.

"Hey!" That soft voice, those kind eyes, brought me an instant sense of calm. Seeing Sujit felt like home. With Sameer, it was always heat and agitation. All fire and brimstone.

"Hi there. Are you working out? You look all hot and sweaty," I said.

"No, just got out of the shower. I'm wet, not sweaty."

"So... you're naked?"

"Yes, very naked and very wet." When he smiled, his deep dimples set off the laugh lines around his eyes. He was a shy, bashful man, and I never missed a chance to tease him about it.

"Show me your chest." He blushed, then moved the phone away from his body to show me his wet, naked torso.

"Mmm." I summoned the deep, seductive voice I rarely used. "Wish I was there."

"Okay, you have to stop. I'm already getting a little too worked up."

"Can you show me how much?"

"No, I'll save myself the embarrassment."

I laughed but didn't yield. "I could've helped you out, you know. Maybe with a warm oral compress?"

"Damn! You know you're killing me, right?" he said, wiping his hair.

"Yes," I said, then softly added, "I miss you."

"Me too." He smiled. "Especially on the weekends. I feel lost without you here."

"You know what I miss the most? It's your smell."

He laughed. "That's a weird thing to miss."

"No, it's the most natural thing. We're animals, first and foremost."

I closed my eyes and inhaled deeply to recall his scent. A heady, woodsy fragrance filled my head, and my heart rumbled at a recent memory. Sameer's full lips, the way he looked right through me and saw everything. My face turned warm, and my pulse quickened. I gasped and opened my eyes, my heart hammering as if I had been caught cheating.

"Well, go put on some clothes, then call me," I said, suddenly anxious to get off the call.

"Actually, I'm going out to dinner. Talk to you tomorrow?"

"Tsk-tsk. I've been gone only two weeks, and you're already going out on dates."

"No, darling, it's just a business dinner. We'll be talking about the new software."

"That's boring. Okay, stay safe, and get back home at a decent time."

"Yes, ma'am." Then he gave me a warm smile and added, "I miss you so much. Wish I could touch you right now."

"Me too. Call me when you're up tomorrow. I love you," I said.

He frowned. "Did you just say what I heard you say?"

I sat upright in an attempt to defy the gravity of my words. "No."

A few months ago, on a playful evening, I went on a rant about how stupid the idea of romantic love was. I had ridiculed the importance assigned to the phrase "I love you" in our shared cultural imaginary. Desire is more amorphous, more fluid than the edifice of "I love you" suggested, I had argued.

"It is rebellious, and transgressive, and dangerous. So, don't ever expect me to say BS like *I love you*," I had scoffed.

Only now, my words had come back to bite me in the rear.

Sujit threw his head back in his joyful, infectious laugh, his sculpted torso shaking with delight. "I could've never pried those words out of you. Looks like distance is doing wonders for our relationship."

"You'd want to believe that, wouldn't you?"

"Oh, absolutely! You finally went for that BS," he said, still laughing. "Can't wait to hear it again."

"*Again* ain't happening. Ever again," I teased, trying hard not to break into laughter myself.

When his laugh simmered to a smile, he said, "Well, here's something that might ease your angst. I love you too, Ms. Tara Kadam. Only I had been bullied into never saying it."

This time I laughed. "Alright, get off the phone now, or you're going to be late for your *date*," I teased.

"Talk soon, darling. Have a wonderful evening. Love you, for real," he said with a wink before hanging up.

I shook my head with a smile, then lolled on the couch, but a faint thought made me sit right back up. "I love you, Sameer," it whispered like a fool.

Desire was rebellious, alright!

TARA

*S*ameer Rehani was the bane of my life. My first crush, my first boyfriend, and the one who left me with a broken heart. Back then, it wasn't difficult to be smitten with him. He was the boy every college girl dreamed of: tall, confident, handsome. A sharp nose under bright, intelligent eyes. A firm jaw that didn't have to work too hard to support his cocky smile. For, behind the charisma that made him the most desired male on our college campus, bred the arrogance that comes with a lot of money.

He believed the world revolved around him, and it did. That was the power of wealth. A power I could never possess because I could never afford it. We ended up as friends only because his cousin Amar was my friend. Otherwise, high-flying rich boys like Sameer didn't make friends with small-town girls like me. And this small-town girl had much to lose if she didn't keep her head in the game and her vagina tucked tight in her pants.

Some people know their calling from a very young age. I wasn't one of them. Like all bright kids around me, my future path was predetermined. I'd be an engineer, my father had declared, a great one. The first female engineer in our family, one of the very few in our community. I was destined to be a trailblazer. This responsibility, I took very seriously. While I was expected to fulfill my duties, helping Aai cook and clean, I consistently ranked among the top three in my class throughout grade school.

But my earliest fond memory was of my brother teaching me how to use oil paint on canvas. It was a picture of the elephant-headed god, Ganapati. Dada was an art prodigy, proficient in every medium he touched. He could sculpt, mold, paint, and sketch with equal expertise and passion. As a child, he used to help our neighbor build massive statues for the Ganapati festival.

I grew up borrowing his colored pencils and crayons. I wasn't a serious artist. I dabbled, so I didn't get any of my own. We didn't have money for frivolities like individual colors and drawing instruments, but Baba always spared a little for him. Even a cynic could see how good he was. And I imitated him. In particular, I loved the smell of oil paint, the tactility, and how different consistencies and strokes could represent different emotions on a blank canvas. But Dada was the artist. I was a mimic.

That afternoon was the first time Dada had trusted me with his oil paints. It was a rite-of-passage ritual for the little artist in me. With laser focus, I followed his instructions while our mother yelled from the kitchen for me to drink my warm milk. It remained untouched on the table before me, tepid, just the way I liked it. It would be cold and undrinkable, Aai reminded me rather loudly, even though that had never been an issue for me.

When she finally emerged from the kitchen, with the edge of her saree, her padar, tucked in at the waist in war pose, she was an inch away from going goddess Kali on me. Dada, a teenager himself, put his hand out in a shocking display of courage and disobedience, fending her off while I finished my work. Aai was reasonably stumped and gaped at us with wide eyes, which softened quickly when she looked at the makeshift easel before me. What she saw on the canvas, what Dada had stopped her from interrupting, was clear to both. I had talent.

Three years—that was the age gap between Dada and me, just like it was with everyone else around us, thanks to the family planning policies of a young India battling population growth. *Hum do, humare do* was the motto: *The two of us* (a heterosexual couple), *with the two of ours*. Planned at least three years apart for the benefit of the mother's health. My parents had two children, exactly three years and four months apart: Aditya and Tara, Sun and Star. Both destined to shine in our own light. Except only one of us did.

Like Dada, I had done well on my twelfth exams, enough to get into the College of Technology and Engineering at the M.S. University of Baroda. Enough to be eligible to choose any branch except computers, which had moved to the top of the hierarchy in the last few years. I opted for the next rung, electrical. But the day I returned with the admissions paperwork secure in my hand, I couldn't sleep. That night, when Aai came to my room before bed, she caught me weeping silently.

"What's wrong?" she asked, caressing my thick, wavy hair.

"I don't know why I'm crying, Aai."

"Did something happen? Did someone touch you inappropriately?" she asked, her back ramrod straight in protective-mother mode.

"No, nothing happened. I was so happy today. I'm going to turn Baba's dream into a reality. I'll be the first female engineer in our family." I burst into inconsolable tears.

Aai moved in and wiped my eyes with her saree. "Do you remember Vinu Mavshi?"

I looked up at her through my tears. Aunt Vinu was her cousin. "When Vinu got married, I was twelve. I remember feeling thrilled that I would get to wear new clothes and put mehndi on my hands. But when we visited to congratulate her, she looked sad. I thought that's how it was supposed to be. She'd be leaving her parents' home soon. My mother asked my sisters and me to stay over to cheer her up. That night, while my older sisters tried to console her, she wept like I hadn't seen anyone weep before. She wept the whole night and all the way through the wedding day several months later. When I look back now, I know why. She knew she was marrying the wrong man. She's never been happy. They have nothing in common, and some days he doesn't even talk to her. She feeds him and takes care of the house, but she has no love. That's her life. Back then, we didn't have much choice. Families decided the match for you."

"Why are you telling me this, Aai?"

"She wept because her subconscious was warning her against a bad decision, and now she's miserable. I don't want you to be wedded to something that will make you miserable, Tara. What's your subconscious telling you that you're not heeding?"

I bawled at her words, like I had just lost a loved one.

"What do you see yourself doing in a few years? If I ask you who you are at your core, what will you answer me, Rani?" Rani was her pet name for me. Queen.

"I'm an artist." It was the first time I had acknowledged it, and in an instant, a weight had lifted off my chest. In that single breath, I felt like all the pieces of my life had snapped into place. "But art is Dada's thing. He's the artist, not me!"

"Yet we made the same mistake with Aditya. But we should learn from our mistakes, shouldn't we? You get to be who you want to be, my rani, because I didn't."

I gasped as she smiled.

That was the day my life changed. Everything good in my life came because I owned my identity as an artist that night.

But when Baba learned about this little development the next morning, he refused to pay for my college because art wasn't what

I was supposed to do with my life. I was throwing my life away on a hobby after everything he had done for us. Behind closed doors, my parents fought. It was the first and only time I heard Aai raise her voice against Baba. When he stormed out of the room, I saw Aai's smiling face and assumed she had managed to placate him and to convince him to pay if I got in.

And I did get into that coveted program with a partial scholarship. The rest, Baba paid, I assumed. Until my accidental discovery that it was Aai who sold her jewelry to pay for my college. I had once asked to borrow her necklace to wear to a friend's engagement party. Her first excuse, that she couldn't find it, quickly turned into a feeble explanation that she had lent it to her youngest sister.

But one keen look at her told me that the usual gold chain around her neck and a set of her solid gold bangles were also missing. Realization struck like a lightning bolt loaded with guilt and shame. I was the reason Aai had to give up her inheritance. But she was a proud woman, so I never mentioned it again and resolved to pick up the rest of my expenses by tutoring kids. Taking my eyes off the target, even for a moment, would mean reducing my parents' sacrifices to dust.

That's how Amar and I became friends. I knew him from a couple of courses we had in common during the first semester. When I put the word out that I was looking for tutoring jobs, he referred me to the people he knew in the city. And he *really* knew people. Within a matter of one week, I had five jobs teaching art and elementary math to kids with families that didn't haggle over my fees. They even offered to pay extra for additional coaching during examinations. At the end of the first month, with my wallet fat with cash, I took Amar out to dinner to say thank you. His kindness, along with the gentleness of his soul, took me by surprise, and I ended up sharing my story. Then, he peered deeply into my eyes and shared his deepest secret, one that he hadn't told anyone yet. Some friendships are tethered by the soul, and ours was one of them.

Amar was a good-looking boy, tall and lanky with a head full of bouncing curls. He came from a very rich family but didn't brag about it. That cast him as weird and invisible. I was a lower-middle class girl who didn't speak correct English. Whoever said institutions of higher education were meant to level the playing field had clearly missed sending the memo to caste and class elitists and Anglophiles. They judged me by the color of my skin, laughed at my pronunciation, and often asked in coded language if I had gotten in on the "quota" reserved for disadvantaged castes and classes. Because with my English, I couldn't have been talented enough to get in on my own merit.

For the most part, I refused to let the bigotry and the putdowns rile me. My maternal grandfather had been an anti-caste activist in his village, and I had been brought up with his values. I had learned to deal with the everyday microaggressions, but when I learned that my friend's roommate at our hostel changed her sheets and washed her clothing if I accidentally touched it, the specter of untouchability rose like an all-consuming monster. I had marched into her room and lectured her on casteist discrimination and the provisions of the Indian Constitution that banned the practice of untouchability, as if irrational beliefs about human inequality could be overcome through logic and reasoning. But their judgment brought us closer—Amar, me, and four other friends who had been similarly marked for our deviation from perceived normalcy.

Sameer's arrival on the scene a year later drastically changed these dynamics. For one, our group of pariahs was suddenly thrust into the spotlight, with the gorgeous Sameer now hanging out with us. Except for the good looks they shared, Sameer was the polar opposite of Amar. Where Amar was quiet, dignified, and talented, Sameer was flamboyant, cocky, and barely bothered to attend his classes. Where Amar accessed his wealth with humility and grace, Sameer was happy to flash it around. Sameer spent his time chasing women and trouble. Fair maidens from across the university thronged to the fine arts campus to catch a glimpse of the rich, handsome, bad boy from Delhi. For his turn, Sameer, who thrived on attention, encouraged the cortege. It completely wrecked whatever little social life we enjoyed.

The six of us, including Amar, tried our best to avoid him. We'd slip away to the library for our study group or go to the movies on the sly, then make an excuse that it was a spur-of-the-moment decision. One evening, we planned a cookout at Amar's apartment and "forgot" to inform Sameer. When he finally caught a whiff of our evasive behavior, he took us to task one evening on the steps of our main building.

"Why are you all avoiding me?" he'd asked haughtily.

Instinctively, everyone looked at me, as if it were my de facto job to bell the cat.

"Well, Tara?" he demanded.

"Why me?"

"Everyone's looking at you, so apparently you're the one who has something to say. Say it," he demanded with hands on his hips, an impatient tap in his foot.

"Rehani," I began patiently. "You're too popular. We can't study or hang out without the spectacle of women draped over you."

There were gasps, followed by a sudden stillness as everyone froze in place. I snarled at them for their betrayal while Sameer gaped at me in disbelief.

"What do you mean?"

"Well, you can make other friends, no? You don't have to be stuck with us just because your cousin is our friend."

Now Sameer glowered at Amar. "Brutus."

Amar jumped up. "I'm leaving. Let me know how it goes," he

said and walked into the building, his curls catching up with the rhythm of his footsteps.

I let out a theatrical sigh and turned to Sameer. "See, now you've upset Amar," I said, attempting to mimic his antics.

"Cut it out," he replied pointedly, then sat down beside me while the rest of my friends took the chance to disperse quickly and quietly.

As a group of students walked toward the building, Sameer scooted closer to give them way. His arms and thighs slid against mine, his pleasant rich-guy scent taking over me brazenly and without warning. At the next inhale, I became aware of my body. My nipples puckered stiff, and my thighs clenched tight to stop the tingling feeling between them. But as my eyes drew to my feet, I saw my brown skin against his glowing light color, my pedestrian clothing, discordant against his expensive faded jeans and name-brand sneakers. My untamed toes retracted into my slingback sandals, bought not at a high-end store or even at a mall but at the bustling city market of Mangal Bazar.

I should've walked away that second, but my body had other ideas. I was enjoying the touch of his skin, basking in the titillating sensation of his thigh against mine.

When I finally found the conviction to move, he gripped my wrist and stood up with me. A shiver ran through my body as I ended up looking into his face, gazing into his eyes. I quickly sat back down. He followed suit, this time sparing a few inches between us.

"You don't know how difficult this is for me," he began. "But... I'm sorry."

"Difficult?" I frowned. "Have you never apologized to anyone before?"

"Never sincerely." He looked at me, and I hastily took my eyes off his glamorous face.

"We didn't mean to exclude you." I twisted the tassel on my

cotton bag between my fingers. "It's alright to have your exciting life, but you can conduct your extracurriculars when you're not with us, yes? We can't spend any quality time as a group because your giggly friends are everywhere, hanging on your every word, falling all over you." I rolled my eyes.

"Umm, okay?"

"And you hog all the attention in the group. You hijack every conversation. Can you at least try and listen to what the others have to say?"

He gawked at me, his magnificent eyes wide with disbelief.

"What?" I asked at his expression of incredulity.

"No one has ever spoken to me this way."

"Like what, tell you the truth?" I countered with a defiant frown.

"Something like that. No one has ever called me out on trying to hog all the attention."

"Well, do you?"

"Of course I do!" he replied. "That's who I am. That's how I've always been."

I shrugged. "Friendships are a give and take. How can you get attention—willing attention—if you don't give anyone yours? Why would we be interested in your stories if you have no patience for ours?"

"Are you saying you don't enjoy my tales of valor?" He let his skin sink into mine in a flirty nudge.

"You're deflecting, Rehani." I slipped into Hindi, looking straight into his eyes, and he turned serious. He lifted his shoulders and straightened his back. "I know how you feel about Amar. I can see you're fond of him, you respect him. But I also see the jealousy in your eyes. In your behavior. Whenever Amar is in the spotlight, at the center of any conversation, you redirect it to yourself. You don't need to do that."

He swiftly shifted away, and I felt the heat explode from his body. "Who do you think you are to speak to me this way?"

I could have detonated, blasting him with words he'd never forget. But this was bigger than my ego. This was about the well-being of my friend, and the things I knew about him that Sameer didn't. Things that could leave emotional scars.

"Amar is my friend. You can walk away if you want. But I'll say what I need to."

He didn't walk away. Although his body stiffened beside mine, he chose to stay.

"Don't you think it's odd that everyone wants to be your friend, yet you hang out with possibly the lowest-status group on campus, just because Amar is with us? Sometimes you hurt him and don't even realize it. You're a smart guy. You don't need to be envious of him. You don't have to feel like you're living under his shadow and try to outdo him. You can be your own man."

That struck a raw nerve, because he jumped up and growled at me like a wounded tiger. "You might think you're the smartest person around, but you aren't. Stay out of my life and my relationships. Don't mess with things you can't handle, girl," he hissed at me through clenched teeth and stormed off.

That was alright. I was a big girl, and unfortunately such infantilizing language wasn't the worst thing I had heard.

But he returned in a few seconds, raked a hand through his hair, and plopped down beside me. "Shit, I'm sorry."

I kept my gaze off him because I wasn't sure what I would read in those eyes.

"I mean it, Tara. I'm sorry for saying that. I have trouble controlling the nasty from slipping out, but I'm sincere about this apology too."

I nodded and glanced at him before promptly returning my eyes to my feet.

"Do you love him? Amar?"

It was a loaded question. At that time in India, at least in the society I grew up in, there was only one context in which the word was used. Romantic love. Sexual relations. Not platonic love or friendships. And I wasn't mature enough to change the discourse. Neither did I have the gumption to flip the script on its head and say, "Yes, he's my friend and I love him." So I responded the only way I knew.

"No."

If there was a singular instance of regret in my life, that would be it. That one word nullified everything I felt for Amar. He was the first male who saw me as a friend, not a girl he would eventually land in bed. Amar respected me and protected me in ways I had experienced only with female friends before. I didn't know friendships across gender lines could be full of love, respect, and loving touches that didn't turn into sex. Amar gave me all that, and I had negated it all with a callous "no."

"He's my best friend, and I'm looking out for him the same way he looks out for me," I added, in a desperate attempt to assuage my guilt.

"Okay," Sameer said after a few minutes and sat up straight. "Okay. This is a new beginning for me. A fresh start away from home. Maybe it's time for a new me."

I smiled. I wasn't sure how different a new version of him would be, but it was refreshing to hear him say it.

"And now I'm truly jealous that Amar has you as a friend and I don't."

My body turned warm. I didn't know if it was from the compliment or from his confession that he wanted me in his life.

"Friends?" he asked, extending his hand.

That's when I should've said "no", but I accepted his offer and shook on it.

SAMEER

ara Kadam is spunky. She's quirky. She's brilliant. She's mine.

She used to be. You messed it up.

I woke with a start, drenched in sweat, breathing heavily, with my heart pounding in my head. It took me a moment to realize I was in my parents' home, sleeping in a room they called mine, although I had never lived here. I fumbled for my phone on the nightstand. It was 3:02 a.m. I fell back on the bed, trying to recall the dream that had roused me so violently, but all I could remember was a feeling. A sinking feeling of loss and hopelessness. And rage. At Amar for bringing Tara into my life. At Tara for re-entering my life.

I swiped open my phone to view her website. The homepage showed her professional picture in a formal smile. I thumbed the screen for more images. There were several. Most of them were of her art or her side profile as she worked on something. A few were with the co-founder of her art consultancy firm. I kept scrolling. Then I saw it. It was a picture taken in Rome. She laughed unin-hibitedly as the wind blew her hair across her face. Her body was bent forward, her nose scrunched from heartfelt laughter. That was the Tara from my memories.

At the sign of first light, I put on my running gear and went for a quick jog around the neighborhood. It was a pleasant morning and running often helped clear my mind of its burdens. Not today. When I returned, the heaviness around my heart persisted. Still, I looked forward to spending time with Mom before Dad woke up.

After a lazy shower, I slipped into a pair of jeans and a t-shirt and sprinted down the stairs with my holdall in tow. The scent of paneer paratha wafted to my nose, prompting happy memories from childhood. It smelled like home. I could always count on Mom to give me just the thing I needed.

Durgaben did most of the cooking for them, but whenever I visited, Mom made some of my favorites herself. Lately, the onset of arthritis caused her trouble, but she never denied me the joy of her paneer paratha. The sizzle of oil caramelizing the onions and spicy paneer between thin layers of dough was seductive enough to fully awaken all my senses.

"Hi, Ma," I said, sliding beside her as she stood by the stove.

"Good morning!" Though still in her nightgown, she looked bright and cheerful. Cooking for her kids always made her happy.

"Smells amazing." I grabbed a plate from the cabinet and slid a hot-off-the-griddle paratha onto it.

"There's the spicy mango achar you like," she said, pointing to a pickle jar on the table behind her. "And Amul butter."

I smiled and settled at the table. "How long until you join me?"

"Just two more to roll. That way, I won't have to return to the stove when your father and Durga come for breakfast."

"I'll wait for you," I said, but I knew she'd insist otherwise.

"You start. I'll join you in two minutes."

I chuckled. Growing up, *two minutes* used to be her standard reply to all my questions.

How long will you be? Two minutes.

I'm hungry. Is the food ready? Two minutes.

I am bored, Ma. Can we leave? Two minutes.

"What's funny?" She turned around with a smile.

"Nothing." I smiled back. "Has he been sleeping in these days?"

"Sometimes." She returned to the griddle. "Depends on how much he's had to drink."

"Do you ever talk about his drinking?"

"No." She looked back at me with the rolling pin in her hand. "I don't bother."

And she resumed rolling. Old habits die hard. Mom had always been hardworking and meticulous. I wondered how she put up with my father's haphazard habits and dubious scruples. I looked at her and felt a twinge of sorrow for the woman who was compared to a flower in her younger days.

"Come Ma, I want to eat with you. We can talk."

She removed the last paratha from the griddle and covered the leftover dough and paneer mixture before settling down at the table. "Okay, I'm done."

"Mmm, this is good," she said after taking a bite of the paratha dipped generously in the spicy pickle.

"Of course it is. You made it."

"You're a sweet talker like your father." It wasn't a compliment. It was an instruction to rein it in. "Have you talked to Juhi lately?"

"No." I chewed.

"Call her sometime. She's alone there." My sister Juhi lived in Australia with her loving husband and his family. But since none of us were close to her, she was alone in Mom's book. But I didn't argue. "Okay."

Juhi had married and moved to Melbourne just before the mountain collapsed and buried us alive. She still didn't know the full extent of what Mom and I had gone through. And she didn't know the truth about how much money it cost me to keep our past at bay.

"Is there something you want to talk about?" Mom asked.

"No," I blurted. "Why?"

"You were jumpy all evening."

My chest tightened. If anyone could understand what I was going through, it would be her, but I couldn't bring myself to talk about Tara. "It's about the engagement."

She looked at me with soft eyes as we continued eating. "Don't let anyone pressure you, Sameer. Take your time. You shouldn't rush into marriage if you're not ready."

I changed my mind. I could use her advice, but just as I opened my mouth, my father's heavy voice carried from the living room.

"We're in the kitchen," Mom called out. "Join us for breakfast if you want. Durga, can you please make chai?"

Durgaben emerged with a fresh face and put a saucepan on the stove.

And just like that, the moment was gone. I would've spilled my heart out to Mom if we'd had a moment more, but things work out the way they're supposed to. Case in point: Tara's re-entry into my life. My mind drifted to her as I nursed my coffee. Despite her outright rejection and hurtful accusations, all I wanted was to see her again. I craved that happy feeling. If only I'd had the courage to tell her everything years ago, we wouldn't be here. I wouldn't be faking affection for Aarti while secretly pining for Tara. The familiar feeling in my chest returned as I thought about my impending engagement.

As if on cue, my father walked into the kitchen and sat down at the table.

I instinctively stood. "I'm off now. Thank you for the paratha, Mom." I kissed her on the cheek. "And thank you, Durgaben, as always, for everything you do." I pulled her into a side hug.

"When will I see you next?" Mom asked.

"Hopefully soon. I'll call you."

"You haven't had your tea yet," my father cried.

"He doesn't drink chai, Rehani bhai. He is a coffee drinker." Durgaben's cheeky response made my day. I gave her a warm smile, picked up my bag, and jumped into the car.

My family's housekeeper knew me better than my dad, but that hadn't always been the case. Although my sister, the first-born, was the apple of his eye, we used to be close. We were like friends. He was the one who allowed me my first cigarette and showed me how to drink responsibly. He taught me how to drive and let me borrow his expensive cars even when I only had a learner's permit.

He was strict, but not a disciplinarian. His rules were *ad hoc*. He insisted on following them when it was convenient for him, when they worked in his favor. Other times, he encouraged us to give the world a big middle finger and do what we wanted.

My mother was the one who ensured our stable emotional and intellectual development. She had rules, and her rules were rigid. She didn't impose too many of them, though, because rules stifled creativity, she held. But she wouldn't tolerate lies and insolence. All her rules revolved around those two principles. That I was a fantastic liar now was thanks to my father. It was a gift that kept on giving, transforming me into a person I hardly recognized anymore.

I shook off my dark thoughts and commanded my car's system to dial Mihir.

His sleepy voice responded. "Hello."

"It's me. Are you still sleeping?"

"What time is it?"

"Nine thirty."

"It's Sunday," he said with a groan.

"It's Saturday."

"It's the weekend. Let me sleep."

"All right, but I still need to talk to you. Call me when you're up."

He hummed an affirmative.

"Is Abby with you this weekend?" I inquired about his current girlfriend.

"No," he mumbled. "Let me sleep."

I scoffed and disconnected. At the next red light, I texted him that I would be at our usual coffee shop if he woke up and wanted a pick-me-up.

SAMEER

I turned onto McKinney Avenue and navigated the one-way streets toward *Cups and Cookies*. It had been my favorite coffee shop since I moved into my condo five years ago. Like all hipster joints, this one had a cheeky name and an industrial design with open rafters and exposed pipes. But unlike a great many of them, it had good coffee and spacious seating, which is why I frequented it more often than any other.

As I parked the car, I thought I saw a familiar figure walk into the café. The woman wore loose linen pants and a short top, like Tara did in college. I shook my head in reproach for conjuring her everywhere. There was no way I'd casually run into her because I wasn't that lucky. My luck had run out a long time ago.

As I walked into the café and removed my sunglasses, I spotted Tara placing an order at the register. A warmth engulfed my heart. This had to be a hallucination. Just then, her eyes drew to me and she pulled herself upright. I wasn't hallucinating.

Quickly gathering my wits, I walked up and stood beside her as she paid for the order. Her glossy hair was wrapped up in a loose bun at her nape.

"Are you stalking me now?" she asked coolly.

I stole a look at her beautiful face before turning my attention to the barista, who returned my smile.

"I was going to ask you the same question, Ms. Kadam. This happens to be my favorite café, one that I visit every day. Are *you* stalking me?" She responded with a stern side-eye, while I smiled at the barista again. "My usual please, *John*."

John nodded, much to my delight and Tara's chagrin.

She picked up her coffee and walked toward an isolated booth by a large window at the rear. Her slight heels peeked from under the flowy pants as her proud figure strutted away.

While I paid up and waited for my order, I fought the urge to turn around. I could feel her eyes on my back, searing through to my heart. Those beautiful eyes, rimmed with liner and mascara, reminded me of the first time I had seen her in makeup.

It was Navratri, the goddess festival of nine nights, celebrated with great vigor in Gujarat, especially in Baroda.

Colorful fabric banners were strung from bamboo poles erected around the open courtyard of our college campus, flapping against the jubilant fall breeze. Cascades of string lights added a festive glow. At the center of the courtyard stood a dais for the musicians, decked with garlands of marigolds and roses. The gaiety, the frenzy, the hullaballoo were a little over the top for me, though perfectly normal for the city. Tara told me that the College of Fine Arts was known for its garba, a traditional folk dance of the region, sans modern musical instruments, microphones, or speakers. Students hosted the traditional dance played to the rhythm of the harmonium, the dhol, and the tambourine.

I had been waiting with Amar, both of us wearing kurta and Indian leggings, when Tara walked in with her friends, looking completely different in her embroidered flared lehenga and blouse, chaniya choli. Her usual simplicity of "the girl next door" was transformed into the seductiveness of an enchantress.

Her long, narrow waist was deliciously naked to the curve of her hips except for the breadth of the dupatta on her right shoulder and draped over the midriff. Her hips swayed with the flow of her full-length skirt like they never did in her baggy pants. Deep red lips, kajal-rimmed eyes. Big earrings that bounced gleefully with every step she took. A pair of three-pronged chains ran from her ears to hook into a flirty, messy bun. A long necklace of oxidized silver swung over the swell of her gorgeous breasts. She wore a black bindi on her forehead and three dainty black dots in the shape of an inverted triangle on her chin.

I had never been much of a kinkster, but watching her that night aroused delightful fantasies in me. Smearing the kohl dots off her chin with my forehead as I slid down to dip my tongue into her navel, just below that delicate waist chain. Naughty earrings and boisterous anklets responding with different tones and cadence to my deep thrusts into her naked body. My hands clasping her perfect, round breasts, her bangles clinking against my ear as she clutched my hair hard until I cried out in pleasure.

When I turned to the campus wall to adjust myself, Amar broke into a smile that was equal parts amused and nasty. "Careful, brother. You might seriously want to reconsider that."

I had just enough time to mouth him a "fuck you" before Tara approached us, and he burst out laughing.

"Navratri is my favorite festival." She told me when we danced ourselves into exhaustion, our bodies glistening with sweat, shuddering gently in the light chill. I sat with her on a thick concrete tree guard around a Peepal. Our friends had exited the garba circle to fetch water and snacks, but I stayed behind. Despite my mediocre dancing skills, I followed her as she dashed, jumped, and twirled, chasing that final beat of the drums.

"You're a terrific dancer," I said.

A sweet smile rippled across her red lips, and I felt a thrill run up my thighs.

"I love garba, but that's only partly why I enjoy the festival."

"Yeah?"

"It's a celebration of femininity and female power. You know the songs we play during these nine nights, the garba and raas songs?"

"The songs are in Gujarati, I didn't understand a word."

She smiled again. "They fall under two main categories: songs of worship for the Mother Goddess and songs of love and desire for Lord Krishna."

I nodded.

"Mother Goddess is Adi Shakti, the original source of energy, of nurture, and of life on this earth. She symbolizes everything that is good. That's what we celebrate."

I nodded again. The heat from her body, her intoxicating smell—not her usual rose, but a seductive amber—hit me hard. I swallowed and tried not to stare at her lips.

"But the songs addressed to Krishna acknowledge women's unabashed, unapologetic desire."

"Yeah?"

"They talk about women lusting for Krishna, moaning about wanting to spend more time with him. They sing about losing themselves to the sound of his flute, bickering for exclusivity when he was tomcatting around... you know, like you. Even the so-called modern songs are about love and female desire. Just imagine, the same people who celebrate Radha's affair with Krishna are the ones who criticize women for falling in love and having sex." She rolled her eyes like she did, playfully, gracefully.

"Sounds familiar. Women are always fighting over me." Except the one I wanted.

"You wish," she said with a playful scoff.

I slid my hand next to hers on the concrete, and for the first time, she didn't recoil. Her touch sent a happy thrill down my spine.

We had been friends for a few months, but unlike her friendship with Amar and the other guys we hung out with, we hadn't breached into the physical. Unlike the others, we didn't nudge each other after a joke, casually fling an arm over the shoulder while we sipped tea at a stall, or give a low five, which I learned was something they did a lot in this part of the country. Even after an accidental touch, she would apologize. Always an awkwardness, as if we secretly liked each other but were too afraid to confess, in case it messed up what we had. And I had certainly messed it up.

The smell of coffee in my face pulled my attention back to John. "Here you go, Sam," he said, smiling with his newly aligned teeth. "Freshly brewed. It's a different blend. I think you'll like it."

"It certainly smells promising." With a smile, I grabbed the cup from the counter, and as I turned, I caught Tara hastily shifting her gaze from me to the laptop before her.

I smiled and walked over. "Mind if I join you?"

"*Arey deva*!" she cried in Marathi, and I had been with her long enough to know what that meant.

"Invoking God, I see. Was that a cry for help or a cry of exasperation, Ms. Kadam?"

"Knock it off, Rehani."

"Oh, we aren't playing anymore?"

"*You* were playing. I was serious," she said, but spotting no animosity in her tone, I took the liberty of slipping into the banquette facing her.

"I see your wardrobe hasn't changed much."

She scalded me with a glare. "Neither has your condescending attitude."

I smiled. I had expected nothing less. "Truce?" A standard question from our past.

"Why?"

"Can we talk?"

"Why?"

"Don't be difficult, Tara." She served me another glare, and I tossed it away just as quickly. "Your coffee is getting cold, but that's how you like it, isn't it?"

She returned her attention to the machine, her nimble fingers flying over the keyboard. "I'm not sure we have much to talk about, Rehani."

It usually took more than a gentle nudge to dissuade me. "Did you find a place to live around here?"

With an audible sigh, she pushed away the laptop and nursed her gargantuan coffee cup. The slender, tapered fingers, finished with professionally manicured nails, evoked fuzzy memories of cold nights in a warm bed. I tried to focus on her face instead, but her plum-colored lips on the thick rim of the cup did me no favors either.

"Yes," she said softly. "About a block away."

"I'm about a five-minute drive from you," I said.

"What do you want, Sameer?"

"A chat with you."

"We have nothing to chat about. You made that clear years ago."

"Will you give it a rest? What I have to say has changed in the last thirteen years and in the last twenty-four hours."

She pulled herself upright, but the expression on her face remained unaltered. "All right, get to it then. This is your chance. Say whatever it is you want to tell me, because after today, I don't wish to see you again."

"What if you accidentally run into me like this?" I grinned playfully. "How will you avoid me then?"

I thought I was being clever, but she gulped down her coffee, shoved her laptop into her shoulder bag, and slid out of the booth. "Like this."

I quickly reached for her wrist. "Please." With her body still attempting a getaway, she turned her head and gazed into my eyes. I'm not sure what she saw in them, but she set her bag down.

"I need another coffee. Anything for you?" she asked, retrieving her wallet from the bag.

I shook my head. By virtue of old habits and male socialization, I would've offered to get her the coffee, but I knew better. I hoped to remain on her good side for at least a day before she blackballed me again. In college, she had always been bluntly honest about her tight finances. Her furious sense of dignity and her fierce self-respect had me completely defenseless even before I fell in love with her. I had never expected it, nor had I experienced anything like it, so I didn't know how to react except to offer veneration. And that's what I did.

That same night of Navratri, as I'd sat wrapped up in her perfume, we'd smelled something else.

"What's that strange smell?" she asked as a young couple walked past us sharing a joint.

"It's what they're smoking," I whispered.

"That doesn't smell like cigarette. Is it a flavored stick?"

"You really don't know?" I asked with genuine surprise.

"Know what?" She turned to me with a slightly gaping mouth, eyes blinking with innocence.

I had to smile. She was smart and savvy, yet totally clueless and childlike in some matters.

"It's weed."

She gasped. "How do you know that?"

"Because I've smoked it."

Another gasp from her made me laugh out loud, just as our friends returned with water. I grabbed the bottle Amar tossed at me and said, "She hasn't smoked weed."

This time the others gasped, and I burst out laughing again.

"Have you all?" she asked.

Everyone either nodded or shrugged matter-of-factly. Even the good-boy extraordinaire Amar had smoked with me when he came home that summer.

"Then I want to try it too! You know, I read somewhere that a good artist needs to immerse herself in every experience, every emotion."

"Yes, academic curiosity is the only reason you want to smoke weed," Amar said with his usual dry wit, and she giggled.

After a few days of the right kind of flirting and a few nights of debauchery, I managed to locate a reliable source for the good stuff in the new city. But when I brought the information to the group, Tara said she'd have to wait until the end of the month to get the necessary cash. Any of us could have offered to loan her the money, but we didn't. We knew she would uphold her dignity even when she was breaking the rules.

So, we waited until she got the money from her tutoring, then spent the weekend in a weed-induced daze at Amar's apartment. That was the first time I kissed her, or she kissed me. I'm hazy on the details, but I have a distinct, vivid memory of locked lips, tangled tongues, and our bodies wedged tight for several minutes. We never spoke of it again, though, not even after we slept together, because it was an aberration between friends and best left unaddressed.

"What are you thinking?" She returned with a steaming cup and sat down across from me.

I knew it would remain untouched until it became tepid. I used to give her a lot of flak for that in college. The cutting chai—a very tiny portion served at tea stalls—was the perfect size for her. A normal-sized beverage was wasted because by the time she got to it, it would be unpalatable for almost everyone else. But Tara wasn't like everyone else.

I smiled. "The past. We're as much in the past as we're here right now."

"But not in the future." She established without blinking.

I swatted that away too. "How are you settling in?"

She took a moment, but answered, "Alright, I think. I don't know anyone in the city, so it's been quiet, but I'm doing okay."

"Well, I'm here if you need anything or want a friend to talk to."

She looked at me pointedly. "What are you doing, Sameer? What are we doing here?"

"What do *you* think we're doing?"

"Don't mess with me," she growled. "I'm not that tame girl anymore."

I smiled. "Two things. I *am* going to mess with you, that's just who we are, but more to the point, you were *never* tame."

"I fell for you once Rehani, it's not going to happen again. I'm not nineteen, and I'm not smitten with you anymore."

"Wait...you were smitten with me?" A deep color rose to her cheeks. "I thought I was the only one with the raging infatuation."

For a moment, we both gazed at each other with a look of mild shock in our eyes. Then she remembered herself. "This conversation is over," she said and pulled out her laptop. "Get lost."

"This isn't over, Tara." *We* were not over. "We need to talk."

I felt heroic, Bollywood heroic, as I strode away from the booth before she had a chance to react or retort.

SAMEER

$\mathcal{M}$y movie-perfect exit was ruined when Mihir walked in, and we literally bumped into each other at the door.

"We're leaving." I grabbed him by his arm to tow him out, but taller and stronger, he resisted me easily.

"Why?" He slipped out of my grip and back into the café. "I need a coffee."

I followed him in with a grumble and silently directed his attention to Tara, who had resumed working on her laptop.

"Who's that?" he said, then immediately recognized my expression. "*Tara?*" he mouthed with a frown.

I shrugged.

"What's she doing here?" he whispered and sauntered across to the register. I had little choice but to follow.

"That's what I wanted to talk to you about," I said in a hushed voice. "She's here on a job. I ran into her at the museum where she's consulting."

He studied me, then scoffed as he paid for his black-with-an-extra-shot and a scone. "You didn't just run into her. What aren't you telling me?"

I looked away.

"Okay," he said and grabbed his coffee. I thought he'd follow me out, but to my morbid embarrassment, and in what was a clear defeat for my ego, he walked straight over to Tara.

"Hi, sorry to bother you...Tara?"

She looked up from her computer and responded with a tentative smile. "Hi?"

"I'm Mihir, Sameer's friend." He pointed to me standing within earshot, and I managed a sheepish wave. "He's trying to flee this establishment. I guess that's your doing?"

Tara blushed at his irresistibly good smile and lowered her eyes for a moment. "I plead the fifth," she said, interlocking her fingers under her chin.

"Ah, I like you."

Were they actually flirting? I scowled at Mihir's back.

"Well, you're too late. Sameer and I are over," she replied, snubbing my beautiful exit line. "So, you don't have to like me, Mihir."

"May I?" he asked.

When she nodded, he slipped into the seat opposite her, his long legs barely fitting under the table, almost touching her.

"But I can like you regardless, can't I?" He smiled and took a sip from his cup. He was a devilishly handsome, suave bastard, and I could see the effect on Tara, who leaned in slightly with a sweet smile on her face.

"Well, you're not obligated to, which makes me wonder, what's your ulterior motive?" Tara was nothing if not devastatingly admirable.

Mihir grinned, and I shuffled awkwardly, debating whether I should join them or take my humiliation outside with me. But Tara nodded at me, so I approached.

I was about to slide in beside Mihir, but he spread his legs wider and said, "Sorry buddy, you'll have to sit there." He signaled to the seat next to Tara. "Woes of a tall body," he added for effect.

Tara tucked her bag closer to the wall and scooted over. I smelled her beautiful, aquatic floral perfume as I settled beside her. The warmth emanating from her glowing skin felt familiar even after all this time.

"Sameer and I have issues," she said, looking at Mihir as if I wasn't at the table. "But otherwise, I'm a nice person. It's wonderful to meet you, Mihir." She extended her hand across the table in a choreographed move.

Mihir played along and took her slender palm in his big paws. Ignoring my fiery glare trained on him, he held on to her hand a moment longer than necessary.

"In my line of work, one can never have enough rich acquaintances, preferably ones with dubious tastes," she teased with a straight face. "You're rich, right?"

Mihir only smiled.

"He has a girlfriend," I blurted for no apparent reason but intense jealousy.

"Good to know." She smiled, her eyes still on Mihir. "I have a boyfriend...And you, Sameer?"

The crushing feeling sprang up in my chest as I offered a feeble nod.

"Good, now we can all be friends."

Her sarcastic words seared my soul as she turned her attention back to Mihir.

"I'm sorry. I'm usually not this disagreeable," she said to him.

Mihir waved his hand. "It's all in good fun. Do you mind if we talk more, or would you like us to leave?"

With a shy smile, she asked, "What do you want to talk about?"

"Tell me about your work, *Tara*." Mihir turned up his charm, uttering her name in a decadent, seductive manner.

She smiled, pushed a non-existent stray lock behind her ear, and gave a quick swipe of her tongue over her juicy lips. Was she doing it deliberately, or was it an unconscious reaction to Mihir's charisma? Whatever it was, it pissed me off.

"I'm an art advisor."

"She's also a phenomenal artist," I said as a reflex, though I hadn't meant to say out loud.

Her soft eyes now turned to me. "Do you mean that?"

I shifted my body to face her. "I just spent a ridiculous amount on your painting. Do you think I would've if I didn't think it was absolutely worth every penny? You know I wouldn't lie to you about that."

Her gaze traveled down to her clasped hands. "Thank you."

Mihir cleared his throat, bringing us back to the moment. "What exactly does an art advisor do?"

"Um, well." She stole a glance at me. "We look at our clients' requirements, the décor, layout, budget, then recommend artwork that would best accentuate the space. We also help procure the pieces we recommend, providing a platform for new and lesser-known artists. We advise collectors on what to buy. Art education is a big part of what we do for private collectors. Every so often, I work with galleries and museums to authenticate and appraise paintings, trace provenance, that kind of thing. Oil paintings are my area of specialization." She snuck another glance at me before smiling at Mihir.

"Sounds exciting," he said.

"It can be. Although most of my work involves long hours of examining old paintings and a lot of research."

"What would you recommend to a new collector like me?" Mihir asked.

"Since when are you a collector?" I scoffed.

"A *new* collector." He shot me a scalding look.

Tara's eyes darted between us. "I know you're only trying to prolong this conversation, but alright, I'll bite. From whatever little I've gathered about you, I'd recommend original works that define the renaissance and impressionist canon, because nothing less will gratify you. They're difficult to get your hands on, but that's a part of it, the thrill of the chase, that excites you. And none of the feminist and queer art that's so much in vogue now."

When I turned to accost her, I found her unfazed eyes and sweet smile resting on Mihir.

"You're not serious," I accosted her. "You'd never recommend that. To anyone!"

"No?" She turned in her seat to me. "What do you think I'd say?"

"You'd introduce him to the wider world of newer, postcolonial artists. Smashing the cannon—that is the thrill he enjoys and you know it. And you're not fooling anyone with the *none of that feminist and queer stuff*. I know your work, Tara Kadam. Your MFA thesis was on Nilima Sheikh's oeuvre, and your own work subverts the male, colonial, heteronormative gaze. For fuck's sake, you wrote a paper on the caste and class juxtaposition of the woman who was our nude model in college. I helped you edit it. Ask me what else I know." With arms across my chest, I leaned back in the seat.

She slipped me a sly smile as if she had expected my reaction. "Not bad, Rehani. What else do you know about me?" She crossed her arms to mirror mine.

I drew my brows together and fumed with recalcitrance.

She smiled at Mihir. "I apologize for the misdirection, but he's right. That's exactly what I'd recommend. After all, the true purpose of art is to disrupt the status quo an—"

"—and unsettle the soul." I completed her sentence. That earned me a subtle but unmistakably warm smile.

Mihir studied us for a moment. "I think I need more coffee. Anyone want anything?"

"A cup of water for me, if you don't mind," Tara replied.

As Mihir walked away, I wondered if Tara and I had just crossed a critical threshold in our current relationship, as it stood.

"We should talk," I took the opportunity to suggest.

"About what?"

"About what happened. Why I left. Did Amar not tell you anything?"

She offered a gentle frown in response. "Amar is a loyal friend. He knows the virtue of keeping a secret."

I sucked in a breath. "Yes, he does." Precisely why I had trusted him not to spill my shame to Tara.

Her eyes flickered for a brief moment. "Tell me honestly. Why didn't you reach out in all these years?"

"Would you have responded if I had?"

She took a deep breath and exhaled. Lying didn't come naturally to her, so she had no choice but to opt for the truth. "Probably not."

"Give me a chance to explain what happened. If we are still not sure we can be friends after that, I won't insist. Just one more chance, that's all I'm asking."

A shuddered breath shook her, and she nodded. "Alright, one more meeting."

"At least two. I don't think I can bring myself to tell you everything all at once." Honesty was the only way to regain her trust.

"Alright, two more meetings."

"Next Saturday? Same time, same place."

She nodded and looked at me. "Sameer?"

"Yes?"

"How do you know so much about my work? And why?"

I shrugged and leaned in. "Do you really want me to answer that?"

Before she could respond, Mihir returned with coffee for himself and water for her. Just then, her phone buzzed on the table.

I felt her stiffen, but she answered it with a bright voice, "Hey, good morning." Judging by her smile and demeanor, I knew it was the boyfriend. "I'm at a coffee shop. Can I call you when I get back to the apartment?"

"About half an hour," she said and slipped the phone into her bag. "Okay guys, I need to leave. Mihir, it was very nice to meet you. Hopefully, we'll see each other again." She pulled out two cards from her bright, quilted wallet and handed them to us. "If you're ever in the market for art but don't know where to begin, get in touch."

I slid off the booth to let her out.

She stared at me for a long moment. "I'll see you Saturday, Sameer," she said quietly as if she didn't want Mihir to hear it. I nodded, and she disappeared.

Mihir reoccupied his spot in the booth, and I slipped into mine. He was the only friend who knew about my family's murky past. He also knew every little detail of my relationship with Tara.

Mihir's father and my uncle were old friends. Years ago, during one of my drunken stupors, I had poured out my heart to him. How much I missed Tara, and how my juvenile decision to disappear from her life still hurt. Back then, he was just a guy I hung out with because our families were close. After that night, he became a friend.

His reaction to my life's story was neither pity nor ridicule, as I had feared. He had taken a sip of his drink and calmly said, "Look at yourself now, and tell me you're not a fighter."

It was a powerful thing for me to hear in my inebriated state, especially from Mihir, whom I had come to admire and respect. It felt like he had cut open the stagnating wounds of my heart, releasing the rot of pain and bitterness. I had never cried so much, not even when we relinquished our comfortable life in India and moved here. He had been my champion ever since, a mentor, though he was barely two years older. He was a powerhouse in his own right, and those who knew him professionally called him ruthless and cutthroat. The image went well with his six-foot-two, broad-shouldered frame, dark eyes, and a bearded face.

"So, what do you think?" I asked, bouncing my feet.

"She's quick, smart, assertive," he observed with furrowed brows, then laughed. "She's way out of your league, man. How did you get her to go out with you the first time?"

"I have no idea what she saw in me." I sighed and fell back in my seat. "Now, she has a boyfriend who makes her face light up like that."

"Don't sell yourself short. You're smart, well-read, moderately successful," he teased with a slight smile. Like Tara, he had kept me grounded all these years. "Have you told her?"

"I've tried."

"And what about Aarti?"

I looked at him and drew my fingers through my hair. "You know it's not that straightforward. I can't jeopardize our future and my family's fortune. Not again. If things don't work out with Tara, I'll lose everything. Right now, I'm still hanging on to the shreds of my life."

He sipped from his to-go cup, which looked like a toy in his large hand, his eyes peering at me over the rim.

"You don't approve."

He kept staring at me with his deep, black eyes, then threw me a light shrug. "It's not my place to disapprove."

Damn straight, it wasn't his call. It was my life, my future on the line.

"Alright, enough with the wallowing." He stood and patted

my shoulder. "Come on, let's get something to eat." With strong arms, he pulled me up effortlessly.

"Here's something that'll cheer you up," he said as we walked out of the café. "She still likes you. Tread carefully, though, because she's hurt and angry. But she showed her soft eyes for you every time she thought you weren't looking."

TARA

A week later, I was back at the café, sitting in the same booth. I had arrived early, wondering if I'd be sitting across from Rehani, a friend, or Sameer, the boy I'd loved.

It was the only time I had chosen to put myself first, ahead of my family, my career, my life goals. Like the foolish girl of twenty that I was, I had spun daydreams of our life together, a family with three kids, a Spanish-style bungalow with a large, detached studio in the backyard where we both would work. Careers we'd be proud of. A legacy we'd leave our children. Little did I know I was building castles in the air.

Truthfully, our friendship was never a smooth, easy one because at its heart lay my intense infatuation for him. The furious debates, the incessant discussions, the unnecessary arguments were ways of being with him while keeping my feelings at bay. I wanted him, but we were not in the same league. Not by a long shot. The social differences between us were too real, too palpable. Then one day it all changed, when I fell into his arms, literally.

That evening, under the old banyan tree, we sat on a concrete guard heated by the October sun, debating aesthetics, quoting Kant, Hume, Pollock, and Warhol. Our arguments were sophomoric at best, but carried the weight of our existential angst. When the shrill call of a bird interrupted our conversation, we looked up to find that the thicket of trees had swallowed the sun.

"We just got scolded by a bird," I said.

"Huh?" He gave me quizzical look.

"It's nightfall. The birds are trying to sleep, and we're bothering them. Come on, let's go."

He smiled and leapt off the tall concrete with a valiant jump. In hindsight, it was a mistake to attempt an emulation because I wasn't nearly as athletic. I realized mid-flight that I was going to miss my landing, but Sameer caught me, breaking a fall that would have injured my ankle or worse. With my body in shock and my heartbeat erratic, I gripped him to steady myself. My chest landed flush against him, his arm around my waist, a pair of beautiful brown eyes gazing down at me. As an electric pulse coursed through my body, I hastily pulled myself away. I couldn't falter. There was more at stake—not in the least, my self-respect.

"I hate these sandals," I cried.

He stepped away to observe my feet. "I like them," he said with his head cocked. "The way your toes peek out. It's very sexy."

My heart bubbled, but I tamped it down. "Don't tell me you have a foot fetish."

He grinned playfully. "Only yours."

"Says the playboy to every girl he meets." I rolled my eyes.

Then, as I heaved my overstuffed bag to my shoulder, my ankle twisted again, only slightly, but enough to compromise my balance. Sameer's arm was around me again, preventing another fall. It was becoming undignified.

"I'm alright," I said, promptly shrugging his hands from my shoulders.

"Hey, it's alright to lean on others sometimes."

I readjusted the broad strap of my bag and calmly said, "I can't afford to."

He peered into my eyes and as if he knew exactly what my words meant, he said, "It doesn't make you weak, Tara."

He always said I saw right through him. I had no idea he saw the real me too. He had just voiced my deepest fear.

"I can't let people think I need help. That I can't handle it on my own."

"People who care about you will never think that. Amar doesn't. I don't."

He smiled at me with a warmth that reached his eyes, and I lost all purpose. As I inhaled the night-blooming jasmine studded along the campus wall like a carpet of stars, I said, "I missed dinner. Do you want to eat at the laris outside?"

The moonlit night cast long shadow of old trees that danced on our bodies as we walked across the street to the west wall of Sayaji Baug. Every evening, food stalls lined the iconic garden, turning it into a popular place for the mingling of minds and bodies. Traffic had thinned out, and the night had turned breathable. Tantalizing smells of garlic and spices wafted through the air, and the sizzle of oil and water hitting the hot woks and griddles whetted appetites.

A group of high school students gathered over plates of Indo-Chinese noodles, "Schezwan" chicken, and chili paneer, laughing their carefree, youthful laughter. An animated group of poli-sci majors tore into flaky, egg-laden Mughlai parathas while fighting over the validity of a multi-party system for a country as diverse as India. Around them, young couple sat at makeshift tables, making little effort to hide the lust in their eyes.

But every sight, sound, and smell faded away as I looked into Sameer's eyes. Our order of piping hot pav bhaji and spicy vegetable-cheese sandwich sat between us when my body erupted in unfortunate goosebumps. He spied this sign of arousal on my arms and flashed his cocky grin. I looked away.

"I'm going to ask you something, and you'll promise me you won't lie," he said.

"I'm going to lie, and you'll catch me at it," I replied with a straight face.

"I'm serious. Do you like me, Tara?"

I picked up my sandwich and bit into it. The dome of cheese, sprinkled liberally with the tangy chaat masala, smeared across my lips. I licked them clean while he kept gazing at my mouth.

"Because I like you," he continued. "So much, I keep worrying I might lose you if I tell you."

"You just told me."

"Am I going to lose you?"

I kept nibbling on the sandwich while the spicy mash of mixed vegetables lay untouched before him.

"Let's go back to my place," he said.

The desire in his eyes unnerved me. It was what I had wanted to see since that evening on the steps. I wiped my mouth with a paper napkin. "I haven't been with anyone yet."

He lurched back in the plastic chair. "Oh!"

"Does that scare you?" I took another bite.

He shook his head. "With you, no. Does it scare you?"

I picked a slice of cucumber from my sandwich, studying the traces of spicy green chutney on one side and smooth, salty butter on the other. "There aren't many things that scare me, Rehani. But I need you to know because I like you too. Enough to be worried about losing myself."

A wave of relief mixed with triumph washed over his face when I looked up at him. His body relaxed in the chair before he leaned in again. "We can start slow. I'll be gentle, I promise."

"Now, why do I not believe that?"

"Oh, I can be very tender if you know how to play me right. And I have a feeling you do."

"Hmm, what if I don't want tender?"

He burst into a laugh so loud, we got judgmental looks from everyone around us—from the chatty high-schoolers and heavy debaters to the relaxed uncles and aunties enjoying an evening out without kids. I brought the cucumber slice to his mouth, and he pounced on it with a grin.

"Tell me what you want, Tara."

"Do you know my caste?"

He frowned. "Do you know mine?"

I shook my head.

"Do you need to know?" he asked.

When I shook my head again, he said, "And I don't need to know yours." Then he grumbled with a deeper, angrier frown. "Why are we even talking about this?"

"It is a fact of my existence, Rehani. One that I'm made to live with every day of my life. How can I assume it won't be an issue between us?"

His frown ironed out instantly. "I'm sorry. You're right, but it's a nonissue for me."

"That's a privilege I don't have."

We let the silence between us get swallowed by the sounds of heavy spatulas banging on cast iron griddles, plastic chairs and tables scraping against the asphalt as people vacated them and new patrons settled in. More laughter, different chatter. An aura of happiness all around us.

"I like you, Tara, so I'm going to ask you again. What do you want?"

This time my answer found the fire I felt in my heart and my spirit. "I want you, Sameer Rehani."

"And I want you. All of you. Every bit of you."

"Every bit?" I asked with a cocked eyebrow. "Now let's see if you can keep that promise."

He rocked in his chair from another belly-laugh, and this time we got envious looks from the couples around us, young and old.

"Well, here's something I do promise. You won't lose yourself, ever. And you won't lose me either. Even if we don't work out, there's no power in this world great enough to prevent me from being there for you as a friend. You only have to ask."

I refocused my eyes on the empty seat across from me, still hazy with memories of that night, and smelled the scent that had tormented me for a week.

I glanced up and saw Sameer standing by me in stylish jeans and flawless hair. I stole a glance at my clothes, into which I had put little thought, except for the bright lipstick I'd had the good sense to choose. My trademark liner and mascara were merely a bonus.

"Can I get you a coffee?" he asked with a bright smile.

I pointed to my cup. "I already got mine."

"Tara," he cajoled. "Just for today, please."

When you've grown up in a struggling family, not accepting favors and freebies becomes a matter of self-respect. But this was Sameer. "Latte, please."

"And a Danish? Muffin? Bear claw?" The question was gentle, teasing.

I smiled. "Raspberry Danish."

By the time he settled across from me with the coffee, two perfectly flaky pastries, and a gorgeous smile, my nerves were already jangling.

"Thank you for agreeing to meet," he said after a few uncomfortable moments, during which I avoided looking straight into his eyes.

"This is weird, isn't it?" I asked.

"A bit."

"How come it wasn't last week?"

He shrugged in the cute way I remembered. "Last week we had our claws out, but today we have to behave like mature adults."

That made me smile. "So where do we begin?"

"Where we left off?"

My jaw clenched and my fingers tightened around the cup at the memory of him leaving me humiliated and alone.

"Maybe not," he said, looking at my hand.

"I still carry a lot of anger, and one coffee date is not going to miraculously erase it."

"No. No, it won't." A heavy sigh and a loaded pause. He relaxed his back against the well-padded seat. "Tell me what brings you here, then."

Work, that seemed like a safe, neutral place to start.

I tore a piece off the Danish. "I'm appraising the paintings a local oil dynasty has donated to the museum."

"Would that be the Arlington family?"

I raised my brows. "You know them?"

"Not directly. Through a friend. She's a friend of their daughter."

"Hm, seems you've made some pretty influential friends here too." I meant to tease him, but he squared his jaw and looked away.

"Well, anyway, I'm also helping curate a new wing they've donated. And I get to showcase my work at the upcoming exhibition." I smiled. "I have three pieces, including the one you extorted from me."

"Extorted. Right," he replied, his smile brimming with mischief.

I rolled my eyes. "I'll have you know, I'm donating that money to a very good cause."

"It's your money. You can do whatever you want with it."

"Are you upset I'm giving it away?"

He shook his head. "Never. Are you upset you had to sell it?"

"I was furious. But I'm grateful for it. I've been intending to donate to a scholarship program for girls in my hometown, and this money is enough to set up a decent endowment. And my agent says it's upped my cachet in the market."

"You're welcome."

"That wasn't a *thank you*," I said, and he laughed. The laugh that made my heart take a tumble.

"Are you happy, Tara?"

"Yes. This is a big break for me, and a huge show of confidence from Dr. Hadden."

"When I spoke with her, it looked like she knew you well."

"She and I go back a few years. I first met her when she was at a museum in Boston. They'd hired the firm I worked for to appraise some paintings. She was impressed with my attention to detail and my *breadth of knowledge,* as she put it. I didn't know how big of a deal it was until the firm's director sent me a bouquet and personally came over to congratulate me. Then, after I quit and started my consultancy, she sent many clients our way. She's an institution, and her word carries weight. I wouldn't be here without her, in every sense of the phrase."

"Then it's safe to assume the paintings are worth your while."

"Oh yes! They're specially commissioned pieces of the family and the estate created during the early twentieth century and of great significance to the history of Texas art. But there are these two artists that have me puzzled. I feel like there's some connection between them. I still haven't figured out what. Their styles are different, as is their palette choice, but I feel it in my gut—" I recognized the smile in his eyes and stopped. "What?"

"I'm happy to hear you talk like this again, passionately. I wish I could see the paintings. They sound intriguing."

"I can sneak you in someday if you're interested. Maybe you can help me solve the mystery."

"I'd love that." He smiled, and my cheeks warmed. "But that's not what I asked. *Are* you happy?" His voice was gentle, bordering on concern. "Is this what you want?"

"What do you mean?"

"You're an exceptional artist. Are you happy with this advising slash consultation business?"

It was my turn to shrug. "Even exceptional artists need to put food on the table. I couldn't afford to remain jobless for long, waiting to be discovered. It's not a fair world."

"It isn't."

"Do you know I got to work with D.G. Groh?"

"Groh! *The* Devon Groh?"

"The very one." I grinned. "I was in a month-long student apprenticeship program with him. He's so humble and unassuming. It's unreal for such a famous artist."

"Unbelievable."

"He's the one who referred me to my first job as an advisor. I was a struggling student with visa restrictions, and it gave my career a new lease. I learned a lot, the pay was decent, and they eventually processed my green card. I worked there until my mentor convinced me to go into a partnership with her at the new firm she was starting. I did, and now, here I am."

"I'm very happy for you, Tara. And proud."

The sound of those words, the look of authentic care in his eyes, knocked down the wall I had built between us. "Until last year, I worked around the clock, till my eyes wore out and my body gave up. I was so tired, Sameer. The opportunities felt surreal, and I couldn't afford to waste a single second. I read and learned and did everything I could, like a greedy, starved person, and yet I felt I wasn't doing enough. Now, I embrace every success and every bit of happiness that comes my way."

"You deserve to be happy," he said, but I caught a glint of something strange in his eyes, like love, admiration, pity, and concern, all blended into a distasteful concoction.

I sat up with a bright smile. "But it wasn't all bad. I had a great time too. During my master's, I got to take courses in folklore theory and Black feminism. And I went to Rome! Those were the best fifteen months of my life. I traveled across Europe and witnessed the glorious pieces of art and architecture that I never imagined in my wildest dreams I'd get to see. Never had too much money, but the friends I made were resourceful and inventive."

"I love your picture from Rome. The one with your hair flying across your face."

My cheeks flooded with warmth to learn he had looked me up. "You know everything about my life, but I know nothing about yours," I accused mildly.

"I follow you on social media. I only know what you've made public."

My back straightened. "You aren't on social media."

"I am." He leaned in to meet my eyes. "Hiding behind a different name."

"I tried looking for you." I regretted the admission immediately. My stomach twisted and my brows creased. "Maybe this wasn't the best idea."

"We need to do this, Tara. Even if it's upsetting."

"It's beyond upsetting," I said, trying to keep my hot head from exploding. "Everything you've done to me is unfair."

"Yes, I've been unfair to you. But it hasn't been easy for me either."

"But you are the one who made all the decisions. I didn't."

His gaze lowered to his cup, and I looked into mine. The beautifully stained rings of foam had now deflated and hugged the ceramic walls in the hope of holding on just a little longer. I pushed the cup away.

"Get me another," I said to him.

"Same?"

"Extra shot."

He nodded and left me to my thoughts. The weekend he'd sent me the text, I had returned home to see my parents, looking for support. But before I could summon the courage to tell them, Baba had a heart attack. A mild cardiac event, the doctor said. And we could get him timely medical attention only because I was lingering outside his room, working up my courage to approach him when I heard the thud. I rushed in and yelled out for Aai and Dada. The ambulance arrived fifteen minutes later. If I had told him, I would've surely killed him.

I ran my fingers through my hair, trying to make sense of my turmoil. Because despite all of this—my heartache, humiliation, and pain—I still a felt a visceral draw to Sameer. He was the only one who recognized my spirit, my hunger. He could tell from the way I held a brush what my next stroke was going to be. He'd take one look at me and know what I was thinking.

Placing a fresh cup before me, Sameer retook his seat. A gentle steam arose from the cup like a mother's consoling hand.

"Tara..."

"Don't." I retorted and tore open multiple tiny packs of sugar, dumping them into my cup.

"I want to make things right," he said softly.

"How? How can you make things right? Can you bring back my father? Can you give me back those years I spent afraid and unsure? Unwilling to trust anyone with my heart? I didn't have a relationship until I met Sujit. I was thirty-two! That has to mean something, Sameer." I stirred my coffee furiously.

"Neither did I, Tara. I could never replace you."

"But you did."

He didn't respond, merely stared back with a tenacity that scared me.

"I have a life, a career," I said. "I'm in a relationship that makes me happy."

"But *are* you happy?" he pressed again.

This time, I refused to respond.

"I want us to move past the hurt and the pain, to be able to talk, share, laugh like we just did. Right now, I'll settle for that," he said.

"To what end?" I argued. "We have different lives now. We don't need to be friends."

"And yet, here we are."

Move past the hurt and the pain. Maybe that's what I needed. For all these years, I had been weighed down by it. Maybe we could get to a point where I could think about him without bitterness in my heart. Maybe that would help me heal.

"You've always been a part of my life, Sameer, a part of me even when I didn't want it. I haven't been able to cut you out. But I can't..."

I looked at my coffee again. It had lost its steam and so had I. "Let's talk about you. Are you happy?"

"No." He let his undaunted eyes meet mine, but I chose deflection.

"I don't even know what you do for a living."

He waited a few breaths, then answered. "I run an investment firm. I took over from my uncle when he retired some years ago."

"Huh!" I said, lifting the cup to my lips.

"What's that?"

"Nothing. I thought things had changed. *You* had changed."

"What does *that* mean?" he demanded with a deep frown.

"You've always had everything handed to you, everything laid out right at your feet. Here I thought you would've accomplished something on your own merit. You surely have the potential. But it's the lack of inclination that was always the problem, wasn't it?"

I knew I was being cruel, but I wanted him to hurt like he'd hurt me.

His fair face turned red. "What is your problem, Tara? I've been nothing but civil."

"Civil? Is that supposed to be my consolation? My problem is that you're still a spoilt rich boy, cruising through life, riding on the wave of your privilege and wealth. Demanding me back as if you're entitled to my love, to me. I hoped you'd changed, but you are still the same. How could you understand what I've been through? While I was busy busting my ass trying to find a foothold in the world, you were busy crushing people like me with the weight of everything you've inherited, not earned."

In one swift motion, he grabbed his phone from the table and slid out of the booth. "*This* is unfair. I said I would tell you everything, but until then, you don't get to sit here and make judgments about me. If you have issues with me because I'm rich, that's your problem, Tara, not mine. I've always respected you, but you don't get to sit here and insult me like this." He took two steps toward the exit, then turned around and added, "You're right, this wasn't the best idea."

With angry steps, he strode away. This time, he didn't come back.

Turned out, work wasn't a safe neutral subject, after all.

TARA

$\mathcal{M}$y fingernails dug into the heels of my palm as tried to calm myself. I didn't regret what I'd said, only how I said it. Thinking about my father, who had worked hard all his life, filled me with a sadness that had quickly turned to anger. I had taken it out on Sameer because neither subtlety nor diplomacy were among my virtues.

I texted Sona to see if she was free for a call. An early riser, she meticulously kept to her writing schedule, even on the weekends. She called me back promptly.

"Hey, what's up?"

"Are you writing? I'd hate to interrupt."

"No, just came back from a run."

"I really need to talk to you."

"What happened?" I imagined her sitting on the couch with her feet on the coffee table.

"I saw Sameer again and said some really horrible things to him," I confessed in Marathi.

"Oh, are you alright?" It was only under very specific circum-stances that we broke into our native language, so she was understandably concerned. I told her everything as calmly as I could manage.

"Okay...did you mean to hurt him?"

"I don't know!" I threw my head back, still talking in Marathi. "It just came bursting out, and I didn't stop it."

"Tara, can I ask you something?" Sona switched to English.

"Hmm."

"Why do you care?"

"What do you mean?"

"You said those hurtful things. He got annoyed or angry or whatever, and he left. Why does that bother you? Why does it matter to you that he's upset?"

Her question stumped me into silence.

"You've been angry at him for a long time," she continued. "You said you wanted nothing to do with him. If this episode burns the bridge between you two, isn't that a good thing?"

Again, I had no response.

"Unless you were actually trying to mend that broken bridge. Were you?" she added softly.

My breath shuddered. She wasn't too far from the truth.

"I don't know," I confessed. "Why can't I let him go, Sona?"

"Because you haven't had closure, my love. You haven't told him what's hurting you. And you haven't heard why he left. Maybe you should talk to him and get it out of your system."

I leaned back and closed my eyes. "All I know is that what I said was impulsive and vindictive."

"Well, what's done is done. The question is, what do you want to do now? You can try and talk to him, be the bigger person and apologize. Or you can both carry your resentments and move on with your lives. How do you want to resolve this, babe?"

"I haven't decided," I said, and I heard a sigh at the other end. "How's my mom?"

"She's good. I went over for dinner last night. She made mutton curry. We called, but you didn't answer."

"I fell asleep on the couch. I called her this morning, but she must've been asleep."

"Oh, we went to the park together. I ran. She walked."

"Dammit, Sona," I wailed. "You're getting all the motherly love that's rightfully mine."

She chuckled. "Then come back soon. She misses you. We all do. Especially your knight in shining armor."

"Don't start. Alright, I'll hang up now. I need to call him too."

"Wow, great friend you are! You'll hang up on me to call him."

I smiled. "Yeah, yeah. Talk to you soon? Hey, thank you for today. I love you."

"Love you too. Stay sensible."

I laughed and hung up. Cramming my stuff into my bag, I left the café.

Last year, a friend had introduced me to Sujit Rao, who was looking to buy artwork for his family home as a gift for his parents. He was a striking man, intimidating with his tall figure, and commanding in the way he conducted himself.

We met at a fancy bistro to discuss his preferences.

"I need to be honest with you," he said, looking at me through his clear glasses set in stylish metal rims. "I'm clueless about my aesthetic sensibilities. I've no idea what I like or what looks good, so I'm hesitant to contact a gallery."

I smiled. "At least you know that. You might not know what you want, but I have a feeling you'll know when you see it."

"I'm looking for something that speaks to my family, to us as individuals. Do you think that's too ambitious, or too vague?"

"Not at all. But to know where to begin, I'll need to know a little more about your family and you," I said.

He responded to what was a professional request with a mischievous smile that revealed two perfect dimples in his cheeks. "That means we'll need to meet up again," he said.

After two more meetings, we drove upstate to his family home so I could see the dimensions and style of the place. It was a perfect day, with a chill in the air and gorgeous fall leaves along the road. Contrary to my first impression, he was a gentle, almost shy man, a pleasant travel companion, funny and genuine. Sharp-witted with a naughty side so subtle, it was easy to miss if one wasn't paying attention. When I'd looked him up before the meeting, I learned that he had started a healthcare-based software company, which had sold for a few billion dollars, and then founded a startup focused on education.

When we pulled up to the driveway of a giant house, I couldn't help commenting, "You're very polite for a person who lives in a mansion. I knew someone rich once who was obnoxious and insufferable."

He broke into a hearty laugh as he closed the car door behind me and said, "If it makes you feel any better, I don't actually live here. This is sort of a family home we use during the holidays or when we have out-of-town guests."

One look at the space, and I knew exactly what it needed. A traditional Raja Ravi Verma-esque portrait in the stately dining room to complement the glittering crystal chandelier. For the living room, which was set to more contemporary tones, I recommended three pieces by newer artists. Each of the several bedrooms had distinctive furniture, which made my job easier than I had imagined. As we turned pages in the portfolio I had brought along, our hands brushed, and he let his touch linger without imposing. My heart did a little flutter before I gently withdrew my hand.

We drove back in contemplative silence, and as he dropped me off at my apartment that chilly autumn night, he asked me out. When I hesitated, he began to apologize.

"Don't say sorry," I said. "It's just that I'm still working for you as a consultant. But I hope you'll ask me again when I'm done and our contract ends."

He smiled at me, and our relationship had taken a gentle turn.

I placed a video call to him. He also gave me updates about Aai. "Thank you for looking in on her," I said.

"Hey, we've talked about this. I don't like it when you thank me. I'm doing this for me."

My heart thumped hard. "How are your parents?" I asked.

That got him talking for another half an hour. He told me about a gathering they had with his extended family at their big house, how everyone raved about the new art, and how he bragged that I had selected each piece personally.

"I wouldn't stop talking about you until I got a few eyerolls."

"Enough gushing already," I rebuked gently. "We've known each other for a while. Don't you think the fascination should've worn off by now?"

"Are you kidding? How can anyone who knows you not be fascinated by you?"

"You're biased. Your opinion doesn't count," I argued with a smile.

"Of course I'm biased, darling," he said with a wink. The dents in his cheeks turned deeper.

Suddenly, I couldn't breathe. I felt like the room had become smaller, the air thicker. My skin felt cold and clammy. I stole a quick breath.

"How's work?" I asked, opting for the ever-handy deflection.

He told me about a new software his company was developing, and I told him about the enigma of the two paintings. He listened politely, but I found myself missing the reaction I had seen on Sameer's face. Sujit was excited *for* me, but it wasn't the same as being excited *with* me. The same way that I didn't share his excitement about the new software. I tried to stop myself, but my mind kept drifting to Sameer.

No! This had to stop.

Instead of dwelling on what happened that morning, I redirected my energies to my accounts and answered emails that had accumulated over the last two days. When my stomach rumbled around five, I realized I had skipped lunch. While I fixed a quick snack, my eyes fell on the invitation card to a cocktail party at the Arlington home that evening.

When I received the invitation two weeks ago, I had intended to pass on it, but Dr. Hadden had stopped by my office to make sure I was going. What does one wear to a cocktail party at the home of an oil baron? I did a quick online search and decided that my black sheath with full-length sleeves would work perfectly. Hitting just above the knee, it had a lace-lined, deep-cut back and a modest neckline.

I queued up my favorite music on the phone—melodious retro Bollywood songs—and began my primping ritual. It was almost meditative. First I straightened my hair into a glossy cascade with a side part. Then I applied sheer makeup, shaped my brows, highlighted my eyes, and swiped on a matte wine lipstick that complimented my brown skin. A pair of strappy kitten heels and diamond studs completed the look. Simple, but chic.

The same way that I played with colors on my canvas, I loved playing with clothing and makeup. My body was my canvas. I had always been an outsider in the art world, whether it was my caste, class, place of origin, or skin color. In the early days when I was starting out, I had erroneously believed that hard work and merit would make everything else irrelevant. But I quickly learned that the world doesn't work that way. I needed to mark my body in specific ways to find a seat at the table.

I learned to expertly apply makeup, which I came to realize I loved. I also played with my clothing, dressing quirky for artists' meet-and-greets, donning business formals when I first met my clients. Later, as I established my command over the field in their eyes, I could dress down, casual or playful. And as I did, I had a great laugh, because here I was, a dark-skinned woman from a community whose artistic contributions were denigrated as "the crafts," handing out proclamations on the value and validity of high art for people with way too much money and clout. It gave me a kick that was beyond what I had ever expected from my work.

But I would be lying if I said I did it all for the thrill, because the fear of being labeled an outsider was an equally strong motivation. Despite everything I had achieved, the feeling that I would be accused of not belonging in that space, in the profession, in the field did not dissipate easily. Identity is a fickle friend. It can desert you at the slightest hint of self-doubt.

To alleviate these fears, I wore designer clothes with an ease I didn't feel in my heart. I carried a prized saffiano bag that I had gifted myself after my first successful consultation. I could afford more bags now, but I didn't need them. Because, despite my experimentation with clothing and makeup, I didn't really change who I was at my core. I only tweaked people's perceptions of me, like adding a little sugar of playfulness to the milk of my personality. Neither changed its true nature, but made the liquid sweeter, more appealing.

The phrase comes from a Gujarati tale I read as a child, *Dudh ma Saakar*, "Sugar in the Milk." The kingdom was Sanjaan, the period circa eighth century CE. Fleeing persecution, Zoroastrians traveled from Persia to the shores of Gujarat. The leader of the Zoroastrians, a wise priest, sent a messenger to the court of the king Jadi Rana to seek asylum. The king handed him a bowl of milk, filled to the brim. When the messenger came back with the bowl, the Zoroastrian leader added a handful of sugar, stirred it with caution so the milk didn't spill, then sent it back.

The king smiled and granted them entry into his land. When his people asked the leader what it meant, he explained, the king's message was that his kingdom was full like the bowl of milk. But the leader said we'll blend in like sugar. Zoroastrians who became Parsis, adopted the language, food habits, and dressing style of Gujarat, while still retaining their faith and identity. They have been an integral part of India since.

True or not, I loved the story, the simplicity, the wisdom in it. It was a tale of survival and hope, of starting over in a new land without losing the essence of who you were. This was my hope each time I started over in a new life, a new career at a different place on the globe. I adopted changes to my wardrobe and language as necessary to my survival but without surrendering my identity or forfeiting who I was, like sugar in the milk.

Sweet, I appraised myself in the mirror and sent a quick selfie to Aai and Sujit before calling for an Uber.

TARA

The palatial house was already bustling with people when I entered through its massive doors.

Dr. Hadden caught my eye and waved me over. Instead of the usual nod, she grabbed me in an excited hug and tugged me along to be introduced to the hosts—the great-grandson of the original oil baron and his wife. They welcomed me with grace and sophistication, but with a decided warmth in their eyes.

"Your paintings are in expert hands, Jenna," Dr. Hadden said to Mrs. Arlington. "I wouldn't trust anyone else with them," she added, sans smile or any other glimpse of warmth. She wasn't complimenting, merely stating a fact.

Mrs. Arlington smiled at Dr. Hadden's words and asked if I'd be interested in seeing the other paintings in their collection. With an overeager, possibly unprofessional nod, I accepted the offer as an unexpected privilege. She reacted with a surprised laugh and summoned Peter, one of their "people," to show me around.

Peter escorted me out of the grand room, into the living area, and to the interior of the house, waiting patiently by every painting as I studied it. Despite my best intentions, I ended up taking long minutes to appreciate each.

"I'm sorry to take up so much time," I said to Peter as we circled back to the grand room, where the soirée was now in full swing.

"It's my pleasure. We see them every day, and they kind of blur in the background, you know. It was interesting to watch you admire them."

Before I could respond, I stopped in my tracks. Ahead of us, standing out in a sea of handsome, elegant people, was Sameer.

His bright eyes scanned the crowd, his strong smile captivating everyone in his vicinity. On his arm was an equally gorgeous, slender, and very well-dressed woman. The couple owned the room, and they knew it. My heart twisted as I saw heads turning to admire the stunning pair.

"Is everything alright?" Peter asked.

"Yes, I thought I saw someone I know," I said, turning to him, and extended my hand. "Thank you so much for showing me around, Peter. I really appreciate it."

He smiled and returned to resume his duties. It took me only a quick moment to deliberate if I should approach Sameer and quell the fire between us or become invisible on the other side of the large room. There was a fair chance Sameer hadn't seen me, so I chose the latter. There was an equally good chance I'd end up stoking the fire instead of quelling it. I considered myself a good person, but I wasn't above petty emotions like jealousy. That woman was gorgeous. *Perfect's the word you're looking for*, my brain prodded, but I shut it down quickly.

I found Dr. Hadden talking with our host. As I thanked him for the opportunity to see the paintings, I couldn't help bringing up the two pieces that perplexed me.

"I think I might be obsessed with them. I keep talking about them to anyone who'll listen." I laughed. "They're challenging me in interesting ways and giving me grief, all at the same time."

He nodded as if he knew exactly what I was talking about, then let a cunning smile slip. "Let me show you something."

We followed him to a wall behind the grand room, where he pointed to a painting hiding in the shadows. When he flipped a switch for a recessed light above the frame, my eyes flickered with excitement. The signature was the same as one of the artists of my affliction.

"Do you mind if I spend some time with it?"

"Be my guest," he said, then squared his shoulders and returned to the party.

"What do you think?" Dr. Hadden asked me.

"I'm not sure. There is something I can't figure out."

She patted my shoulder. "Well, have fun with it. I'm going to get another drink."

"Sure," I replied absently, and began my investigation.

Standing before the painting reminded me of Sameer's words, but that particular ship had clearly sailed. I studied the piece till its colors began to blur my vision. What I needed was to rest my eyes and hit the reset button. Perhaps get a drink. I walked back into the grand room, but before I could reach the servers floating around with elegant flutes of white wine and sassy goblets of red, I ran into Sameer.

"Tara!" he said, his eyes wide with disbelief.

My heart jumped at the way his shoulders filled out the tailored jacket. In my heels, I was almost as tall as him, but in that moment, his towering figure overshadowed me.

I did my best to project disinterest. "Oh. Hi, Sameer."

"Didn't expect to see you here."

"Ditto," I replied in the same haughty tone he had used.

His gorgeous companion turned to us with a brilliant smile

on her perfect face and stood close to him. Too close. She put a hand on his back.

"Aarti," Sameer said, his eyes averted. "This is Tara. She's Amar's friend from Baroda. Tara, my girlfriend, Aarti."

The slight guilt working its way into my heart disappeared fast.

I extended my hand. "Nice to meet you," I said as her brows hit the roof.

"Wow, that's an old connection."

I smiled, wondering how she'd react if she knew about our real connection.

"How do you know the family?" Aarti asked.

In other words, where might I stand in the hierarchy of the social elite?

As far away as I could put myself.

"I'm appraising the paintings they've donated to the museum," I said, wishing I had a drink in my hand to hold as a barrier.

Her brows flew higher. "That's wonderful." She looked impressed, but I couldn't decipher if it was genuine appreciation or derision. I wasn't good at these things. Sameer was. I looked at him.

"Aarti's an old friend of their daughter." Sameer's voice, firm and guiltfree, conveyed the private message loud and clear. The *friend* who knew the family was the *girlfriend*. Sneaky, but I was impressed he had managed to keep her out of our conversation this morning.

"Yes, Mary Beth is visiting after a long time since her wedding." Her eyes beheld Sameer in unmistakable admiration, and my stomach did a funny flip.

"Well, it was wonderful to meet you, Aarti. Nice seeing you again, Sameer." I faked a big, broad smile, and walked away.

Grabbing a glass of red, I returned to my refuge behind the wall. It was safe to assume he hadn't told her about buying my painting for that exorbitant amount. But judging by the designer cocktail dress on her, twenty-five thousand dollars was probably pocket change for their lot. I resisted the urge to spiral down into thoughts of him and his gorgeous girlfriend and redirected my focus to the painting.

Suddenly something clicked. The painting snapped into relief. I moved in closer, then immediately stepped back in shock and disbelief. *It had been right before me all along.* I just needed someone to confirm my theory, a desire that took precedence over my anger and heartbreak in that moment.

I found Sameer at the other end of the grand room, talking and smiling. As I approached, hustling quickly through people holding drinks, his smile faded.

"I'm sorry, but can I borrow you for a moment?" I asked him, then looked at Aarti.

She smiled. Sameer managed a micro-expression as he set his drink aside. I felt my heart thumping against my eardrums as we weaved back to the landing behind the wall.

"I need to run something by you. See what you think." He responded with a solemn nod. "Ok, tell me what you see." I pointed to the painting.

His eyes stayed on me. "Tell me what you want me to see," he replied with a gruff breath.

"Sameer," I said sharply, and his frown ironed out. "I need a moment's détente. This is important." He responded with a slight nod, and I directed him to the painting once more. "What do you see?"

He scanned it, dispassionately at first, then with a series of knowing blinks. "Is this the same artist?"

"One of them."

I pointed to specific parts. "What do you see here?"

"I...are those eyes?" He stepped closer to the wall, and I closed my hand around his wrist. I kept my eyes on him as he gazed into the canvas, his pulse steady against my fingers. Notes of musk and tobacco flirted with the drifty oud in his mysterious, seductive cologne. The smell alone was enough to make my heart race. Then I saw it—a twinkle in his eyes, a smile at the corners of his mouth—an expression I knew too well.

"These aren't benign-looking landscapes, it's symbolism."

"Yes!" My fingers clenched tighter around his wrist.

"These trees look like shrouded figures, and the withering tall grass resembles prostrating humans."

"You see that, right?"

"But the sky is pink and white, and my first thought was *Love and Loss*. You used pink to depict our first time together, didn't you?" he asked, his sight trained on the canvas.

"Yes, why? What are you thinking?"

"I'm thinking rapture, ecstasy. A transcendental experience of some kind."

"Spiritual?"

My eyes were glued to the painting, but I felt him shrug.

"Or sexual."

"Or both?" I glanced at him. "The liminal space between the sexual and the spiritual, human and nature?"

A liminal space. Wasn't that also where we stood?

He turned to me. "That's for the expert to figure out." The familiar smile warmed my heart, and I found the nerve to thread my fingers through his. His touch felt the same—thrilling yet comfortable. Warm, soft, yet firm and commanding. We were so close, he could've kissed me without moving an inch. Perhaps I wanted him to. But he turned to the wall. "This is brilliant, Tara! *You're* brilliant."

"Couldn't have done it without you." I found myself grinning like a giddy teenager. "Told you I'd need your help solving the mystery."

"You solved it. I only corroborated after the fact."

"But two artists using similar symbolism seems untenable."

"Maybe one was an apprentice. Did you find a difference in technique?"

"They have distinctive strokes for sure, but I was on a completely different tangent, so I'll have to look again."

As I savored the warmth of his hand in mine behind that sturdy, faithful wall, we found ourselves in a moment of complete bliss. On the other side was a cruel, unfair world, full of pain and heartache.

"Thank you for sharing this with me. It had been a long time. I didn't think I had it in me anymore."

"You'll always have it," I whispered. "Nothing can take that away."

When he rolled his thumb over my hand, it was all I needed to get through one lifetime. "So, Amar's friend, huh?"

"I was angry," he said, his eyes back on the painting. It was then that I tried to withdraw my hand, but he tugged it back and held on tight. I stood looking into the painting but not seeing it. His grip tightened and my breath turned heavy. "You look beautiful."

My heart began sprinting again. I waited for something to happen—a sound, a breath, a touch. Nothing changed, but my body was preparing itself for something. Then I heard it. *Footsteps.* High heels on the polished wood floor. I quickly disengaged my hand and backed up a respectable distance from Sameer just as Aarti came around the corner.

"There you are!" She gave a friendly smile. "What are you doing here?"

He quickly stepped toward her. "Tara wanted to show me something."

"What?" she asked and looked back and forth between us.

"Just something silly we used to debate about in college," he said. The smile that accompanied it could be easily misconstrued as adoration if one didn't know him. But I could spot his discomfort from a mile away. He slid his hand around her waist and looked at me over his shoulder. "See you around, Tara."

See you around, indeed. I threw back my wine and ambled into the grand room where the hot couple blended seamlessly among the rich and powerful. I walked over to Dr. Hadden and stayed with her until the first guests began to leave.

Out the door I walked, along the path flanked by a rambling lawn, only to end up in Sameer's presence for the third time that night. He stood by the large marble fountain, talking on the phone, and hung up when he saw me. An uncomfortable moment elapsed as I flashed back to the swift arm he had slipped around Aarti. Fire and brimstone, that was us.

"I was waiting for you. How are you getting back?" he asked, and I felt my anger spike.

"I'm calling a cab," I said while scrambling to open the app on my phone.

"I'll drop you." Not *can*, will.

"Thank you, but I'll be alright."

Just then, a few other guests walked out, and he smacked me with a stern reproach in Hindi. "Zid mat karo."

I glared at him. He glowered back and placed a call on his phone. "Aarti, I'm going to drop Tara," he said, and started walking toward the parked cars. "She lives five minutes from mine. You head over. I'll see you there."

Bile rose in my throat. Furious that I followed him like an obedient pet.

"I wasn't being stubborn. I'm furious," I finally responded to his reprimand, as he held the car door open for me.

"Yeah? So am I," he said and slammed the door in my face.

The car glided out of the gates. "I'd thank you for the ride, but I didn't need it." I was prepared for the quick glare he tossed in my direction. "Why did Aarti not drive back with you?" I asked, and he frowned hard.

"She came directly from hers."

"But she's going back to yours?" When that fetched me an irate look too, I quickly added, "I'm sorry, it's none of my business."

"Yes, it's none of your business, and yes, she's spending the rest of the weekend with me, which she does whenever she can."

The words, carefully chosen to inflict pain, did have the intended effect. But I pushed back the humiliation.

"She's gorgeous. You both look good together."

"She's not you," he said with his eyes on the road and an angry frown between them.

"No," I said with a sigh. "She isn't. She's perfect, and she's with you."

"You can stop it, Tara. You've already hurt me enough. You don't need to take it any further. You have no right to judge me when you know nothing about my life."

My heart wrenched. I had never intended to hurt him, but I had, twice. I looked out the window as we zipped along the empty roads. Sona said I had a choice to make. I could apologize or let it fester into an irreconcilable affair. But by the time we arrived at my apartment, I still hadn't decided what I wanted.

"I'm texting you my number," he said as his dexterous thumbs glided over the screen. We stood by his car underneath my building. "I'll wait here until you're in."

"You don't have to do that. I'm a grown woman. I know how to be careful."

"Give me your apartment number," he added as if I had silently acquiesced to his first demand.

I unleashed a resigned sigh. "1707."

We stood in silence with the sound of an occasional car driving past in the cool night.

"Good night, Tara." Another command.

I heard the distance in his voice. "You have every right to be angry, Sameer. But for what it's worth, I didn't mean those things. I've been holding on to a lot, and I guess I snapped. But that's not how I really feel about you. I want you to know that." I started walking away, then turned. "But if you'd trusted me with your past, we wouldn't be here."

"You didn't give me a chance," I heard him say, but I kept walking.

Riding up an elevator as empty as I felt inside, I entered my apartment and texted him.

> In. Thank you.

Then, I kicked off my heels and collapsed onto the couch in tears. It felt like my heart had burst open again. How could this happen to me twice? Weren't there rules for heartbreaks? How was it fair that I had to live through this pain again? I couldn't decide if I was hurting more from having wounded Sameer or from the visions of him spending the weekend with his glamorous girlfriend, tumbling around in bed having sweet sex. A fresh stream of tears erupted at the thought.

My cell phone vibrated on the coffee table. I blinked away the tears and saw Sameer's number flashing on the screen. I didn't answer. The last thing I wanted was to make him a witness to my breakdown, a defeat of my wits against his perfect life with his perfect girlfriend. He called again. I let it go to voicemail. And again.

When the phone buzzed for the fourth time, it was a text.

> SAMEER
>
> Open the door.

I rushed to the door and peeked through the peephole to see

him standing outside. I wiped my eyes and reluctantly pulled the door open.

He entered and closed it behind him.

"I knew you'd be crying," he said, holding my arm. "I'm angry, Tara, but I can't be the reason for your tears. Never again." He threw his arms around me and drew me into his chest.

"I hate myself for hurting you," I said before breaking down and lining his fancy jacket with my tears.

"It's okay. We're in this mess because of me."

His hands slipped under my hair and touched my bare back. It was an accidental touch, and I felt him hesitate, but the next instant, I heard him inhale a quick breath against my cheek. His fingers dug into my skin and clutched me tighter, my breasts pressing into his hard chest. His warm breath landed on my neck, his smell reaching deep inside me and turning my knees to jelly. Wrapping my arms around him, I sank deeper against him and felt his lips draw closer to my cheek. I held my breath. I was ready. I knew what I wanted.

"Sameer, I—" It was a gentle tremor from his jacket that stunned me into silence.

He pulled out his phone. "It's Aarti. She's at my place. I should go."

Like the fool that I was, I stayed in his arms a moment longer than I should've before I stepped out and wiped away my tears.

"Will you be alright?"

"Yes."

"We should talk, Tara."

"There's no need. You just made your decision very clear."

"Tara..."

"Leave."

He hesitated at the door but left anyway, and I crumbled on the couch.

SAMEER

I had heard Tara weeping before she came to the door. Her tears smudged her makeup, and I saw the pain on her face. The same pain that now stabbed at my heart as I drove back home. I'd just had a glimpse of how she must have hurt when I left her years ago. All I wanted was to stay with my face nuzzled in her neck, holding her in my arms.

Instead, I was driving back to Aarti. Why? Because I had promised her. And because I was too much of a coward to come clean to either woman. I should've broken it off with Aarti the moment I realized Tara still harbored feelings for me. And I should've trusted Tara with my past.

But there was more at stake. After our disgraceful exodus from India, breaking up with Aarti would make my family a social pariah again. For Dad, my marriage promised the merger of our fortunes and the linking of our family name with theirs. It meant security and status. Aarti's family didn't care about that. They didn't need to. For them, I was the trophy partner who looked really good on Aarti's arm. That I wasn't a major-league asshole was what had clinched this relationship for them.

The Bhatia name held a lot of clout in the region, especially in the South Asian community. A single misstep would ruin me, cutting me off from every important social and economic connection I had cultivated. Years of my hard work had made the company larger than it had ever been. It would cost me more than the stigma of a failed relationship if I messed this up, something I couldn't do to Mom again. I banged my hand on the steering wheel as I cursed aloud in the privacy of my car.

Everything I had done since that fateful night, every single decision I made, had been with the sole intent of protecting Mom. Within a span of twenty-four hours, she'd lost her home, her wealth, and her name. All on account of the man who was her husband. He'd shattered her entire world in a blink, and she'd deserved none of it.

Mom was a queen, in looks, grace, and demeanor. Her family wasn't exactly royalty, but they enjoyed the wealth and lifestyle that would make blue bloods green with envy. Life in a palatial haveli in Punjab with numerous servants bustling around, catering to their every whim and fancy, was her normal. Her wealth was ancestral, and Mom remembered her childhood as decadent yet disciplined before they settled in Delhi, where her father had set up his businesses.

As the youngest child and only sister to three brothers, she was doted on by everyone around her. Her oldest brother had moved to the U.S. in the 1970s for higher education, fell in love, and settled into a life here. But when they lost the two brothers between them—one to a road accident and one to heart disease— he brought Mom over. He had no children and raised Mom like his daughter. By the time she graduated with a master's degree in finance, she was also a U.S. citizen. But unlike her brother, she missed having her parents around, and much to his displeasure, declared her intention to return to India. To appease him, she promised to retain her U.S. citizenship and to confer it on her own children.

Upon her arrival in India, Mom had only one condition for marriage: she wanted an educated man. She had seen enough women in her family smothered by the weight of wealth and traditions. She wanted someone who'd see her as a partner, not merely a wife or an asset. And Dad did that, initially at least. He had the trifecta when it came to arranged marriages. He was educated, handsome, and comfortably rich, the founder and owner of a small but successful pharmaceutical company. Mom thought she had hit the jackpot and unhesitatingly pumped all her wealth into his business. Success worshipped them, and they took the company public around the time I was in middle school. Dad was appointed CEO, and we moved into the echelons of the Indian super-rich. This change in fortune accounted for much of my cockiness growing up, until it all came crashing down like a house of cards.

Mom's brother saved her grace. Uncle invited us to the U.S. and shared his wealth with a generosity we didn't deserve. He paid for my education and trained me at his firm, then sent me to business school. I worked hard, attending college in the morning and working with him in the afternoon. I had no friends and no social life. I severed all ties with my former lifestyle, surviving on the wages he paid me, which were comparable to others employed at the same level. When Uncle bought a monstrous mansion for my parents, I insisted on renting an apartment I could afford on my own, opting to live in a community that housed graduate students and newly employed young people struggling to start a new life like me.

My uncle offered me access to whatever I wanted, but I wouldn't accept what I hadn't earned. Through the years, Tara remained the standard against which I measured myself. I wanted the dignity and respect she commanded. Tara had been right in her accusations. I had inherited the company and the wealth, but this time, I had earned it, made myself worthy of it.

Six years ago, after his wife passed, Uncle became severely depressed and gradually handed me the reins of his company. The keys to the firm, however, came with responsibilities. The professional ones I grasped quickly and conducted competently, but the social burdens caught me off guard. My visibility demanded the apropos performance of success in clothing, cars, and behavior, cultivating the *right kind* of accent, maintaining the delicate balance between my Indian and American identities. I couldn't be too Desi, especially because I grew up in India, but I also couldn't come across as so American that I couldn't be trusted to be a good Indian. I had to be a good son to be viewed as a good person. But I had to display enough independence from my parents to be considered good husband material.

I changed myself to become the man I had never imagined I'd be. Amar was the achiever in our family, I was a lost cause. My only worth would've been to inherit Dad's wealth. Until there wasn't any.

But my attempts to rebuild our life did little to heal the scars on Mom's heart, especially when Dad resisted making the effort. He wallowed in conceit and complacency, refusing to mend the cracks he left when he shattered her life, punishing her for my offenses. So now it was up to me. I had to redeem myself by reinstating Mom's life to its former glory and give her back the social stature she once enjoyed before he besmirched her name.

As the elevator dinged for my floor, a strange realization hit me. None of this would matter if I had Tara. None of this would matter *to* Tara. As the memory of her sweet face drenched in tears resurfaced in my mind, I realized she was right. I *had* left her for money.

The elevator doors opened and closed twice before I could bring myself to exit. Then I stood outside my apartment, preparing to slip into the role of the loving boyfriend. Killing the uneasy clog in my chest, I unlocked the door and stepped inside.

"I'm in here," Aarti called from the bedroom as I dropped my keys on the counter.

"Okay, give me a minute." I detoured to the kitchen and poured a glass of water to buy myself a few more moments. Then, leaving the glass untouched, I headed to the bedroom.

Aarti looked up from her Kindle and straightened. "What's the matter, baby? Are you alright?"

I smiled. "Yes."

"You look pale."

"It's been a long week."

I threw my jacket on a chair and went into the bathroom with a change of clothes. She was still reading when I returned. I knew where we were headed, but I couldn't do that to Tara. I couldn't do that to myself. I climbed into bed and lay on my back.

"Sameer, you'd tell me if something was bothering you, right?" She locked the Kindle and placed it on the nightstand.

"Of course!" I forced a reassuring smile and tucked her hair behind her ear. "Really, I'm just tired. Too much going through my mind."

"You wanna talk about it?" She let her slender finger trace my jawline.

I took her hand and kissed it. "Not today."

She snuggled against me with her head on my chest, and I snuck my hands under my head to avoid putting them around her.

"Can I ask you something?"

"Hmm."

"Does it have anything to do with Tara?" She looked up at me with wary eyes.

My heart thumped. "What?"

"Who is she, really?" She tried to soften her tone, but I felt the fire in her words.

"She's Amar's friend. We overlapped at the art college." I made sure to maintain the equilibrium in my voice. "Why?"

"I got the feeling you two had been close."

"We were friends for a year. That's why she dragged me off to share some ridiculous theory about the painting. I don't know those things anymore."

Aarti was no fool, but I was a good liar. I had probably managed to convince her because she nodded and sat up with a smile. "What do you want to do for your birthday next weekend?"

"Next weekend?" I hadn't realized it had already been a month since Tara arrived in Dallas. That funny hole in my chest reappeared.

"Hello-ooo." Aarti's singsong voice beckoned me.

"Sorry, yes."

She shook her head and tousled my hair. "Silly boy," she said, and placed a gentle kiss on my lips. "I asked if you wanted to go away for the weekend or have friends over?"

"When you say have people over, you mean here, right? Not at my parents' place?"

"Not unless *you* want that," she said with a naughty smirk.

"Here sounds good. Let's have friends over and get some drinks and pizza."

She grimaced. "Pizza?"

"Why?"

"Because you're not fifteen."

"Okay, then whatever you want."

"It'll be lowkey, but let's get some decent food. Maybe some sandwiches and some kind of spread. No, scrap the sandwiches. Let's make it a Mediterranean spread, kebab, shawarma, gyro. And something vegetarian. Maybe rice and pita and three dips at least. Oh, a baklava cake with honey buttercream frosting. I had it at a party last month." She eyed my checked-out face and smiled. "I'll have Shirley arrange it."

Shirley, her event-planner friend, catered to Aarti's whims as frequently as she did her parties.

"I thought we were keeping it casual."

"We are. Very casual," she said with a naughty grin.

"If Shirley's involved, it's going to be anything but casual." I shook my head and smiled back.

"Well, she knows how to keep me happy."

"That she does. Better than me," I blurted, then instantly regretted my words. I had internalized the habit of pleasing her despite how I felt, a habit that was sure to blow up in my face soon.

"I wouldn't say that." She snuggled against my side and slipped her hand down my pants. Employing both enthusiasm and seduction, she tried for a while but gave up with a frown on her pretty face.

"I'm sorry. I'm very tired," I said when she pulled her hand out.

"You're not even trying. Look at your hands, just stuck under your head. Maybe if you slipped them under my shirt, we could get some heat going." But a smile quickly replaced her frown, and she dropped a light kiss on my lips. "That's alright, baby," she said. "Consent works both ways."

I rolled to my side and kissed her forehead. "Thank you for everything you are, Aarti. And I'm sorry for everything I am."

She peered into my eyes, and I prayed she didn't see the guilt in them. "Don't be silly. It isn't a big deal. I appreciate who you are, just the way you are."

My breath caught between my throat and lungs. I was fucked up, and she deserved better. Tara deserved better. And I deserved neither of these phenomenal women. *What the hell was I doing?*

When she buried her soft body next to me, I mustered up

some courage to wrap my arms around her. But at the first sign of her deep, peaceful breath, I snuck out to the dark living room with my phone.

Are you up?

I texted Tara and waited. Across the room, two green dots on the oven clock blinked steadily, counting moments wasted on misgivings and heartache. Fifteen silent minutes later, I returned to bed, pulled Aarti's hand from under her, and fell asleep holding it.

The next morning, Aarti insisted on going to her favorite brunch place in Plano. With one eye on my phone, I pretended to enjoy her company, but felt a deepening ache as I heard nothing back from Tara. We returned to spend a lazy afternoon watching TV, all the while feeling like the imposter that I was. When Aarti left that evening, I was tempted to rush over to Tara's, but her furious silence had been her response.

Later that evening, Mom's name lit up my phone.

"Hi, Ma," I said.

"Are you busy?"

Her tone startled me. Something was up. "What's wrong?"

"Is Aarti with you?"

"No, she left. Why?"

"It's about Sangita."

My anger spiked at the mention of that name. The veins in my head throbbed. My body went rigid with rage.

"Whatever it is, I don't want to hear it, Ma. I'll have nothing to do with that woman anymore. And you shouldn't either."

"Sameer, just listen to me for a minute, will you?"

"Haven't we had enough?" My angry voice ricocheted off the walls in the cavernous apartment. "Haven't we done enough?"

"Sameer." Her voice hardened. "You know I'd never talk about her unless it was important. Don't you trust me anymore?"

"Yes." Pulling in a soft breath, I ran my fingers through my hair.

"She's not well."

My hand flew up in disdain. "Wow, that's new!"

"I don't appreciate that tone, Sameer. Call me back when you're ready to talk like an adult."

"I'm sorry, Ma. Go on." Quickly and quietly, I resigned to Mom's reprimanding me as if I were a child and asking me to be an adult in the same breath. It was a battle I couldn't win.

"She has cancer. It's serious."

I lost my tongue for a moment. Basic human decency mandated that I feel sorry for her, but given her history with the family, my defenses were rightfully up.

"Is this a ploy to get more money?" I asked gently, not wanting to alienate Mom.

"I sent her to Vishal. He's been treating her."

Mom's cousin, Vishal, was an oncologist in Delhi.

I paused for thought. "When did she call you, Ma?"

"A few months back," she said after a deep silence that I didn't break for effect.

"When, Ma?" I demanded in a voice I had never used with her before.

"He's been treating her for almost a year now."

"A year!" I jumped off my seat. "Why didn't you tell me?"

"For this reason. I knew how you'd react. I didn't want to involve you unless it was necessary."

"My involvement is *always* necessary when it comes to her." I rubbed my forehead with my free hand as I paced around my living room. "But you shouldn't get involved, Mom. And how does she even know how to get in touch with you? I'm paying the lawyers an outrageous amount of money to keep her out of our lives."

Mom chose silence again.

"Ma."

"I had sent her my number two years ago." She confessed in a barely audible voice.

"What? Why?" I cried. "Why would a sensible woman like you do something like that?"

"For Riya. In case she needed anything."

"Mom!"

I couldn't decide who the target of my anger was at that moment. Mom, who had reinstated the woman back in our lives after I had spent the better part of my youth trying to keep her away? Or Sangita, who had managed to crawl her way back to us? Or the universe that had played this cruel joke?

"I know you're angry," Mom said softly, "but it's not the little girl's fault. She shouldn't be paying the price for her parents' mistakes."

"It wasn't a mistake. It was cheating, knowing and deliberate."

"What's the use of rehashing all that, beta? We know what happened, and we moved on."

"It's not over though, is it? Here she is again."

"The only person who matters now is Riya. She'll need you if anything untoward happens to Sangita."

But I didn't want to think about that little girl, who must be almost a teenager now.

"Is she asking for money?" I asked to redirect my own thoughts.

"No, but I've been paying for her treatment."

I sighed. "You should've told me, Ma."

"I didn't want you to go through it again," she said.

"And I don't want you to go through it alone."

Mom cut through the bullshit. "Riya will need a home, Sameer. Sangita is deteriorating. We might not have enough time."

"Yes, I'll take care of it. I'll talk to her tomorrow." I exhaled hard. "And please don't entertain her calls. She shouldn't be calling you."

"She doesn't know how else to reach you."

"Through. The. Lawyers." I threw my hand up in exasperation.

"But these aren't normal circumstances to conduct business as usual."

"How are you not angry?" I asked.

She sighed. "Because it doesn't help. Bye, beta."

TARA

A *re you up?* Sameer had the balls to text me after leaving me in tears to rush back to his girlfriend. Had he texted me before or after having sex with her? I couldn't believe I was about to give up my loyal and kind Sujit for the fickle, heartless Sameer. I decided I had to stop obsessing over him and rid myself of the dark shadow I had dragged along for all these years. I was bound to run into him, but now I was going to be indifferent.

Four days later, still fighting my bitterness, I stretched a new canvas to paint away my deepest feelings. Usually, it worked, but today I was smeared in paint, and the canvas resembled a murder scene. I stood staring at it with my head cocked, questioning its redeemability, when the phone buzzed with an unfamiliar number. I swiped it open with the only clean section on my pinky finger.

"Hello?" I said, putting it on speaker.

"Hey." A vaguely familiar voice responded. "It's Mihir." I took a moment trying to put a face to the name when he added, "Sameer's friend."

"Oh, yes, of course."

"How are you?"

"I'm alright. How've you been?"

"Good. Great. What're you doing this Saturday?"

"Are you asking me out?" I asked with a light laugh. "You know I'm seeing someone."

He apologized with a deep, throaty laugh. "That came out wrong. Let me start over. I've been invited to a party, and I want you to come along as my guest."

"Aren't you going ask *if* I want to come?"

"Ah, see I knew you'd say that. I also know you'll refuse if I leave the decision to you. So, what do you say?"

"How do you know I'll refuse?" I smiled at the memory of our lighthearted exchange at the café.

"It's Sameer's birthday."

My smile vanished. I knew his birthday was next Tuesday, but I wasn't planning on sending a message. I hadn't for all these years, and now was definitely not a good time to start.

"Mihir, I appreciate what you're doing, but if he wanted me there, he would've invited me."

"He's not invited anyone. Aarti's doing all the planning."

"Then I absolutely shouldn't be there."

"Tsk, where's the fun in that? If you come along as my guest, he'll have to behave, and you get to rub it in."

"Rub what in?" I wondered how much Sameer had told him about our past.

"He's still hung up on you, but can't bring himself to own it."

"Oh, he owned it alright! He owned it with one arm tightly wrapped around Aarti."

"Exactly."

I heaved a big sigh. "Why would you do this? I thought you were his friend."

"To give you both a second shot."

"What if I don't want one?"

"That's your choice. I'm trying as Sameer's friend, perhaps yours. You can always refuse." His voice held a veiled challenge, and I found challenges very hard to resist.

I took a moment to mull it over. It would surely fluster Sameer if I showed up unannounced at a party his girlfriend was throwing. It would also allow me to demonstrate how completely over him I was. *Which I was*, I asserted.

"Okay, I'm in," I said. "What's the dress code? I don't want to be caught under or overdressed among the rich and the bratty."

He chuckled but it was a sophisticated sound. "Casual. Very casual. Pick you up at seven?"

"Perfect."

Summer had set in bright and strong, and in keeping with the season, I chose an off-the-shoulder yellow midi dress that Saturday. Instead of using a flat iron on my hair, I fluffed my naturally playful waves. With matching yellow polish on my nails, red lips, and flirty tan heels, I was dressed to provoke. I had found the perfect gift for Sameer, with the perfect message written inside. Grabbing the shoulder bag that I hauled everywhere, I waited for Mihir.

Game on!

When he pulled up, he gave me a quick once-over. "Not bad."

"Thank you," I said as we rolled out of the driveway. "I must admit though, I feel like I'm making a dreadful mistake coming uninvited."

He threw me a reassuring glance. "You aren't coming uninvited. I RSVP'd for two. You're my plus one. And this was my idea, and I don't make mistakes."

I was starting to like this troublemaker.

"Okay, but I'm leaving immediately if it gets awkward."

"Of course, if you're even the slightest bit uncomfortable, give me a sign and I'll drive you home."

In about a minute, we arrived at Sameer's luxury condominium complex, with an emphasis on luxury. Suddenly, the picture of Sameer with the perfect Aarti made complete sense. But it wasn't jealousy I felt at that moment. Indifference, perhaps. But that didn't mean I wasn't going to play.

We exited on the twenty-third floor, and while Mihir pushed the doorbell, I took a moment to run my nervous palms over my dress. Sameer answered the door, saw me, and stood dumbfounded.

"Happy Birthday, buddy," Mihir said with a painfully loud slap on Sameer's back as he brushed past him. Sameer blinked, then let me in.

"Abby was busy, so I brought a friend," Mihir said to Aarti, who approached us with a smile. "I hope that's alright."

"Of course!" Aarti said, and she gave him a hug. "Good to see you again, Tara. Come in, please." While she led us inside, I found Sameer still standing speechless by the door.

A small group had congregated in the living room, and all eyes turned to me.

"Everyone, this is my friend, Tara," Mihir said. "She's a terrific artist and an expert art appraiser, so if any of you are trying to pass off fakes, she'll smoke you out." A tide of polite laughter rolled around the room, and everyone took turns introducing themselves.

"Grab a drink," Mihir whispered in my ear as I placed my bag on a corner table. "Oh, and laugh like I said something funny."

"That's your play? To make him jealous?"

"Yes, now play along."

"I can't laugh on cue!" I said between clenched teeth. "How about a fake smile?"

"You're taking the fun out of this," he said and walked toward the kitchen, where the food and drinks were set up.

I smiled, not a fake one, and spotted Sameer in the kitchen.

Taking the beautifully wrapped gift from my bag, I walked up to him.

"Happy Birthday, Sameer," I said, handing him the gift.

"Thank you," he said, holding himself in perfect poise for a second before abandoning the pretense. "What're you doing here?" His annoyed frown was my first reward that evening.

I whipped out my sweetest smile. "Mihir invited me."

He looked at Mihir, who glared back before taking a swig of the beer he had just opened. "She's my guest. She better be welcome."

Sameer didn't reply, just held his friend in a steady gaze, then took my gift and walked away toward the anterior rooms. I struggled to suppress a grin.

"People are going to talk about us." I rolled my eyes and poured myself some whisky over ice.

Mihir picked up a meatball on a stick. "Does that bother you?"

I shrugged and took a sip of the very expensive, very smooth liquor. "I don't live here. These aren't my friends. I hope you don't find yourself the subject of a rumor," I said, although something told me that wouldn't bother him.

He picked up another meatball on a fancy stick and handed it to me. "Try this. It's really good."

"Of course it is," I said, scanning the spread of Mediterranean food—fresh, decadent, and beautiful.

"Stop being grumpy and work your magic," Mihir said just as Sameer walked back to us.

"What are you two whispering about?" Sameer asked with narrowed eyes.

"We weren't whispering," I said, pushing myself off the counter with a playful grace that earned me Mihir's approving smile.

When I rejoined the group in the living room, people were

curious to know more about me. What did my work entail? Where was I from, *really from*, because my accent didn't sound *Indian*.

What does an Indian sound like to others, I wondered. Eventually, though, I faded comfortably into the background.

When the doorbell dinged again, we dispersed to get more food and drinks. Relaxing on the couch, I had struck up a conversation about art with a woman named Jessica, when we were interrupted by a little boy who came hurtling through the front door.

"Oh my god, Bryson!" Jessica squealed and hugged the little boy.

A well-dressed woman came rushing after Bryson, followed by a man carrying a baby bag. "We're so sorry. Our sitter had an emergency, and we didn't have time to find a replacement. I hope you don't mind," the woman said, looking at Aarti, who welcomed her in.

"Of course, not." Aarti smiled warmly. "We love having Bryson."

"Hi, I'm Amanda." She extended a hand to me. "My husband, Ben."

"Tara, very nice to meet you," I said to Amanda and waved across the room to Ben. "I'm a friend of Mihir."

Amanda smiled. "Bryson is almost ready for bed. Just a few more minutes and he'll be out like a light."

I smiled at the young child, who stood gawking at me with big, curious blue eyes. "Hi, Bryson, I'm Tara."

When he gave a shy smile, I put my drink on a side table and slipped to the floor on my knees.

"Would you like to draw?" I asked and watched his eyes gleam.

"Come with me."

He looked at his mom.

"It's alright, Bryson."

"Catch your breath," I said to Amanda.

With a huff, she flopped down on the couch.

Bryson held my hand and followed me to a table by a large window. Propping him up on a chair, I pulled out paper, pencils, and oil pastels from my bag. Beautiful city lights twinkled outside. The Bank of America Plaza was lit up tall and proud, and the Fountain Place stood out in its distinctive shape. The Reunion Tower was slightly hidden from this vantage point, but its glory remained unfettered.

I had loved my job as an art tutor in India and had continued to volunteer at my local public libraries. There was nothing more beautiful than seeing the world through the art of a child. "What do you want to draw, Bryson?"

"I wan draw circle," he said confidently.

"That's good! Here, take this pencil and draw a circle. Let me know if you need help, okay?"

He nodded and gripped the pencil in his fist, making curves on the paper.

"That's good. Can you draw another?"

He threw in more curves, squiggly lines, and a partially decent circle. Then we filled the shapes with color as the party moved along. Mihir joined us, and Bryson pointed to several drawings and shared their stories. I understood about half of what he said. The baby talk garbled the rest. When Bryson was tired, Mihir helped me clean up, and we moved back to the living area. But the kid refused to leave my side, resisting his mother's attempts to take him to bed. I settled down beside Amanda, and he slipped between us. As he began to recline against me, I caressed his light-colored tresses with faint *shhh* sounds. In about two minutes, he was fast asleep with his head in my lap.

"You're very good with kids," Amanda whispered, gushing with gratitude.

"I have a lot of friends with kids." I smiled back at her, and then my eyes caught Sameer, watching me intently from across the room.

"We'll put him inside," Amanda said, nodding at Ben to take him.

"I can take him, if you don't mind," I offered.

With the slight boy cradled in my arms, I followed Sameer down the hall to the guest room, where he turned on a quiet lamp. I walked around him to the bed, laid the boy down, and tucked him under a light blanket. He wriggled but didn't wake up. As I turned around, Sameer blocked my way, standing so close I could see the individual hairs in his stubble. His eyes glowed like fire in the soft light. I clutched my dress for a small second.

"What's this new game, Tara?" he growled in my face.

"*Game?* What game? Showing affection to a little kid is a game for you rich folks?"

His eyes continued to burn amber. I turned my head to look at the child, cozy in sweet slumber. "Or are you embarrassed that I look like a dark-skinned nanny to a rich, white kid?"

His mouth dropped.

"Oh, is that what's really bothering you? You're ashamed of how your rich friends might perceive me?" I stepped toward him. "I'm not of your world, Sameer. I don't share your values, I don't have to play by your rules."

"Dammit, Tara, stop trying to pick a fight every time we talk." He blew out an angry breath.

I smirked. "*See you around*, Sameer."

"Tara." I heard his soft voice when I reached the door. "Let it go."

"What the hell are you doing with Mihir? Enough with these ridiculous games. If you want me, just come out and say it."

I turned around and whispered, "I did, and you flew out of my arms to rush back to Aarti."

"Don't do this, Tara. You know—"

"Go be with your girlfriend, Sameer. Go back to your perfect life."

I walked out to find Mihir in the kitchen, opening another bottle of beer. He stopped midway through twisting the top when he saw me. "Do you want to leave?"

"No." I sighed. "But for the record, this hasn't been your most brilliant idea."

"Well, I'm not ready to call it yet," he said just as Aarti shuffled past us. "I think she's jealous of all the attention you're getting today," he whispered.

I drove my fingers through my hair. "What am I doing wrong, Mihir? Why won't the pain go away?"

He chugged from his bottle. "You won't let it."

Turning my face to him, I said, "Listen, I'm sorry I misled you. I'm not here because I want him back. He left me humiliated yet again, and I came here to have a little fun at his expense, but now I feel horrid about that too."

"Alright."

"*Alright*? What does alright mean?"

"It means I get it." He smiled as he broke open an expensive scotch someone had brought as a gift and poured a splash in a glass.

"Here, drink this and relax. Don't be too hard on yourself." His warm words and intent eyes reminded me of Dada. "The pain won't go away because you gave *him* a second chance, but you never gave yourself one."

"How's that?"

"Let yourself feel vulnerable again. Whoever you want to be with, Sameer or your boyfriend in New York, let it flow. Don't restrict it, don't put conditions on it."

I gulped down the contents of my glass. "So, who exactly are you, Mihir, a reincarnated wise sage who enjoys a stiff drink?"

He smiled and gently bumped my shoulder.

Past midnight, as we thanked the hosts for a fun party, Mihir slipped an arm around my waist with the polished brazenness of 007. I wish I had seen the look on Sameer's face, but not watching him was half the fun.

SAMEER

Sometime past one that night, we closed the doors behind the last guests. Aarti squeezed me into a tight hug and planted a kiss on my cheek.

"What's that for?" I asked.

"I'm so relieved," she said, gripping me in another hug.

"About what?"

"When I saw Tara here tonight, I thought there was definitely something between the two of you. I mean, why else would she show up uninvited?"

"What?" I feigned a frown.

"Don't worry," she cooed. "You're in the clear because she's obviously sleeping with Mihir."

"You really think so?" I frowned again, involuntarily this time.

She scoffed. "Didn't you see them? They were together all evening, all smiles and whispers. I'm sorry I doubted you," she said, and began gathering bottles scattered around the living room. "Looks like Abby's out, Tara's in."

"You don't have to clean up. I've called the cleaning service for tomorrow."

She shrugged. "That's alright, I'll just put the bottles away. It's not a big deal."

"Here, give me those." I took the bottles from her and deposited them in the recycling tray. "It was a great party. Thank you for making it perfect, as always." I pulled her into my arms and gave her a quick kiss of appreciation.

"I'm glad." She smiled. "I love it when I make you happy."

Aarti's lowkey was never really so. She had obsessed over every small detail for the past week, and when we hit the bed that night, the fatigue finally caught up with her. I snuck out of the bedroom and called Mihir. It was almost 2 a.m.

"Hey," he said, sounding surprisingly alert for that time of the night.

"Is Tara with you?"

A deep inhale. "Why?"

"Is she?"

"It's late, Sameer. What do you want?"

"What the hell were you thinking bringing her here? Are you screwing her?"

There was a pause. "That's none of your concern."

"Answer me. I need to hear it from you."

"You're happy with Aarti. Why do you care?"

"Then you are."

He hung up without another word.

I called him back. "Don't hang up, dumbass. I need to talk to you." He didn't respond but didn't hang up either. "Sangita has cancer."

"Shit!"

I slumped down onto the couch behind me.

"Is it bad?"

I told him what had occurred over the past few days.

"Riya?" he asked softly.

"Yes, Mom's worried about her too."

"How can I help?" And just like that, he was a trusted friend again.

"I've initiated the paperwork to get her here if...*it* happens. Mom's been taking care of the bills, but she didn't tell me until last week."

"You should've told me."

"I know, but there's been so much going on. Nothing is ever okay, Mihir! Every time I think I can breathe again, something else goes wrong."

"Does Aarti know?"

"No," I said with a deep sigh. "What do I tell her?"

"And Tara?"

"She doesn't know either."

"I'm not sleeping with Tara," he said after a long silence.

"I know."

"Neither of us would do that to you."

"I know."

"You're a knucklehead."

"I know that too."

"Wise up, Sameer," he instructed in his brusque, pithy manner.

"I'm trying," I managed feebly.

It wasn't the first time I had let my insecurities get the better of me. In fact, that's how our story began. I met Tara in college through Amar. Tall, slender, and dusky with perfect, gentle curves, she always wore the same kind of clothes: a short t-shirt or top over loose-fitting cotton or linen pants that showed off just a sliver of her waist. She smelled like delicate roses in an evening breeze. Gorgeous as she was today, but unaware and unconcerned with it. Despite her allure, the ugly truth was that I initially wanted her only because I was jealous of her close relationship with Amar.

My first cousin on my dad's side, Amar was a few months

older, and we had grown up together. Quiet and polite, even as a child, he had a generous heart and a mind that was wise beyond his young years. An old soul, they called him. He never answered back, never broke a toy, let alone a rule, never roughhoused. We grew up like siblings, but I soon began to glean how much more my parents, sister, and everyone else loved him over me. Mom never had a bad word to say about him. I, on the other hand, was bratty and mouthy. And while Mom's parenting philosophy didn't include aggressive verbal or physical assaults, she never failed to take a stern tone with me, one that she never used with Amar.

Despite our rivalry, however, I loved Amar immensely, and he loved me selflessly. It was my family's behavior toward him that irked me. The closer we grew, the more resentful I became. Because, although he never suggested it through words or behavior, I knew he was seen as the worthy son. I was the black sheep.

Amar and I were both good artists with a keen eye. When Amar declared that he was going to an art college after high school, he broke ranks with his father, one of the most prominent lawyers in the city, who had hoped Amar would join him at his firm. Tauji was upset but ultimately supported Amar's decision. More reason for me to feel envious. Not only did I lack the vision to choose a vocation for myself, but I also lacked the courage to imagine a life without the cocoon of my father's wealth. I cowered and took a more traditional approach, opting to study chemistry like my father. I wasn't necessarily interested in the field but thought a science degree would come in handy when I took over his pharmaceutical business.

What I had miscalculated was the correlation between intelligence and hard work. With a complete but grossly misplaced faith in my abilities, I spent the year smoking weed and engaging in mindless sex. I picked fights with goons of the college in a bid to become the big, bad boy on campus. Of course, I ended up in the hospital a couple of times, but that didn't deter me. I continued with my pigheaded behavior until the college kicked me out at the end of the first year.

Deeply ashamed, my parents paid a huge amount in donations to get me a seat at the art college in Baroda the following year. They hoped Amar would keep an eye on me. But the more insidious reason was that they didn't know many people in the city, so it wouldn't hurt their social reputation if I continued with my disgraceful behavior. Just another option in the repertoire of the wealthy—ship your difficult kid to an obscure city or a foreign land to take the heat off the family.

But now that I was head-to-head with Amar, I had come in ready to sabotage him. I knew he was better than me in every possible way, so I chose to become who he wouldn't be. I bedded my first woman in Baroda within two days of my arrival and thus took my new identity. I was a playboy—rich, visible, available.

Meanwhile, Amar hung out with his nondescript group of friends. They went to cheap, standalone theaters with suspect air conditioning at a time when multiplex theaters were erected in every corner of the city. They traveled in autorickshaws, while I drove Dad's car. They ate at roadside food stalls and drank tea at roadside stands. But when I saw how close the six of them were, jealousy reared its venomous head again. Their friendship wasn't loud and braggart but soft, gentle, and caring. They didn't need to blow money to have fun and feel connected.

I couldn't stand to see Amar happy when I wasn't. I wanted what he had. I wanted Tara. It was petty, but that's who I was until she called me out on it one evening.

When I accosted her for excluding me from their group gatherings, she not only had the balls to point out my disconcerting behavior but actually used the words *jealous* and *envious*. As if I'd handed her the script to my life. In what became a moment of reckoning for me, she called bullshit on my confidence, my bravado and flamboyance. She said I could be my own man and didn't need to live under Amar's shadow. My wealth, the car, my clothes meant nothing to her. She only saw what I was capable of achieving on my own merit. It was the first time anyone had shown faith in me, and it shook me to my core.

I stormed off, angry at being seen so clearly. But almost instantly, I craved the validation she was gifting me. I could be who she thought I was. Suddenly, I saw who she was too. A goddess with a philosopher's mind, Saraswati herself; a loyal friend who loved and protected her people with the same fierce dignity she showed for herself. I took a chance and asked her point-blank if she was in love with Amar. To my surprise, she uttered the word I was silently praying for, "No." At that moment, everything changed.

A year before, if someone had joked that I'd be enamored with a simple, small-town girl who wore no makeup and whose English accent left much to be desired, I would've wagered my dad's shiny new car. I was a rock fan, while she reveled in mainstream Bollywood music, a clear déclassé in the eyes of the Indian rich. We came from two completely different worlds. But that strong, fierce girl was no joke. She could cut you down to size, even in her less-than-perfect English, because she was brilliant. And it wasn't that she couldn't speak the language. Her English was grammatically on point because she was an avid reader, but she hadn't had many occasions to converse, so her pronunciations didn't always land.

The first time we had sex, she mispronounced *condom*. Jarring as it sounded to my unaccustomed ear, when I saw her in the dim light of my table lamp, it became superfluous. Those beautiful eyes, rife with desire, saw me and liked what they saw. I often felt naked beneath her gaze. It was a heady feeling, the freedom of being who I wanted to be—tender and vulnerable, angry and impatient.

That magical night, after we flopped onto my rumpled bed,

naked, exhausted, and satisfied, she threw in a quick, clinical lecture to inform me that not all women bleed during their first intercourse. And it shouldn't hurt to the point of agony unless there is a medical reason or a case of gravely mismatched genitalia, which is very rare. And that lube could play a very important role in pleasure.

"So, was it good for you?" I said, picking up the tube of lube and placing it on the side stand.

She smiled with a hand on my heart. "What you did with your tongue was amazing. I never expected to have such a strong orgasm my first time."

"If this was your first time, how do you know what orgasms feel like?" I asked like a typical nineteen-year-old fool.

She frowned. "Why, do you think only boys DIY?"

"No," I cried feebly. "Can I confess something? It's the first time I've done that with my tongue."

"Oh, so I was your guinea pig?"

I laughed. "Or maybe I was saving it for someone special."

"No, you weren't. You were scared."

I groaned. "Why don't you ever let me live my lies?"

She smiled and closed her eyes.

"What is it I was scared of anyway?" I asked.

Her big, sleepy eyes opened halfway. "You weren't confident you'd do it right. You didn't want a messed-up act ruining your reputation with women, one that you've cultivated so carefully."

"If that were the case, why didn't I hesitate with you?"

"Because I'm not one of your conquests, playboy, and you know it."

"Darn it, woman. Let me revel in my persona!"

She stared into my eyes. "Can I kiss you, Sameer?" That was the first time she'd called me by my name.

"Why do you need to ask?"

"I don't know. Maybe that was it for you. Maybe you've lost interest now that we've done it."

I pulled her closer and wrapped my limbs around her soft, glowing body. "You are not one of my conquests. You can kiss me any time you want. But you wouldn't mind if I used my tongue to play with other women, would you?" I asked with a cheeky grin.

"It's your tongue. You can stick it wherever you like," she whispered. Why did I think I could fluster her?

"There's only one place this tongue wants to be. Well, two, actually."

I wiggled my fingers at her waist, and she shrieked in giggles. Then, I let her take my mouth with the same frantic urgency I felt in my body.

That day, I knew what true surrender to someone felt like.

As Aarti slept, I tiptoed to the guest room where I had stashed Tara's gift. I didn't want to share it with Aarti. For one, I wasn't sure what was inside that deceptively beautiful wrapping. I hadn't known Tara to be particularly decorous when she was pissed. She hadn't come over in the stunning yellow dress and the provocative red lips to make nice.

A blank canvas and a set of artists' oil pastels greeted me when I tore open the package, along with a beautifully handwritten note.

Sameer,
Happy Birthday!
A small gift to create your own perfect picture.
Tara

I wanted to be mad, but I had to smile at her audacity. And I knew exactly how I was going to get back at her for this.

SAMEER

*T*wo days later, when Amar called to wish me happy birthday, he shared news of his own. After trudging through several temporary gigs at smaller colleges around the country, he'd finally landed a permanent position at the most reputable art college in Mumbai.

"I'm thinking of coming for a visit before the semester begins," he said. "I don't know if I'll get a chance again soon."

Amar had visited us almost every year since we'd moved to Dallas.

"That's great." I smiled. "It'll be good to see you again. Ma's going to be over the moon."

He held his silence for a moment. "Is everything good?"

"Of course, why wouldn't it be?"

"Okay, I'll book my tickets and text you the details."

My relationship with Amar was no longer marred by envy. When my life broke into pieces, he held me like a true brother and helped me get back on my feet. That's when my love for him underwent a complete reformation.

Two years later, on his first visit to the U.S., I came clean to him. I laid bare all the jealousy and resentment that had hollowed me for all those years. I abandoned all trepidation and confessed how much I had hated his kindness and generosity.

"I've never not loved you, Amar," I confessed. "But it was exhausting trying to be as good as you. Everyone around us thought you were the perfect child, the perfect son, and I hated being the second best, always. But I see it now. You've always been rightfully worthy."

He'd barked a long, hysterical laugh. "Isn't that fucking hilarious!" It was the first and only time I'd heard him curse. It was also the only time I'd seen him agitated. "I've never been the son they wanted, Sameer, even when they thought I was. Not for my parents, and neither for yours, I suspect."

When I had given him a drunk, dumb look, he said, "I'm bisexual, Sameer. I've known for a long time but didn't have the guts to tell my parents until now."

"They know?" I had asked with raised brows.

"They haven't disowned me, if that's what you're asking. They have no choice. I'm the only heir to their hard-earned crores," he had spewed with bitter sarcasm. "But I see it in their eyes—the disappointment, the pity. So you have nothing to worry about, brother. *You* are the worthy son, fucking straight as they wanted."

Pouring himself another big glass of whisky, he'd continued. "You gave me that look too, you know. The shock, the disbelief, as if I'd just confessed that I was a murderer. But I don't take it to heart. Everyone has given me the look, or variations of it, even my most well-meaning friends. The only one who didn't was Tara."

"Tara knows too?"

He'd taken a valiantly big gulp from his glass and bobbed his drunken head. "She's the only one who knew until last month. And guess when I told her? At our very first meeting. The very first time I'm talking to her, and there's something about her that's so genuine, honest, and decent that I spill my guts without thinking."

I had waited while he steadied his gaze. "She didn't make a big deal out of it but didn't underplay it either. She just recognized it as a part of who I am and supported me the way I needed, quietly and staunchly."

Every memory of Tara I had wished away when I left India came barreling back. We had been so young then, barely out of adolescent immaturity, and I was still behaving like an entitled prick, when Amar had trusted Tara with this delicate secret. And she had held him up when he had no one else to rely on. That was more than I had ever done for him. I had pelted him with jealousy and aggression at a time when he most needed a friend. So, regardless of our current status quo, I knew I had to be gracious to Tara during his visit. She was the knot that bound me to Amar, and he was the thread that led me to her.

When I saw Amar at the airport later that week, the now-familiar feeling of pure happiness flooded my heart. He wasn't the skinny boy anymore, but he still sported a head full of curls and an expression of open-hearted kindness.

"Looks like you work out," I said as I drove him to my parents' home. "I see muscles."

He shrugged, Zen as ever. "How's Aarti?"

"She's good." I flinched inwardly at the way my voice rose in pitch. "You'll see her the day after tomorrow. Mom has invited us to dinner. Apparently, you're an important guest, and our presence is required," I teased.

"I'm not a guest. It's my home as much as it's yours."

"It's all yours. I want nothing to do with that house or that man."

"Still bitter, I see," he said, casually peering out the window. "It's so much less green than the last time I was here."

"The metroplex is growing in all directions," I said, then snapped. Enough skirting the issue. "Why don't you just straight up ask me?"

"There's nothing I need to ask you, dude," he said, and continued gazing outside with an interest that was at odds with the bland concrete buildings and the giant network of highways rolling alongside.

"Then you know Tara is here."

He smiled like he had won the game. "Yes, we talk. She called me when you bought that painting anonymously. That wasn't very smart." He chuckled. "Now, Tara, on the other hand—"

"Yes, she's always been smarter than me."

He caught the warmth in my voice and said, "I hope my being here doesn't complicate things for you."

"It doesn't. I'll always honor your friendship with her, no matter how I feel."

"And how do you feel?"

A deep sigh was the only way I could respond to that question, and he took the hint.

"Heard about Sangita. I'm sorry. I wish I was in Delhi to help."

I glanced at him. "Thank you, but there's very little we can do anyway."

"Have you talked to Riya?"

I shook my head.

"Well, I don't need to tell you what the right thing to do is. She's a little girl, and she's your blood," he said, as if I could ever forget that.

I responded with another audible sigh.

"Okay, no more lectures." He flashed a smile. "Can't help it. It's my profession."

"Congrats, brother. I'm glad you finally found what you wanted so badly for so long."

"You too."

"Not yet," I replied. "She hates me...and I don't know what I want. I don't think she does either. Every time we talk, we end up fighting."

"You've always had your disagreements," he said matter-of-factly.

"But this time we're hurting each other."

He looked at me. "So, what are you going to do about it?"

"Nothing. I can't lose sight of what's on the line."

"What's that, your happiness?"

"You know as well as I do that's not the priority."

"Well, I'll be here when you need me."

I smiled gratefully. "I know. That's the one thing I can count on, no matter what."

TWO DAYS LATER, I arrived at my parents' home with Aarti in the hopes of sitting down to a nice, intimate dinner with my family. But when I parked the car, I saw Tara in the rearview mirror, exiting a cab.

"Tara! What a nice surprise," Aarti said to her at the door. I looked for hints of unpleasantness in her tone but found none.

"Aarti, good to see you again," Tara replied, completely ignoring me as Amar answered the door.

"Amar!" Tara gave him a heartfelt hug. "It's been too long."

"Good to see you again, Amar," Aarti said as Mom came to the door to welcome us.

"You have a very beautiful home, Mrs. Rehani," Tara said.

"You can call her Aunty. There's no need to be formal," Amar said and looked at Mom.

"Of course." Mom smiled. "Amar is my son, and you're his dear friend. I'd love it if you called me Aunty." With her arm gently draped around Tara's shoulder, Mom led us to the living room.

Dad sat on the throne of his favorite armchair with a drink in his hand. After quick introductions and pleasantries, we settled down.

"What would you like to drink?" Amar asked Aarti and Tara.

"White wine," Aarti said and smiled at me, and I stepped over to the dry bar at the far end of the room.

"Wine's good," I heard Tara say.

I poured Aarti some sparkling white. After Amar poured for Tara and brought it to her, I signaled him to join me at the bar.

"Why did you invite her?" I frowned.

"I didn't." He calmly poured himself some whisky. "Chachi did."

I narrowed my eyes at him. "Ma doesn't even know her."

"I was talking to her about Tara, and she asked if she'd like to join us for dinner tonight." He gave me an arm-pat and turned to Mom. "Chachi, some wine?"

"No, thank you, beta."

Mom turned to Tara, who exuded ease and confidence, but I could tell she was quaking in her shoes meeting my mother for the first time. Perhaps she hadn't thought it through when she accepted the invitation, and it tickled me. She wore a beautiful embroidered Indian short top and jeans, paired with oxidized metal earrings and stylish pumps. But with delicate eyeliner and a subtle shade of lipstick, she looked uncharacteristically demure for the feisty woman that she was.

"Tell me, what do you do, Tara? Are you an artist like Amar?" Mom asked.

"Yes, and I'm also an art consultant." She explained her job and what had brought her to Dallas.

"That's wonderful." Mom looked at Amar and Aarti with pride. "You kids are so accomplished."

Dad found his opening and wasted no time. "Do you know Sameer also attended your college?"

"Yes," Tara said politely.

"Do you know why he was sent to a small city like Badauda?" he asked with visible disdain.

"Because it has one of the best fine arts colleges in the country?" Tara delivered the tart reply with a sweet smile, and I tried to suppress a chuckle. *Atta girl!*

But Dad recovered swiftly. "Yes, Amar said they were the best years of his life."

"It's a beautiful city with a rich history and warm people," Amar added.

"Yes, but that's not the reason we sent Sameer there." My insides burned with anger and humiliation at Dad's efforts to prove his point.

"Shall we eat?" Mom redirected in her gentle, classy manner.

"Yes," Amar and I blurted in unison.

When we gathered around the table, I turned my attention to Aarti. Amar and Tara sat across from us, with Mom on Tara's right. Dad was at the head of the table.

"I would love to see your work someday." Mom smiled as she passed Tara the chicken korma.

"Would you like to come to the opening with Amar?" Tara asked with raised brows. "I can send your invitations with his."

"That would be wonderful," Mom replied, turning to me. "Are you both going?"

I nodded.

"So, Aarti, how are your parents?"

"They're well, Aunty. Although they're getting impatient that we still haven't decided on a date." She looked pointedly at me. "Sameer keeps dragging his feet. I've started to doubt if he's at all serious about us." When she placed a teasing hand on my arm, my heart began racing.

"We also want you to decide soon." Dad jumped in. It was his favorite subject, after all.

"They're getting engaged, but we want a proper ceremony, so we're asking them to pick a date that works for them," Mom explained to Tara.

This time, I couldn't avoid looking at her and saw sorrow and disappointment flash across her face. But she followed it up with a big smile. "That's wonderful, congratulations."

She smiled at Aarti, while Amar warned me with a stern look that said, "What are you doing, dude?"

I scuttled to change the subject. "Guess what?" I draped an arm around Aarti and said, "*We* managed to snag a Selfia for the office. It was a bidding war, but Aarti's agent is quite clever."

Aarti beamed. "Sameer wanted it so badly, she was determined to make it happen!"

I scanned Amar for a reaction and caught him exchanging a look with Tara before offering Aarti a conciliatory nod.

"What, no compliments, no felicitations?" I prodded.

"That's because he knows Anthony Selfia is an overrated hack," Tara blurted.

Amar shook his head at her, but I didn't expect him to jump in and defend me because, as he'd once put it, he preferred to remain non-aligned in the face of our Cold War. Only not all our wars were cold.

"I can't believe someone like you would say that!" I fumed at Tara. "How can you claim to run an art advisory firm and not appreciate Selfia?"

"Exactly. It's my job to advise people against buying junk."

"Junk? *Junk?*" I cried. "Did you just call my five-figure piece of art junk?"

"Five figures? Did you just throw that much money at that

worthless hack? This is exactly why he's overrated. People with a lot of money who know zilch about art blindly follow whatever the current hype is."

The gloves were off. My face was hot as I retorted, "Oh, excuse the rest of us mortals, who didn't graduate with high priestess degrees from eminent art schools! What did they teach you there? New rituals to offer reverence to the same old dead artists?"

"Don't condemn the masters to compensate for your own shortcomings. You know, if Selfia was a woman, he would've been scoffed off the field years ago. When female artists dared to bring private emotions into art, they were condemned as airing dirty laundry in public, quite literally. Then artists like Selfia come along, rip off ideas and techniques, and are hailed as trail-blazers!"

"It's no different in literature," Aarti interjected with her cool demeanor.

"Thank you, Aarti." Tara offered her sweetest smile. "I'm glad one of you has good sense."

"Don't encourage her, sweetheart," I said to Aarti. She consoled me with a nod, then exchanged a private look with Tara.

"Aarti's right. When women wrote about their relationships and emotions, it was called *domestic fiction*." She made air quotes. "When women write romance, it's seen as fluff, drivel. When men write about female emotions, as *they* interpret them, they appear on bestseller lists. When women write about their desires, it's vulgar. When men do it, it's art. Women sketching their own bodies is blasphemy, when men do it...argh, men have been doing it for ages."

"I can't believe this." I shook my head while clambering for a crisp response but came up empty.

"I have to agree with Tara on this," Aarti said in a calm voice, then took an elegant sip of her wine.

"Let me get this straight, you think I value Selfia's art only because he's a man?" I fumed, hotter than the steaming rice on my plate.

"No, you value Selfia because you don't know the difference between art and hype," Tara said with a condescending smile.

"And you would know, wouldn't you?" I banged down my spoon, violating every etiquette rule Mom had ever instilled in me. "You'd know the value of absolutely everything."

"Yes, because I do it every day. It's my job." Tara's conceited cool irked me even more than her angry retorts. "Do you have any idea how the art market works?"

"No, how would I? I only have the money to make or break that market."

"Don't be smug," she said. "You and your ilk would be nowhere without us. All you have is money, but no taste, no aesthetic sense."

"And you do, do you?"

"My resumé and net worth say I do," she said and looked at Aarti. They exchanged a smile, raised their glasses, and sipped their freaking wine.

I snarled at Tara as my insides turned to lava. "Give it up, Rehani. You're just another zombie following the dead crowd to nowhere."

"Guys..." Amar drew our attention back to the table. "This is exactly why we couldn't leave you alone in a room during college."

I felt Aarti's body stiffen at his words. "Is this how they've always been?"

"No, this is an escalation. They used to argue, but they were always respectful and considerate. Never devolved into personal slander. Now they both harbor huge egos," Amar said while calmly helping himself to more chicken and rice.

He was the king of admonishments. You wouldn't realize how hard you had been whipped until you went home and reflected on it. Only then would the cicatrices become evident—the scars you'd carry for life. I suddenly pitied his students.

"I'm sorry, that was rude of me," Tara said, looking at Dad, then at Mom.

"Not at all, my dear." Mom placed a hand on hers. "I learned something new today."

Tara's shy eyes lowered to her plate.

"I'm sorry too," I said to no one in particular.

"The food is amazing, Aunty," Tara said.

"Thank you. Durga is a very good cook."

When Durgaben came in with a basket of warm, buttered naan, Mom introduced Tara to her. Tara detected her accent and spoke to her in Gujarati. Durgaben's eyes lit up and her smile widened as they exchanged a few sentences.

"The food is absolutely wonderful," Tara said in English. "Reminds me of home."

"Yes, Durgaben is super talented," I chimed in. Durgaben blushed slightly from all the attention.

"Thank you," she muttered, and shuffled back out.

"Aarti, your nail color is so trendy," Tara said. "I can never find such fun colors to suit my skin tone."

"Oh, thank you," Aarti gushed. "I'll give you the name of a brand I like. It's got a lot of great colors for Indian skin tones."

"That would be amazing!" Tara showed her fingers to Aarti. "Look at this drab color I have on." I thought the color was just fine, but Aarti disagreed.

"You're right." She frowned. "It clashes with your undertones."

Whatever that meant.

"So have you two picked out what you're wearing for the engagement?" Tara asked Aarti.

She was determined to avoid me and was doing a fantastic job.

"Ah, I wish!" Aarti blew out a sigh. "I can't even get him to talk about a date."

"Western or Indian?"

"Most likely, Indian." Aarti squeezed my hand. "What do you think, Sameer? It will look glamorous, won't it?"

"Sameer, you're not eating," Amar said. I shot him a fierce look, and he grinned back.

"What's the matter, beta?" Mom quickly turned to me. "Is the food not to your liking today?"

"Everything is perfect, Ma," I said with all the calm I could muster.

All through dinner, Tara continued to bond with Aarti. When she and Amar recounted some outrageous stories from *their* college days—I was conveniently excluded—even Dad managed a few chuckles. Aarti was having a splendid time. She had decided that Tara was smart and funny.

By the time Durgaben brought out bowls of deliciously cold kheer, flavored with cardamom and saffron, Aarti was regaling us with wild stories from her college days. Everyone seemed to be enjoying a perfect evening. Except me. I was seething with unresolved emotions.

The moment we returned to the living room, Dad poured himself another drink. Mom sighed. Clearly she'd lost count of how many he'd had that day.

But I had other things on my mind. A worry about Tara, for starters. I pulled Amar aside. "It's late, and Tara will insist on taking a cab back. Ask her to stay the night. It's the weekend anyway. She doesn't have to go in to work tomorrow."

He frowned as he tried to gauge the intent behind my suggestion.

"I can offer to drop her back, but we both know she'll refuse. Adamantly."

That convinced him. "Tara, it's getting late. Maybe you should stay here tonight? We have spare rooms, right, Chachi?"

"Oh, of course!" Mom said. "I'll ask Durga to make a fresh bed."

"I'll do it, Ma," I said. "Durgaben must be tired."

Mom graced me with a smile.

"It's alright, Aunty. I think I'll go home." Tara politely refused the offer. "I didn't bring any extra clothes or anything else for that matter."

"That's alright, beta. I'll give you some nightclothes and other things." She stood from the couch to make the necessary arrangements. "Anyway, Amar is going to Sameer's for the weekend. Maybe they can drop you off on their way. Where do you live, Tara?"

"Uptown."

"Oh." Mom turned to her. "Are you close to Sameer's place?"

Tara shifted in her seat. "A few blocks away."

Mom looked at me, then at her. I directed my calm eyes at Aarti.

"I'm sorry to cause trouble, Aunty," Tara said. "This is really awkward."

"Don't feel awkward, beta. You're Amar's friend. This is your home," Mom reassured Tara with a smile.

I followed Mom upstairs while she instructed me on the proper way to prepare for a guest.

When I returned, Aarti was ready to leave. "Sorry, I can't stay," she said as she kissed my cheek at the door. "Got an early morning tomorrow."

Things couldn't have turned out better if I had tried.

SAMEER

*W*hen Dad retired to his room, Mom cast me the same knowing look again. I had put off talking to him about Riya for two weeks now. Shame and guilt were the two main culprits, although my anger was a worthy accomplice.

I found Dad in the monstrous armchair in their bedroom with his hand wrapped around an empty glass, as if that were the only thing keeping him alive. A proud decanter of whisky stood by him on a table. During the day, its facets caught the brilliant light streaming in from the bay windows. Right now, it looked restrained, much like my father.

"Dad, I need to talk to you. It's important."

His dazed eyes traveled up to me.

"It's about Sangita," I said, lowering myself to the edge of the bed. He turned his head away from me. "She's unwell."

The soft tone I used was a calculated move to invoke some emotion, but I found nothing more than dispassion in his glassy eyes.

"So? Throw more money at her," he cried. "You're good at that."

"She has cancer, Dad. She might not make it." This got me the intended reaction as he struggled to sit upright. Terror had now replaced the indifference in his eyes.

"Can I pour you another?" Stepping over to the table, I poured him a splash. He gulped it down. I dispensed another shot and gently placed the glass in his hands.

"Riya will need a home," I said. "I'm working on bringing her here."

"So now that bastard child will live with us?" he cried with anger. It wasn't long ago that I had used the same vile word to describe her.

"Don't say that. I regret how I handled things with Sangita, but I'm especially sorry I left Riya when she was only an infant. I want to make up for my mistakes. Can you support me?"

He scoffed. "So now the all-powerful Sameer Rehani needs my support? When did you ever heed my word? I told you thirteen years ago, but you decided you knew better."

"You didn't tell me, Dad." I corrected him gently. "You threatened me."

"And you threatened me back—" His gaze darted behind me.

I turned around to see Mom standing at the door. She made strong eye contact with the both of us before turning on her heel and walking away. With a sigh, I crouched to the floor in front of Dad.

Placing my hand on his, I said, "Will you help me bring Riya here? You know I can't do it without your signature on that paper. She needs her father. She needs you."

He dropped his head back on the chair and nodded. "Okay. But I need details. You took away every authority, every bit of power I had. I want to know everything you've done with my daughter since that day. Every decision you made for her and her mother, everything you know about where they are now. I want a copy of every legal document that bears their names." Despite his inebriated state, he arrested me in a stern look.

I returned a weak nod as my heart pumped heavily in my chest. "I'll get you everything."

I stood and crossed to the door.

"Who's the girl?" he asked.

"Who?" I knew he was talking about Tara, but I didn't want to put her in his path.

"Tara. Who is she?"

"She's Amar's friend," I replied.

He glared at me, but I kept the confused look on my face until he nodded and returned to his drink.

Relief washed over me as I walked out of that room. I found Tara and Amar in the dining room, helping Mom clear the table. The light and laughter in this part of the house stood in stark contrast to the darkness and gloom I'd just walked away from. I could have all this—the smiles, the jokes, the love. Tara's warm body against mine, her genuine spirit guiding mine like she did once before. When I walked up to them, I saw a light in Mom's eyes too. She looked truly happy, unlike the façade she put up during Dad's parties. I had seen her happy like this only in the presence of one other person, Mihir's mom.

A smile bloomed on my face. "What's going on?"

"Amar and Tara were sharing some memories," Mom said.

I glanced at Tara, but she promptly retreated to the kitchen.

"Can I help?" I asked Mom.

"We're almost done here," she said. "Go see if Durga needs help."

I strode to the kitchen, and a burst of excitement coursed through me as I imagined myself in the same space as Tara. I found her putting away leftovers in glass containers.

When I stood beside her, she pointed to an empty container and a bowl of korma. "Make yourself useful."

I poured the curry out, and snapped the lid closed. She handed me the rice next. When we were done, Mom and Durgaben retired to their rooms. We strolled into the backyard with a bottle of port and a perfectly aged Glenlivet. A gentle breeze flirted with the tiny lights around the pergola, and they twirled with glee. With my eyes set on Tara, I breathed in the beauty of the night.

After sampling both, Amar chose the wine, while Tara and I favored the liquid gold, as I knew we would. It was comforting to know some things hadn't changed. We didn't talk much. A few words between sips. But when I returned from a trip to the restroom, I caught Tara's hushed voice. The air turned still as I stopped around the corner.

"...he's a really nice guy. You'll like him."

"I'm happy for you," Amar said, then after a moment. "What about Sameer?"

"What about him?"

"Have you told him?"

Silence.

"Are you going to?"

"It's been years, Amar. I know he's your cousin and your loyalties lie with him, but he was the one to cut off all contact when he left."

"I meant it might be one way to help you move on." In my mind, I could see his smile, like mine but warmer and kinder.

"I know, I'm sorry," Tara's voice was softer now. "You were there for me when it mattered most. I can never forget that."

A sigh, but I couldn't tell whose it was. I wanted to burst right in and confront them, but my evil, competitive side convinced me to continue eavesdropping.

"How do you feel about him?"

I held my breath.

"You just heard, he's getting engaged. So that makes the question irrelevant now, doesn't it?"

Another sigh. Amar's.

"Don't worry, this time it's for the best," she said.

I heard shuffling and the barking of a neighbor's dog. As I turned the corner into their sight, I saw Amar's arm around her and her head on his shoulder, and I surmised what the conversation was about.

I rejoined them, and we sat in silence until Tara excused herself to turn in for the night. "I'm well-fed, drunk, and happy," she declared. "This has been a great evening. My heart is full, truly." She gave Amar a big hug. I showed her to the room I'd prepared, but all I got was, "Good night."

Out in the backyard, I poured us another round. "I overheard you both earlier," I said to Amar and took a sip of my scotch.

He looked at me. "And?"

"Did you two hook up after I left India?"

He dragged a sip at the end of a sigh. "Would it bother you if we had?"

"What do you think?"

"Does it change how you see her?"

My nostrils flared. No. But it did change how I felt about them. *Resentment* was the word. They had continued to grow closer as Tara and I drifted apart.

"You left, and you didn't tell her why. How does it matter what she did after that?"

"Don't do this to me, Amar. You know you're more than a cousin to me. Please tell me you didn't betray me."

He put a leg over his knee and relaxed into the sofa. My mind drew up images of them together, and I raced to prevent it. "I thought she was your friend," I finally protested like a pouty child.

"She is." He kept his unblinking gaze on me. "She's still one of my closest friends."

"I want her."

"I know."

I poured a splash into Tara's empty glass and gulped it down. I felt her lips on it, smelled her fragrant breath.

"What's your problem, dude?"

"She thinks I left because I was done with her. That I cast her aside like she was some sort of accessory, expendable."

"Then tell her the truth. Game-playing is not the flipping way to get her back."

I blinked at him.

"And why are you still with Aarti?" he asked with a gentle frown.

Again, there was nothing I could say.

"You've been through a lot. I understand that it's hard to accept that your father had an affair and a child from it while he kept playing the doting husband and loving father to Chachi and you. Your world was shattered, but you bounced back, and you're in a good place now. Don't throw it away. There's only one way to get Tara back, and you know what it is," he said sagely, and swallowed the rest of his wine. "Go, grovel before her." He smiled and walked away.

SAMEER

$\mathcal{T}$he next morning, I woke early and lay in bed checking emails and reading the news on my phone, trying to get past the thought that Tara was asleep in the adjacent room. When I went downstairs to make myself some coffee, I saw Mom at the kitchen table with a steaming cup of tea.

She looked up from her phone and smiled. "Couldn't sleep in either, huh?

"No. Good morning." I walked to the coffee machine and turned it on. "Everyone's still asleep?"

"Yes, it's Durga's day off. She'll probably go see her daughter later." She paused. "Do you want to eat? I can make paratha."

"No, Ma, I'm not hungry. And you don't have to cook. I can make some eggs for everyone later."

She smiled. "Never thought I'd hear a sentence like that from you."

We returned to reading on our phones after I settled down by her with my coffee, but I caught her stealing glances at me.

"What do you want to ask me?" I said, my eyes still on the phone.

She looked at me. "Nothing."

"Ask. We both know you will, sooner or later."

"How well did you know Tara when you were in Baroda?" she asked as if she was trying to frame the question just right.

I put my phone down and looked at her. "*Well*."

"And?"

"What do you want to know, Ma?"

"Do you like her?" Her eyes were steady on me, as were her hands gripping the phone.

"There's no simple answer to that."

"It's a yes or no question, Sameer."

I sighed. "Yes. But it's complicated."

"Because of Aarti?"

"It's not just that. Tara has been burned and doesn't trust me."

"What do *you* want?"

"I want her, Ma." I met Mom's eyes with conviction. "But I cannot *will* her to want me, can I? I also know what happens if I break it off with Aarti prematurely."

"What do you mean?"

"I can still hear people whispering about us, Ma. About you and Dad."

"But this isn't about our past, Beta. It's about your future."

"But I'm so close to making it. No one will ever dare talk down to you again."

"What are you going on about?" Mom's brows creased in genuine confusion.

I told her everything that had been weighing me down. "I want to give you back the life you deserve, the life Dad promised and didn't deliver."

"Oh, my child! Come here!" I pulled my chair closer to hers and put my head on her shoulder. "People will always talk. Haven't you learned that yet? Even when we had everything, people talked. They talked about us behind closed doors. After it was ruined, they just found the gumption to say it to our faces. But you don't need to carry that burden, my baby," she said, patting my head. "That's *our* burden, mine and Pavan's. I got the life I chose. I was foolish and blinded by love. But you can't live my life for me. You need to figure out what's good for you, what you want."

I pulled myself away and looked at her. She took my hand between her soft ones. "Your reaching the top, whatever that means, guarantees nothing. Not for me, and neither for you. Your father was at the top when we lost everything. You need to ask yourself, what are you chasing?"

"But I've worked so hard, I can see the summit. Was that all for nothing?"

"Then let's finalize your wedding plans. Aarti said you're dragging your feet. That will clinch it, right?"

The familiar pain of a cold clamp around my heart made me squirm in my seat.

"That's what I thought. You want to use Aarti to get ahead, to get something you think I deserve while depriving yourself of the happiness you want. Then what? You'll cast her aside? How long will that take, and will Tara keep waiting for you? Aarti deserves better."

The truth hit me like a lightning bolt. Dad had used Mom and her money to get ahead, and Mom deserved better. I had spent my days trying to become the man that my father wasn't, but that's exactly who I'd molded myself into. I was my father!

"You're clutching my hand too hard," Mom cried, and I dropped it. She brought it to my cheek. "Don't hold on to the wrong things, Beta. I saw how Tara looked at you last night, and I've never seen you this happy with Aarti. I choose happiness for you."

"I choose happiness too. For me and for you."

"I made my choice, Sameer. If I wanted the world, I wouldn't have married your father. I would've married the man your grandfather chose for me. He was a royal descendant, and he promised me the world."

"Do you regret not marrying him?" I surprised myself with this question, but Mom didn't flinch.

With a steady gaze, she answered, "I didn't know that man, so I can't say with certainty I would've been any happier with him."

"Do you regret Dad?" I found the courage to ask.

This time, she allowed herself to exhale. "No," she said quietly. "I've raised two strong, wonderful kids with him. And despite everything, he has always respected me, my person, and my intellect. He has always trusted me, and that's something you should know."

I gaped at her, trying to bring myself to accept her logic. But it was her marriage, her life, and she had the right to decide how she felt about him.

Her bright smile shattered my daze. "What I'm saying is, you can hate him all you want, but you don't have to hate him for me. I can do that myself."

Of course he respected her, she was brilliant, smart, and witty.

I placed a kiss on her hand. She crossed her arms delicately and said, "Now, tell me about Tara."

I held nothing back. Well, except for how hard we fucked. "She saved me from who I was before. She saved my friendship with Amar. If it wasn't for her, I would've drowned after what happened in India. She's my anchor to this world and myself. I want her, Ma. I need her in my life."

"Talk to her, Beta, and resolve it. I hate seeing Aarti's happy face when she's with you."

I nodded and dragged my hand over my head. "I wish I hadn't agreed to go along with Dad in this sham of a relationship."

Her stern glare shut me up. "There's a lot I dislike about your father, but you can't blame him for this mess. He didn't force you. He didn't knowingly push you away from Tara and toward Aarti. This was your choice, your doing. Don't blame others for your own bad decisions like he does."

I lowered my gaze to the table. She was right. She was always freaking right. This one was on me.

"What do you think of Tara?" I asked quietly.

That brought out Mom's bright smile, like the sun peeking from behind a dark cloud. "She's smart, successful, and lovely. And she knows how to keep you humble," Mom said with a soft chuckle. "She makes you happy. What more can I ask for? I especially liked how she stuck it to your father," she whispered.

"Oh yeah, she's got a smart mouth, that one."

"Morning."

I zipped around with a start when I heard Tara's voice behind me.

"Good morning," I said, but threw Mom a nervous look.

How much had she heard? Judging by the bright smile on her dewy face, not much. In the light of the morning and the conversation I had just had with my mother, I felt a renewed kinship with her. I felt closer, but that could've been because she was wearing one of my pajama sets, swimming in them like a cute vixen. My insides turned warm at the thought of her full breasts brushing against my clothes.

"Coffee?" I asked.

"Yes, please."

"Come, sit." Mom pulled a chair next to her. "I hope you slept well."

"Yes, I slept soundly. Thank you for everything." I'd never seen her this shy and restrained. "Thank you," she said to me when I handed her a freshly brewed cup.

"Don't be so formal, Tara," I said, now emboldened by my

mother's approval. "Consider this your home." Mom couldn't hide a chuckle at my words.

A little later, Amar came downstairs, and Mom made him her special spiced chai. We sat at the table, the full house giving me a weird sense of déjà vu. Just a fleeting glimpse, like I'd been here before or maybe I'd dreamed about this moment. Mom, Tara, and Amar bonding over morning tea, their laughter flooding the entire house in a soft, golden light.

We decided to get breakfast on our way back to our apartments. When Tara went upstairs to get ready, I continued chatting with Amar and Mom while Dad had his tea. His good mood from the previous night had carried over to this morning. Seeing Amar usually softened his remorseless heart.

But when the topic of our conversation veered toward relatives in India, I knew we were only moments away from Dad bringing up my wedding. I excused myself and sprinted up the stairs, two steps in a stride, and caught Tara scrambling away. She stopped and turned around when I reached the landing.

"Hey," I said. She was still in my night clothes. "Did you need something?"

She quickly scanned the stairs behind me. Then, in a hushed voice, said, "I was looking for a bath towel but was too embarrassed to come ask for it."

"Oh, I'm sorry! Mom asked me to put a set in your room last night, but I guess I forgot after I changed the sheets."

She smiled. "No problem."

"And you don't need to hesitate. This is Amar's home, as good as yours. Here..." I stepped over to the linen closet in the hallway and pulled out a set of fluffy towels.

"Bath, hand, and a washcloth." I beamed.

She pressed her lips together. "Impressive!"

"Mom taught me that."

"Hmm, I never would've guessed."

We shared a quick chuckle before she approached and took the matching set from my hands. "I was beginning to think I made a mistake staying over, but you and Aunty made me feel right at home this morning."

"Yes, Mom's amazing that way," I smiled back. "Hope you were comfortable last night."

"Everything was perfect. And thank you for the toothbrush and toiletries."

"Except I forgot the towels."

She tossed her hair over her shoulder. "I forgive you."

"Oh? That's mighty generous of you."

Her eyes creased with a heartfelt smile, then drifted downward to the towels.

"Tara, I'm sorry for being a jerk these past few days. I know you're angry, but it was never my intention to upset you."

She looked up and shook her head. "I don't want to carry this anger any further, and I should be the one apologizing. I shouldn't have gone off on you in the presence of your family and Aarti."

"We're both hurting."

She stepped away. "Yes, and it needs to stop. I'm happy for you, Sameer. Aarti is phenomenal, and she really likes you."

I wondered if this was my moment to break into the confession that I dreaded. "I was wondering if we could talk about that, actually."

She shuffled before setting her weight on her right foot. "I need to tell you something too."

"Now?"

Her reluctant nod coincided with her phone ringing in the room. "It's probably Sujit," she said as her fingers curled tight around the soft cloth. "Let's talk after the opening this Friday. I'll be a nervous wreck until then."

I smiled in reassurance. "Your art is the last thing you need to be nervous about. I wouldn't have bought your painting unless it was worth it."

She raised an eyebrow. "You know you lost all credibility when you bragged about buying that Selfia." Then, with wide eyes and a gasp, continued, "Oh my god, promise me you won't put mine in the same space where you hang that hack-job! Ah, my dignity just suffered a massive blow."

"Stop," I chided with a smile. "When did you become this dramatic?"

She shrugged. "Another survival tactic." Her phone had stopped chiming, and she lingered for a moment longer.

"You don't need to worry about surviving anymore, Tara. You're thriving."

The exuberant smile that blossomed on her face took us both by surprise. She quickly replaced it with the fake one I had taught her years ago. "I'll see you at the opening?" she asked.

I thought I spotted a hint of anticipation in her eyes. "Yes, I'm looking forward to seeing your other two pieces."

She put up a warning finger. "Don't try to buy them. Let others have a chance to own a Tara Kadam original."

I raised my palms. "I'll try, but I can't promise. If I like them, I'll outbid the hell off others."

She rolled her eyes. "Funny, but no one is dying to bid on my work yet."

"It's only a matter of time."

Her dark eyes gazed into mine so hard, I felt my heart take a tumble. "Let's talk next weekend. Does that work for you?"

I nodded, and we both retreated to our rooms in silence.

TARA

*I*t was the most important day in my art career, the culmination of my hard work and persistence. Being a consultant was one thing, but being recognized as an artist in my own right was a different high. This was my one chance to shine, to show the world I was worth taking note of. But this could also be my chance to drown. My future as an artist was riding on it because I wouldn't get a similar opportunity anytime soon. I could not blow this.

Imposter syndrome had stalked me everywhere over the past week as I witnessed the museum come alive with activity. The staff worked around the clock, setting up exhibits, installing descriptions and artist information, and getting the paintings lit to perfection. I snuck in a couple of times on my way to the restoration room and stood in awe at the amount of labor and care involved in the process. The exhibition, showcasing emerging artists like me, promised to attract an ensemble of critics, collectors, and art lovers.

Maybe my anxiety would have been allayed if Sujit and Aai were coming, but Sujit had a conference he couldn't miss, and Aai didn't want to travel unaccompanied. If I had known I would be this nervous, I would've flown out myself and brought Aai along. But then, I also hadn't predicted the effect my interactions with Sameer would have on me.

I returned home that afternoon to dress up for the evening. It would be the first time I would wear a saree to a professional event, a tribute to my mother, and her sacrifices that had brought me here. I would stand before an audience that evening as an artist with enough credit to play by my own rules and be taken seriously. The black saree with an antique gold border and turquoise paisley motifs was designed by a dear friend, who paid handloom artists in India a fair price to weave her own unique designs. Her special blend of linen and silk promised long hours of creaseless wear. I paired it with a beaded blue turquoise necklace handcrafted by another friend. I straightened my hair, highlighted my eyes, and swiped on a subtle brown lipstick.

After I applied a final coat of mascara, I flashed my practiced smile in the mirror. The last time I used that smile, I was standing in the empty corridor with Sameer, ready to tell him everything before my phone began trilling. Perhaps it was our impending talk that added to my nerves. Once I had confessed my past to him, there would be no going back. No way forward too, I suspected, as I dabbed my lips with a tissue to set the color. Then I swiped another coat of the lipstick and repeated the dabbing. Would that end my connection to him?

Tumultuous as our relationship had been, a part of me had always trusted the artist, the critic, the friend in him. I wouldn't hesitate a moment to put my life in his hands. The only thing I couldn't trust him with was my heart. Yet it was his warm smile that I saw reflected in the mirror because years ago, it was his critical feedback that helped establish my credentials as an artist.

That year in college, I became the youngest recipient of the *Maharaja Fateh Singh Rao Award* for the best original oil painting. Later that year, he helped me edit a paper that got nominated for the best undergraduate research at the *National Conference on Gender in the Visual Arts*. Sameer and I had two major disagreements before I set aside my ego to accept that he was right and made amendments to the paper. Despite the intimate nature of our relationship, he never showed mercy when we debated, and it was this connection that had kept me bound to him all these years.

But being with him had thrust me into the limelight like I had never wanted. This lower-middle-class girl with her imperfect English had suddenly become the envy of the campus. I detested the attention, as if being Sameer's girlfriend was my only identity. But Sameer never imposed on me. He never coaxed me to change my lifestyle, my wardrobe, or my accent. He respected my space and my friendships.

Then there were things that I *did* learn from him, like how to elegantly wrap spaghetti around a fork and how to savor fine whisky without drowning it in Coke. He showed me how to fake a smile without flashing my teeth, which had come in handy as a consultant. It was the same fake smile that I saw in my mirror right now.

Limelight, I didn't do well under it, and one would be on me tonight.

With a thudding heart and sweaty palms, I gave myself a once-over and headed out the door.

Little did I know I'd get the surprise of my life at the reception. It was Sujit and his date, a small woman on his arm, who caused my heart to stop and a small scream to escape my lips.

"Aai! I can't believe my eyes!" I took her in a big hug and looked through watery eyes at Sujit, who smiled back.

"Surprise!" Aai said in English. "Sujit teach that to me."

I laughed out loud. "My heart is beating so fast," I said to her in Marathi. "I've spoken to you every day. How did you keep this a secret?"

"Sujit made sure I didn't accidentally spoil the surprise. Called me every day to remind me," she said in Marathi, returning his smile. When I relayed it to Sujit, he laughed and gave her a side hug.

"And you!" I cried in complaint. "I'll deal with you later. I'm...I can't tell you how happy I am."

"You look beautiful," Aai said. "The saree looks perfect on you. I could never miss this proud day."

As we walked inside, Sujit whispered in my ear, "You look amazing, I can't wait to get you alone later. That naked waist is killing me." I looked at his handsome face, and instinctively my eyes darted to Sameer.

I caught him watching us, holding a wine glass, with no expression on his face. I quickly turned back to Sujit. "You never talk like that. Who are you and what have you done to my boyfriend?"

"Maybe I've missed you too much," he said.

"I still can't believe you're here. You're devious!"

"I can't stay, though. I have a meeting tomorrow I can't miss. We have a late-night flight back," he said with his usual straight-forwardness.

"What? But tomorrow is Saturday."

"We're starting a new project, darling. There are no weekends."

I looked at Aai. "Are you leaving too?"

She nodded. "I can't fly back alone."

I looked at them both. "That's not fair!"

"We can fight about it later." He hooked his arm in mine. "This is your day to shine."

I was back in the spotlight, only this time its glare dazzled me. It wasn't my first time showcasing my work, but it was certainly the first time I was swimming in this depth of love and support. Paradoxically, it made me nervous.

"Let me introduce you to my friends," I said, walking toward Amar and Sameer.

Aarti's eyebrows shot up again when I introduced Sujit as my boyfriend. Perhaps the ruse Mihir and I had cooked up that evening had worked too well. But as we stood around talking, another bout of self-doubt hit me. And it hit hard.

I needed time alone. I rushed toward the restrooms and halted next to a bench, trying to gain control of my breath. A sinking feeling overshadowed me, like the world around me was melting and pulling me down to drown. I looked at my phone. I had a few minutes to get a handle on myself, but my fingers trembled, my eyelids felt heavy, and my body sagged against the wall.

SAMEER

a sharp pain imploded in my heart at the sight of Tara with Sujit. He looked at her with such adoration, and the way her face had lit up when she saw him walk in. I understood how she must feel every time she saw me with Aarti. Yes, I loved Tara, and yes, she knew it, but the painful reality of her having to confront Aarti and me together, every day, hit me as I shook hands with Sujit.

He was a striking fellow, a couple of inches taller than me, with skin smooth and dusky like Tara's. As if that wasn't enough, he had dimples when he smiled. And I got to see a lot of those dimples that evening. They made a stunning pair. I hated myself for thinking it, but he seemed to make her happy. Tara gushed about how he'd made it to her opening night despite his busy schedule. And he had brought along her mother, who displayed the same familiarity as if he were her own son. I had acted like a selfish, immature prick by announcing to her and half of my immediate family that I was still in love with her. For, though Tara and I might be pining for each other, here was a devoted man who would make her a better partner.

Stable, grounded, and soft-spoken, he was the yin to her yang. He was the calm Parvati to her turbulent Shiva. Tara and I were perhaps too alike, too volatile, and the events of the past few weeks had proven it. It was best that I gracefully removed myself from her life. I had a chance, and I blew it. Now it was sheer selfishness to demand her back in my life when she had finally found the happiness she deserved from the start.

This sudden resignation felt strange, at once liberating and cloying, as if the boulder that had just landed on my heart was also my path to moksha. As my eyes landed on a happy Aarti, I decided I couldn't deceive her any longer, but I needed to wait until it was the right time for her. I looked at Sujit, and a strange calm washed over me. I had made the right decision. Slowly, my gaze turned toward Tara. Her eyes flitted nervously, and her smile was vacant.

Something was wrong.

She excused herself and hurried toward the restrooms, but no one else seemed perturbed. Sujit and her mother were oblivious to her distress. But I knew. I felt it in my body. I counted to fifteen, then excused myself.

As I turned the wall separating the large gallery from the restrooms, I found her sitting on a bench with a distant look on her face. I rushed over and crouched before her.

"Hey." I took her hand. "What happened? Are you alright?"

Her palms were cold and sweaty. There was a slight tremble in them, and her eyes looked dazed. Her breathing was heavy, as if she were having a panic attack.

"Tara, look at me." I rubbed her hands between my palms.

She sucked in a sudden, jagged breath and grabbed onto my hand. "I'm scared, Sameer."

"Scared of what?"

"I feel this weight so heavy I can barely breathe. So many people watching me today, I need to do right by them."

"Look at me, sweetheart." I lifted her chin, and her eyes met mine tentatively. "You don't have to do right by anyone but your-self. Do you hear me?"

"My chest hurts," she said.

I moved closer, and her grip on my hand got tighter.

"Listen, you're brilliant. You don't have to prove yourself to anyone. You are you. You're the best at what you do."

She kept her beautiful, dark eyes on my face.

"Have you felt like this before?" I asked. "Is this a panic attack?"

She shook her head and looked down at her hands.

"Keep looking at me." At my words, she lifted her gaze back to me.

"We'll figure it out, okay? Right now, you need to show the world how brilliant you are. You don't have to prove it, just show it. Let your work speak for itself."

She nodded.

"Don't doubt yourself. You said you trusted me, right? You trust me to tell you the truth? I'm telling you, you're a marvel. Nothing and no one can take away your genius." I kept rubbing her palms. "Now breathe. Deep breaths. Keep breathing."

After a few minutes, color returned to her face. Her breathing slowed to normal. I dropped beside her on the bench, still holding her hand.

"Growing up, I didn't have much ground for confidence," she said slowly, looking into the distance. "The only way I could succeed was by working hard and believing in my abilities." I rolled my thumb over her hand. She looked at me. "You always admired how strong-willed I was, but it didn't come naturally. I had to train myself to be that way. To overcome doubt and fear. To take nonsense from no one."

"Especially from a rich boy like me."

That brought out a tiny smile. "My confidence is drawn from deep within me, like a well. I draw from it over and over. After a while, the well dries up because I'm asked to prove myself again and again. Opportunities like this help rebuild my confidence, but it also means I need to draw from that well even more. It's exhausting, until one day all I come up with is sand and grit from the bottom of a dry well. Today is that day."

I'd never met this side of Tara, and for good reason. She was a trapeze artist without a safety net. She couldn't falter, and she didn't. She couldn't show her vulnerabilities because they would be misconstrued as inherent unworthiness. I stood up and held out my hand. She gripped it with a smile and pulled herself off the bench.

I kissed her forehead. "I'm going to give you a hug now, is that alright?"

She nodded, and I took her in my embrace, breathing her in. Her arms came around me as she sank her head into my neck. For a minute, the world around me faded away, and my resolve weakened. How could I live without her? How could I deny her my love?

"How do you feel?" I asked.

She lifted her head and smiled. "Better."

"Tara." I put my hands on her shoulders. "You're one of the smartest people I know, and I really mean it. Never second-guess yourself."

As she looked up at me, standing so close I could feel her breath, I saw Sujit coming around the corner. I promptly stepped away and turned to him.

"She wasn't feeling well," I said.

His protective arm came swiftly around her. "Hi, darling, are you alright? What happened?"

I began to walk away as she vanished in his embrace, but her eyes stayed on me. They followed me as I disappeared into the claustrophobic crowd. Amar threw me an uneasy look, but I turned my attention to Aarti and Mom.

When Hadden introduced the artists, she gave a special nod to Tara as a guest of the museum and the only non-Texan to be featured in the exhibit. Hadden's invitation for her to say a few words seemed to take her by surprise, but she eloquently described how she fell in love with the city and its heritage.

"I want to extend my deepest gratitude to the museum and to Dr. Hadden for this incredible opportunity to have my name in the same catalog as these stellar artists," she said. "I came to this city with a dream in my eyes and hope in my heart. I shall return with stars in my eyes and love in my heart. And for that, I thank you all. I'm grateful for your generosity and warmth. Thank you for coming this evening." She finished with a luminous smile.

Sujit's face radiated pride and joy, like he truly appreciated and cherished her. She avoided me for the rest of the evening, while Sujit stayed by her side, and her mother could hardly contain a proud smile. Overall, it was a great day for the Kadam-Rao clan. Another bad one for the Rehanis.

After the event, Aarti decided to spend the night with me. My body heavy with emotional fatigue, I couldn't think of a convincing way to refuse her. So I took the coward's way out again and acquiesced. There was always a tomorrow to resolve things.

Around ten that evening, as Aarti and I lounged in the living room watching a movie, my doorbell dinged.

"Are you expecting anyone?" she asked.

I shook my head and dragged myself off the couch to answer the door. Tara stood outside, still in her saree, with a smile on her face and a glimmer in her eyes.

"Who's it, Sameer?" Aarti called from inside, and Tara's smile dropped instantly as she hung her head and tugged at the edge of her saree.

"It's Tara," I said and let her in.

"I'm so sorry to barge in like this," she said with tiny beads of sweat on her forehead.

"Oh, not at all," Aarti said. "Come in."

Tara took a few steps inside. "I just came by to thank you both for coming today. It meant a lot to me."

"Come share a drink," said Aarti. "It was such a fantastic day, you deserve a toast. Yes, Sameer?"

"Yes," I said meekly, and excused myself to grab whatever sparkling drink I had. I never bought champagne—I hated it. But Aarti enjoyed a sparkling white wine. I brought it out with three flutes. We drank to Tara's success, but she was jumpy and rose to leave immediately after.

"I'll go drop her off," I announced.

"No, it's alright," Tara objected. "It's a pleasant night to walk."

"Actually, it might rain. There's a storm passing through," Aarti said. "Sameer, go drop her off, please?"

She smiled at us, and I grabbed my keys off the counter.

"Where's Sujit?" I asked as we pulled out of the garage.

"They flew back," she said in a low voice. "He has an important meeting tomorrow, and Aai didn't want to fly back alone."

I let several deliberate minutes pass in silence before I asked, "Why did you come, Tara?"

With a feeble attempt to conceal her labored breath, she replied, "I wanted to thank you for talking me through my crisis of confidence today."

I glanced at her. She was lying, but I didn't push. When we arrived at her apartment, she unbuckled her seatbelt but didn't exit the car. We sat in silence.

"I watched you with Sujit today," I said.

Her tired, dark eyes regarded me with curiosity.

"It looks like he makes you happy. And you make him unbelievably happy," I said with a smile. "You two are good together, Tara, and I was selfish to thrust myself back into your life again. I'm sorry. It's time for you and Sujit. You deserve to be happy."

She continued staring at me as I kept my eyes on my hands. Finally, she pulled in a deep breath. "Thank you."

Somewhere beyond the horizon, an angry bolt of lightning flashed across the sky and struck hard. Wild winds jabbed at the trees. We sat quietly as two drops of rain splattered on the windshield, then quickly turned into a heavy downpour.

"We can still be friends," I said with a deliberate inflection in my voice.

She stared at the water pelting the window and nodded. "Yes. While I'm here," she said, shutting down multiple doors simultaneously. "Thank you for the ride."

I pulled the car beneath the covered entrance of her building. "Good thing I came to drop you. You'd have been completely drenched if you had walked," I said gently to diffuse the tension.

"Yes, sometimes things work out for the best. Good night, Sameer."

I watched her walk into the building, her graceful figure slightly slumped.

As I pulled out of the complex, Mom's number flashed on the dashboard.

"Hi Ma," I said.

"Are you okay?" she asked with urgency in her voice. "I've been trying to call you since we left."

"Oh, sorry. I'd put my phone on silent and forgot."

"I was worried sick."

"Why, what's the matter?"

"*What's the matter?*" Her voice went up half an octave. "You met Tara's boyfriend today."

"I'm alright, Ma. I've decided to let it go."

"What are you talking about?"

"I told her she and Sujit make a good pair and will be happy together."

"Why?"

"I don't know, Ma. It doesn't seem worth it to upend her life, especially after seeing them today."

"But she still loves you. I saw it."

"Yes, but she seems happy with him. And I'm all wrong for her."

"What does that mean?"

"I don't think I can make her happy."

"How do you know that?"

"Mom, what are you doing? I'm trying to resign myself to my fate here. Why aren't you being more supportive?"

"Because that's not your fate. And because I can see you'll never be happy without her."

And she hung up. Just like that, all full of sass and badassery.

TARA

*O*ur paths had crossed and diverged again, like railroad tracks at a junction. We were two trains running at full speed without a care for where the other was headed. Of course we were going to ram into each other at some point.

I wanted to hurt. I wanted the pain, but I felt nothing. My heart was in mutiny against my emotions.

Back in my apartment, I flung off my heels as the cell phone whirred in my hand, unusually loud against the jarring silence in my head.

"Hi, Sona," I said with an upward lilt in my voice, but she didn't buy my enthusiasm.

"What's wrong?"

"Oh, Sona. I just did a stupid thing and realized my mistake." I told her how Sameer had consoled me and how I had rushed over after Aai and Sujit left for the airport, only to find him with Aarti. "Like a fool, I stood there, still in my saree, hoping for what?" I wiped my forehead with my free hand. "There was no dignified way to exit. I'm grateful Aarti was kind. But it was like, suddenly something clicked. Sameer and I can never be."

I heard her exhale.

"I went over to get him back, Sona. To cheat on Sujit the moment he left with my own mother in his care. I'm a horrible person."

"Don't say that, love. This is Sameer we're talking about. When has anything involving him been easy or simple? Just give yourself some time. Show yourself some kindness."

"He said he was happy for Sujit and me, that I deserve to be happy. And yet..."

"And yet?"

I sighed and dropped onto the couch. "And yet, he was the only one who saw my distress. Not Amar, not Sujit, not even Aai. No one else noticed."

"Maybe he does love you, but not all love is realized in the same way. He loves you enough to let you go and be happy on your own terms."

"But he just set the terms for me. He pushed me into Sujit's arms, knowing full well I had gone there for him."

"That's what he thought you wanted. Why the heck aren't you both talking about it?"

"That's why I went over, to tell him how I feel and to listen to his side, but he was with Aarti."

She sighed.

"So, what's the use of having someone care for you so deeply if it's ephemeral? If it can't be realized in this lifetime?"

"Books have been written on the subject. However, metaphysics is not my forte, but I'll be happy to talk at length about the contribution of queer of color spaces to feminist theory if you're interested." I heard the shift in her tone from serious to teasing.

"Alright, alright, point taken, Professor Thomas." I had to smile.

"Thank you, young child. Now tell me, how was the opening? I want details. And how did you like the surprise?"

"I hate you all so much. How could you keep it from me? I thought my heart was going to explode when I saw them walk in."

I filled her in on the evening, including Dr. Hadden's commendation and my impromptu speech.

"I'm so proud of you, babe," she said. "And hey, don't think too much. You have Sujit. Sameer is your past. Don't try to erase him. Embrace the power of letting him go."

"That's very sound advice, Professor. Alas, my heart and brain don't operate on the same frequency."

When I rang Sujit immediately after, the call went directly to voicemail. I left him a text thanking him for the love and support that had helped me get through the evening.

It was also Sameer's love and faith in my abilities that had put me back on my feet, but I didn't want to think about him anymore.

I started the week knee-deep in research, trying to figure out the mystery of the two artists while still getting ahead of my work. I felt happier back in my comfort zone, a place where I could stay invisible and sane.

I exchanged a few texts with Amar, who was off visiting relatives on the West Coast, but we didn't bring up Sameer, who had kept his distance since that evening. He did text me early that week to congratulate me on the critical coverage I had received in two local newspapers.

SAMEER

So proud of you

I underplayed it with a simple

Thank you

He had taken the hint, and I didn't hear back from him for the rest of the week.

By Saturday morning, I had settled into a quiet routine of work and research that I didn't want to break for the weekend, so I decided to take my work bag to *Cups and Cookies*. I was about to leave for the café when I got a call from my brother. I hadn't spoken to him since I brought Aai over to the U.S., and seeing his number on my phone screen made my heart thud.

It was Saturday evening in India, and he was drunk. He lived in Gujarat, a dry state, so most likely he had been boozing on something cheap because he was too broke to buy decent liquor illegally. Using the choicest of abuses and curses, he accused me of having messed up his life. He recounted how I thought I was better than him, that I had taken away every bit of his happiness, and in a final cruel stroke, even snatched his mother away.

Her love was the only thing helping him cope, and I had stolen it. Unaware that I was in Dallas, he demanded to speak to Aai. I fended him off, threatening to call the police if he tried to contact her, but he was too drunk to realize the absurdity of the threat. My only reassurance was that he didn't have Aai's U.S. number. Unless overcome with motherly love, she had shared it with him. The thought terrified me, so I kept him on the line, indulging him as he hurled abuse at me until he passed out and I heard him snore.

Five minutes later, still standing in the same spot where I had answered his call, my skin turned numb. My hands began to tremble. I needed to sit down, but I couldn't move.

I tried breathing like Sameer had shown me that evening. I took deep breaths and closed my eyes to Sameer's image. I saw him holding out his hand for me. I grabbed it and steadied myself. I was still holding on to him when my other hand began to vibrate. With a jerk, I looked at the phone. It was Sameer. By sheer reflex, before I could stop myself, I answered the call.

"Hello," I said blankly.

"Hey, it's me. I'm sorry to call, but I'm meeting Mihir at *Cups*. I was wondering if you could join us. We have an interesting proposition for you."

I heard his voice but not his words. All I took in was Sameer, confident and reassuring, telling me I was loved.

"Tara? Are you there?"

"Yes." My voice cracked as a tear rolled down my cheek, and I heard his breath quicken.

"Tara, do you want me to come over? Just say the word."

"Yes," I said again, my voice still small.

"Give me twenty minutes. I'll be there, I promise."

"Okay."

Asking for help had always been impossible for me. I wasn't always fine, but I always ended up fine. What happened on the journey from not-fine to fine was my burden to carry. That day, I decided to share the burden. I needed a shoulder to lean on, and I chose one. I knew I could rely on Sameer.

I managed to walk to the couch and lower myself onto it. How could my own brother say such horrible things to his little sister? I had loved him for most of my life, and he would've died for me at one time. How had we gotten here?

When Dada finished high school, I was in the ninth grade. He had scored very well, way beyond what he or Baba had hoped for. He had his heart set on going to an art school, but Baba said it would be a waste of his talent and energies. Just like he would say it to me three years later. But while I got to study art, Dada paid the price.

He went off to one of the best public universities in Mumbai to study civil engineering. Proud, but never happy. He cleared the first semester with a flourish, but every semester after that, he either failed a course or barely managed a passing grade. When I graduated high school, he was repeating his second year. Perhaps it was this resentment that grew into the pot of bile that drowned us both. He thought I was living the life that should've rightfully been his, because I certainly wasn't living the one that would've been chosen for me.

My parents had bravely resisted the social pressure to marry me off early like some girls I knew. They let me become my own person. I never had to protest. They kept the snakes at bay, repelling every venomous comment targeted at me. It was this sense of gratitude and obligation that silenced me when Baba declared that I would become an engineer. If Aai hadn't coaxed me to be forthcoming, I would've become an engineer, probably married, with two kids exactly three years apart. I'm sure Dada would have reveled in the predictability of such a life. A stable job, a two-income household, and two kids. But it wasn't the life I wanted.

When I returned home toward the end of my second year at the art college, Baba had a heart attack. Dada was visiting for the summer, and he never went back to school. The hospital bills piled up fast, but when I offered to quit my studies, it was Dada who convinced me that I was doing well while he was flailing to stay afloat. It was better if he quit his studies and found a job. And he did. He was happy for a few months, but a monotonous, low-skill job with the brilliant mind of an artist was a cocktail for disaster. He began drinking each day after work, but for the most part, Baba had kept him on the straight and narrow.

After Baba passed away five years ago, Dada's drinking began in earnest. Soon he would be drunk at all hours. Baba had left a surprisingly large sum in life insurance. Dada kept whining to Aai that he could do so much with that money if she would only trust him with it. One day, she gave in, and before long, he had squandered away every last rupee. Soon he was back to square one, except now, Aai was broke too. Baba's pension was enough for daily expenses but left little for Dada's wasteful habits. I used to send Aai a little money, maintaining the delicate balance between helping her and respecting her dignity.

Two months before I came to Dallas, I was with Sujit when I got a call from Aai. It was only the second time I was at Sujit's for the weekend. She was sobbing, trying to tell me she was hurt, but in the same breath, desperate to protect her son. In his drunken state, he had demanded more money, which she had refused because she didn't have any. In a blind rage, he'd thrown a brass vase that hit her forehead.

Frightened and distraught, she'd locked herself in a room and called me. I was on the next flight to India. She pleaded with me not to call the police on him despite the injuries to her head. I packed her a light bag and brought her back to New York. Her multiple-entry visa from when they had come for my graduation allowed her entry into the country. Now I was protecting her the same way she had protected me all these years.

TARA

I was seated at the edge of the couch when the doorbell rang.

Sameer had only taken twelve minutes to arrive. I opened the door and fell against his chest. His touch and smell invoked a familiar, comforting memory that said it was alright to be weak, just for a day.

He stepped in and closed the door. I broke into tears, which turned into sobs that escalated to breathless gasps.

Wrapping his arms around me, he let me weep. "It's okay. Let it all out."

I wailed some more. Of course, I was no longer ashamed of showing him my tears, not after that evening at the museum. He had scooped me up and consoled me, as if he knew exactly what to do, what I needed.

"Let's get out of here," he whispered against my cheek.

"No, I can't let anyone see me like this."

"Then let's go to my place."

When I tried to step out of his arms, he pulled me closer. "Don't resist. A change of scene and some fresh air will do you good." He lifted my chin with his forefinger and smiled. "Come on, I brought my convertible."

"I hate convertibles," I said, wiping my eyes with my fingers and the backs of my hands. Some errant tears ran down my arms. "They mess up my hair."

He laughed. "Fine. We'll keep the top up and crack a window."

I blinked away the rest of my tears. "I want ice cream."

He smiled. "I know just the place. Go change."

I took two steps, then turned and said, "Just because I'm leaning on you today, doesn't mean I've changed my mind about us. I need you as a friend, that's all."

"I understand."

Pulling on a white eyelet dress, I bundled up my hair into a loose bun. I brushed on a light coat of mascara and refreshed my muted red lipstick. No, I wasn't dressing up for him. I didn't go to the grocery store without lipstick.

With the top up and the windows down, he drove us to a local creamery. At ten in the morning, it was deserted. "I wonder why people waste their time on breakfasts and brunches when there's ice cream." I snorted as I settled down at a table.

"Yeah, silly people," he said, using his phone to pay on a fancy register.

I had chosen the biggest cup they had with three flavors that didn't go together, or so Sameer informed me. I responded with a stink eye.

"Are you sure you don't want any?" I asked as he pulled out a chair across from me.

"No, I'm one of those silly people who prefers to have break-fast in the morning."

"Your loss!" I scooped a spoonful into my mouth.

He smiled.

"Keep those judge-y eyes off me while I eat away my grief."

"I don't have the audacity to judge you, nor the moral authority."

"That has never stopped you before." I stuffed my mouth with another big scoop as his phone buzzed on the table. His smile faded.

"Text from Aarti?"

He breathed and clenched his jaw.

"I'm sorry, not my concern."

"Yes, you've made that very clear."

"*You* made it clear that night in the car, Sameer." I tried to produce a scoff, but it sounded off-tone on account of my cold tongue.

"Let's go," he said, pushing back his chair, keys jangling in his hand. "Before this turns into another fight."

I pointed to my bowl of dessert. "And this?"

"Eat it on the way."

"You're still heartless, aren't you?" I cried as I followed him to the car.

Neither of us said a word as he drove us to his place. I considered asking him to drop me back at mine, but his crestfallen face discouraged me. The least I could do was be a good friend to him.

It was the first time I saw his condo in daylight, and the sun streaming in made the tastefully decorated space even more appealing. I had heard everything is big in Texas, but it was enormous, at least five times bigger than my apartment. I could see his artistic vision in the arrangement of furniture and the choice of accent pieces. Big, open glass windows stood in lieu of walls on two sides, inviting in the bright Texas sunlight.

"I never got a chance to tell you what a beautiful home you have," I said to break the ice between us.

"It's not a home yet. I'm hardly here during the week, and some weekends I spend at my parents'. Would you like to see the place?"

"Sure." He went around the house, and I followed him with a sturdy grip on my ice cream bowl. The decor was minimalist but perfect. Everything looked like it had a purpose, and nothing was out of sync.

"Would you like something to drink?" he asked as we circled back to the kitchen.

I held up my bowl, and he gave me a restrained smile.

"Do you want me to leave?" I asked.

"Why?" He frowned.

"I'm upset. I need to sulk. But if you're going to do that too, I'd rather be by myself."

He smiled. "Sorry, I didn't know we couldn't share the sulking. Take turns, perhaps?"

I shook my head and put the bowl to my lips to drink up the last molten bits of the cacophonous flavors, which tasted absolutely fine to me.

He held out his hand, and I placed the empty bowl in it. "Thank you."

"You're going to have a stomachache, a headache, or both. I'm waiting to see which hits you first."

"I'll gladly take either over the bloody heartache," I said.

"There's enough of that to go around. Aarti texted about setting a date for our engagement."

"I'm not sure how or why to feel sorry about that."

He let out a deep sigh. "You still don't mince words, do you?"

"Sorry, I—"

"Don't bother," he said. "Sit."

We settled on the couch in the living room, facing the skyline. "So, are you going to tell me what happened? Those were some tears."

But as I met his eyes, I lost my nerve. How could I reveal the grim, dark secrets of my family?

Before I realized it, I was on my feet. "I think this was a mistake."

He held my wrist and gently said, "Hey, if you don't want to talk about it, that's alright. Stay, we can talk about something else."

I hesitated but sat down. "Is Aarti coming here today?"

Another sigh from him.

"I'm only asking because I don't want to be here when she comes."

"No, she's not coming this weekend. I wanted to work."

I sat up straight. "I didn't realize. I keep barging in on your life. Maybe it's best if I left." I stood again.

He held my hand and coaxed me back to the couch. "It's never a bother, Tara. You know that."

After a few minutes of silence, he said, "I'm hungry. Is it okay if I make some eggs?"

I nodded and followed him to the kitchen. He pulled out eggs from the refrigerator and pointed to a barstool at the island.

"Have a seat," he urged. "I had just come back from the gym when you called. Took a quick shower and headed out."

I slipped on to the barstool. "I can't believe rich boy is cooking." I couldn't mask the sarcasm and incredulity. "You didn't cook when you lived alone in Baroda."

He gave a restrained smile and said, "Times change."

With a serrated knife, he cut precise slices off a loaf from a gourmet bakery I had seen around the corner and put them in a slot toaster. Then he turned on a fancy coffee machine that ground fresh beans before brewing. The sweet smell of a specialty roasted coffee replaced the delicious, yeasty aroma of the bread.

"How's the response to your work been since the review?" he asked, working on the eggs.

"Good, a few other media outlets picked up the story, and now I've got two people bidding over *Healing Love*."

"That's great, Tara." He appeared genuinely proud of my achievement.

"Yeah, my agent is hyping me up as the next big thing."

"And I have the honor of being the first to own a Tara Kadam original."

I smiled at his back. "And you've got the best one yet."

"Hey, did you solve the mystery of those artists?"

I sat up. "Yes! It's so intriguing. It was the same artist. Can you believe it?"

"How did you figure it out?"

"When Mr. Arlington showed me the painting, he flashed this sly, crooked smile, which stuck with me because it was at odds with how he had been all evening. So that got me thinking, and instead of focusing on the paintings, I began to research their family history. In one obscure biography, I found a clue. Turns out, Bayles, the artist who was hired by the estate, had a torrid affair with one of the daughters-in-law of the patriarch. So they ousted him and destroyed his early work. But the couple continued their clandestine relationship, and he used a pseudonym to sneak in several pieces depicting sexualities cloaked in landscape art. Dr. Hadden is ecstatic."

"Then how come they still have the ones with his real name?"

"Ah, see, this is why I love talking to you," I said, and he turned around to gift me a smile. "His lover hid them, and they were discovered long after the entire generation was dead."

"That is truly intriguing. Almost like solving a real mystery."

"Hey." I frowned. "It *is* a real mystery."

He cast me a teasing look, and I rolled my eyes. "I had forgotten you do that." And I had forgotten how good it felt when he teased me like that.

"So..." I exhaled. "When did you move to the U.S.?"

"Thirteen years ago."

He didn't even flinch when he unloaded that piece of information on me. Realization struck me like a lightning bolt as I figured out why I couldn't reach him anymore. He hadn't changed his number. He had moved out of the country.

"How could you not tell me, Sameer?"

"Let's eat." He transferred the fluffy eggs onto two plates, put the toast beside them, and carried the plates over to me.

"I'm not hungry." I pouted.

It was partially true, but I was also furious.

"Eat a little or you're going to be sick." He placed a plate before me, then took a seat at the island.

"I know it's too late, but I'm really sorry about how I left things," he said and placed a hand over mine.

I withdrew my hand, grabbed a fork, and stabbed the egg on my plate. We ate in absolute silence, except for the clink of the silverware. After I helped him clean up, I declared, "I should leave."

"Stay."

"I'm mad at you, Sameer."

"I know, but we're here now," he said softly and poured the fragrant coffee into two huge mugs.

We returned to the living room and stared at the city drowning under the bright summer sun. A small button on a tiny remote drew the shades, and just like that, we slipped into a refuge of our own. Away from the noise and bustle of the city, away from the prying eyes of the sun. Wrapped up in a cocoon of safety. The coffee mug felt cozy in my hands. I moved closer to him, pulled my knees into my chest, and relaxed against his shoulder. Soon, silent tears began flowing down the side of my face, and I allowed them to run unchecked. When his arm wrapped around my shoulder, my story spilled out.

"My brother was devastated when he sobered up and realized what he had done," I said. "He cried and pleaded and apologized, but I couldn't trust him anymore. I asked him to keep the family home because that's all he would get. Every so often, I send him a little money, even though I know he's not buying groceries with it. He texts me, sometimes thanking me for the money or asking how Aai is doing. I avoided his calls for months, but I never imagined he could say those things. I can't believe he's carried so much bitterness in his heart. Among other things, he called me a whore, Sameer. It sounds worse in Marathi. Like a stab through the heart. In a flash, it strips you of all humanity and all sense of dignity, no matter who you are. You become a word in someone else's mouth, to be used at their will, to be dragged through the dirt, to be trampled upon."

"Oh Tara, I'm so sorry!" He gathered me in his arms and kissed the top of my head.

"I won't repeat what else he said, but no one should hear such cruel words from a loved one. I understand he's an addict, and perhaps I shouldn't have left him alone like that, but we put him through three different rehab programs over the years. Expensive ones. He came back, stayed clean for a few weeks, then started drinking again. He blames me for not giving him the money that would put him back on his feet instead of wasting it on rehab," I added with fresh tears. "But my life and my work are here now. I can't go take care of him every time he relapses."

"You're right," Sameer said against my cheek as he continued to hold me. "Neither you nor your mother should blame yourselves. He's a grown man. Grown adults need to take responsibility for their own actions, not expect others to clean up their messes."

I moved out of his arms and threw my shoulders back. "Sujit stood by me like a rock through it all." He needed to know the depth of my feelings for Sujit. "He helped me get my tickets and booked car rides and hotels while I was on the way. He's also helping me get her stay extended. He's the reason I'm not worried about her."

Sameer pulled me closer and kissed my temple. "I'm glad you have him."

"I'm not a citizen yet, which means I can't sponsor her immigration. We'll have to wait and see what happens. Worst-case scenario, she'll go back to India for six months. I might go with her or have her stay with a relative until I can get her back. But I can't knowingly put her in harm's way again."

"I'm also here for you, Tara," he said. "Let me know if I can help."

I nodded and relaxed against his shoulder.

SAMEER

*S*he lifted her head from my shoulder and asked, "What time is it?"

Her tears had ceased a while back, but she had stayed in my arms. I grabbed my phone from the table. "Just past two."

"I should leave. I took up your entire morning."

"No, you're not leaving feeling like this."

She offered a weak smile and picked up her bag. "I'm much better now. Thank you for...today."

"Stay," I said. "Let's order some lunch, or I can try and cook something for you. How about pav bhaji?"

She blinked. "*You* are going to cook pav bhaji?" she said and burst into a hearty laugh. Like a clear wind-chime clinking in the breeze, her sweet sound sliced through the silence of my apartment, and a word flashed across my mind, *home.*

"Okay, okay, that was a foolish thing to say."

"You think? You can't even list the ingredients that go into it."

"Well, obviously, there's pav," I said, referring to the pull-apart rolls. I was blissfully ignorant, of course. I had never cooked anything beyond eggs and the occasional cup of tea in my life.

"Yes, and?"

"There are vegetables in the mix."

"Obviously. Which ones?" Watching me fumble had lit up her face. "What kind of spices?"

"You win. I give up."

"I bet you don't even have the basics in this fancy house of yours, let alone the pav bhaji masala."

"I have things," I protested. "Durgaben stocks my pantry."

"Why does she do that? Doesn't she know rich boys don't cook?"

"For some strange reason, she loves me, dotes on me, and checks up on me from time to time. Sometimes she brings me meals for the week."

"That is strange. There's nothing remotely lovable about you," she said with a frown.

"May I remind you, there was once a very sassy girl who was quite fond of me?"

"She was naïve and stupid."

"She wasn't naïve. And she's still the smartest person I know."

Tara smiled and said, "Let's check the pantry."

Organized in neat rows in the walk-in pantry were some staples: Basmati rice, yellow moong dal, a bunch of pasta, and some canned and jarred goods.

"How about dal chawal?" she asked with a twinkle in her eye. It had been months since I'd had a fresh homecooked meal.

"Sounds perfect. I don't think this house knows what dal smells like." The thought of the tempered yellow lentils over steaming rice invoked fond memories of a different life that would never return.

"Well then, let's introduce it to the simplest of life's pleasures. Hey rich boy, you think you can manage chawal?" she asked with a playful hand on her hip.

"I might have a rice cooker somewhere." I walked into the pantry and returned with one. "Found it. Thank you, Durgaben!"

"That should work. Now measure out one cup of rice and rinse it twice. Then put it in the cooker with two cups of water," she directed.

I nodded and pulled out pots and pans from the cabinets. "Then press this button...see this one here?" She grinned.

"You're enjoying this, aren't you?" I said and proceeded to measure out the raw rice.

She rinsed the dal and put it in a pot with water over the stove. I went back to the pantry for a jar of pickled raw mango. "My mom's special," I announced with pride.

While the grains cooked, we set the table. She instructed, and I followed. She even located a masala dabba in the back of a cabinet.

"I like Durgaben. She's meticulous." Tara gestured toward the stainless steel container. "Look at this."

Stocked with dry masalas and turmeric and suspicious-looking tiny grains that Tara said were broken fenugreek seeds, the masala dabba was a kaleidoscopic delight of potent flavors. Accompanying it was a small bottle of the pungent asafetida.

"I didn't see any fresh vegetables in the fridge. Do you have any frozen fries?"

"I might." I pulled open the freezer drawer and produced a bag.

"How about masala fries?"

"You're a wizard in the kitchen, Tara. Master of color, mistress of spices?" I said, and a warm smile appeared on her face.

When the oven was hot, she slid a tray of frozen fries into it. Then she fluffed the rice and tempered the dal with such grace and expertise that not a splatter ruined her pristine, white dress. When the fries were golden and crisp, she tossed them with mustard seeds, chili powder, and turmeric.

I stood by her at the stove, and she instructed me like a TV chef. "It's best to check for seasoning at this stage."

I nodded, but my heart ached as I watched her move with familiarity and comfort in my kitchen. This could've been my life —the two of us cooking, cleaning, and feeding little ones. Tired but wrapped in her arms at the end of an exhausting day.

She looked at me tenderly and said, "What are you thinking, Rehani?" Then shook her head.

Don't go there.

By the time we sat down to a very late lunch, she was herself again, happy, bossy, and impetuous. We reminisced about past days and old friends as we ate. The food was spot-on. There was only one other person I knew who could create such perfect flavors from the limited ingredients I had.

"This is absolutely wonderful. It reminds me of—"

"Don't say it," she cut me off, spooning dal over a small portion of rice on her plate.

"What?"

"Don't say it reminds you of your mother." She looked at me pointedly. "Apart from being a terrible cliché, it's creepy."

"That's not what I was going to say." It was exactly what I was going to say.

"What, then?"

"I was just going to say, it reminded me of...Durgaben's cooking." I scrambled.

"Ah, nice save."

"No, she's a really good cook."

"Drop it," she ordered with a faux stern expression. "I know what you were going to say."

"Okay, but you made it sound so weird."

"It *is* weird to look for your mother's qualities in your girlfriend. No one wants to hear that," she said without realizing she had forgotten to add the "ex" in that sentence. Freudian slip? I smiled and ate another mouthful of the soul-soothing food.

Quietly, we put the leftovers in the fridge, cleaned up the kitchen, and loaded the dishwasher.

"This is the first time my dishwasher is getting a full load," I said. "Coffee?"

"Sure, I love whatever expensive beans you have. I'm sure they cost more than what I make in a month."

I tuned out the sarcasm and turned on the coffee machine.

She leaned against the counter while the coffee brewed. "Thank you for today."

"You never have to thank me, Tara."

"Why is this so easy, yet we seem...impossible? It should be easy."

I looked straight into her eyes and the answer was right there. We never had a fair chance.

When we returned to the living room with the hot coffee, she settled down at the other end of the couch from me and pulled up her legs.

"Do you remember that attendant in the dean's office?" she asked, her slender fingers wrapped around the mug.

I nodded. "He had that strange look in his eyes, as if he could peer into your soul and know what you were thinking."

"Yes, he was always kind to students who looked sad or distraught. Oh, how he hated you, Rehani." She laughed. "As if he saw through to your dark soul."

"That's funny because I distinctly remember he didn't like you much either."

"That's because I didn't carry my emotions on my sleeve. He never saw me upset, even when I was."

"Yes, he only saw your haughtiness. No surprise there."

"You're one to talk! But the real reason he hated you was for your extracurriculars. I saw how he glared at you when you tried to woo young women."

"Hey, I didn't need to woo anyone. If anything, I was the one being wooed."

"Oh yes, of course, women were tripping over themselves falling for you," she said with an exaggerated eye roll.

"Over themselves and each other." I winked.

She shook her head. "You're shameless."

I placed my mug on the coffee table. "What else do you remember?"

"Everything!"

"Wanna bet who remembers more?"

"What are the stakes?" she asked, depositing her mug on the side table. She could never resist a challenge.

"Whatever you want."

"Then let's make it fun." Her tone matched the naughty glint in her eye.

"I sense trouble..."

"If you fail to answer my question, you'll have to sit through an entire Bollywood song of my choice. And if I fail to answer yours, I'll suffer through whatever loud music you want. What do you say?"

I grinned. "You'll never give up, will you? How long are you going to hold that against me?"

She tilted her head with a cute smile. "Until you concede that Bollywood is good music."

"If those are the stakes, you're on."

"I knew it, you egomaniac. You wanna go first?"

"Sure, let me think...okay, what was the name of the eatery that had the best sandwiches?"

"*Testy*, with an 'e'. Amar's favorite place," she said with a beautiful, toothy grin. It was *Tasty* misspelled.

"Not bad."

"My turn. What was the name of the hostel warden who used to check our rooms for contraband?"

I furrowed my brow. "Mrs. Mehta, right?"

"What was her first name?"

I couldn't recollect, so I cried foul. "I didn't live there, so I think it's an unfair question."

"Alright, Rehani, I'll give you this one. Her first name was Devika."

"Ah, I remember now. Devika Mehta, terror personified!"

"Your turn!" She grinned.

This time, I was ready. "Do you remember the night we sat chatting under the tree before we went off to my place?"

"Yes?"

"What were you wearing that night?"

"Oh!" That was an undeniable yelp. "Umm..."

"Isn't that the sound a loser makes?"

She narrowed her eyes and growled. "Give me a minute."

"Sure, I'll wait," I said, pulling out my phone. "While I browse for a song."

When no sound left her lips for two full minutes, I smirked at her. "Although your silence is like music to my ears, you should give up, Tara."

She let out a dramatic sigh. She wasn't one to accept defeat graciously. "So, what was I wearing?"

"Ivory linen pants and...ahem...a tight little burgundy top." I remembered being envious of the looks she had fetched all day.

"You always had a dirty mind, didn't you?"

"But you saw right through me."

As her smile faded away, I cleared my throat. "Okay, hope you're ready. I'll now torture you with some obnoxious metal that even I don't listen to."

"That's not fair," she whined.

"Your terms, missy. Here we go." The loud noise that blared

from my phone was some crappy experimental music a friend had once forwarded to vex me. It was tone-deaf and disturbing, to say the least, and the perfect way to annoy her.

"Ugh, stop," she yelled over the clamor of disharmonious metal sounds, clamping her hands over her ears. I turned down the volume. "Congratulations, I'm officially hard of hearing."

Her lips turned into an unintended pout as she inserted her slender fingers into her ears. How I longed to pull her into my arms and kiss her at that moment! But wasn't I the one who had pushed her away?

"My turn, but how about we raise the stakes?" she said, and I focused my eyes back on her. "I'll ask one last question, and if you answer correctly, you get to ask me anything you want."

"And if I don't?"

Her eyes sparkled with devious intent. "If you don't, you'll *dance* to a Bollywood song."

I smiled. "I'd be so scared right now if I didn't know you. But I accept, because I know I can never lose!"

"Such misplaced arrogance!" She smirked. "Alright then, tell me who was the first girl you slept with in Baroda?"

I frowned at her. "Really? That's crass."

She raised her brows. "Crass! Since when does Sameer Rehani care about crass?"

I squeezed one eye closed in thought. "Okay, let me think."

"Oh yes, it's quite a list. You'll need more time. Maybe I could come back tomorrow?"

"Hush...I don't remember her name..."

"You never did."

"...she had long hair, wore a fruity fragrance...an economics major."

She whipped out a wicked smile and shook her head. "Tsk, tsk, get ready to wiggle your hips, mister!"

"Wait, you can't just reject my answer. It's my life, I know, for the most part."

"She had short hair, wore a dark lipstick, and had a very artistic eyeliner. A psych major. She was right up your alley."

My jaw dropped in disbelief. "How do you know that?"

"I have my sources." She put a finger under my chin to close my gaping mouth.

"No, really. How on earth do you know that?"

"Why?" She frowned.

"Because she had a boyfriend, and no one was supposed to know."

"Pfft, big deal. It was college, who cares?"

"I promised her, so I care. Seriously, no one knew. Were you, like, obsessed with me and spying on me?"

"Puh-leeze," she scoffed. "I'm very observant. I spotted the hungry look in your eyes right away. You had been in town for what, two days? You met her when you joined us at the café across the liberal arts campus and chatted her up. It doesn't take a genius to figure out what happened next. She was totally into you, by the way."

I shook my head. "Wow."

"So, you just wrote her out of your history?"

I shrugged.

"And she went back to her boyfriend after she shagged you?"

I shrugged again.

"Oh yeah, I forgot, you never slept with anyone more than once."

"Except you."

"Shut up."

"Although in this case, I did sleep with her again."

Her eyes went wide. "How did *that* happen?"

I wondered how much to tell her without raking up our past. "Do you remember the weed incident?"

She sat upright. "You got the contact from her? Did you sleep with her for that?"

I nodded. "She got it from her boyfriend, but she set the terms of our...interaction."

"*Interaction*?" Tara narrowed her eyes at me. "Is that her word or yours?"

I stifled my chuckle with a cough.

"That one was for you," I said in a near-whisper.

As Tara looked up from her phone, I asked, "What's taking so long?"

She took the hint and dropped the subject. "I'm looking for the worst item number I can find." That was Bolly-speak for a song that had no relevance to the story. *As if any of them did*, I scoffed. To myself, of course. I wasn't bold enough to say it to her.

"Ah, here we go," she said and turned on a loud, raucous, raunchy song. "Time to shake that booty, Rehani."

It was the worst kind of double entendre, set to loud hip-shaking music, and yet it sounded strangely erotic. I willed myself off the couch and flung my arms and legs around to match the rhythm.

"Yes!" She rolled on the couch laughing. "Dance to the music you loathe, rich boy." I "danced," watching her revel in schadenfreude, before pulling her off the couch. "I can't be doing this alone. You're dancing with me."

She swayed her hips, moving gracefully to the music that I had trouble keeping up with. When she turned her back to me, I brought my hands to her hips and pulled her flush against my body, taking in her smell and absorbing her touch that, until yesterday, was only a memory. She danced without a care, cheering me on in my humiliation. For the first time in years, I abandoned all inhibitions and cavorted like she wanted me to. By the time the song ended, I was out of breath, and tiny beads of sweat glimmered on her forehead. We flopped down onto the couch together.

"How did I forget you're such a terrible dancer?" She panted, reeling in her laughter.

I covered my face with my palm and said, "That was humiliating! You won't breathe a word of this to anyone."

She brought her chin to rest on my chest and removed my hand. "Serves you right, Casanova," she said. As her eyes met mine, her breath shallowed, her pupils widened, and her smile disappeared. She lifted herself off with haste and moved away on the couch.

"Why did you come over that night after the opening, Tara?"

This time, she met my curious gaze with grit. "I was so overwhelmed by what happened that evening that I thought if you could handle me at my worst, we'd be able to face anything together. I gave myself the wrong idea that you wanted me."

I bolted upright and rubbed my hands over my face. "You know what I want, Tara. You've always known."

"We've been at these crossroads twice before, Sameer. It's not fair to me. It's not fair to Aarti and Sujit."

"I want you to be happy."

"It's not that simple. Are you prepared to give up Aarti?"

"I'm breaking up with her after her parents' anniversary party next weekend."

She frowned in confusion. "Why?"

"Why am I breaking up, or why after the party?"

She blinked. "Both."

I let out the breath I was holding. "I realized life is too short to spend with someone I don't love, but I still wouldn't want to be cruel. I don't want her to feel dumped and unwanted at an event she's spent an awful lot of time planning."

"You *have* changed," she said with a weary slump. "But you don't know the whole story."

"What story?"

She clutched her hands together and heaved a breath. "It's what I wanted to talk to you about that morning at your parents' home. Sameer, when you left, I was pregnant. I learned a week later. I tried to get in touch with you desperately because I wanted you to know." She took a shaky breath and kept her eyes on her hands. "I didn't carry the pregnancy. It wasn't the right time for me. Amar was my sole support during that time. I couldn't do it alone."

My heart pounded in my head, and I felt heat creeping up my neck. My forehead wrinkled into a frown, and I felt sweaty and unwell. It took me a moment to gather my thoughts to respond.

"And you thought this would somehow change my mind about breaking up with Aarti?"

"It might change your mind about us. I don't regret the decision, only the circumstances."

I blinked in disbelief. "Fifty-seven," I whispered.

She looked up with a quizzical frown.

"The number of times you called that week, and the number of times I didn't answer."

She gasped as tears pooled in her eyes. I reached out to hold her hands and dropped my forehead on hers. "I'm so, so sorry, Tara, for deserting you when you most needed me. Why would you think this would change anything? And why did Amar not tell me?"

"He didn't know until you cut off all contact with me. Now I know you had already left for the U.S. by then," she said in a hollow voice.

"I left because I had no choice."

It was time to tell her everything. The words poured out of me. I abandoned all my excuses and disclosed the shame I had kept buried for all these years.

"The deeper we dug, the more dirt we unearthed. Turned out

Dad had incurred a huge personal debt. We were forced to liquidate every asset we owned to repay it. We lost everything. There was no choice left but to flee. Mom deserved none of it, and I've worked hard to give her back everything she lost. She was the doyenne of high society. Classy, cultured, and proud, but always kind. She never spoke ill of anyone, never indulged in gossip, yet life dealt her a hand that made her the subject of gossip, a target of bawdy jokes. I heard what rotten words they used for her, although it was Dad whose misdeeds had led to our downfall."

Tara brought her hand to my cheek as a tear slipped down hers. "I'm so sorry, Sameer. Why didn't you tell me all this sooner?"

"I was so ashamed. I'm still ashamed. How could I have dragged you into the ruins of my life? I never intended to be cruel, but I was so out of my depth. I had no idea what I was doing. It has taken me all these years to get past it."

"So, where does that leave us? Where do we go from here, Sameer?"

I looked into her eyes. "Years ago, I asked you this, and I'm asking you again today. What do *you* want, Tara?"

This time, I didn't get the answer I wanted.

"I don't know. I'm scared," she said.

We stayed in the same spot on the couch, our hands clutched tight and our foreheads touching, until the sun shifted in its track to cast an evening shadow through the west window. When my phone chimed on the side table, she stirred and relaxed her grip on my hands.

"I better leave." She scooped up her shoulder bag from the recliner and dashed out the door.

TARA

*T*he soft click of the door closing behind me sounded like a gong in my head as I walked away feeling conflicted and discombobulated. The thought of crossing the dreaded threshold back into his arms terrified me, but that's exactly where I wanted to be.

I rushed back and rapped on the door. It flew open as if he had been waiting on the other side.

"I still want you, Sameer Rehani," I cried and threw my arms around his neck.

"And I want you, all of you," he said.

"But if we do this, there's no going back. If you disappear again, it will destroy me. Do you understand?"

He nodded. "I'm not going anywhere."

"I'm scared, but I'm trusting you, Sameer."

"I know I haven't given you many reasons for it, but I'm right here."

I flung my bag on the floor and held his face in my hands. "Don't say that." I touched my forehead to his. "But you can't change your mind again."

"I've never changed my mind, Tara. It's always been you."

My heart gave out a flutter, and my knees quivered at those words. My entire body trembled. I pounced on his mouth so wildly, I almost knocked him off his feet.

He staggered but held on to my shoulders and steadied himself. "Easy, easy, baby."

I knew I didn't want to wait any longer. "Kiss me," I rasped with need.

I watched his smile fade away as he stepped back. His strong gaze considered me for a moment, then he said, "Nah, I changed my mind."

I felt myself turning to stone. My heart stopped for a second, then plummeted. One tear had already slipped out of my eye when his mouth turned up into a crooked smile. He leaned in and said, "Damn, Tara, that was way too easy!"

I swiftly wiped away the tear and pushed him to the couch. My dress rode up my thighs as I climbed on his lap and clutched his t-shirt in both my fists. "If you *ever* do that again, I'll bite your dick off," I growled against his lips.

Of course, he didn't flinch at the threat. "That's tough talk from a tear-shedder," he said. But the tenderness in his eyes belied the smirk on his lips.

I sat back and waited. "Well?"

"Well?"

"I'm not going to kiss you. It's your turn."

As I shimmied my shoulders and leaned in, his eyes drifted to the generous cleavage peeking out of my neckline. He leaned in and brought his mouth upon mine.

The kiss, slow, deliberate, and intentional, was nothing I had expected. I was prepared for fireworks and pyrotechnics, I got cotton and clouds. His plush lips were soft, his body firm against my melting flesh. "I've missed you so much," he said every time we broke for breath. His mouth moved gently across my jaw and neck, placing soft kisses where I had expected scratches and teeth marks.

"Oh, Sameer," I cried breathlessly, and felt him harden against my thigh.

He wrapped his hands around my waist and showered tender kisses all over my face. Pausing at my left cheek, he regarded the scar cutting across my eyebrow. He traced it with the lightest touch of his finger, then kissed it as if he was afraid it still hurt. My heart squeezed. I could handle the fire and brimstone, but this tenderness was uncharted waters.

"Sameer, are you being gentle because of what I told you?"

He smiled and nuzzled his head in my neck. I kissed his cheek and whispered in his ear, "Because I still don't do tender."

He looked up with heartfelt laughter below teary eyes. I wiped them with my palms and dropped two gentle kisses on his eyelids. He straightened himself against the couch and sniffed.

"In that case..." As his breath shifted, the air became charged. The warmth from a moment ago turned to raging heat when he kissed me again. This kiss was different, and I knew how to respond. I brought my arms around his neck and kissed him back, lips, tongue, and teeth. The next instant, he lifted me and pressed me against the wall.

He clutched my earlobe between his teeth. Gone were the soft lips. His stubble scorched my skin. His hands found the zipper on my dress.

"Wait!" I cried, and he stopped. "Just one question before we do this."

He nodded.

"Do you still have that Selfia in your office?"

He threw his head back in a silvery laugh. "No, I unloaded it on some other chump and made a tidy profit doing it."

"Alright, I'm all yours."

He swung me around, pushing my stomach against the wall,

and slid down my zipper in a flash. Torturously sweet kisses landed on my neck and back as goosebumps rippled across my skin. Turning me around to face him, he flicked the dress off my shoulders. It slipped down without protest to pool around my feet, leaving me wearing nothing but a thin, white-lace bra and matching panties.

"Damn!"

"This is a coincidence, I promise! It's the only white pair I brought here," I said earnestly as he yanked off the pin holding my hair up. It tumbled down my back.

"A perfect coincidence," his needy voice rasped in my ear as he took his hands to my bottom, setting it on fire. He grabbed the soft flesh popping out of the cheeky panties, before planting two surprisingly well-placed spanks, sending shivers up my body.

"I'm so going to enjoy digging my teeth into them," he said. I wrapped my hand around him and grazed along his sculpted back, then traveled from his butt to the front of his jeans. He jumped slightly as I pushed my greedy fingers into the waistband.

"Mmm, is that what you want?"

I moaned. "So bad."

"Yeah?" He pulled my hands out. "But you'll have to wait. There's something else we need to do first."

I moaned as his kisses turned into bites, his grip loosened, and I pushed my hands into his luxurious hair. But he was on to me. "What's cooking in that brain of yours, babe?"

I returned my hands to his jeans while attempting a quick descent to my knees. But he was faster. In a flash, he pulled me up and pinned me to the wall. When he nudged his leg between my thighs, I bent into a squat to rub my core against him. With a loud moan, I pushed my breasts into his chest, my palm rubbing the front of his thick denim. "I can't wait any longer."

He kissed the swell of my breasts and whispered against my skin, "Tara...babe...today's game is pleasure. And to achieve it, you need to give up some control and a little bit of power. Today is not about outdoing me. We're both winning, my love." He placed a firm kiss on my lips. "So, are you going to behave?"

I bit my lower lip and nodded.

"No mischief." He held up an index finger. I bobbed my head again.

He kneeled and began kissing my stomach. A touch, a graze, a tease. My ticklish body wiggled. Holding my hips in place, he looked up at me. "Relax."

My hands gripped his shoulders. I breathed deeply and let him travel further down, kissing my hips, thighs, and the lace of my panties. Electric shivers fizzed across my skin.

Hooking two fingers in the band of my panties, he slid them down. "This is new," he said and kissed my soft, waxed skin. My face felt hot as he came up to kiss me while his fingers continued to caress the tender skin. "I love it," he said, and I savored the sound of his breathy, greedy words in my ear.

He propped up my right leg on the wooden console and knelt again. His soft lips took over from where his determined fingers had left off, kissing me right to my core.

Pleasure, he had said, was the game. Does pleasure have a superlative, I wondered. And would I be able to make it to that peak without unraveling? In response, he pushed my legs open and ran a firm, warm tongue along my wetness. I came so undone, my head banged on the wall behind me.

His head snapped up at the sound. "Are you alright?"

"Yes, don't stop," I cried.

I flashed back to his apartment in Baroda, his clean-shaven face wedged between my thighs. "Keep them open," he had insisted. I tried, and my body began levitating off the bed, suspended to his playful strokes. I remembered clutching the bedsheet in my fists, begging it to ground me, but he drove me higher and higher, like the kite I used to fly every Uttarayan day. I soared in open skies, uninhibited, strung only to his mouth, which kept tugging me along closer to the light. Then, when I thought I could fly no more, that golden light exploded into a thousand shards of white, brilliant sparks flying everywhere. I had struggled to breathe. But he was right there to catch me, reviving me with slow, loving kisses, and I was reborn in his arms.

I wanted what my nineteen-year-old self had found that night. I dragged my fingers through his hair and held on to him. This time I knew what I wanted, and I let my hands guide him. I felt the hot burn of his stubble on my inner thighs and on my swollen lips as he chased me closer to the edge. He pushed me open wider and took charge. The tender licks and light flicks had given way to an intense, rhythmic sucking.

My breasts felt heavy and flushed with heat. A storm was already gathering below my stomach, rising steadily, threatening to wash me away. When he pushed a finger in, I cried out his name, softly at first, then as I approached devastation, my insides exploded in a deafening scream. I trembled in his mouth, and my foot slipped off the console. He caught it in his hand and kept going, but my shaky knees became too weak to support me. He held me in his arms and gently placed me on the rug. My insides spasmed, and the tremors refused to quell.

"Please don't stop," I begged with clenched eyes.

He covered my mouth with his and pushed two fingers in. His thumb rubbed my clit in tight, perfect circles as he carried me through another violent squall to the other side. My hips thrust up as I clamped down on his fingers, and he fought against me to keep going. It felt interminable. Exhilarating, exhausting, before the calm finally washed over me.

I panted in his mouth. He smiled into mine.

This was the only way I wanted to feel powerless to him.

TARA

"*S*ameer." I breathed a satisfied whisper as he held me in his arms.

"I've waited thirteen years to hear you say my name like that," he whispered back.

I opened my eyes and looked at him. "Something's wrong."

"What do you mean?"

"I'm naked. You're not."

He closed his eyes and laughed. "We can fix that, can't we?"

I mounted him and pushed his t-shirt up, inch by inch, licking the soft hair on his stomach. My breath rattled as I unveiled his magnificent body. With every touch, I went further up, unwrapping him slowly like the prized treasure that he was. When I pushed the t-shirt to his neck, he lifted himself halfway, pulled it off, and tossed it away. The heat from his naked torso hit me hard, making me ravenous. The fine, light-colored hair on his chest was sexier than I remembered. I went down his body, kissing, licking, nipping, as he let out soft sighs. When I undid the jeans, he lifted his hips, and I slid the pants and underpants off him. My heart vaulted when I wrapped my hand around him and stroked.

He groaned helplessly but raised himself up on his elbows. "No," he said, coaxing me back to the rug. "Today is all about you, Tara." He straddled me and caught me between his thighs.

I frowned. "What if that's what I want?"

"Not today. Remember what I said?" He held my arms at my side and bit into the soft flesh spilling out of my bra. I moaned as he sucked and kissed the bite. While his teeth gripped the delicate skin again, my mind scrambled to recall that quote about sex and power.

"Oscar Wilde," he said, and flicked my taut nipple through the lacy material.

I groaned. "What?"

He rolled his tongue over my nipple and sucked hard. "'Everything in the world is about sex except sex. Sex is about power.' Oscar Wilde."

"How..." I gasped aloud before I could complete the thought because he had my other nipple clamped tight between his teeth. I fought hard to breathe, to think.

"I saw it in your eyes. We've had this conversation before," he said, then dragged his expert tongue down to my navel, setting fire to all my nerve endings.

"I don't buy it." I managed to gather my wits and struggled to free my arms, but he was stronger.

"Which part?" He bit into the curve of my waist, then licked it.

I grabbed his hair in my fists and tugged. The sweet brutality of his tongue and teeth, the bristly stubble rubbing into my skin, drove me breathless. But this wasn't a conversation, it was a competition. And I couldn't lose. "Sounds like... something... Foucault would say..." I managed.

He got off my legs and flipped me over.

"...or Freud," I added as he nibbled at my shoulder and my head rose up in response. This was in my wheelhouse. I couldn't let him win.

"Hmm..." He flicked open the hooks on my bra, and the delicate lace retracted without a fight. His tongue zigzagged down my spine to my buttocks, with wet kisses peppered along the way.

"...or Catherine MacKinnon...." I stole a quick, jagged breath as his tongue rolled over my buttocks.

"Are you bothered by the fact that the quote might be wrongly attributed to Wilde...or that the quote itself is false?" He bit into my fleshy bottom as promised, and my head rose up again.

But I was too consumed with what he was doing to my body to respond to how he was messing with my mind. I surrendered to my body. "Do it again."

He went down my legs, tormenting me with his mischievous tongue, the brusque caress of his stubble, and the light tease of his fingers. He bent my leg at the knee and kissed my feet. Pushing my legs apart, he began his journey back up. Kisses, nibbles, tickles, right up to my buttocks. Only this time, I was exposed.

He dipped his finger in and dragged it to my bottom. Twice. My hips flexed. With a wet finger teasing my bottom, he dug his teeth into my buttocks again. Delicately at first, then with increasing pressure until I yelped in pain. He withdrew inside the threshold and bit me wild.

Then he rolled me over and grabbed my unconfined breasts in his hands. With a teasing gaze trained on me, he brought his hungry mouth onto them, and the sensations traveled down to my already slick core.

"The quote is wrong," he said when he returned to kiss my mouth.

"I don't care anymore. It's my turn. You know what I want." I held him down and climbed onto him.

He gave me his most flirty smile, the one he used on women he said were *hard to get*.

"It's not going to work on me." I grinned.

"Okay then, sex is not *about* power. Sex *is* power. As are pleasure and the erotic." He pushed his hand into my hair and grabbed it in his fist. He knew my weaknesses, and his disarming smile was not one of them.

"Audre Lorde?" My back arched, and I moaned. "And semantics? You're full of surprises, Sameer Rehani." I let him take me through a rough, wild rollercoaster of a kiss. "Fuck me, Sameer," I whispered, writhing on top of him.

He gathered me in his arms, rolled over, and lifted me off the rug. He wanted to carry me to the bedroom, but I was too tall and heavy, so we kissed instead. After pretending to drop me on the bed, he pulled out a fancy condom packet from his nightstand, rolled it down with incredible speed, and entered me with a familiarity that felt both weird and reassuring. I moaned, and my back curved up.

Holding my hands above me, he settled into a pulse, his eyes set on my face. "You're so beautiful, Tara. I've missed holding your body against mine."

I savored his weight on me, moving with him, submitting to his rhythm. His striking features and the adoration in his eyes rendered me helpless. Those gorgeous light brown eyes that perfectly complemented his deep brown lashes and light skin.

Heat coursed through my body as I kept staring into his beautiful face. "Go deeper."

He growled. "Want to ride me?"

I nodded and pulled him into a kiss before he rolled over. I climbed onto him, setting my own pace, feeling him deeper inside me. His hands covered my breasts, and I felt myself dripping on him. He felt it too.

"Fuck, Tara, you're so hot," he said, and thrust up to meet me, pushing harder, going deeper.

His hands worshipped my breasts, pressing, kneading, and bouncing with me as I rode faster. But when I felt the heat in my face, I slowed down and bit my lip in fear of the approaching torrent.

"Don't stop. Don't hold back," he said, lifting his head to look at me. "Let me feel it, baby."

My eyes pinched shut as I grazed against him. In seconds, my insides clenched tight around his thickness, and I heard him groan. My toes curled behind me, and my thighs squeezed around his hips. But I made no sound. I didn't want to expel the power of my orgasm just yet.

Keeping his grip firm and steady on my breasts, he pumped hard. When I was finally ready to scream, ready for it to end, all I could manage was a whimper. A soft whine of complete satisfaction.

Happy and spent, I collapsed onto his chest, inhaling his scent before taking him to his peak. I remembered what he liked as if we had never been apart. When I felt him pulsate, I bent over and bit hard into his shoulder. The loud groan that emanated from his chest traveled to my stomach, and I trembled as he erupted inside me.

I slid down beside him, panting hard. "That was incredible, Tara. Just...incredible," he said, and a gush of pride and joy surged through my body.

He kissed my cheek and rolled me over to hold me from behind, our naked bodies flush like two matching pieces of a jigsaw puzzle.

While our bodies cooled, he flung his hand idly over me, strumming my nipple.

"What happens now?" I asked, extending my hand to his thigh.

"Now I have you and I don't care what happens to me."

I turned over to face him. "How bad are we talking?"

He exhaled against my forehead before planting a firm kiss. "Nothing compared to how happy you make me, Tara."

He leaned in for another kiss. "You know, Amar led me to believe you both got together after I left. And I thought, it's alright. I can never be cross with either of you."

"*What?*" My knees pulled into my stomach as I burst into a fit of laughter.

"What's so funny?"

I touched his cheek. "You're such a silly, insecure man."

"Hey!" He frowned with indignation.

"Amar is my friend. He's been my friend since before I knew you, and that has never changed. Why would you think that about us?"

"I asked him, and he didn't deny it."

I smiled and moved my hand to his heart. "Sameer, if we're together again, we need to trust each other. You let your insecurity ruin every close relationship in your life. You have to let it go. You can't let it ruin our relationship—any relationship—anymore. Do you understand?"

He nodded.

"That's the reason it was so easy to fool you when I came to the party with Mihir. You assume I'm too good for you, that I deserve someone better. Someone kinder like Amar, more successful like Sujit, or an alpha like Mihir. That I would easily fall for any of them over you."

His eyes widened, and he held my hands tight as my words sank in.

"But I want you. It's how *you* make me feel. We're all messed up in our own way, Sameer. The idea of perfection has never appealed to me. *Perfect* is an illusion, a ruse to hide imperfections.

Believing in the beauty of the imperfect is how I learned to love myself. How I came to love you. The imperfect is beautiful because it is real. So however flawed you think you are, I chose you all those years ago, and I choose you today. I will always choose you, and you need to trust that."

"And I deserve you." He blinked with sincerity. "I hesitated to contact you all these years because I was convinced I didn't. But I do."

"Yes, you do." I cupped his face. "You deserve me just as much as I deserve you. You're a good man. I need you to trust me on that too.

"I trust you. I trust you with everything I have."

"Including *Love and Loss*?" I asked, borrowing his cheeky grin.

"Except that." His voice immediately turned from soft to commanding. "That's mine, Ms. Kadam, as we've already established." And I burst out laughing again.

He pulled me over his body and kissed me hard. I looked into his eyes and ran a finger over my bitemarks on his shoulder. "You always made me feel good, Tara, only now you also know how to fuck me hard."

I grimaced as he grinned and enveloped me in his arms.

When we finally exited the bedroom, the hot sun had mellowed into an evening breeze. We retreated to the balcony with coffee, then ordered Chinese. The setting sun cast a soft glow on Sameer's handsome face, and I was instantly reminded of Sujit. I sucked in a ragged breath as I felt myself coming back down to earth.

"I need to talk to Sujit," I said while we waited for the food to arrive.

"It won't be easy breaking it to Aarti."

"She loves you, you know."

"Tara, if you want me to end it before her party on Saturday, I'll do it. Whatever decisions we make from here on out, we'll make together. Do you want me to?"

"No," I said in a hushed voice. "I don't want to be unkind either, Sameer."

He nodded, and his gaze traveled to the city behind me.

"She invited me too, but I'll tell her something's come up. I can't imagine going to her party, drinking her wine, and eating her food after having slept with her boyfriend." I pulled my hands over my face. "Am I a horrible person, Sameer?"

"Neither of us expected this to happen today, but I've waited for it too long to let myself be bogged down in guilt and shame. I only want to feel happiness now. And you give me that."

I lifted my head to look at his face, happy and relaxed. I wanted it for him, and I wanted it for me, too. I held my hand out to him, and he grabbed it to pull me onto his lap. "I'm going to let you in on something, but you can't laugh."

"You know I will when you ask me not to," I said, and he gripped my earlobe between his teeth.

"I'm going to dance with Aarti at the party. But it's not just us. It's this whole choreographed thing with her parents and us, and her brother and his wife, and her parents."

"I see. You don't have a problem wiggling your hips for her, but you pout when I ask you to do it!"

"There's no hip-wiggling, I promise," he said, placing a kiss on my cheek. "I just want to get it over with, so I can finally talk to Aarti."

"Are you going to tell her about us, about today?"

"I'm not sure. I was going to end it anyway, so why put her through more hurt?"

I nodded. I wasn't sure what the right course of action was either. It wasn't like we had extensive experience cheating on our partners.

I tapped his chest and got off. "I'll have a quick shower before the food gets here."

I left the room feeling a heaviness settle around my shoulders.

TARA

*T*empted as I was to spend the rest of the weekend with Sameer, I knew I couldn't do it unless I had a chance to talk with Sujit.

"It's not right," I said at Sameer's sulking.

"But why are we hiding it, and from whom?"

I raised my brows. "Really? Are you forgetting you have to play the doting boyfriend until Saturday?"

He grumbled.

"And what if Aarti decides to drop by and finds me here? Just one more week, my jaan. I'll talk to Sujit at the first chance I get, and after Saturday you can tell Aarti. We can start over after that."

"Did you just call me Jaan?"

"You don't like it?"

"I love it. You're also my life, my jaan." He held me close, and I hoped it would be enough for us to survive on until the next weekend.

But the euphoria of reconnecting with Sameer did little to ease the guilt of having cheated on Sujit. A dark echo from my past returned. I had chosen to put myself first again, ahead of my career, my family, and Sujit. The last time I did that, I lost a tiny bit of myself. And yet I craved the happiness that only Sameer seemed to give me. The thrill, the surge of energy coursing through me when I was with him was unlike anything I had ever experienced with anyone else.

Just one more week, I reminded myself when Sameer dropped me back that evening. My first instinct was to call Sona, but I couldn't tell her what had happened until I had spoken to Sujit. She was truly fond of him, and I felt like I had betrayed them both.

I texted Amar about the development, even though I suspected he would've already heard.

> AMAR
> I know! Are you happy?

> Very happy!

> Then I'm happy for you. I'll see you soon.

While I was responding to him, Aai called. Since her visit to Dallas, I sensed tension lurking in the background whenever we spoke. She had delicately asked me about Sameer, and why I hadn't mentioned him before when she had heard so much about Amar. I had brushed it off with a feeble explanation about how he wasn't a close friend. But since then, our calling ritual had also undergone a change. Before, I used to call when I had the time. After her visit, she began checking in more frequently, asking me tenderly how I was holding up, as if she could read the invisible ink on my heart.

I answered her video call, but a few seconds into our conversation, she paused to look at me. "I wish you would come back now."

"You must be lonely. I'm sorry, Aai. Maybe I can bring you here for a few weeks."

"No, I'm just fine. I'm worried about you."

"Me? What's there to worry about? This is a very safe city."

"It's not that...."

"What, Aai?"

"Okay, don't be cross with me, but that Sameer boy was looking at you with unusual fondness."

My heart lurched as I prepared to lie. "He's a friend, Aai."

"No, it's different. See, Amar doesn't look at you that way. Sameer looked at you like..."

"Like what?"

"The way Sujit does," she said, stunning me into silence. "Has he said anything to you, Tara?"

I responded with an exaggerated shake of my head.

"Okay. Just be careful, Rani."

"Careful about what, Aai?" I cried. "It's not like he's going to force himself on me."

"No, Tara, I'm talking about the heart. Be careful."

I didn't know if it was a mother's instinct or her keen perceptiveness, but in that moment, her uncanny ability to read my life felt like a mythical superpower. For the first time, though, she didn't bring up Sujit.

Over that weekend, I tried calling Sujit two more times, but he was busy, and I saw no way to squeeze into the rushed conversation, *I'm sorry, I think I'm still in love with Sameer, and also, I slept with him while you were mired in work.*

Luckily for me, the week started out busy. A shipment of paintings had arrived from Naples, Italy, on loan for a new exhibit. Even though it wasn't a part of my assignment, I was enthralled by their large collection of oils and offered to help with cataloging. This left me with little time to think about Sujit or miss Sameer. I managed to catch up with Sameer during my lunch hour, and he told me about the dance moves he was learning. He didn't mention Aarti, and I didn't pry. Between his evening choreography sessions and business dinners, I didn't get to see him much that week. By Thursday, I was missing his touch and his smell. I texted him that afternoon and took a cab to his apartment after work.

When I arrived, Mihir answered the door with a beer in his hand.

"Tara!" he said, a gentle frown marking his otherwise equanimous face. "What are you doing here?"

"I...I wanted to talk to Sameer about something," I fumbled, then cursed myself for offering such a flimsy pretense with such little conviction.

He gave me a quizzical look. "Really? About what?"

"Umm, is he in?" I strained my neck to see around him, but he didn't budge. His big, tall frame blocked the door, preventing me from peeking inside.

"Let her in," Sameer's reproaching voice called out.

He came around Mihir, who was now grinning.

"He's messing with you. He knows." Sameer smiled at Mihir, then pulled me into a hug and whispered, "I missed you." My body relaxed in his arms.

"Talk?" Mihir smirked at me, "Is that what you kids are calling it these days?"

"You don't want to know what the kids are calling it these days." I grinned as he took me in a big hug.

"I'm happy for you two knuckleheads."

I hugged him back with vigor. "Thank you, but right now I need food and a drink."

"Sameer has ordered Thai and insisted I stay for dinner. You've made him efficient and attentive. How did you manage that?" Mihir walked to the kitchen and poured me red wine. I followed him.

"I didn't," I said. "Maybe Aarti did? That's convenient for me. I'd get a fully-trained hu—"

Mihir laughed, slapping my arm, and walked out to Sameer.

"I heard that," Sameer yelled from the living room, where he was buried behind his laptop screen. "It's okay, Tara. You can start thinking of me as your husband. I'm not scared of the M-word."

"We'll cross that bridge when we get there. Let's first get past our current situation."

When the food arrived, I regaled Mihir with the details of the dance that Aarti's entire clan was participating in.

"I can't wait to see that." He jeered at Sameer.

"Terrific." Sameer sighed.

"I texted Aarti, but she's insistent on having me there," I said, gripping a perfectly charred piece of broccoli between my chopsticks. "I've made so many excuses, she probably thinks I'm either a snob or that I hate her. She even asked me if she'd done something to offend me. Now I wish I had said 'no' when she first sent me the invitation. But things were different then."

"Don't make it too complicated." Mihir, in his authoritative voice, advised. "Unless you're ready to come clean before Saturday."

The three of us exchanged grave looks before Sameer and I shook our heads, hung low.

"You can ride with me." Mihir offered. "We'll be out of there as soon as it's polite to leave."

I nodded. "Thank you," I said, then looked up at him. "But I'd hate to be a third wheel if you're bringing a date."

He shook his head. "I'm currently single."

"Again?" Sameer asked, holding his chopsticks halfway to his mouth.

"What do you mean, again?" I asked.

Sameer smirked. "Do you want to explain or should I?" he teased Mihir, who gazed back with insouciance.

Sameer turned to me. "Remember all the names you called me —playboy, Casanova, womanizer? Mihir here puts all those to shame. He's the real bad boy."

"Oh?" I gawked at Mihir, who continued to work on his pork-and-veggie Pad Kee Mow with expert chopsticks. "Rich, handsome, brilliant, with just enough gruffness to add mystery?"

"But with a heart of gold. Oh, and great in the sack," Sameer added with a grin. "Or so I've heard."

"Maybe we should find someone to tame him." I nudged Sameer. "Someone who could tug at the strings of his heart."

"Are you both through? Just because you found someone doesn't mean I'm looking for it." Mihir placed the chopsticks down on his empty plate and left the table to fetch another beer while Sameer and I shared a giggle.

"*This* man can't be tamed." He returned to his seat and flipped open his bottle with a flourish. "And those things you listed—all hearsay, all bullshit."

"Oh, so you're terrible in bed?" I sipped my wine and blinked at him innocently. Sameer winked at me, then burst into a laugh.

"Except that," Mihir said, tipping his bottle at me.

When Mihir dropped me off at home, I called Sujit again. He texted back to say he was busy and would call back later. He apologized for being unavailable these past few days and said he missed me. Two more days, I reminded myself as I turned in that night.

TARA

The next evening, I called Sujit again, almost absently, like I had done for the past week. Only this time, he answered.

"Hey, *darling*," he said, and I was totally unprepared.

"Hi," I managed.

"Okay, before you get mad at me, let me say that although I've been busy, I've been thinking of you all the time. I couldn't go see Aai either, but I call in every day to check on her. I also called Sona to make sure Aai doesn't need anything."

My breath hitched, my chest tightened, and my eyes stung at the thought that I had so ruthlessly cheated on this kind, generous man.

"Tara?" he said when I didn't respond.

I swallowed my tears. "I'm here."

"How mad are you?"

"Not one bit. I could never be mad at you. Tell me about your new project," I said, stalling.

His voice sparkled with joy as he talked passionately about software that would change education for kids with learning disabilities. By the time he hung up to attend a conference call, I had lost my appetite. How could I break his heart over the phone? I would need to go to New York and speak with him in person.

I skipped dinner and called Sameer, but he didn't answer. A few minutes later, I got his text

SAMEER

It's busy in here. Anything important?

No. Talk to you tomorrow

Early the next morning, I went to *Cups and Cookies* and drowned myself in work. I didn't call Sameer. Sujit's kindness stood in sharp contrast to my resentment for Sameer as he hobnobbed with Aarti's family. I stopped myself from going down that rabbit hole, but not soon enough. I had asked him to trust me, but did I trust him? Could I?

He had been upfront about his ambitions and how he thought Aarti would help him regain his lost status. I possessed neither her looks nor her wealth. Was he ready to give all that up to settle into an average life with me? Could his feelings for me coexist with the loyalty he felt toward his mother? Or would he be willing to sacrifice me for the goal that had kept him going all these years?

That's why, when he called me that morning, I responded with a text.

At Cups, working

Half an hour later, he walked in, looking way too sexy for that early in the morning. I pretended I hadn't seen him. He got his coffee and joined me at what had become my favorite booth.

"Hey." Slipping an arm around my waist, he kissed my cheek. "You smell like flowers."

"Hey," I responded without looking up from my laptop.

"Uh-oh, what did I do now?"

I kept typing.

"Cold shoulder. That's new."

I cast him a blazing glare.

"What's wrong, baby? What did I do?"

"Absolutely nothing. You didn't call me when you returned home last night. Nothing this morning. Having too much fun with Aarti?"

Amusement flickered in his eyes as he grinned. "Yes, they had a full house, and you know how much I love making small talk. Then Aarti found a moment to sneak me up to her room, where we had rough, hot, sweaty sex. It was so satisfying."

I gave him a stink eye. "You think you're funny, but given your proclivities, I wouldn't put it past you."

"And you're not remotely bothered."

I scoffed.

"Okay, Jaanu, I'm sorry. I returned very late. Thought you'd be asleep, and I didn't want to disturb you. I called as soon as I woke up this morning. But that's not why you are upset, is it?"

I hated that he knew me so well. "I spoke to Sujit last night."

"And?" He sat upright.

"I couldn't do it."

"What do you mean? Are you having second thoughts?"

I narrowed my eyes at him. "You'd love that, wouldn't you? Then you can go running back to your pretty girlfriend."

"Then why couldn't you tell him?"

"I didn't want to blurt it out over the phone. I need to look him in the eye when I tell him. Every time I talk with him, I feel like I didn't deserve him in the first place."

"Don't say that. Apart from being blatantly wrong, it's unkind to yourself. If you were unworthy of him, you wouldn't be beating yourself up about it."

I looked at him.

"I know you, Tara. You'll run yourself down with guilt, but Sujit is just a boyfriend, isn't he? You haven't committed to him or promised him anything."

"He's more than a boyfriend, he's my champion, a trusted confidant, and a close friend of my mother's. I need to at least show him the respect of doing this in person."

"We haven't done anything wrong. We were impulsive, but not wrong." But his conviction failed to persuade me as I stuffed the laptop into my bag. "Do you want to come over to my place? We can spend a little time before the party."

"No," I said. "I'll go back to mine."

"Can I come?"

"No, it's best if we wait until after I've talked to Sujit and you've broken up with Aarti."

"This is ridiculous." He huffed and stood from the booth to let me out. "At least let me drop you back home. It's hot already."

I nodded. "Okay."

We pulled up to my building, and I placed a chaste kiss on his cheek.

"I love you, Tara. Nothing's going to change that. You know that, right?"

I nodded and managed a smile. "Can't wait to see you in your sherwani. I bet you'll look like a prince from a culturally appropriated children's movie." He laughed and blew me a kiss before he drove off.

I entered my apartment, consumed by a strong urge to paint. This had become a thing. Every time I saw Sameer, touched him, smelled him, my insides stirred, pushing me to create something new. Initially, I had chalked it up to the novelty of it, seeing him after all these years, and the unresolved emotions. But I soon realized it was more. He truly was my muse, although I would never tell him that, lest it should go to his head. I smiled as I dipped my brush in paint and puttered on a fresh canvas.

It was early evening when Sameer called from his car on the way to Aarti's place, and I decided to clear up the mess I had made and start grooming.

I had chosen a dark Byzantium full-skirt, off-the-shoulder gown with delicate ivory and gold embroidery. The event demanded elegance, but I wanted to remain as inconspicuous as I could. A bare neck balanced the look of my big kundan chaand-bali earrings. I debated between highlighting my eyes and empha-sizing my lips and finally decided to wear matching matte lipstick with subtle make-up on my big eyes. Muted gold heels and a matching clutch completed the look.

Mihir arrived looking every bit the upper-crust man he was, in a gorgeous, tailored suit and meticulously coiffed hair and beard.

When we arrived at the ranch where the festivities were planned, Mihir offered me his arm. People mingled over drinks while soft music played in the background. As if to complement the sedate opulence of the evening, a gentle breeze whispered sweet songs of summer.

"Relax, it will be over soon," Mihir said, patting my cold hand on his arm.

I saw Amar, and my heart eased a little. We approached him as he stood with Sameer's mother, who held me in a luminous smile that reflected off the rich Banarasi saree she wore. When Mihir stepped away to greet a friend, she took my hands.

"I'm very happy for you and Sameer," she said in a low voice, and my face dropped with shame and guilt. She patted my hand and said, "I understand this must be uncomfortable, but I'm proud of you both. There is no substitute for kindness, and I'm glad you chose to put Aarti first today."

When a tear formed in my eye, she quickly grabbed a dinner napkin and swooped in. "The time for tears is gone, Beta," she consoled, and I gave her hand a grateful squeeze as Sameer walked over to greet us before returning to Aarti's side.

Mihir introduced me to his friends, and I pretended to enjoy myself with an untouched cocktail in my hand. I was chatting with Sameer's parents when Aarti walked over, looking like she had just walked out of a real-life fairy tale, and my heart clenched. She was by far the most glamorous woman I'd ever seen in my life.

"I'm so glad you made it, Tara," she said with a big, happy smile on her face, and hugged me. We had never hugged before. "I was starting to suspect you were going to renege."

"No, you were very persuasive," I teased to diffuse the clog in my chest.

She laughed, then leaned in. "I'm just a little nervous."

"Why? The arrangements are fabulous, and you look beautiful."

She nodded. "It's just... such a big night. I hope everything goes well."

When it was time for the Bollywood-themed, song-and-dance bonanza, I wanted to stay hidden in the shadows, but Aarti tugged me, Amar, Mihir, and a few of Mihir's friends to a prime spot near the stage. The sequence of events began amid wild cheers with Aarti's parents exchanging floral garlands as a way of renewing their vows. The music faded in gently, and the anniversary couple began their dance.

Despite the fun I had poked at Sameer, the choreography was tasteful, not frivolous. Delicate, sensible steps for the older couples and graceful, romantic ones for the younger. It wasn't as cheesy as Sameer had made it out to be.

Of course, I wouldn't tell him that. No, I'd tease him for the rest of my life. This would be a story I'd tell our grandchildren, I thought with a smile, as I waited for Sameer and Aarti's segment to begin.

They came in last. I had imagined he would be awkward and stiff, but he swayed gracefully. Mihir chuckled in his urbane manner, while Amar and I tried very hard to suppress our laughter.

As the music began to fade out, petals of roses showered down on the couple, and Aarti's parents re-entered the spotlight. Someone produced a microphone for Mr. Bhatia. Sameer stood in the shadows with Aarti, both looking breathtakingly gorgeous. She held his hand, but his eyes never left my face.

"Ladies and gentlemen, friends," Aarti's father began when the sound of clapping died down. "Thank you for being here today. When we sent out the invitations, we thought we'd be celebrating our anniversary. But I have an announcement to make. This special day has become even more cherished as we also celebrate our daughter, Aarti, and her boyfriend, Sameer. Come here, you two."

Loud claps resumed, and Aarti dragged Sameer into the spotlight. His smile had changed. Frozen. This was his Sameer Rehani smile, absolutely striking but full of pretense and false bravado.

Mr. Bhatia continued. "Sameer, I made a decision last week. I've decided to offer you a twenty-five per cent share in SB Real Estate." Loud cheers and whistles interrupted him again. "That now makes you worth more than I am! I'm no longer the biggest baddie in this town." He barked a loud laugh as people cheered. "But I'm more than happy to be replaced by a good, honest man. Someone better than me, for sure.

"But with great power comes great responsibility." Mr. Bhatia paused for the groans and jeers that arose from the audience. "I know, I know, but I couldn't resist." He chuckled. "Well, this partnership comes with a responsibility, Sameer. Are you up for it?"

All eyes were on Sameer as he smiled and bowed graciously.

"The responsibility I'm expecting from you is to keep our dear child Aarti very happy."

And before he could react, before anyone could, Aarti went down on one knee.

Her father held the microphone near her lips as she cooed in her sweet voice. "My dearest Sameer, will you marry me?"

Sameer's smile vanished, his face went blank, and he took a step back. His eyes darted to meet mine. I felt like someone had punched me in the gut and stopped me from breathing. I saw Sameer smiling with his frozen face at Aarti as I stumbled backward. An arm grabbed me, and I heard loud cheers and whistles. The last thing I saw was Aarti slipping the ring on Sameer's finger before Mihir and Amar led me away from the crowd. Mihir settled me on a chair while Amar miraculously produced a glass of water and instructed me to sip it. I put my hand on my midriff, taking deep breaths.

Mihir crouched before me. "Everything will be okay, Tara."

"How? He just hit the jackpot! He got everything he wanted."

"He's going to break it off, you know it," he said in a voice that matched the confidence I saw on his face.

"Mihir, half the city is at this party. All of the important members of the community are here tonight. This will no longer be a simple breakup."

"He'll do it," Mihir said.

I looked at Amar. His face was a mask of complete ambivalence.

"Can you take me back?" I asked Mihir, my voice cracking. "I'm sorry to pull you away from the party like this, but..."

"Don't worry." He offered me his hand. "I don't care about staying."

As people thronged around the happy couple, offering smiles and felicitations, Mihir led me toward his car. This time, though,

I didn't shed a single tear. I was shaken, but not sad. As if I had already prepared myself to lose him again.

The ranch faded in the rearview mirror as we left the bright lights behind and drove into the dark silence of the empty road.

SAMEER

good, honest man, Mr. Bhatia said about the person intent on hurting his daughter.

For a moment, I couldn't breathe, couldn't think. I saw Tara watching my every move. I wanted to run into her arms and declare it all a sham. But Aarti slipped a platinum band on my finger and handed me a diamond to put on hers. I did, numb and robotic. She kissed me as more rose petals rained down on us.

I was now engaged to be married to the woman I had planned to break up with the next day.

I watched as a few rogue petals caught the night breeze and disappeared into the trees. I longed to escape with them, but Aarti gripped my hand and guided me off a stage that was now strewn with the corpses of dead flowers. Crowds surrounded us, shook hands, offered congratulations, and all I could think of was Tara.

My queen in the purple gown. Where was she? How was she? I hoped she knew I intended to quit this relationship. Was she crying? I needed to find her. My eyes skimmed the crowd. I saw her standing by the stage, and the next instant, she was gone. I couldn't spot Mihir or Amar either. I needed to get away and make sense of what had just happened.

How did an innocent anniversary party turn into my engagement soirée? Why was everyone important that I knew at this party? Did Aarti know I loved Tara? Is that why she planned this *surprise*? A million questions whirled around in my head as my eyes scanned for Tara and I smiled, muttering "thank you" to the people around me.

When I saw Mom standing by a table, I excused myself to speak with her. Anxiety marked her lightly furrowed brows.

"Did you know about this, Ma?" I growled.

"Of course not! Do you think I would blindside you like this?" she retorted with indignation.

"What the hell happened?" Ordinarily, she would have admonished me with a single word, *language.*

But not today. "Have you talked to Tara?" she asked.

I shook my head. "I can't find her."

I saw Amar approaching us, and my body perked up. "Where's Tara?" I asked him.

"Mihir is driving her home. What happened, Sameer?"

Apparently, no one knew. I had to ask Aarti, but she was busy showing off her ring to her friends, who gushed about her being the luckiest woman on earth.

Suddenly, a sick feeling gripped me. "Where's Dad?" I asked Mom.

"Not sure."

The three of us looked around and spotted him in the distance talking to Aarti's parents. I felt blood rushing to my head. Mom grabbed my arm.

"Don't make a scene," she warned.

She signaled for Amar to follow me as I stormed toward my father.

"Ah, there he is! Our son." Aarti's father beamed with pride.

"Congratulations, Beta," her mom said, "we're so happy, so proud of you both."

I managed a gracious smile. "Thank you."

"I was just telling your father what a fantastic idea this was," Mr. Bhatia said, confirming my fears. "Our special day is now your special day too."

My father cast me a villainous look cloaked in an affectionate smile. "Yes, you're now bound by more than love," he said with a laugh, then softly added, "I just want the kids to be happy."

But the vicious look in his eyes betrayed his words.

"Can I talk to you for a moment?" I said, excusing us from the Bhatias.

"What did you do?" I asked quietly, trying to rein in my anger. Amar stayed by my side to *prevent me from acting recklessly*. Mom's words.

"You don't need to thank me, son." He smiled as if this were a tender father-son moment. "The look on your face is thanks enough."

My fingers curled into an angry fist at this betrayal.

Just then, Aarti approached us with a wide smile, and I eased the grip on my fist. "Hey, you!" she said. "Are you happy?"

I had no choice but to respond with a nod.

"I was so nervous," she said, wringing her hands. "I was worried you'd walk off or something because we never talked about it. But Uncle convinced me you'd be happy." She looked at my father standing beside me and leaned in to put a hand on his arm. "Thank you, Uncle."

"All we want is for you to be happy." He patted her hand and directed his smile at me, menacing and vindictive.

"That's why I invited Tara," Aarti continued. "I wanted your friends to be a part of this special evening. I'm glad Amar is here too."

Amar shuffled in place before returning a weak smile.

"Where *is* Tara? I want to show her my ring. You are happy, aren't you?" She looked at me expectantly.

"Yes," I lied with a strained smile.

"A word, Sameer?" She pulled me aside. "I want us to go back to your place. This is a big night for us, and I can't wait," she said with a coy smile.

"Yeah, sure, let's talk after the party."

She nodded and placed a kiss on my cheek. "You look so handsome. You literally take my breath away." She wiped the lipstick off my cheek with her thumb and left.

My chest tightened. There were too many fires to put out. I had to talk to Tara. I called but got her voicemail. I called Mihir, but he didn't answer either. I needed to settle the score with my father and had to discourage Aarti from wanting to spend the night with me. How had I ended up trapped like this again?

When my head stopped spinning, I looked around. My father had found himself a drink and was no longer concerned with what was going on around him. Aarti beamed with the happiest smile on her face before disappearing from my sight. At that moment, I decided everything else could wait. My fight with my father could wait until tomorrow. Appeasing Aarti could wait. I needed to be with Tara. As the party began winding down, I shamelessly used my mother as a crutch and told Aarti that she was feeling unwell and that I should stay over at their house in case she needed me in the night. Aarti didn't doubt me. She accepted the ruse and even offered to help. Trust is a liar's most useful ally.

I drove straight to Tara's and rode the elevator to her apartment. She didn't answer the door or her cell. But I wasn't budging until I had spoken to her. She could ignore my phone calls, but she couldn't avoid me. I planted myself down against the wall in the carpeted hallway.

About half an hour later, the elevator doors opened, and Tara walked out, her makeup still intact. No runny mascara, no streaks down her cheeks, no red eyes.

She froze for a moment as I stood.

Retrieving a key from her clutch, she asked in a voice that was neither angry nor annoyed, "What are you doing here?"

"I wanted to make sure you're okay."

"Why wouldn't I be?" She approached the door with calm steps.

"I tried calling. Where were you?"

Throwing me a dispassionate glance, she slid the key into the lock. "Shouldn't you be by your fiancée's side right now?"

I took a step toward her.

"See you later, Sameer."

When she tried to close the door in my face, I thrust my foot against the jamb and stopped the door with my palm. "I'm not leaving until we talk."

She turned and walked inside. I followed and closed the door behind us.

Gracefully stepping out of her heels, she stowed them in a small shoe cabinet. Her gown rustled against the carpet as she walked to the kitchen, filled a glass of water, and downed it before moving inside toward the bedroom.

"Tara," I cried, unnerved by her apathy.

She looked at me and kept walking. I followed her into the bedroom, where she proceeded to remove her earrings.

"Say something, love. How are you not angry?"

She glanced at me in the mirror, standing behind her, but she continued to hold her silence.

"Where were you?"

"Mihir took me to some exclusive club to get a drink. We couldn't go to a regular bar dressed like this. He seems pretty well connected."

Her nonchalance was now beginning to annoy me.

"Are you drunk?"

An angry frown. "Now," she said, turning to me with her hands on her waist. "If you could please leave, I need to change."

"I'm not leaving."

She grabbed a t-shirt and pajama bottoms from her dresser and started toward the bathroom.

"How're you not angry? I thought you'd be in tears."

"Are you ending your engagement?"

"Of course," I said.

"Then why should I be angry or in tears?"

My mouth dropped.

"On the other hand, if you won't, why should I waste my anger on you?" She faced me with fierce eyes, hands on her waist. "You need to figure out how to fix this mess. Don't expect me to cry and wait for you. I won't. Not this time," she said, still in her power posture.

Ah, this was the Tara I was looking for.

She blinked. "Let me ask you something. How many tears did you shed for me? How many nights of sleep did you lose after you disappeared from my life? I cannot be the one to cry every time, Sameer."

"Tara—"

"I'm sad, but I'm done shedding tears. My tears are precious, just like my love. You must earn them, deserve them. Go away, Sameer. Go spend the night with your fiancée or spend it alone. Go fix your messes, then come back and earn my love and my tears."

I stood rooted to the spot, looking at her. "I'm not leaving," I repeated for a third time.

She pulled in a deep breath. "Can you handle the heat after you end it with Aarti? Are you strong enough? Can you come to terms with the fact that our passionate dispositions make us explosive, that we'll always be at loggerheads? Can you accept that I'm just as fierce and hotheaded as you, and will fight dirty for what is mine? If you claim to be mine, I'll fight for you. Every single time. I'll stand with you against the world. But I need to know you'll fight for me too. I came to you the night of the opening, and you pushed me away yet again. You seem to give up on us at the slightest hint of tension. Why would I expect today to be any different? You've been pegged into a relationship in the presence of family and friends, all those social contacts that are so important to you. You've been handed the keys to the kingdom. How am I to assume you're ready to give it all up for me? When did you ever give me an indication that you're willing to fight for me? Fight for me, Sameer. If you think you deserve me in your life, fight for me. Show me how much I mean to you."

I removed the ring from my finger, put it on the dresser, and stood before her. She hugged her clothes to her chest and turned toward the bathroom.

"No, Tara, don't walk away." She stopped and stood with her back to me. "I heard you out. Now you've got to listen to me, babe." She remained unmoving. "Look at me. I need you to look me in the eye."

She turned and met my eyes with grit. I stepped toward her. "I'm here. I'm already fighting for you, can you see that? I'm here when the woman I just got engaged to wants me in her arms tonight. You want me to be invested in this relationship, but I already am. I'm devastated and distraught by what happened this evening. I expected you to be sad, not because I want your life to revolve around me, but because I know how much I mean to you. I'm not demanding your tears, Tara. I deserve them because I love you so fiercely. I need you to feel about us the way I do.

"I made a mistake by not coming clean with Aarti sooner, and I regret it. I regret hesitating the night of the party and the night of your opening. I was afraid, but no more, babe. I said I'm ready to give up Aarti and everything that comes with it, and I haven't changed my mind. But I can't do this alone. I need you. I need your strength. You said you trusted me? I need you to believe it. Trust me to do right by us."

She blinked.

"Now, do you want me to leave?"

She responded with a shake of her head.

"Come here, babe." I threw my arms out. She tossed her clothes on the bed and rushed into them. "I know I haven't given you a good reason to trust me in the past, but I'm here now. And you're right, it is my turn to fight for you."

She lifted my chin with her forefinger and placed a light, reassuring kiss on my lips. My body slacked down to her bed.

"What do we do now?" she asked and sat beside me.

I fell back, my legs dangling off the side of the bed. She laid down, turned on her side, and placed a gentle hand on my chest. I covered it with mine. "Nothing has changed, my jaan. I'll talk to Aarti tomorrow. It will be tough, but I never expected it to be easy, so a mere ring on my finger is not changing anything for us."

"Will you hold a grudge against me for getting in the way of your ultimate goal?"

"My goal was to return happiness to Mom's life, and I think you've already done that. I saw how happy she was the other day. Everything else was my folly."

"I'm thinking of making a quick trip to New York to see Sujit."

I kissed her hand. "You're wrong about one thing, though. I did cry for you. I've cried and hurt for all these years."

She let out a choppy breath, then her eyes glazed. "Did you lock the door?"

I shrugged.

"Go check," she said, and I pulled myself up.

"Yup, all locked up and safe," I said as I returned and laid down by her side.

I loved it. It felt normal, domestic. Something couples do.

SAMEER

*S*he pulled her knees into her stomach and placed a hand on my heart. "Tell me what you're feeling."

I let out an exhale. "Turn over."

She smiled, turned over, and snuggled into me. I pushed her fragrant hair over her shoulder and wrapped my hand around her waist.

"I feel like I can breathe again," I said. "I was suffocated when I came here. Now I feel relieved. I don't need anything else."

She stroked my arm, and I placed a gentle kiss on the back of her neck just as my phone vibrated violently on the dresser. She turned around.

"It's Mom," I said, glancing at my watch. Reluctantly, I pulled myself off the bed and answered the phone.

"Yes, Ma?"

"Sameer, I'm sorry. I know you're with Tara, but this is urgent."

"It's alright. What happened?"

"Sangita called," Mom said without a preface. "She's at the hospital again,"

"Oh!"

"You'll need to be there for Riya if anything happens, Sameer. You need to get there as soon as possible."

I looked at Tara's calm face. She sat up and smiled at me, but I couldn't smile back. I didn't want to lose this moment with her, but I also didn't want Riya to end up an orphan if Sangita passed. How was I ever going to tell Tara about her?

"Yes, Ma. I'll come right over, and we can hash out the details." I evaded Tara's eyes as I ended the call.

"Sameer?" Her sweet voice demanded.

"Another fire I need to put out." I sighed as I lowered myself to the edge of her bed. "There's something urgent I need to attend to in India."

"In India?"

"There's one last thing I haven't told you yet."

When I finished telling her about Sangita and Riya, her hands covered her startled, gaping mouth.

"You have another sister! This is huge, Sameer!" She blinked. "Oh, my darling!" She leapt forward to grab me in a hug. "No wonder you've been hurting for so long." She held my face in her hands. "Did I just mess up your life again, Sameer? Please tell me the truth."

I smiled a weary smile. "No, my love. You made everything right. Can we talk about this when I'm back?"

"Are you leaving now?"

"As soon as I can, possibly tomorrow morning. I'll grab a bag with some clothes from my place then head over to my parents'."

She sat up and hugged my back. "It will be alright, Sameer. You're doing the right thing. I'll be here when you return."

I took her hand and kissed it, then willed myself off the bed.

On my way to the condo, I called Mom. "Ma, I'm going home to pack a bag. I'll stay at yours tonight, then leave on the next available flight."

"Okay," she said.

"Does Dad know?"

"No." She dropped her voice "But we might have to tell him now."

"Wait for me. Don't tell him anything yet," I cautioned. I wasn't sure how he'd react. I didn't want Mom to bear the brunt of his temper. I wanted to be there to give him what he deserved.

In my apartment, I changed into jeans and a t-shirt, pulled out a bag from the closet, and shoved some clothes and essentials into it. I retrieved my U.S. passport and Overseas Citizen of India card, which would allow my entry into the country. I had been gone a long time. It would be strange to be back there and see the place with different eyes.

When I arrived at my parents' house, Durgaben let me in. Dad lounged in the recliner in his study with the television on. I didn't have to guess that he had a drink in his hand. Amar and Mom had changed out of their party clothes and sat in the family room, anxiety and fear marking both their faces. Mom rushed over and hugged me.

"It's okay, Ma. Everything will be fine. I'll take care of it."

Just then, Dad ambled in with a tight grip on his crystal glass. "Ah, the ungrateful son returns."

"Ungrateful?" I fumed. "Do you really think the stunt you pulled today won't come and bite us in the ass?"

"Language..." Mom muttered under her breath. But I threw her a stern glare, and she looked away.

"What the *hell* were you thinking suggesting that bullshit to Aarti? What did you tell her anyway?"

"Well, you're going to be rich and happy for life, aren't you?" he replied, unfazed.

"Are you serious? Did you really think it was wise to jump into formalizing a relationship with someone as well connected as the Bhatias without first cleaning up our own backyard?"

"What are you talking about? They know all they need to know."

"Really? And what happens when they learn about Riya?" I frowned with anger. "Do you think they'll be cool with that?"

Dread filled his eyes as he staggered, groping for something to steady himself. Amar and I rushed over. Amar took the glass from his hand while I lowered him to the couch.

Leaving him alone with a refilled glass, we went to their bedroom.

"Keep a cool head," Mom said, "and be kind. There is nothing greater than kindness at this time."

I hung my head low. "Yes."

"Make the girl feel loved. She's at that tender age where she's not a child anymore. She knows things even if she doesn't understand them completely. If she needs to come here, she should be happy about it and not feel trapped. Do you understand? We're her only family. Sangita's parents have broken all ties with her. They will want nothing to do with Riya."

I gave her a meek nod just as Amar walked in with a laptop in his hand. "I found two first-class tickets for an early morning flight tomorrow. Expensive, but I guess it's alright?"

I nodded and handed him a credit card. "Wait, why two?"

"Amar is going with you," Mom said.

I looked up at him, and he reassured me with a light nod.

"I'm sorry you have to cut your visit short," I said, but I was grateful for his support.

"You'll stay at Tauji's while you're there," Mom said.

"I'd rather stay at a hotel." I looked at Amar. It was his home, after all.

"I don't care," he said. "Whatever works for you."

"Zid mat karo," Mom admonished. "And don't argue. You and Amar will stay at his parents'. End of discussion."

"I'm guessing you've already spoken to them?"

"No, I'll talk to them after you leave. I have no idea how to broach the subject."

Amar and I said nothing. This was between the elders of the family, and we *kids* were instructed never to interfere.

TWENTY-SIX HOURS and one layover later, we landed at the Indira Gandhi International Airport in Delhi. Being there again after everything that had happened evoked mixed feelings. Although I was born in the U.S., I grew up in this city. All of my formative memories were linked to this place. It was home. At least, it used to be. But thirteen years is a long time in a rapidly changing world. The city had changed. I had changed. My relationship with it wasn't the same. I almost didn't recognize some parts as we drove to my uncle's home.

"Worried about seeing Riya?" Amar asked upon reading my face.

I nodded. "And Sangita."

"Don't worry. People have a way of surprising you when you least expect it. I'll be with you all the way."

"I'm glad you're here," I said as the driver pulled up into the driveway of a stately home.

My anxiety was not unfounded. I was facing Tauji and Taiji after a long time. While Amar had made multiple visits to the U.S., Tauji continued to hold a grudge against us. It was moralistic righteousness, but that was his prerogative.

Taiji gave me a warm welcome. Her husband remained somber but wasn't bitter. I think having Amar with me softened the blow.

Early the next morning, I called Vishal Mamaji. He said

Sangita had shown positive signs after her first two chemotherapy sessions but had deteriorated since. She had become too frail to endure another round. We discussed the possibility of other medical alternatives, but he didn't voice much hope for their success.

"Get her affairs in order," he said curtly. "And yours."

"Yes, Mamaji. Can I visit her? I was hoping to see Riya."

"Yes, she visits after school. Come by in the evening."

That evening, Amar and I walked into the luxury hospital with its polished tiles and tasteful décor and took the elevators up to the fifth floor. I stifled an anxious breath as I prepared myself to meet the little girl who I had last seen when she was a nine-month-old baby. How would I introduce myself to her? What had Sangita told her about me? My feet halted outside the giant doors of the oncology unit.

"What will I say to her, Amar?"

"You'll find the words when you see her," he reassured.

We found Sangita's room and knocked softly. A young girl answered the door, and I took an unconscious step back. The resemblance was unmistakable. Amar and I exchanged a quick look.

"Riya?" I asked.

"Yes." She sounded courteous but confident.

"I'm Sameer," I said, still outside the door.

The slight smile on her face disappeared as she blinked rapidly, and an angry frown began taking shape.

"Can we come in?"

She put a hand on the doorjamb, trying to decide if she should let two strangers in, for that's who I was to her—a stranger.

She turned and looked behind her. "Give me a minute," she said, and closed the door on us.

Several minutes passed before she let us in.

My eyes landed on Sangita. She looked completely different from the last time I had seen her. She had aged beyond her years. Her eyes had sunk deeper into their sockets, and her already pale complexion had gone from healthy pink to sickly white. She looked frail.

"Yes, cancer will do that to you," she said.

"I'm sorry." I took a step toward her, but Riya's hand blocked us.

"Don't get too close. She's weak and prone to infections." She pointed to the chairs by the wall, across the room. "You can sit there."

I nodded, and we sat.

"I'm sorry to see you like this," I said to Sangita.

She turned her gaze toward Riya. "Can you give us a minute?"

Riya stared back with undaunted defiance. "I'm not leaving you alone with him," she said to her mother.

"It's alright," Sangita reassured her with multiple weak nods.

Riya frowned and pouted before walking out and closing the door behind her.

"Do you want me to step out?" Amar asked in his gentle, calm manner.

She responded with a tired shake of her head. "I'm grateful you're here, Amar." He nodded and returned a small smile.

She looked at me. "Let's cut to the chase, Sameer. I called your mother because I'm dying, and I want Riya to grow up with you all. I don't want her living like an orphan in India or with my parents, who haven't met her yet. Whatever our history, I know I can trust you to do right by her. I know you will love her the way she deserves to be loved. You're not a cruel man, or you wouldn't be here."

I hung my head.

"I had hoped it wouldn't come to this, but here we are. Riya has her passport, and she'll give you whatever else is needed. I've entrusted her with all the important documents and legal papers. We got the visa appointment, but I've no idea how long I have. I can sign over the parental rights too if you want."

"No," I said with an emphatic shake of the head, "I want her to be with you..."

"As long as I'm here. I appreciate it." She nodded. "For what it's worth, I'm sorry."

"You don't have to say that. It wasn't entirely your fault."

"Even so, I willingly entered into a relationship I knew would wreck lives."

I looked at her across the span of the long room. "Do you wish to see him?"

She was too frail to sigh, but made a sound that was close to it. "No. It was never meant to be. I don't want to be conflicted in my last days."

"I'm sorry, Sangita. I shouldn't have left you and Riya alone to fend for yourselves."

"You didn't. You've been generous. Without the financial support you ensured, we wouldn't be where we are. Riya is thriving at the elite school. She's smart, like you." She managed a brief smile. "She's a natural genius and has a very bright future. You need to make sure she fulfills her potential."

"I'll do everything to make things right," I said as a lone tear slipped out without warning. I sniffed and swiped it away quickly.

"I see you're still a kind man, Sameer. I'm very proud of who you've become, if I may say that."

I gave a slight nod. "You've been brave. I can't imagine being in your shoes, being this charitable toward me after how I treated you. Thank you for trusting me with her."

An impatient knock interrupted us, and Riya stuck her head in. "Can I come in now?"

"Actually, I'd like to speak with you outside, if you don't mind," I said, looking at Riya, then at Sangita.

Something transpired between them with an exchanged look. Sangita nodded, and Riya slumped her shoulders. I stepped out of the room with her and walked over to a bench near the big windows at the end of the hallway.

"Do you know who I am?" I asked.

She nodded, her eyes on her hands.

"What has your mom told you about me?"

Anger flashed across her face, but she took a deep breath. "I hate you, Sameer," she said calmly.

"I know, and you have every right to."

"But Mumma trusts you. She says you're the only one I can trust when she's gone." She held her head high. "But I'm not ready for her to die."

"I understand."

"You don't understand," she said. "Have you lost a parent? How can you understand? I lost my father, and now I'm losing Mumma."

"You'll have your father back," I reassured her. "And a brother."

"Too late," she declared with a firm look. "I can never love anyone else like I love Mumma."

"No one can take her place in your life. But we can have a different relationship, a different love? Friendship, perhaps."

I spotted distrust in her eyes.

"Your mom wants you to come with me to the U.S. if..."

"You mean *when* she's dead." She was a firecracker who reminded me of Tara. The two would get along well. She didn't mince words—no euphemisms for death. *Dead.* As if using it would allow her to come to terms with reality. Treating her like an adult, not the child that she was, seemed like the smartest way to gain her trust.

"I'm sorry I didn't talk to you before I started the paperwork, but I want to ask if you're okay with it. I don't want to do anything without your permission or against your wishes."

She considered me for a long minute.

"Yes." She exhaled. "Mumma trusts you. So I do too."

When we left, I thought I saw a faint smile at the corners of her mouth. I took it as the beginning of a new relationship.

TARA

I was in the restoration room Monday morning when Sameer called. Two of the Arlington paintings had shown traces of fading, and it was more of an obsession than a necessity that I spent my days trying to ensure that the integrity of the paintings was maintained through the restoration process. When I got back to my office around noon, I turned off my *Do Not Disturb* and texted to see if he was up. He called back promptly.

"Hi," I said with a smile.

"Hey, love." He sounded weary.

"Long day?"

"It was emotionally exhausting. Facing one's past is no small feat."

"How did it go? Did you see Riya?"

"Yes, better than I had expected. I miss you so much, Tara. Makes me wonder how I lived without you for over a decade."

"I miss you too. I can't wait for you to get back. How's Amar? Is he happy to be back in India?"

"He's a contented soul. He's happy wherever he is."

"Hey, you forgot your ring at my place."

"Oh!" he exclaimed. "I didn't even notice it was missing."

"What did you tell Aarti about the sudden departure?"

"Business trip."

"She didn't ask why? Especially when you had nothing planned until the night of?"

"No, but I said a new opportunity had come up and I needed to attend to it immediately." He sighed. "She trusts me."

"We need to tell her, Sameer. This isn't right."

"I know," he said, and sighed again.

There was a brief silence.

"I'm planning a weekend trip to New York," I said. "You and I can begin on a clean slate when you come back. When will you be back?"

"Not sure yet. Too much is hanging in the air." He paused. "Alright, I'll let you get on with your day. I'll try and call whenever I can."

After the call, I booked my return tickets to New York and called Sujit, Aai, and Sona to tell them I was coming. I kept the conversations brief. I still wasn't sure how I was going to break it to Sujit. What would he think of me, but more importantly, how much would this hurt him?

After work on Friday evening, I took a flight to JFK. When I landed, I saw Sujit at the airport, despite my strict orders that I would take a cab. A wide grin, a warm embrace, a familiar kiss. My heart thumped hard, and my hands shivered with mixed feelings of happiness and guilt. I was beginning to feel sick to my stomach.

"I can't wait to see Aai," I said when we were in his car. "I wish I had your patience to keep a secret. But then, I think Aai would have a heart attack if I showed up unannounced."

He glanced at me and smiled. "She's waiting eagerly."

"Sujit, there's something important I need to talk to you about," I said before I lost my nerve.

"Sure. What about?"

"Can we spend some time together tomorrow? Alone."

"Uh-huh. Ms. Tara Kadam, I don't trust you to behave yourself when we're alone. Maybe I should get some reinforcements?"

Guilt and shame weighed down my breath.

"Where's the laugh?" he said, glancing at me. "I thought that was very cute."

I turned to him and smiled. "It was. You are terribly cute."

"But?" He glanced at me again.

"But nothing. No buts. You're cute. Period."

"Uh-oh! That sounds ominous. You're never this nice. Something's up, isn't it? You're breaking up with me." He was smiling with his eyes on the road, confident in his joke.

"How's work?" I asked.

"Meh, same old. You?"

"It's been a good two months. I got to learn some characteristic features of the Texas landscape in art." Ah, small talk, the refuge of those who wish to avoid talking about real emotions. "Colleagues have been supportive. Can't complain."

I saw Aai on the balcony, and she waved at me as I exited the car. She was already at the door when we reached upstairs. Sujit helped me lug up my carry-on laden with paintings that I had brought back.

"Okay, I'll let you both be," Sujit said. "I'll see you tomorrow."

"Please come inside. For long time, she doesn't see you, so please come and sit with us. You will not disturb us," Aai said to Sujit in her tenuous English.

He smiled. "Thank you, Aai, but it is late. And I will see her tomorrow." He had learned to pace his words so she could understand his curved Rs and soft Ts. This was the considerate Sujit I was preparing to devastate tomorrow.

After a very late but hearty dinner that included my favorite bhendi chi bhaji and poli, and tomato-onion koshimbir with crushed peanuts, Aai and I settled on the balcony with hot cups of tea. The sound of crickets stridulating in the distance, the light clouds hanging below the night sky, and the delicate smell of herbs and lilies wafting up from the downstairs balcony all reminded me of home. Aai, Baba, Dada, and me on our terrace on hot summer nights, playing cards, laughing hard. Sometimes, when my aunts, uncles, and cousins visited us, Dada, Baba, and I teamed up to cheat, winning round after round of rummy. When our scam was discovered, we had to agree to treat them to ice cream for a whole week. I smiled at the memory of my father's warm face.

"Do you want to eat mutton tomorrow?" Aai asked.

I smiled again. Aai's mutton curry used to be Baba's favorite. It was the one thing he was most vocal about—his love for her curry and his disdain when others cooked it. Aai often reproached him for it.

"I've missed your mutton, Aai. But I'll be out with Sujit tomorrow. I don't know what the day looks like, so let's not plan anything elaborate. Simple food is good."

She nodded, took a sip of her tea, and watched me. "Something about you is amiss." She didn't beat around the bush this time.

"Aai, I want to tell you something."

"Is it about Sameer?"

I pulled in a deep breath. "Yes."

She nodded.

"Aai, we knew each other in college."

Knew, a euphemism because I couldn't bring myself to tell her in explicit words that I was consorting with a young man when I was supposed to be focused on my education.

Another nod from her.

"I liked him a lot. He liked me too. When we reconnected in Dallas, we realized we still liked each other."

Like, another euphemism.

"Hmm," she said with a thoughtful frown. "Then what about Sujit?"

"I'm planning to tell him tomorrow."

She gave a slow, thinking nod. I wanted to tell her everything that was passing through my mind, but I couldn't. I merely stared at her beautiful face with its soft, aging features. I got off my chair and paced the balcony, sipping silently from my cup.

"Look, Rani, you're smart, educated, and you have traveled the world. I'm a simple woman with very little exposure to the world beyond my own, so I can't tell you what the right thing to do is. All I can say is that you need to be absolutely certain, because such relationships can make or break your life. A single decision can be the difference between a happy life and a life full of regret. Now, I can't say who can give you that happiness—Sameer or Sujit. For that, you will need to trust your own instincts." Aai gulped the last of her tea and placed the cup down on the table. "The voice inside you will tell you what the right thing to do is. What does your voice tell you?"

"I like Sujit. I like him a lot. I respect him. But I like Sameer with an intensity I've never felt for Sujit. I feel it painfully in my heart, in the pit of my stomach."

"Yes," she said slowly. "I saw that."

"What?"

"I saw it in your eyes when I was in Dallas. That's why I asked you to be careful."

Growing up, desire was such a taboo subject. Sex and love were accepted as natural, even normal, but never spoken about openly with parents out of respect for them. But the past few years had brought us closer in unusual ways. Now Aai and I relied on each other for love and survival.

The next morning, I was ready in a pair of jeans with a simple top, waiting anxiously. Sujit arrived at 11 a.m., dressed sharp, business casual, gel in hair, stylish sunglasses, and happiness etched in his dimples.

"Who are you meeting all dressed up like this?" I teased.

"There is someone special," he said, then gave a shy smile as he saw Aai watching him intently.

"I'm going to my room," she said.

"No, we are leaving," I said to her.

Sujit looked at me and remained steady in his place.

"What?"

"Can you put on something nicer? We're going somewhere special." I gave him an eyebrow raise. He was the last person who would be bothered with what I was wearing.

Aai had already disappeared into her room behind a closed door. If this were any other day, I would've moaned into his chest, asking him the reason for such a request. But this wasn't just any day. This was the day I was breaking up with him.

"Okay." I smiled. "A dress?"

"Yes, wear the blue one I like. You look great in that."

"What's going on, Sujit? You're never like this."

He pushed his hands into his trouser pockets and shrugged. "Maybe I missed you more than I thought." He smiled, and my stomach turned again.

I quietly retreated to my room and changed into the blue dress. I had to swap my earrings for another pair to match the dress, and I picked a different shade of lipstick as well.

"How's this?" I asked when I returned to the living room.

"Perfect. What's wrong, darling?"

I forced a smile. "Nothing."

"You look tense. I'm sorry I asked you to change."

"No, it's not that." I comforted him with a quick squeeze of his arm. "Come on, let's go, I'm hungry."

But instead of driving us to a restaurant, he made leisurely stops, first at a florist to buy me a beautiful bouquet, then at his favorite bakery to pick up cupcakes. He took almost fifteen minutes trying to decide what he wanted. When we finally returned to the car, he began to drive us out of the city.

"Where are you taking me?" I asked, befuddled by his behavior.

His response was a sly grin.

"Are we going to your family home?"

"Darn, you're smart, aren't you?"

"Why are we going there? I'm hungry, Sujit. There better be food, or I promise I'll gobble you up."

"You can gobble me any time you like," he said with a naughty smile.

"Oh my god, what the hell happened to you?" I said, part annoyed, part amused. "Who made you into this raunchy person? You got a flush when I first used dirty talk."

He only shrugged.

"Don't say it was me," I warned, holding up my index finger. "I *do not* take responsibility for whatever is going on right now."

He burst into a throaty laugh. "Oh, Tara, how I've missed you. I don't think I've laughed from my belly since you left."

Suddenly, the hollow in my stomach wasn't from hunger. "Sujit, maybe we should talk somewhere quiet first?"

"What's on your mind?"

But I didn't want to blurt it out so casually, so callously. Maybe going to his family home was the perfect idea. It would be isolated, and that's where our relationship began, kind of. Although the awkwardness on our ride back would be painful.

But then, I wouldn't ride back with him, would I? I could call rideshare...

"What are you thinking?"

I smiled and shook my head. "It's a beautiful day," I said, looking at the bright sun and lush greenery floating past the car windows.

"It is." I heard the happiness in his voice.

When we pulled up at the house, a strange feeling hit me. I saw no cars in the street or the driveway, but the house didn't exude the same quiet quality as the other times we had been here.

"Is anyone else joining us?" I asked.

He evaded my eye and shook his head. "No."

But when he pushed open the large front door, I noticed it was unlocked.

"What's going on, Sujit?" I hesitated outside the door. "I'm not getting a good feeling about this."

"Oh, come on in!" He held my hand and gently pulled me inside.

The house appeared still, but I smelled food and heard a clink from some distant corner.

"Sujit—"

"*Surprise!*" A unified roar sliced through the silence of the cavernous house.

I trembled violently. Sujit's arms engulfed me before I spotted Sona and Aai among a room full of strangers. Of all the faces in the room, only my mother's matched mine, a visage of horror and sadness. She looked as stricken as I felt, so I knew she hadn't known about the surprise when I left her this morning. I also saw a young couple and an older one, who I guessed from the resemblance were Sujit's family.

"Happy early birthday, my love!" Sujit planted a firm kiss on my cheek. I exchanged a quick, uncomfortable look with Aai. Sona had a bright smile on her face.

"I don't know what to say..." I turned to Sujit, my shaking hands gripping his to hold myself upright.

"We won't see each other for your birthday, so I thought this was the perfect way to celebrate." Gently, he pulled me toward his family.

"Amma, Nanna, this is Tara. Tara, my parents, and my brother and his wife."

Everything felt out of sync, like an erratic dream. This was not where we were supposed to be, not what we were supposed to be doing—meeting his family for the first time at my surprise birthday party. My mind struggled to piece the day together. I longed to be in Sameer's arms right now. I cast a guilty glance at Sujit. He was smiling as if this was the happiest day of his life.

The lunch was set up in the beautiful dining room, flanked by the paintings I had helped choose. Each piece of art looked down on me with contempt as I hung my head in shame while smiling all the smiles I could muster.

His family was warm and unassuming. They made me feel welcome and loved. It was already getting more difficult when Sujit brought out a cake frosted to look like one of the paintings in the living room. I might have mentioned that it was my favorite piece. My hands got clammy as Sujit handed me the knife. I cut a sliver, as if that would somehow compensate for the slash I was going to rip through his life. *Breathe*, I told myself.

It was almost twilight when the party began to break up. I learned from Sona that Sujit had arranged for a car for her and Aai. He had confided in Sona about the party, and after he had picked me up that morning, Sona called Aai. That was the reason for the detours we took before landing here. He was buying them time to arrive before us. I hadn't told Sona the real reason for my visit. When the gravity of the event came crashing down on her, she sucked in a quick breath.

"That's why your mom has been so quiet." She cast a glance at

Aai, who was talking to Sujit and his parents. "She looked sad on the ride over, but I couldn't figure out why. Now I know. You've told her?"

I nodded. "Last night...I can't breathe, Sona."

She covered my hands with hers and patted them. "I know whatever you decide will be the right thing for you. Trust yourself, okay? I love you. I'll come over when you're back. You're not alone, Tara. You have me. You know that, right?"

I nodded with my eyes lowered, resisting the urge to hug her tight.

"Do you want me to stay with you?" she asked as I squeezed her hand.

"No, I'll text you when I'm back."

Aai walked over to us. "Are you still going to tell him?" she asked in Marathi.

"I don't know. Maybe not today."

She kissed my forehead before she and Sona left for home. Sujit's family left too. His sister-in-law and mother gave me warm hugs before driving off in their separate cars.

"We're alone, now," Sujit said, closing the door behind them.

"Yes. Thank you so much for such a special day."

I smiled and gave him a formal hug.

"You can do better than that," he said, gathering me in his arms. "I still haven't given you your birthday present yet."

"Sujit..."

"Yes..." He smiled suggestively.

"I don't feel well..."

"Oh!" He released me and held my shoulders. "What happened?"

"I feel nauseated."

It wasn't entirely a lie.

"Okay, just relax. Here, sit here." He led me to the couch. "Do you want some water?"

I shook my head. "I just need to rest for a bit."

"Okay, take your time. There's no rush. I'll put out the trash quickly and get you some water. Is that good?"

I nodded, and he scurried away. Taking in deep breaths, I tried to regulate my heart rate, but it was a futile endeavor. When he came back a few minutes later, he smelled of floral hand soap and expensive cologne.

"Any better?" he asked, handing me a cold bottle of water.

"No, but I'll be alright." I twisted the top open and sipped.

He dropped onto the couch beside me and relaxed, our heads resting on the back, our chests rising and falling.

"Oh, I forgot to tell you." He turned his head toward me. "The immigration attorney called. I was in a meeting, but he left a voicemail saying he has some good news. I'll call him back on Monday for details."

I looked up at the ceiling. Could this day get any more difficult?

"Thank you, Sujit."

"Hey, haven't I told you never to thank me?"

That's what Sameer had said, *you never have to thank me, Tara*. A tear rolled down my cheek before I could stop it. Sujit saw it and moved closer.

"Hey, what's the matter? You didn't like the surprise?" He wrapped a gentle arm around me. "Was it too much bringing in my family without telling you first?"

"No, they are wonderful people." I sniffled through my tears. "Everything was perfect. It's just me. I haven't been myself."

"Yes, I noticed. Is that what you wanted to talk about?"

I wiped my tears and stood.

"It's nothing. I'm overwhelmed seeing you after so long. I think I need some rest. Can you drop me back home?"

"Yes...of course...sure," he said, and got up reluctantly. "Let me lock up."

We drove back in silence.

"Thank you for the lovely surprise," I said as he dropped me off, but he was visibly upset.

"Was it something I did, Tara?"

"No, Sujit." I smiled. "Never. You can do no wrong. You're a kind man. You'll never hurt me in any way."

Usually, when he dropped me off, I would ask him up. We would have tea or talk for a while. This time I bid him goodbye in the car and walked away without looking back.

TARA

*A*ai came rushing to the door when I entered the apartment. She had changed out of her dressy saree into the simple cotton one she wore around the house.

"What happened?" she asked.

"Couldn't tell him." I slipped my heels off and kicked them against the wall. "He was so happy. It would've ruined his day."

"You're my good child. I don't know if I've ever said it, but I'm very proud of you."

"Don't be," I said brusquely. "Nothing I'm doing right now is worth being proud of."

"Don't say that, my rani."

Just then, my phone dinged with a text from Sona.

SONA

Are you back?

Yes

I replied and started toward my room. "I'm going to take a shower," I said to Aai.

Back in my room, the small carry-on I had brought along lay open on the floor, the paintings arranged on my work desk.

"What's all this?" I said to Aai, pointing to the paintings on display.

"I was checking to see if you had any laundry, and I found these. Did you paint them after you saw Sameer?"

"Yes, why?"

She looked at the paintings, then at me. "I think you made the right decision with Sameer."

"What are you saying?" I cried with weary exasperation. For the past few weeks, my life had felt like a series of random, bizarre, disconnected events that I couldn't make sense of if I tried. And this was the epitome. "Last night, you were sure Sujit was the right man for me. Today he shows how much he cares, and suddenly you flip sides? What changed, Aai?"

"I saw these paintings," she said, as if it made perfect sense.

"What does that have to do with anything? And how do you know so much about art, anyway?

"I don't," she replied. "I don't know art, Tara. I know you. I know how you feel about Sameer. He makes you happy, but he also lights a fire in you. You want that. You need that. It's in your nature. You cannot go through life with someone who doesn't ignite that passion, that hunger, in you. You'll never be happy without it."

I slumped on the edge of my bed.

"You got all this from looking at my paintings?"

"No," she said in her soft voice. "I got it from watching you at the party today. You looked like me when I was younger. Stifled, unsure, unable to breathe. I don't want that for you. You're confident and fierce when you're with Sameer. Look at these colors." She pointed to my art. "That's the Tara I raised."

"There's more to the story, Aai," I said before breaking down into inconsolable tears.

She came around to sit on the bed with me and took me in her arms. I sobbed on her shoulder, then in her lap like I did when I was little. She stroked my hair and wiped away the tears running down my face.

"I need to tell you something," I said, and sipped the water she had fetched. She led me out, away from the mass of paintings scattered in the room.

When we settled on the couch in the living room, I kept my eyes lowered. "I'm afraid you won't love me the same way after you hear what I'm about to tell you," I said, and tears trickled down my face again.

She stroked my back.

"I was involved, physically, with Sameer in college. I thought I was in love. Then suddenly, he was gone." She continued her gentle patting, but I couldn't bring myself to look up at her. "Except he wasn't really out of my life. A week after he left, I discovered I was pregnant." This time, I felt her hand leave my back. "It was the most difficult time of my life. I couldn't figure out why he had left, and I couldn't get in touch with him. Amar was also in Delhi, and when I texted him, he said I should ask Sameer. I wanted him to know, but there was no way to do that. Lost and distraught, I came home that weekend."

Aai looked at me, but I kept my gaze on my knees. "The weekend that Baba had his heart attack, I was there to tell you both about it and seek your guidance. But before I could, Baba fell, and my first thought was that if I had told him, it would have surely killed him! I would have killed my father because of my self-ishness."

Aai's hand returned to my back as I sobbed. "So I went back to Baroda and waited for Amar. When he returned two weeks later, he emptied out Sameer's apartment. 'He doesn't want to ruin your life,' Amar said when I asked about Sameer. So, I broke down and told him. He wanted to talk to Sameer, but I forbade it.

If Sameer wasn't taking my calls, I didn't want Amar to be my conduit. I knew I wasn't going to continue the pregnancy. Because I knew what you had done, Aai." I finally looked up at her, and she returned a questioning frown.

"I know you sold your jewelry, your inheritance, to send me to college. I've always known. You and Baba went through so many hardships, and there was nothing that could stand in the way of my success. Then Dada quit his studies. I didn't hesitate for a single moment about my decision. But Amar was my only support during that time. He stayed with me through everything like a true friend. It was the only time I accepted financial help from anyone. He accompanied me to the clinic and took care of me until I healed, both physically and emotionally."

A fresh burst of tears erupted and continued for minutes. Aai kept caressing my back.

"I'm not upset, Tara," Aai finally broke her silence. "I wouldn't have wanted you to be a mother at twenty, and an unwed one at that," she said with her old-school sensibilities, but I didn't interrupt. "I'm sad because you had to go through it alone. You should've told me. I don't know if I would've supported you in the right way, but I wouldn't have let you go through it alone, my rani." She put her hand on my head and pulled me onto her shoulder, her tears dripping onto me. She kissed my temple, and overwhelmed, I cried some more.

"You feared I would love you less, but I think you acted like a responsible adult. I wish you were sensible enough to avoid getting pregnant in the first place."

"Like not having sex?" I whispered tentatively.

She shrugged. "Or using those things." She meant contraceptives, but couldn't bring herself to say it.

"We did, Aai," I said reluctantly. "It was an accident."

There was another awkward silence before I continued. "But Sujit has helped me so much with you. He just told me his attorney has found a way to extend your stay. How can I be ungrateful to him like this?"

"You can't build a strong emotional bond on obligation, Tara, nor a lifetime's worth of commitment," Aai said softly, at the same time as the doorbell rang.

It was Sona. She entered with a restrained smile, saw my face, and rushed over. "Tara, are you alright?" she spoke in Marathi, as we always did around Aai.

"Yes," I said. "But I still haven't talked to Sujit."

"Then what happened? Why are you crying?"

"She has been with Sameer, and feels guilty about cheating on Sujit," Aai said.

"What?" I stared at Aai.

"What?" Sona's head snapped back to her.

"You think I don't understand these things?" Aai asked with a haughty sniff.

"What's she talking about?" Sona asked me in English.

"I slept with Sameer," I whispered. "I don't know how she knows."

"I knows. And I speak English little bit," Aai teased, forcing me to smile.

I gave Sona the CliffsNotes version while Aai made tea with cardamom, no ginger. Sona hated ginger in her tea. When we settled at the dining table with tea and cookies, Aai kept stealing concerned looks at me.

"Let it go, Rani," she said finally, returning her empty teacup to the table.

"What?"

"This burden of obligation that is weighing you down—to me, to your Baba, to Aditya, to Amar, to Sujit. Yes, we made some things possible, but it's your life. Live it according to your rules. Your dreams. I tried to give you the life that I wanted to live, yet you're living the life I settled for. Release yourself. You've repaid us all with what you are, *who* you are."

When I began to sob again, Aai put her arm around me. Sona put her cup down and took my hand in hers.

"There's no reason for tears, Tara. I'm actually relieved that you, what's that word you used, *slept*?"

Sona nodded.

"Yes, that you *slept Sameer*, because you chose it for yourself. You believed in your own happiness to break out of this cycle of obligations."

The doorbell buzzed, and Aai walked to the door again. "It's Sujit," she said, looking through the peephole. I rushed to the bathroom to clean up the evidence of tears from my face, but one look in the mirror told me it was a lost cause. I heard his voice outside and decided to brave it, red eyes, swollen face, and all.

Sujit took a startled step back when he saw me, and looked between the three of us. "What's wrong, Tara?"

"You both talk," Aai said in English. "Tell him, Rani," she said to me in Marathi and placed a light pat on my arm.

"Talk about what?" Sujit asked.

"She'll tell you," Sona said to Sujit, then accompanied Aai to her room.

The door closed behind them.

"What happened, Tara?" Sujit stepped toward me, his face contorted with anxiety and concern.

"Sit." I lowered myself to the couch while he hovered over the edge of an armchair facing me. "I need to tell you something important."

"Why are you crying? Did I do something?"

"No, this has nothing to do with you." Fresh tears ran down my face as I took a shaky breath. "Do you remember Sameer? You met him at the opening night in Dallas."

His frown ironed out instantly, and he released a knowing sigh. He removed his glasses and pinched the bridge of his nose.

"Sameer is not just an old friend. He's my ex. We reconnected over the past few weeks."

Sujit stayed silent, waiting for me to continue.

"I want to give us—Sameer and me—another chance. But I don't want you to think I'm being ungrateful. I owe you so much for helping me with Aai. If it wasn't for you, I couldn't have brought her over so quickly, and I'm not worried about her being alone here."

"What does that have to do with anything?"

"I'll always be indebted to you."

"Indebtedness is not a substitute for love." Crisp and to the point. Classic Sujit.

"That's what Aai said. I never meant to hurt you, Sujit."

"Do you love me?"

I hung my head. "Why did you come back?" I asked instead, looking up at him.

He returned my look with some anger. "I wanted to make sure you were alright." A brief pause. "You didn't answer me. Do you love me?"

"Yes. If I didn't, this wouldn't be so difficult. I do love you, Sujit, but it's different with Sameer, and I want that," I answered unabashedly because he deserved my honesty. "You're a warm, genuine man—"

"Is that why you're doing this to me?" His caustic words hung between us in the guilt-ridden room, and silent tears began flowing down my face again.

He put on his glasses, stood up, and left, closing the door behind him with a sharp slam.

I helped Aai reheat leftovers from the previous night and coaxed me into eating. When she left, Aai made tea for my massive headache. We retired to the balcony, but I couldn't smell the herbs or the lilies. The crickets had abandoned me too. Aai and I finished our tea in the silence of the suffocated night.

After Aai turned in, I called I. He answered, but from the sounds of heavy traffic and incessant honking, he seemed to be outside.

"I told I," I said.

"Oh, my jaan, are you alright?"

"I will be," I said, trying to hold back my tears. "I, when are you coming back? I don't want to spend another moment without you."

"Soon, Jaan. Listen, I have to go now, but I'll call you tomorrow morning, I promise." He hung up, and I sobbed until I passed out from fatigue.

The next morning, I looked like I had been in a boxing match. No amount of tea or Aai's ointments helped ease my persistent headache. Finally, I took a strong painkiller with my tea while Aai made a quick semolina breakfast. I called me as promised, and we talked for a bit about Sangita's condition. Then I packed and got ready for my early evening flight.

"Aai, now that I is no longer a part of my support system here, do you want to come to I? It's not a long time. We can go around the city a bit."

"No," she said. "It's too much of an effort for me to pack for such a short visit."

"But I'll be worried all the time."

"I is here. Don't worry about me."

"She liked I," I said to Aai.

"Yes, I like him too. But this is your life, not either of ours."

I called I to apologize, but as I had expected, he didn't answer. Instead of leaving a voicemail, I sent him a text, asking for his forgiveness and telling him he didn't need to check up on Aai anymore. I anticipated no response, and I got none.

After I packed and showered, we ate a light lunch. I didn't

want to eat at all, but Aai insisted. We had just finished when I appeared at my door.

"Can I come in?" he asked as I stood dumbstruck. I nodded and moved aside to let him in.

"Hi Aai," he said.

You don't have to call her that anymore, I was tempted to tell him, but I think he used it more as a term of endearment than actually calling her *Mom*.

"Hello, Beta," Aai said with a warm smile. "You talk here." She retreated to her room.

"I'm sorry, I," I began.

"No, I'm sorry for leaving abruptly."

"You don't have to apologize, and you have every right to be angry."

"I'm not angry, I. Don't you see?"

I mustered the courage to look into his eyes. "I'm not angry, I'm devastated," he said, dropping onto the couch behind him. "I went home and spent the night thinking about what you had said. This morning, I was determined to come over and ask—what happens if it doesn't work out with I? Would you give us another chance?"

"I—"

"Wait, I'm not done. But on the way here, I began reflecting on us. And I have a question for you."

I nodded.

"Last evening, you said I could do no wrong. So, I want you to tell me one thing that you dislike about me."

"What?"

"What do you dislike about me, I? What are my flaws?"

"I..."

"That's what I thought. You see me as infallible. That's not love, it's reverence. Notice my flaws, I. See me as impatient. Indecisive at times. Sometimes angry, sometimes timid. If you don't see all that, that's not love."

"You can't decide how I feel about you."

"No, but I know what I want from the person I'd be with. I want her to see me as I am, with all that's good inside me, and bad."

Like I did with I, I mused, looking out the glass door of the balcony.

"So, I'm reverting our status back to friends."

"Unilaterally?"

He smiled with his sexy eyes and dimpled cheeks. "You dumped me last night. I guess that makes us even."

I had to smile. He was always ready with his sharp one-liners.

"Come on, I'm also here to drive you to the airport like we planned."

"Oh, you don't have to do that." I sat up with embarrassment. "I'll take a cab."

"No, you won't. And don't worry, you don't need to feel indebted to me in any way, because that can't be the basis for any relationship— love or friendship. I'm not that person, and you know it."

"Thank you, Sujit, for everything. Everything you are, and everything you've done for us."

I leaped into his arms and held him tight. He rested a gentle hand on my back, waiting patiently through my tears, while we brought closure to our relationship.

SAMEER

*T*wo days after my first meeting with Sangita and Riya, I was back at the hospital.

"I'll accompany her to the visa interview," I said to Sangita. She smiled at Riya, who stood by her mother's bed wearing a glum look.

The visa would secure Sangita's last wish, but far from the silver lining it appeared to be, it was laced with the morbid eventuality of her death. It wasn't an easy situation, yet I couldn't help but marvel at Riya's strength.

Amar and I had taken her out to dinner the previous evening, but it didn't feel like we had formed any kind of authentic bond. Then again, it was unfair to expect her not only to put her trust in me but to also feel emotionally connected. It would take a lifetime, if at all. My only hope was to be with her when she lost her mother and to make her feel safe, protected, and loved.

While we sat at the consulate waiting for our turn, I spotted a tense look on Riya's face. I patted her hand. "It'll be alright. I'm here with you, always," I said.

She nodded with an earnest look on her face. For the first time since I'd met her, she let the young child sneak out. Timid, afraid, and uncertain about a future with a family she hardly knew.

In that moment, it struck me. For years, I had tried to channel the cruel and cutthroat in order to get ahead, but the only reason a sick woman trusted me with her daughter was my kindness. Sangita understood that my intent was to protect someone I loved, even if it meant hurting her in the process. But life had just handed me a second chance at love and redemption, and I was ready to grab it with both hands.

We breezed through the interview because my attorney had done a foolproof job with the application. He was an old friend of Mihir's who had helped with Dad's immigration. Smart and connected as he was, his most appealing quality was his discretion. I couldn't trust anyone else with the delicate secrets of my family.

With Riya's visa in place, it seemed macabre for me to stay on in India, waiting for the passing of Sangita. For the past few days, she'd seemed upbeat, albeit not any healthier, though I thought her skin had regained some color and she smiled more. With the hope of her recovery in my heart, I decided to travel back and return if needed. She was at ease with the decision.

That weekend, Tara called to say she had broken the news to Sujit. Now it was my turn to face Aarti and end our engagement. I also had to navigate that tricky tightrope talk with Dad about Sangita's condition. But despite the difficult conversations that lay ahead, I was looking forward to seeing Tara.

Tuesday afternoon, I landed in Dallas and drove straight to my parents'. As I sat with Mom at the kitchen table, holding a cup of the rich, smooth coffee I had missed, I recounted everything, including the slender hope that Riya might eventually warm up to us.

"She doesn't have much choice, poor girl," Mom said. "We should've been more considerate sooner."

"I was angry, and with so much happening, it was the last

thing I'd considered. I wish I'd had the maturity to foresee that the little girl's life would become collateral damage in the whole fiasco."

"Tell me about her," Mom said with a faint smile. "What does she look like?"

"Like me when I was that age." My face turned hot, and my eyes dropped to the table. Mom touched my cheek gently.

"No one blames you, Beta."

"I do. I blame myself, and Riya hates me. She says she'll trust me only because Sangita does. But why does Sangita trust me, Ma? After what I put them through, how can she trust us with the most precious thing she has?" I tried, unsuccessfully, to quash the lump gathering in my throat.

"She's out of options. And despite it all, you made sure they never lacked for anything. You were bitter, but not cruel. That's the difference. She knows it...I know it too. And there's enough blame to go around."

"But there was never a simple solution, was there? There couldn't have been. Did I make the wrong decision, Ma?"

"I don't know," she said. Her eyes welled, and her upright, dignified figure slumped as she broke down into tears. I put my arm around her. I had not seen her cry in years, and I knew I had to be strong for her and Riya.

Mom wiped her tears and sat upright again. "Go talk to Pavan."

Durgaben walked in with a glass of water and nodded at me. I left Mom in her caring hands and went looking for my father.

He was in his armchair again with the decanter of whisky by him, shining like a jewel in the sunlight. He seemed buzzed, and it was only early evening. It appeared he began drinking sooner and sooner each day.

"We got the visa, Dad," I said softly. He looked up at me and nodded. "We don't know how much time we have, but I'll be there for Riya when it happens."

He turned his head away from me. "You took away my happiness, Sameer."

"I'm sorry," I said, and began to leave.

"I know you're in love with that girl, Tara," he said.

I swiveled around swiftly and saw him staring at me, sipping from his glass.

"Isn't she the one you ran out on in Baroda?"

My heart dipped.

"You used to scream out her name in your sleep," he said, as if it were a perfectly normal thing to happen. "I knew the moment she set foot in this house that she was the same girl. You masked it well, but I know what she means to you."

I felt myself grow heavy and turn to stone.

"She's a sweet girl. Headstrong but real, unlike other girls you were involved with. This girl couldn't care less about your money. She's confident, content with who she is." I remained glued to the spot, listening to my drunk father talk cogently. "You need someone like her in your life. She'll stand up for you like she did when I talked about you. She'll protect you. She'll make you happy. She *makes* you happy." He grinned menacingly. "I couldn't have that."

He pushed himself upright and refilled his glass. "You asked me why I hastened your engagement to Aarti? That's why." He threw back the contents of the glass and glared at me with pure hatred. "You're now stuck in a life without love. I couldn't let you be happy. I *cannot*," he said, and began weeping without shame as if the father and the competitor in him were at war. "I cannot," he repeated amid sobs.

I walked up to him and took his hand in mine. He looked up, surprised, his face drenched in tears. I took the glass from his hand and put it by the decanter.

"I *am* going to end it with Aarti, you know that. I don't care if it scars our social status or ruins my business. You made two mistakes, Dad. I only made one, leaving Tara the first time. I'm never losing her again. I'm going to do it right this time."

I had finally said it aloud. I was going to make it right. As I walked out with my head held high, I heard a frustrated scream followed by a loud shattering of glass.

Jetlag was creeping up on me fast, but the prospect of seeing Tara and holding her in my arms kept me going. On the way to my condo, I texted her that I would come over around seven and spend the night at her place.

> TARA
>
> Can't wait to see you!

When I went over as promised, she opened the door in her apron with her hair tied up but her lipstick and makeup intact.

"You look beautiful," I said.

"I missed you!" she said breathily, taking me in her embrace.

"Me too, my love." The familiar scent of her delicate, aquatic perfume felt reassuring, and the house was enveloped in the warm, inviting smell of spices. "Are you cooking?"

"I thought you needed some TLC after the tough week in India, so I made dinner."

I kissed her. "And later, we're going to have sex," I announced, pulling a handful of condoms from my pocket.

"Oh, ambitious!"

"Sex, Tara, sex. Not tender lovemaking. I want rough, hot, kinky sex."

She rolled her eyes and walked to the kitchen. Small but well organized, it had a little round dining table in a corner. Above it, a lamp hung from the ceiling, making it both romantic and cozy.

"What did you make?"

"Not pav bhaji," she teased me with a grin that showed her

perfect mouth, the front two teeth slightly bigger than the rest. She used to tease me that I had a type. I grinned at the memory and said, "I can smell that." As if I could really tell the difference. But I could never fool her. She narrowed her eyes at me, then smiled.

"I made my mom's chicken curry with roti and rice. And a side salad. Sound okay?"

"Sounds fantastic." I kissed her cheek. "And smells even better."

As I wrapped my arms around her waist from behind, she put one hand on my cheek and stirred the curry. Scooping some with a fresh spoon, she blew on it and brought it to my face that was resting on her shoulder.

"Taste for salt and spice."

"Mmm, it's perfect."

"Is it too spicy?"

"No, it's just right. Different from the curries I've had."

"Yes, this one uses a browned onion and coconut paste that's made fresh."

"You made it?"

She nodded. "It's Aai's family recipe."

"I love you." I hugged her tighter. She turned around in my arms and kissed me.

I took the opportunity and brought my hand to her breast, but she promptly removed it and pointed to a cabinet. "Kinkiness later. Can you set the table?"

"Sure, if you direct me."

"Seriously? How do you not know how to set the table?"

I pulled out dinnerware and flatware while she carried the food to the table. Over dinner, she told me about her visit to New York. She was wracked with guilt at the way Sujit had thrown her a surprise party and at the fact he was still just as kind and considerate.

"Tara," I said with my eyes set on the plate, "I completely forgot about your birthday."

"That's alright." She placed her hand over mine. "You have a lot going on."

"It's tomorrow, isn't it?"

"Yes."

I had reminded myself before I left for India, but amid everything happening, it had escaped my attention. A sudden pang of guilt hit my heart. There was Sujit, whose life was drama-free, and who cared enough to throw her a surprise party. And then there was me, in love with her, engaged to another woman, and trying to redeem myself by becoming the primary caregiver of yet another woman's daughter.

"What's the matter?" She put her hand on my arm when I stopped eating.

I shook my head.

"Sameer, it's not a big deal you forgot my birthday. I don't care about these things. You know that."

The food was exceptional, like everything of Tara's. She was an exceptionally passionate woman. Self-doubt resurfaced in my mind. She said I deserved her, but did I really? I looked at her blissful face as we cleared up the kitchen, then settled on the couch.

"I don't have any alcohol, but I can make some coffee," she offered.

"I'm okay." I patted the couch, and she sat down beside me. I rested my head on her shoulder, and she kissed my forehead.

"Do you want to watch something?" she asked.

"No."

"Okay...Do you want to talk?"

"No."

"Sameer..."

"I'm sorry, Jaan. I had a tiff with my father, and with everything going on in India and with Aarti, I just don't have the energy to share anything right now."

She put her palm on my cheek. "That's okay."

Turning on the television, she muted the sound and began browsing.

I remember closing my eyes for a second, and the next thing I knew, the morning sun was sneaking in through the blinds. I was on the couch with a pillow under my head and a blanket over me. Tara was asleep on her side on the rug by the couch. I pulled her blanket over her when she turned over to face me. I looked at her beautiful face and realized, yet again, how much I cherished her.

TARA

"*H*appy Birthday, Jaan." His deep, sexy voice was the first thing I heard that morning.

Stretching my stiff body, I smiled. "Morning. This is how I want to wake up every day."

"On the floor? Silly girl, why didn't you sleep in your bed?"

"I needed to be with you."

"You're going to be sore all day."

"You can give me a massage later." I tried a seductive smile despite my puffy morning eyes.

"It'll be my pleasure," he said, running a finger along my cheek. "But I have to go in early today to make up for the days I've missed." He got off the couch and stretched his back. "Ooh, I'm stiff too."

I offered to make breakfast, but he refused. "Tonight, at my place. We'll celebrate you."

After he left, I made short calls to Aai and Sona. Sujit had left me a birthday wish at midnight, and I responded with a text. My phone and social media pages were abuzz with messages, but when I considered how I wanted to spend my day, all I could think of was Sameer.

While having my coffee, I cooked up a plan that promised to make the day special for the both of us. I sent a quick email to Dr. Hadden that I was taking the day off. She emailed back promptly, saying I deserved a break after all the hard work I had put in. When the shops opened at ten, I took a rideshare and went shopping.

It was almost noon when I returned. After a quick bite of last night's leftovers, I gave myself a mini-facial and stepped in for a luxurious shower before donning my new purchases. Then I called for a cab to take me to Sameer's office.

A well-dressed receptionist asked for my name.

"Devika Mehta."

"Do you have an appointment?"

"Yes, but I won't be on his schedule. It's a private appointment."

She gave me a blank look. I responded with a sweet smile and held it until she was forced to smile back.

"I'll let his assistant know," she said, lifting the intercom receiver.

"Thank you." I strolled along the lobby, studying the artwork on the walls, glad that it included no Selfia. In about a minute, a scrawny young man of South Asian descent, impeccably dressed, approached me with a confident but gracious smile.

"Mr. Rehani is in a meeting, but you can wait inside." I followed him. I wondered why he had not asked me for more details about the meeting. Did "private meeting" mean something specific in this industry? Maybe they thought I was a rich heiress planning to invest my money with the firm? Or perhaps I was here to service Mr. Rehani. The thought tickled me.

I thanked him as he showed me to a stately waiting area

surrounded by glass offices. Sameer was seated in one of the conference rooms, deep in conversation with two men and a woman. He looked striking in a tailored suit, his confident bearing exuding power. I settled down with my back to him, picked up a magazine from the side table, but returned it promptly. Neither celebrity gossip nor finance interested me. Instead, I pulled out my phone and began reading an article I had bookmarked. In a few minutes, the door opened, and the men and the woman walked out.

The young man reappeared to escort me to a different room. It was Sameer's office, and he sat at his desk with his back to me.

"Lock the door behind you, Ms. Mehta."

I turned the lock with a smooth click.

"Go ahead and strip. I'll be with you in a moment," I heard him say and went motionless.

His hand moved to somewhere around his table, and the blinds on the door and the windows began drawing in the darkness. I didn't move. Didn't breathe. He lifted his head from his file, his back still to me. "I don't hear you stripping, Ms. Mehta. Are you waiting for me to rip those clothes off your body?"

"Uh, Sameer," I whispered.

"That's Mr. Rehani to you." He swiveled in his chair with a straight face and stood up. "You thought you could pull one over on me, Ms. Mehta? As if I could forget you made me dance to that challenge?"

My face flamed with heat.

He advanced toward me with careful, calculated steps. "See the thing is, although you might be an alpha, a tigress, I'm only one tiny step behind you, Tara Kadam. I'm a tiger, fearsome and powerful."

"Is that so?" I purred.

"You better have brought some other clothes with you,

because this dress is getting destroyed." He snapped the buttons and flung the dress off my shoulders with such incredible speed that before I could gather my wits, I stood naked before him. But he wasn't expecting what greeted him when that double-breasted trench dress came off my body.

I stood in an open-bust, black bondage bra with rings and leather straps and a matching leather T-string. In other words, mostly naked. The nice woman at the sex shop also helped me pick out a discreet chain necklace attached to nipple rings.

"What do you say, tiger?" I said, striking a pose.

All he could manage was a desperate groan as he raked a hand through his hair, then loosened the tie at his neck.

I giggled. "You wanted kink, you got kink, baby."

"Oh, you have come to play, my tigress."

I saw the spark in his eyes as he saw my perked-up, taut nipples. But he bridled his excitement and flicked them with his fingers to watch me wince.

Holding a firm grip on my wrist, he led us to his table and, in a swift motion, swiped the contents to the floor. Files and paper flew off the desk like I had only seen in movies. As I wondered who was going to clean all that up and reorganize the files, he ordered me down on my back with my knees spread wide. I redirected my eyes to him and obeyed like a good girl. With a growl, he removed his jacket and flung it away. It landed somewhere in the vicinity of my discarded dress.

With eyes firmly locked on me, he continued, "This is what a tiger does when he is really hot and horny. Are you ready, my tigress?" He attacked my neck and clenched it between his teeth, firmly but not to the point of pain. I giggled hard.

"Unless you have a degree in zoology, I'm not taking your word for it," I teased. "But I did read somewhere that the tiger holds down his mate by the neck to prevent her from slapping him as he enters because it's painful. But apparently, the pain is what enables fertilization and propagates the species."

He looked up and stepped away. "You just killed my sexy tiger with that science lesson," he grumbled with a frown, and I laughed.

I flung my legs back together and sat up. "Don't worry, your sexy tigress knows enough ways to get you hot again. Let's see what she has to offer."

With complete faith in my transfer-resistant, matte red lipstick, I took my mouth to his. His hands explored the cool leather on my bare breasts. He rolled his thumbs over my nipples, then took his hands down to my waist. I squirmed.

"Aah, tickles!" I yelped and jounced out of his arms.

"Okay," he said, and pulled me back.

I inhaled him. "You smell different."

"Yeah?" He kissed my jaw while beading my nipples. "Different how?"

"You smell like power." I put my arms around his neck, and he squeezed my bottom.

"Hmm, does that turn you on?"

In response, I kissed him furiously.

He smiled. "That much, eh?"

I stepped out of his arms and asked, "How did you know I had come here for this?"

"You underestimate me, babe. I'm usually one step ahead of you. I can always anticipate your next move." He leaned against his desk, arms folded, legs crossed at the ankles, holding a smile— the smug one that I hated.

"How about a wager?" I took a step closer. "I'm dying to wipe that smirk off your stupid face."

He remained unperturbed and grinned wider. "What's the challenge this time?"

"I bet you'll come before I do."

"Really?" He raised an eyebrow. "That's bold, borderline audacious. What are the stakes?"

"Isn't winning reward enough?" I asked with a smirk of my own.

He chuckled. "Okay, challenge accepted. Show me what you've got." He rolled his chair over and sat, then planted a conceited smile on his face.

In the dim light of a tall floor lamp standing guard in a corner, I walked to the couch where he had put my bag and pulled out a pair of five-inch stiletto heels to replace the sensible low spikes I had worn to get there. I strutted up to him like a model on a catwalk, kissed him, then kicked his chair, which rolled back and hit the wall.

I wedged my heeled foot between his thighs and said, "So Mr. Rehani, what would you like first?"

I unbuttoned and unzipped him. He slipped off his shoes and removed his trousers and underpants. Kneeling seductively on the carpeted floor, I wrapped my fingers around him. His eyes remained fixed on my red nails as I stroked him, but when I took my red lips to it, they clenched shut as if by a magic spell.

His body slumped in the chair, making it easier for me to take him in. It felt more thrilling than I had imagined. I loved owning this power to make him groan with helplessness. His hand slipped into my silky hair, clutched it, and pushed me in deeper. I stopped and pulled him out.

"Don't force me," I commanded.

With closed eyes, he nodded, and I took him in my mouth again, sliding all the way down his beautiful, thick length. Curling my tongue, I swirled it a couple of times. I wanted him undone. My tongue rolled over the head, teasing the delicate skin. He thrust his pelvis up and let out another groan.

Oh yes, I was so winning this!

He must have felt my smile, because the next instant, he leapt off the chair and cast me an evil grin. "My turn."

The tenderness with which he helped me up from my kneeling position disappeared in an instant when he shoved me down on his desk. It was so hot that I was ill-prepared for the soft touches that followed. He grazed his fingers along my back and peppered my buttocks with kisses. But it was a misdirect, because the next thing I felt was a light spank. I gasped, and he kissed away the sting. He brought his left hand around to my breast and kneaded it softly, then spanked me again, a little harder this time. My back arched.

"Did that hurt?" he asked tenderly.

"No."

"Want more?"

"Yes."

"Harder?"

"No."

His relentless hand came down on me as he continued to knead my breast with the other. After each whack, he kissed and blew on it.

When he pushed me flat to my stomach, my bottom hung out, courtesy of the impractically high heels, giving me the leverage I needed and the access he wanted. Using his legs, he parted mine. I held my breath as I felt him squat behind me, his tongue flicking between my buttocks. They squeezed on instinct, but he used his hands to pull them wide. The tongue kept rolling and swirling, going further down to my already wet core. But I wasn't complaining. He was my tiger.

"Come up, turn over," he said. My T-string came off next and got tossed away.

"Lie on your back."

He pushed my knees up and out, exposing me to him completely.

"I feel really naked," I said.

"You are, and I love it." He bent down and kissed me. Featherlight kisses meant to torment, leave me begging for more. When I jerked into his mouth, he smiled and kissed but didn't yield. "Not yet, my love."

He released his grip on my knees and moved up my stomach, the hair on his jaw scraping my skin, setting it on fire, his beautiful, shapely lips pressing everywhere. My fingers grazed through his hair as his mouth landed on my breasts. His tongue twirled around the metal ring, and when he flicked my bound nipple, my head jolted off the desk.

"Easy, baby." He laughed, but his tenderness reappeared. "Does that hurt?"

"No, keep going, tiger." He kissed my chest, gradually moving down my body. I knew where he was headed. I wanted it, but it also meant my annihilation. He began with a light lick, and I groaned.

"Not a sound, my kitten. Let's see if you can manage that." His warm tongue ran through the cold, wet beads, and my entire body stiffened. He swirled his tongue on me just like I had a few moments ago.

"Cheater. You stole my technique," I whispered.

"Yeah? Are you complaining?"

"No, not me." He took the flesh tenderly between his teeth before turning it over to his soft lips, and I was ready to accept defeat. I had to stop it.

"There's a condom in my bag." I panted. "From the ones you left at my place."

"What's the rush?" he asked, exploring a new zigzag route with his tongue.

I took my lower lip between my teeth to stop the loud moans from escaping my throat before pushing him away.

"Ah, was that the tigress' slap?"

I swung my legs back together and stole a few quick breaths.

"We need to level the playing field. Get the condom."

He smiled and kissed me before walking to the couch where I had put my bag, his disheveled appearance making him sexier. His cute butt peeked from below his shirt, and the tie around his neck had lost its shape and purpose. He was perfectly naked and heavy. I touched myself at the sight while he stroked himself, our eyes locked. Then he rolled on the rubber.

I jumped off the desk. He swung me around and lifted my right leg to rest on the cool wood, bending it at the knee. Then, coaxing me down, he entered. But unlike the torturous experience for the poor tigress, my tiger filled me up smoothly until he was hot and tight inside me. He slipped up the band of my bra, freeing my breasts from their cage, but the nipple rings stayed intact.

He kneaded ever so gently. When he found his rhythm, he pulled an arm around me, sucking on my earlobe and kissing my nape. His pulse quickened as he increased the pace, his breath on my back adding another layer of sensuality. Unintentional, but oh, so good. I was losing fast. He put his palm flat on my back and leaned me over the desk, pumping deeper, faster, making more contact with my core. I knew I wouldn't last long. He knew it too.

I had to prolong it by distracting myself. Instantly, I summoned the multiplication table of seventeen. It had vexed me most as a child, and I had still not mastered it.

Seventeen twos are thirty-four, seventeen threes are ...add, my mind prompted ... *fifty-one. Seventeen fours are ...fifty-one plus seventeen...sixty-eight.* It was working. I was pleasantly focused on the table, and I felt him throb. I had to hold on for a few more seconds, a minute perhaps, until he gave in. Maybe I could hasten it. I clenched my pelvis and continued counting.

"Seventeen fives are eighty-five."

"What?"

"Nothing, keep going."

"Are you doing multiplication in your head?"

"No. Move faster."

Seventeen sixes are...ah, shit, what was seventeen fives?

"Tara...are you doing what I think you're doing?" He thrust harder.

"I've no idea what you mean."

Okay, back to seventeen into five...eighty-five.

So, eighty-five plus seventeen is one hundred and two. It was working again. I wasn't drawn to all the wonderful things happening to my body. I tightened my pelvic muscles again, *seventeen sevens—*

"Tara," he rumbled in a deep voice. He leaned into me, kissed my shoulder, and dragged his fingers down my back. My head rose in response, and my mind drifted to him for a brief, weak moment. "Do it again, baby, squeeze me. Do you know how good you feel? How tight and perfect?"

"Shut up, Sameer. I know what you're doing," I said, and reverted to the numbers dancing in my head. But he kissed my back, and they vanished again.

"Oh, Tara...I want you just like this...everyday...for the rest of my life." He enunciated each words in my ear, and the volcano erupted. My treacherous body responded violently to his words and spasmed, clenching him tight, my orgasm coursing through my body. My head dipped forward and my knees buckled as I felt him pulsate vigorously. With a silent grunt, he emptied himself and collapsed on my back. He beat me by two seconds.

When we descended that high, he removed the condom and trashed it in the bin. "There you go, Tara Kadam, you lose again." With a handful of tissues plucked from the box on his desk, he wiped himself clean.

"You cheated," I said, adjusting the useless bra that covered nothing.

"Says the person who used math to delay her orgasm." He grinned and bent to suck my nipple peeking through the ring.

I pushed him away with a grunt. "Well, congratulations, big winner."

"That's not in the spirit of the game now, is it, *loser*?" He pulled me closer and cupped my butt. "Do you want to remove the rings? Do they hurt? I have lotion in my drawer if you want."

I smiled. "I'm okay. They aren't too tight."

"That was the best surprise anyone's ever given me, babe. You get something special for this tonight, your birthday gift."

"I don't care much for worldly possessions," I said with a dramatic flair. "But I won't say no to having you." I grinned, and he laughed.

"I'm sorry I can't take the day off. With this unexpected trip to India, there's much I need to do."

"That's alright." I flirted. "I can't wait for this evening."

"Me neither. Now let me find someone to give you a ride back. I'll come and get you after work."

"*What*? No way! This will be my walk of shame, if there ever was one. Everyone on this floor knows what we did in this office. Probably heard us too. I'll avoid all eye contact and slip out as discreetly as possible."

"Hey, you got to own it with pride. Plus, no one is going to make eye contact with you, sweetheart. You were in the boss's office," he said with a wink.

"And when has that ever worked out well for anyone?"

"True, but you're the only one who's been in here with me, so that kind of makes you special, doesn't it?"

"Speaking of..."

He sighed. "I haven't yet."

"You still don't have your ring on."

He looked at his hand. "I didn't notice. That's telling."

I caught a hint of anxiety on his face as he tucked his shirt into the trousers.

"Don't worry," I said, placing a hand on his chest. I straightened his tie and put his hair back in place. "It won't be as bad as you imagine." He nodded.

Despite my repeated protests, he drove me back. As I got out of his car below my apartment, he said, "Hey, save this set. I see us using it many times over."

SAMEER

$\mathcal{I}$ remained distracted through my last meeting. Honestly, I was distracted since I dropped Tara off, but I couldn't cancel or reschedule my conferences. With another impending visit to India, I had to make every minute count.

I still had to figure out how to break up with Aarti without hurting her. And I wondered what Tara would think of me when she learned about how I treated Sangita and Riya. Would she hate me? Or leave me for good?

Shoving the negative thoughts back to some dark corner of my mind, I called the caterers to confirm the time of delivery. Instead of taking Tara to a busy restaurant, I had placed an order for a four-course meal and a specialty cake that morning. She deserved to be treated like a queen, my queen. I wanted to shower her with the love and attention she deserved. Something I should've done years ago. She was Tara, a star, my star.

Aarti called just before my final meeting of the day. To say she was unhappy about the fact that we hadn't spoken since the engagement was an understatement. I could hear her disappointment quivering beneath every word, and I had only just managed to placate her when my clients arrived.

One of the earliest lessons Mihir implanted in me was how to manage meetings with bossy, swanky, or presumptuous clients without exuding a whiff of dismissal. My client was none of those things, but I still managed to cut our meeting short while appearing charming and gracious.

I rushed home, showered, and put on the blue shirt that Tara loved. The doorbell sounded just as I finished styling my hair. It was the catering service. With appetizers and entrees in a warm oven, I popped the salad, dessert, and cake into the fridge. While I put everything away, the good man from the caterer's set up the table as requested, complete with candles and flowers. I wanted everything to be perfect that evening. When I was satisfied, I drove over to Tara's. This was going to be our evening.

I found her in the lobby of her building, waiting with a small overnight bag. She didn't need much to look gorgeous, and in the simple, stunning red dress and gold heels, she looked devastating. What caught my eye was her deep neckline, but of course, I wouldn't tell her that. I wasn't stupid.

"You know, I had to take a nap this afternoon," she said when we started.

"Well, be prepared to lose more sleep, because tonight neither of us is getting any."

"Yeah, yeah, I've seen your ambitious plans. You'll be asleep on the couch before I realize you're no longer listening to me."

I burst into laughter. She was the only one who could outsmart me with her quips.

With one hand covering her eyes, I led her into my apartment and to the round table by the windows. The look on her face was worth every effort the caterers had put in. "This looks wonderful!" she said, putting her arms around me.

I lit the candles on the table and pulled out a chair for her.

"What's on the menu?" she asked as I headed to the kitchen to retrieve our first course.

"I thought Spanish would be a good change."

"I love all food, and I trust your choice." She smiled as I put the small portion of Spanish croquettes and patatas bravas before her, then poured us some wine.

"I trust the food will be to your liking," I said with a dramatic bow.

"Everything looks perfect!"

I settled at the table and raised my glass. "Tara, this is a new start for us, and I want to celebrate you every single day for the rest of my life. You are the brightest star in my universe. Happy Birthday, my love."

When I stood and kissed her cheek, the tip of her nose turned a deep pink. "Are you blushing?"

"Don't be ridiculous. I never blush." She took a sip of her wine. "That toast was terribly sappy and clichéd, by the way," she said, but her dusky skin had plum undertones.

I gloated with a smile. "I love you, Tara."

"I'm not so sure," she said, delicately slicing into a croquette. "If you did, you would've let me win this afternoon."

"Oh, you won, trust me," I said, flashing a cunning smile, and found her blushing again. I could get used to this bashful Tara. Again, I wouldn't risk telling her that.

"Mmm, this is really good, Sameer. The saffron aioli is exquisite!"

"I'm glad you like it. It's one of my favorite restaurants here. Wait till you try the entrée."

"What is it?" Watching her eyes gleam with pure pleasure, I decided to spoil the surprise.

"Braised lamb shank. You won't believe how good their recipe is. It's incredibly tender and so flavorful!"

Her eyes held mine in an amused smile. "I didn't know you were this passionate about food."

"Well, just because I can't cook doesn't mean I don't appreciate the talent that goes into making something delicious. Like your chicken curry."

"Is that flattery?"

"It's the truth."

"Hmm, I'll soon have you cooking though, the basic stuff at least. It's a life skill, and you need to learn," she said eating a potato from her fork.

"I love it when you claim your right over me."

After our second course of a fresh, crisp salad tossed in a deliciously tangy vinaigrette, I was about to serve the promised lamb shank when the doorbell rang. I froze, casting a nervous look at Tara. Her face revealed the same fears.

"Sameer!" Her body tensed. "What do we do?"

"It will be okay, love," I said, and we heard a key slip into the lock.

We both left the table and stepped toward the door. Tara stopped near the couch in the living room. As the door swung open, I ended up face-to-face with a smiling Aarti.

"Surprise!" she said sweetly, but turned somber at the look on my face. "Sameer?" She stepped inside, saw Tara, and stopped. "What's going on?" She looked between the two of us.

"It's Tara's birthday," I said. "We're having dinner."

Her eyes traveled to the table and the flickering candles. "An intimate dinner?" Dark shadows crossed her face. Her eyes flitted to Tara, then to my hand. "Where's your ring?"

"Aarti, we can talk about this tomorrow. I'll come over and explain everything."

"Explain?" she cried with an angry frown.

"Tomorrow," I said. "Today is Tara's day. I don't want to ruin it for her. We can discuss everything tomorrow."

Tara crossed the few feet between us and touched my arm. "Be kind," she said softly, and Aarti's face flared into full-blown anger.

"So, I *was* right. You *are* sleeping with her." She turned to Tara with a derisive scowl. "What was that with Mihir? Are you sleeping with him too? Or are you just fucking everyone within reach? Mihir, Sujit, and now Sameer—"

"Watch your mouth, Aarti!" I growled at her, bubbling with rage.

"You bastard," she screamed back. "You're a fucking cheat. A fucking lowlife cheat."

Tara clutched her dress, and her face changed, but she remained silent. I stepped over and put an arm around her. She tried to resist, but I clutched her tight. "You can shout at me all you want, but don't you dare say anything to Tara."

Aarti's eyes turned dark with anger, and her fists clenched hard. "You fucker! You had everything. My father placed the world at your feet. I gave you my love, my whole self, and you fucked it all up for a few nights with *her*? We would've had a glorious life. You'd have been the envy of everyone around you. All you had to do was keep your fucking dick in your pants. You couldn't even manage that?"

My grip on Tara's shoulder tightened, my fingers digging into her flesh, as a bolt from my past hit me. I had heard these same words once before. Tara tapped on my chest before stepping out of my arms.

"Stop it, Aarti," she ordered in a calm voice. "You're hurting him."

"So you're his keeper now?" Aarti fumed.

"Do you want to learn the truth? Or do you want to keep abusing Sameer? You have a choice. You can stay and let Sameer explain. Or leave with this rage and carry the grudge for life. Neither will change the fact of his betrayal, but you can choose how you want to resolve this."

I stood behind Tara, holding my breath as Aarti gaped at us, tears pooling in her eyes. I knew she wouldn't let us see her vulnerable. She rushed to the door but stopped and turned to us.

"You seemed so nice, Tara," she said, tears now rolling down her cheeks. "How could you do this to me?"

"Would you like to hear us out?" Tara asked instead.

Aarti flinched at the word "us." She looked at me with the puppy eyes I had never seen on her before. A pang of guilt and shame shot through my heart as I nodded and walked over to close the door.

Putting her arm around Aarti's shoulder, Tara escorted her to the couch and sat beside her. She signaled me to get water. I brought a glass and handed it to Aarti before taking a seat on a recliner near her.

"I can't figure out what went wrong," Aarti said, tears streaming down her beautiful face. "Did I push you away, Sameer?"

"No, Aarti. It wasn't you at all. In fact, I'm grateful to you for everything you've given me."

"Then what, Sameer?"

"We've liked each other since we were nineteen," Tara explained calmly.

"What?" Aarti's eyes scanned me.

"Yes, and I never got over her." I let those words sink in for a moment. "Aarti, I was going to tell you everything the day after the party. But you proposed, and I was called away to India."

She gave a confused frown and swiped away the tears. "Did your father know about this? Because he pitched us the idea for a surprise proposal. He said you'd be happy."

I nodded. "My father and I have a complicated relationship, and he used you to get back at me. All I can do is apologize, but believe me when I say that I was going to tell you everything. I just didn't want to ruin the day for you."

I rubbed my hands over my face, then dragged them through my hair. When I held them out for Aarti, she stared in disbelief. Tara reassured her with a smile, and she trusted her hands to me. I kissed them and said, "I have to come clean with you, Aarti. I'm truly sorry to have misled you, but the truth is, I would've never loved you like you deserve. I would've always been in love with Tara. You are a phenomenal, successful woman, and you don't deserve to wallow in the loss of a relationship that wasn't worth it in the first place."

"But I do love you, Sameer." She burst into sobs.

"I know, and I am sorry," I said, unable to meet her eye.

Tara put a soft hand on her arm. "It will hurt," she consoled tenderly. "For a while."

"Until you find the one who appreciates you for who you are," I said. "For me, you were a ticket to the big league. I never deserved you. And I'm not saying this to make you feel better. I know you'll still be angry and hate me, and you have every right to."

Tara made sure I saw her reassuring smile. My father was right. I was lucky to have her by my side. She was the one who would stand up for me, fight alongside me, make me happy.

When Aarti left twenty minutes later, she didn't look angry, but tomorrow would be another day. After she had talked to her family and friends, their reactions would determine how much damage this particular train wreck would cause.

I held Tara in my arms. "I'm sorry for what Aarti said about you."

"We hurt her, Sameer. We're the reason for her anger."

"She liked you. I know her. She wasn't faking her admiration for you."

"And I caused her so much pain."

"*We,*" I said, and let out a unified exhale.

"Do you want to finish dinner?" I asked.

"The meat must be dry by now..." she mused distractedly.

"Cake?"

"Sameer, I'm very proud of you," she said with a hug.

"Why? I cheated on her and hurt the both of you. What's there to be proud of?"

"What you confessed today couldn't have been easy."

"Nothing's too difficult if the outcome is a life with you, Tara. I've had enough. I'm tired. I need you, and now I'm going to be stubborn about it." I placed my head on her shoulder and closed my arms around her waist.

"I'm here, my jaan," she whispered in my ear and caressed my hair. "I'm sorry the evening didn't turn out quite as you planned."

"But it's done, and I'm glad." I raised my head to look at her. "And I have you to thank for it."

If Tara hadn't insisted, Aarti would have darted out in anger with only half the truth in her grasp. Emotions would have festered, angers flared, families would've gotten involved, and a drama of epic proportions would've unfurled. Tomorrow would have been too late. Tara prevented it all and saved me yet again.

"What do you think will happen now?" she asked quietly.

"Oh, I do expect a heavy backlash and the possible loss of some big accounts, but it's insignificant compared to how happy you make me. The only person I need to protect from the fallout is Mom, but this time it's different. This time, I have you and Mihir in my corner. I'm not afraid. Not anymore."

She smiled and cupped my cheek with her cold palm.

"Are you alright?" I gripped her icy hands between mine.

She nodded. "We did the right thing, didn't we? I mean, we'll be happy together, right?"

"Tara, look at what's happened in the past month and a half and what has occurred in the last decade. If we're still here, I'm willing to bet anything we'll make it."

I stayed in her embrace until she whispered, "I have an idea."

I looked at her with raised brows.

"I know of a way to reignite our appetites."

"What appetites are we talking about? Is that a double entendre?"

"Maybe," she said, dropping her dress to her feet. She stood in a red plunge bra and a lace thong.

TARA

*W*et, weary strands stuck to my face as I lay wrapped in Sameer's arms, happy and content.

"I really need to start working out if we're going to do this," I joked. "You're so demanding."

"Me demanding? As if you didn't make me work hard. How many times was that?"

I smiled as my chest heaved. "I never count. But this is what you're signing up for."

He pulled me closer and took my earlobe between his teeth. "I work out. I have my routine down. I'm ready for whatever you want, whenever you want."

"That's a tall claim, Mr. Rehani. You better have the means to back it up."

"Oh, I do," he said and slapped my buttock with his exhausted means.

He had rolled me over to hold me from behind, and I felt his breath ease up on my neck.

"You're not going to fall asleep on me, are you?" I teased.

"After this, not a chance. I want more."

"Sameer, when you were in India, I got a call from my brother. He said he's checked himself into the rehab place he was at the last time."

"Well, that's good news, isn't it?"

I turned around at the tone of his voice. He tried to deflect by gripping my nipple between his fingers, but I swatted him off.

"What surprises me is that he'd never check himself in on his own, and he doesn't have that kind of money. So, it makes me wonder how that came about."

Sameer kept his face passive.

"Well?" I demanded.

"Do you really want to know?"

"If you had anything to do with it, I absolutely do, yes."

"Okay," he said with a resigned sigh. "I might have put some pressure on him."

"Pressure? What does that mean? And how?"

"Do you really want to know?"

I frowned. "Dammit, Sameer! Tell me everything *now.*"

"Okay, okay, don't get mad. Heavens! I sent some people over."

"What people? Goons?"

He stroked my arm to placate me. "Not exactly. They're just some friends who can be quite persuasive. I had them contact your brother and make some threats. But no real violence, I promise."

"Sameer!" I gasped with wide eyes.

He continued stroking my arm. "Listen, when your mom was here. I spent some time talking with her. She was pleasantly surprised that I spoke Hindi, and that's how we began chatting. She casually mentioned that she hopes to return to her life in India soon. She has very few friends here and no relatives, and despite your best intentions, it gets lonely. And she worries about Aditya."

"She never said anything to me!"

"She knows you worry about her, and she doesn't want to add to your burdens. She thinks it will upset you."

I squinted in disbelief. "And she said all this to you?"

"Not in so many words. But I can read between the lines. Don't forget, I'm just as smart as you."

"That's what *you* think!"

Planting a kiss on my forehead, he grabbed a lock of my hair to twist around his finger. "No one should be forced to live where they don't want to, Tara, if they have the option. I brought my father here against his wishes, and he hasn't been happy a single day since. He can't return, but your mother can, and she should have the freedom to do so. I asked my friends to talk some sense into your brother and got him into that rehab. Once he's sober, they'll keep checking up on him. I've also talked to someone about getting him a job. One that he likes. Your mother should be able to return if she wants. It is her home."

I pulled in a deep breath. "That's an expensive program, Sameer. You shouldn't have paid for it."

"Hey, our destinies, our fortunes are linked now. It's no longer just my money. It's ours. So are our families, for better or worse. Mostly for worse." He gave a rueful smile. "We have to deal with them together. I hope I didn't overstep my privileges."

"Oh, darling!" I leaned in and kissed him.

He took my hands in his and kissed them, and then I felt him exhale hard against my forehead. "I haven't told you everything about Riya," he said.

I looked into his eyes.

"I was the one who compelled Dad to leave them and come to the U.S. with Mom and me. I left them alone and desolate in a cruel world where an unmarried mother and a child born out of wedlock face the worst kind of stigma. I took Dad's love out of their lives and replaced it with money. Juhi and I were both grown up. We didn't need him, but Riya did, and I stole him away from her."

I gaped at him, speechless.

"There are two things I need to ask you," he whispered. "Can you see yourself spending the rest of your life with a man who would do this to a woman and her child?"

I pulled in a breath at the end of a long pause. "Did they forgive you?"

"Sangita did. I'm not sure about Riya."

"I think you've more than atoned for it, Sameer. You shouldn't keep punishing yourself."

He clutched my hands between his and kissed them. "Thank you," he said as a tear rolled down the side of his face and onto the pillow.

I wiped his eyes with my palm. "What's the other thing?"

"When Riya is here, I might end up being responsible for her. Will you be alright sharing our life with her?"

I smiled and smacked his forehead. "You *are* a silly man. I'm already sharing you with your parents, your friends and loved ones, and I'm happy about it. You're sharing me too, with my family and my loved ones. What makes you think being in love means loving only one person in life?"

"But it's not the same. Riya is..."

"Family," I concluded assertively. "We're not living in the 1980s, Sameer. No one cares anymore, and if they do, it's their problem."

"There will be whispers, eyebrow raises, and questions all the same."

"And we'll tackle them together. Did you really think this would bother me? I'm offended," I grumbled.

He gathered me in his arms, and I breathed in his comforting scent. "When you told me about your pregnancy, my first thought was that she would've been about eighteen months younger than Riya," he said in my ear.

I held my breath. When I finally found my voice, I confessed, "I want a baby, Sameer. I want our baby."

"We'll have as many as you want, my love. We can have a whole cricket team."

I laughed at his ridiculously silly joke, but it flooded my heart with warmth.

"And you're not scared, are you?"

"A bit. But I have you, and I have Riya for a trial run. I bet she'll tell me exactly what my parenting failures are."

"I'm looking forward to meeting her," I said, and he brought his forehead against mine in gratitude.

"Come on, let's have some cake," he said, brushing his finger against my chin. "Yeah?"

"I want to call Dada first."

"Come outside when you're done. I'll get the cake ready." His lips met mine in a delectable embrace. Pulling two robes from his closet, he handed me one. "I'll be outside."

It was early morning in India, and after jumping through several hoops at the rehab center, I finally managed to get in touch with Dada. In his sober condition, he sounded like the brother I had known all my life. "I'm sorry, Tara. I'm so ashamed of myself for what I said to you. You're my baby sister, yet you're the one who's always protected me."

His unabashed weeping had me blinded with tears. "I miss you so much!"

"Baba was right to be proud of you. You're everything he hoped you'd be. Maybe that's why I was jealous. But no more, Chimni. I am very proud of who you've become." It had been years since I had heard him call me Chimni. His little sparrow.

The word "catharsis" gets thrown around quite freely, but I didn't grasp its true meaning until that day. The strange lightness I felt in my soul was something I couldn't express in words if I tried.

"And tell Sameer, I'm coming for him once I get my bearings back. The bastard threatened me!"

I laughed from my belly. "I'd pay to see that brawl."

"You trust me this time, Chimni, don't you?" he asked softly.

"I do, but I need you to trust yourself. You've got a second chance. Make it count."

"I promise."

"I'll call you again tomorrow and every day until you're out. You're not alone in this, Dada. Aai and I are with you, okay? Aai will be home as soon as she's ready," I reassured him with the confidence Sameer had projected.

When I wrapped myself in the robe and walked out, Sameer was sitting at the island, reading on his phone, with a beautiful cake before him.

I walked up to read the inscription, *Happy Birthday to the Only Star in My Universe.*

"Everything okay? How is he?"

I hugged Sameer tight. "He's doing well. Everything is...as good as it can be."

"Scared of using the word *perfect*?" he said, making me laugh.

"He said he's coming for you when he's healed."

He released a guttural laugh. "I'll welcome him with open arms."

Holding the knife together, we cut the cake. Exquisitely flavored chocolate frosting sat between delicate layers of vanilla sponge that melted in my mouth. He smeared a bit of the frosting on my lips and lapped it up.

"That's a waste of cake," I said with faux annoyance.

"You think?" He dug out a small piece with his bare hands,

spread it on my chest, and licked it clean. He smeared another piece across my neck and clavicle.

"What are you doing?" I wailed. "I'm all sticky and greasy now."

"Well, we can take a shower...together." He grinned with a wink and put his mouth on my neck.

His tongue was just about to melt me away when he stopped and said, "Hey, before I forget, I have something for you." He rushed inside and emerged with a canvas in his hand.

"What's this?"

"Your birthday gift to me, remember?"

I tried not to smile, but a tiny one slipped out anyway.

"Yeah, that was pretty smart of you. But here, I did paint a perfect picture, one that I wanted."

In bold oil pastels, the canvas said:

Tara

Sameer

Forever

I hid my smile behind a forkful of cake.

"Yeah, missy. I bested you. Accept it."

"Never," I said, and stuffed my mouth with cake.

He leaned in to kiss me when his phone went off in the bedroom.

"You should get that," I urged.

"Don't move. I'll be right back," he said and walked into the bedroom. When he returned a few minutes later, his face was pale with worry.

I leaped off my seat. "What happened?"

"Tara, I'm sorry, but I have to go back to India."

"Sangita?"

Before he could respond, his phone rang again. "Amar, yes, Riya called me. I'll be on the next flight. Can you be with her until I come? Hey, wait for me if anything happens."

After listening quietly for a few seconds, he said, "Yeah, see you soon."

He stepped forward and hugged me. "I'm scared, Tara."

"I wish I could come with you. But Amar's there. Lean on him. He's your anchor."

"You're my anchor. He's my mast."

SAMEER

I dropped Tara off and returned to pack a quick bag. Amar was scheduled to leave for Mumbai, but I requested he stay back. I would need his support.

Sangita had stopped responding to medication, and even the painkillers weren't enough now. She was in constant pain and ready to give up. I was partially responsible for her being in this state—alone and unloved. My insides churned as I drove to the airport for a 2 a.m. flight.

During the long flight, I made a mental list of things I would need to take care of—hospital formalities, legal ones, social obligations, the cremation, last rites. I was prepared for it all, except for the one thing that really mattered: facing Riya. How does one console a child who is about to lose the only parent she has known?

When the wheels touched down in New Delhi, there was no change in Sangita's condition. She was still with us, Amar informed me. A small consolation. As I entered through the giant doors of the intensive care unit, I spotted Riya and Amar on a bench in the hall-way. Amar rose promptly when he saw me, and Riya's eyes lit up. I walked up and put an arm around her shoulder. She let her head rest against my chest for a moment before pulling herself upright.

"You should get some rest," I said.

"No, I want to be here when it happens," she declared, pushing her palms under her thighs and leaning slightly forward, eyes fixed on the door to her mother's room.

Amar beckoned me away from her to the large windows.

"What's the status?" I asked.

"She's on a ventilator."

"What does Vishal mamaji say?"

"Any time now."

"How did she deteriorate so rapidly? I was here three days ago."

"Her pain is too much to handle."

I raked a trembling hand through my hair. He patted my shoulder and said, "We'll wait."

We didn't have to wait long. Sangita passed away in her sleep that night, painlessly, thanks to the morphine. Riya hugged me as she wept. She stayed close while I finished up the paperwork at the hospital. I asked if she wanted to inform Sangita's parents. She shook her head.

"They never came to visit. We don't exist for them, Mumma said." Sobbing, she pulled a letter from her pocket. "Mumma wrote this last week. She asked me to give it to my father when she was gone."

I kissed the top of her head and took it from her.

We gathered Sangita's belongings and followed the ambulance to a crematorium. According to Hindu customs, it was the prerogative of the husband or the son to light the pyre. It was also their duty to perform the last rites for the transition of the soul into the other world. But Sangita had neither. She had a beautiful daughter.

I asked Riya what she wanted. She was a brave child, but a child nonetheless. I didn't want to impose on her to perform the last rites, nor did I want to take away her agency to decide otherwise. It was a tricky line to walk.

The electric cremation was simpler, with no spectacle, no smell, and no sound of the cracking bones. As Riya, Amar, and I bid farewell to a beautiful Sangita whose life I had ruined, I wept without shame, not caring about the few other families who were there cremating their own loved ones. I had taken away her love and left her to die in loneliness. Riya held my hand tightly as she wept, and I let all my grief and guilt flow out with hers. Her gut-wrenching scream tore through my heart when Sangita's body slid into the chamber and the fire gripped it in a hungry embrace before the lid closed shut. I held her firmly against me, almost carrying her back to the car.

We returned to Amar's home, showered, and had a light breakfast that Taiji had prepared. Riya refused to eat, just as she refused to go to bed. I sat with her on a couch in the living room until she fell asleep against my shoulder. I laid her down and covered her with a light blanket.

"I'll take her to get her things when she wakes up," I said to Amar.

"It will be difficult for her to go back home and not see her mother."

"Do you think I should go alone?"

"No, we should let her decide," Amar said.

"I must get lawyers to sort out the status of that house. I think it's still in my name."

Amar put a hand on my shoulder. "Don't worry about that right now. Those things will happen in time. Just take care of Riya. We'll manage the other things here. Dad's lawyers will get all the formalities sorted."

I hugged him. "Thank you for everything, bhai. I owe you big."

"Keep Tara happy, and we'll call it even."

"That's the plan." I smiled back.

We strolled into the dining room, where Taiji had laid out tea and snacks. When we were alone again, I said to him, "She told me about the pregnancy."

He nodded. "Good."

"You should've called me immediately."

"You had already left India when she told me, and she didn't want me to approach you about it. She feared you'd think it was a ploy to get money from the rich guy who had ditched her."

His words stunned me. "What?"

He shrugged. "You were in a bad place, Sameer, but so was she. I guarded her secret the same way she did mine. You wouldn't have heard it from me, ever."

"I see, professor."

He smiled.

"I can't believe fate gave me another chance after I blew the first one so spectacularly." I threw my head back with a sigh.

"Don't mess this one up. You won't get another."

Our eyes were instinctively drawn toward the living room.

That evening, I took Riya back to her home. She wept continuously as she gathered her life into bags to be carried across the ocean to another country, to a home she had never known. The only consolation, she repeatedly told me, was that her mother had trusted me, and she trusted her mother's judgment. The driver helped us load her bags into the car as she said goodbye to the house she'd grown up in.

On our way back to Amar's, I told her about the rituals surrounding death that I had seen in the family and asked if she wanted to perform any.

"No," she said. "But I would like to scatter her ashes in the river."

I nodded. "We'll do it tomorrow."

"If I choose not to perform any rites, will her soul suffer?"

She was asking the wrong person, but this wasn't the time for rationalistic expositions. "No," I reassured her. "The soul is gone. It can't suffer any longer. What you do from here on is for you, for the sake of the living. The dead have passed on. We can't hurt them anymore."

Fresh tears drenched her already tired eyes.

"Are there any friends you want to say goodbye to?" I tried to change the subject. "Any boyfriends?"

That got me a slight smile.

"Really? Boyfriend or *boyfriends*?" I asked. "And aren't you a little too young for that?"

"Mumma would've been so mad if she heard you talking to me about this," she said, then cried a little.

"So that's a 'yes' to the boyfriend, then?"

She tugged at corner of her cotton top. "Not a boyfriend, exactly. But I like him, sort of."

"Hmm, does he know?"

"I think he does, but we never talk about it."

"Do you want to see him before we leave?"

"Yes," she sobbed.

"You're barely thirteen, Riya. You'll meet many people in life who will make you very happy. Friends, family, lovers."

"Eww," she said from behind her tears.

"What?"

"How old are you?" She grimaced. "Who says lovers?"

"Hey, that's a perfectly fine word to describe someone you love."

"For your generation, maybe," she scoffed.

"Oh, that's what you think? You're going to play the age card with me, are you?" I ribbed. "I'm not that much older than you."

"You are old." She ended the argument definitively.

We talked about the friends she wanted to see before we left. We decided to call them the next day and visit them. We also cooked up a plan to have her see her not-boyfriend and give them some alone time together. She suggested I drive them to a coffee shop or a mall.

At dinner that evening, she ate a little more than she had all day. She still broke down in tears every so often. I didn't want her to be by herself at night, so I had a small extra bed moved into one of the larger guest rooms. After she fell asleep in the large bed, I slept on the extra bed near the door in case she needed me in the night, but she slept through the night without distress.

Early the next morning, we collected Sangita's ashes from the crematorium and drove north toward the river Ganga. We scattered her ashes in the river, sans rituals, and had a quick lunch at a roadside restaurant before driving back. Then we began calling Riya's friends to ask if we could stop by. It was rough watching the young girls lose their cherished friendships. I made small talk with the parents while Riya went into their rooms to chat and say goodbye. It was difficult to explain my relationship to her, so I introduced myself as her cousin. Given our resemblance, people bought the lie easily.

Then I accompanied her and her not-boyfriend to a nice, uncrowded coffee shop. I took my coffee and sat out of earshot. I called Tara, but it went to voicemail. I texted her instead.

> I miss you. Coming back in two days. Can't wait to see you.

When Riya was done talking, they got up and exchanged a brief, formal hug, which led her to cry a little. He put his hand on her shoulder. I let them finish before approaching. Then we dropped him off at home, and the driver took us to Amar's.

"Amar is leaving for Mumbai tomorrow," I said to Riya. "It will get a bit lonely."

"He's very quiet. Not like you. You're chatty."

"Is that good or bad?"

"It's good. I like chatty people."

"You've decided you like me, then?" I asked cheekily.

"No, but I have no choice, right?"

"You always do, Riya. If you have even the slightest hesitation about coming back with me, tell me. I won't do anything against your wishes. If you decide you want to come back to India after a year, we can work that out too. But I'm confident you'll have a good time there. And you'll love Tara. The two of you are so much alike."

"Who's Tara?"

My chest squeezed a little.

"Tara is my...well, you can sort of say she's my girlfriend, but she's more. She's my strength, my life. She's my *lover*," I said and grinned wide.

"Ew, Sameer! You have to stop using that word," she chided me.

I laughed. "How was your meeting with your not-boyfriend?"

"His name is Ayaan," she said haughtily. "It was good. I told him I liked him."

"Yeah?"

"He said he liked me too, but he thought I liked someone else."

"Wow, a triangle at thirteen?"

"No, I don't like that other guy. He's an assho—sorry."

"Don't worry, I'm a heavy swearer myself. Big on the F word."

She smiled. "This other guy, he's rich, good-looking, and he thinks the world revolves around him. He's insufferable. I can't believe Ayaan thought I could be interested in someone like him."

"I was him once," I confessed.

Her eyes widened. "But you don't seem that way now. What changed?"

"I met Tara."

She looked at me with kind eyes.

"Does she make you happy?"

"Very."

"That's good. I want everyone to be happy, including you. I don't want to see the sorrow I saw in Mumma's eyes ever again."

"Riya, I'm sorry about what I did to Sangita. And to you."

"Mumma said she understood. But I don't think I understand. Maybe you can explain it to me someday."

"Tell me what happened with Ayaan."

"Nothing much. I told him. We talked. He said he was sorry about Mumma and asked what I was going to do now. I told him I'd keep in touch over email. For the first time, I felt something in my stomach when he looked at me. Have you had that feeling?"

"Yes." I smiled. "But FYI, I'll be monitoring all your emails until you're eighteen, young lady."

"What? Absolutely not! I'll never give you my password."

"You don't need to. I have hacker friends." I didn't.

She pouted. "You are worse than Mumma."

TARA

$\mathcal{S}$ameer called early that morning, before I woke up. His text said he was coming home in two days. I him texted back.

> Can't wait to see you too

Two days felt like a week. The paintings had been appraised and cataloged. The exhibits had been shortlisted. The documentation was complete. As I went through the list of actions in my planner, I realized I had worked ahead of my timeline. I scheduled a meeting with Dr. Hadden to discuss prospects for a future collaboration. I had previously emailed other galleries and museums in the region about possible collaborations and consultation gigs, and I was in conversation with a private collector about appraising his collection. I tried to keep busy as I waited for Sameer's return.

Late afternoon two days later, I was at work when I got his text.

SAMEER

Just landed. Coming directly to yours.

I packed up for the day to return home. On my way back, I texted him.

Should I make dinner?

No

I entered my apartment, wringing my clammy hands. I was nervous about meeting Riya. Sameer had been worried about my acceptance of Riya, but what if *she* disliked *me*? Would it create a rift between Sameer and me? Had he given it any thought?

About an hour later, the doorbell rang. I was still in my work clothes, a silk blouse and flowy trousers, but I had refreshed my lipstick before rushing to the door. With a wide, albeit nervous, smile, I opened the door and saw Sameer with a young girl.

"Tara," he said, resting his hands on the girl's shoulders. "I want you to meet someone very special."

I looked at her. She looked back at me with Sameer's eyes, and my heart sank at the thought of her as a motherless child.

"This is my sister, Riya. Riya, this is Tara, the love of my life."

She gave me a tired smile. "He could *not* stop talking about you. But you are as pretty as he said."

"Hello, Riya. It's wonderful to meet you. Is it alright to give you a hug?"

She rushed to me with open arms, hugged me, and began crying. "Is she alright?" I mouthed to Sameer.

He nodded with a tired smile on his face.

"Well, Tara, I hope you're ready. We are going to my parents'. We're going to get Riya settled there, then have some amazing food cooked by Durgaben. What do you say?"

"Give me a few minutes to change?" I said, asking them to take a seat.

"Hey, pack an overnight bag, just in case," Sameer called as I started toward the bedroom.

A few minutes later, I walked out with them in a cool summer dress, a small bag in my hand.

"I'm so tired," Riya said from the backseat of Sameer's car.

"It will be a while before we reach the house. Why don't you take a nap?" Sameer suggested as we pulled out of the garage.

"I can't. I'm so nervous!" She looked at me. "I'm meeting my father and Sameer's mother for the first time."

I merely nodded. I didn't want to offer any false hope.

"There's nothing to be nervous about." Sameer looked at her in the rearview mirror. "That is your home now. You can be as bossy and boisterous as you want. I've got your back."

"Why can't I live with you?" She frowned. "You promised Mumma you'd take care of me."

"I'm at work all day, and my home is not equipped to handle boisterous young women. Except one," he added and winked at me. Heat rose to my cheeks.

"Shut up, Sameer!" I muttered under my breath.

"That's alright, she knows we are *lovers*."

"OMG," Riya said and sighed dramatically. "Tara, you *have* to get him to stop using that word. It's vulgar."

I laughed loudly. "You've finally met your match, I see."

"Yeah, now I have two stubborn women who hate my guts."

"Who're you calling a woman, old man?" Riya cried with an angry frown.

"She thinks I'm old," Sameer said to me.

"Well, you are old," I said, winking at Riya. She smiled and leaned in for a high-five.

"Are you two going to be ganging up on me?"

"Absolutely," I said, readjusting myself in the front seat.

With the sweetest smile, he mouthed, "I love you."

"I so totally heard that." Riya rolled her eyes in the back. I chuckled.

"You know, using *so* and *totally* in the same sentence is redundant," Sameer teased.

"You know what's redundant? Explaining redundancy."

I looked at Sameer with wide eyes. He gave me an "I know" look. We shared a smile as I saw her eyes gently droop.

Sameer held out his palm, and I put my hand in it.

"Lot of drama in your life, Sameer Rehani," I whispered when I was sure Riya was fast asleep.

"Not anymore. I'm going to tie up all loose ends today."

"You sound like a mafia boss planning on cleaning house."

"People aren't the loose ends in my life, Tara. Relationships are."

Riya stirred in the back, and we stopped talking. We drove the rest of the way in silence, with a satisfied smile resting on Sameer's face. I loved seeing him that way.

Durgaben's warm smile greeted us at the door when we arrived. She stood stunned for a moment when she saw Riya. Perhaps the resemblance struck her too. But she recovered quickly and invited us in. Aunty came rushing out and welcomed us. She gave Sameer and me a quick hug.

"Riya," she said, looking at the girl's nervous face. "Welcome to your new home."

Riya stepped closer to Sameer and started crying. He put his arm around her and led her to the living room. We followed. With Riya still recovering from her tears, we began talking. Aunty asked me about work, and I furnished details I didn't need to, just to fill the silence.

"You're an artist?" Riya's voice broke our conversation. I spotted admiration and wonderment in her teary eyes.

"Yes." I smiled.

"She's very good," Aunty chimed in.

"The best." Sameer beamed with pride.

"That's so cool!" she said softly, wiping her eyes.

"Let's eat something," Aunty suggested, using the opening to turn her attention to Riya, and led us to the kitchen.

Durgaben had laid out a colorful spread of white and green cucumber-chutney sandwiches, brown and red cookies, and crispy golden pakoras. The gentle aroma of tea infused with ginger and cardamom lingered in the kitchen, drawing in a cozy feeling.

"Do you drink tea, Riya?" Aunty asked.

"Sometimes Mumma lets me. Used to let me," she corrected.

"Well, you can have some if you want. But we also have fresh juice and milk if you prefer that."

"I will take some juice, please. Thank you," Riya said deferentially.

Aunty smiled. "This is your home, Beta. You don't have to say thank you. Learn from Sameer," she chided lovingly. "Behave like he does."

"Hey, I'm terribly well-behaved!" Sameer protested. Riya laughed, though her eyes remained tired and swollen.

We ate amid gentle conversation, and Riya began to relax. When Durgaben joined us at the table, I said, "The sandwiches are really good. I've missed the taste of this cilantro-mint chutney. You'll have to teach me how to make it."

"Yes, I love it too," Riya added.

"Anything you like, you let me know," Durgaben said to Riya. "I can make most things."

Sameer gave Durgaben a warm smile of gratitude, then excused himself. Aunty signaled me silently to follow him.

"Sameer." I caught up with him in the living room.

"Hey babe, I'll be back in a minute."

"Aunty asked me to come with."

He looked in the direction of the kitchen. "Are you both already conspiring against me?" he said with an amused frown, but he grabbed my hand anyway and led me to the other end of the house.

We walked in silence to his parents' bedroom. It was a palatial room with large, open bay windows overlooking a beautifully maintained garden. Sameer's father was seated in a large armchair with his eyes closed. He could've been asleep. I wasn't sure.

"Dad," Sameer said gently, dropping my hand and walking toward him.

He didn't stir. Sameer approached him and touched his arm. "Dad."

He opened his eyes, saw Sameer, and sat up. As he did, his gaze fell on me. He sat upright without acknowledging me.

"Riya is here," Sameer said softly. "Do you want to come out and welcome her?"

He looked out the window. "What is she doing here?" he asked.

"She's family, Dad," Sameer said looking at me, then turned back to his father. "I broke it off with Aarti."

"Yes, Bhatia called to hurl abuses at me. You threw away your future, son."

I shuffled in place.

"I threw away *your* future, Dad. Mine is standing right here beside me."

"Sangita is dead," his father said. It sounded like an allegation.

Sameer lowered his head. "Yes, but Riya is here. Come on, get up. Let's say hi to her," he coaxed.

Sameer's father made no effort to rise. Instead, he glared at me and beckoned me closer. I took a few halting steps toward him.

"Has he told you what he did?" he asked me. "You love him, don't you? You should know this about the man you love. He took away the only woman I loved in my life. He took my baby," he said, and began weeping.

I took a startled step back.

"He hauled me off like a piece of luggage. My baby was nine months old. He took away my happiness." He wept bitterly. "I hate him."

"Dad." Sameer squatted before him. "I was young and impetuous, and worried about Mom. But I did what you asked."

"After you left me penniless! How could I take care of my family without money? I lost everything, and you used it to force me away from them."

"I have apologized. To you, and Sangita and Riya. I know what I did was wrong. I was immature. But what about you? You betrayed Mom. You betrayed our trust in you, you had another family. Yet you've never apologized in all these years. Not to me. Not to Juhi. Not to Mom."

Sameer stood up and paced for a moment.

"You could've done it the right way. You could've divorced Mom, then married Sangita and had a proper family with her. But you didn't. You didn't because your fortune was tied up with us, with Mom, and you chose the coward's way out. Yes, I'm at fault for separating you from your other family, but it was your fault we were in that position in the first place."

His father turned his face away, with the stream of tears still going strong.

"Did you ask her, Dad? Did you ask Sangita what she wanted?" The older man's stubborn neck remained strained away from Sameer. "Did you consider why she asked for me instead of you during her last days?"

That brought his father's face swiveling back to Sameer.

"Because you assumed and imposed your will on her life. On Riya's life. She would've gladly accepted to live with a little less money if it meant living with you. I understand love, Dad. I understand its loss. I understand it perfectly now. I know you loved her. But you did it wrong. You chose the wrong family for the wrong reason. You were smart. You could've started over. Sangita and Riya didn't need your money. They needed you. But you needed the money and the comfort, didn't you? You've always blamed me for the loss of your love, but you were the reason I lost Tara. But this time, I choose Tara. I know what it will cost me, and I don't care."

His father looked at me, and I lowered my eyes. I had been unwittingly drawn into their family drama, but it was going to be my family now, along with all its drama. If he wanted me to leave, he gave no indication, so I remained planted in my place.

"I sought Sangita's forgiveness, as I have sought yours." Sameer's eyes moved from me to him again. "And she forgave me. But you've been so complacent, so unrepentant, lashing out at me for your decisions. Mom thinks you drink because you miss Sangita. But I know it's not her you miss. You miss the unchecked behavior. You sulk because you couldn't have it all. You couldn't have your marriage to Mom, keep your social status, *and* have your life with Sangita, whom you claimed to love. You are a farce, Dad. It is high time you stop blaming me and confront your own sins."

His father's head snapped up at those words. Sameer stared back at him, not in anger, but with apathy for his tears.

"Riya is waiting for you. She needs you. You have a second chance. Don't be selfish this time. And lay off the whisky, Dad. It's time to quit. Time to move on. Riya is here, and we've got thirteen years to make up for."

Sameer took a couple of steps toward me, then walked back to his father. He pulled out an envelope from his trouser pocket and extended his hand.

"Sangita wrote this letter for you. She told Riya to give it to you when she was gone."

His father's eyes welled up again as he took the letter from Sameer's hand.

Outside the bedroom, Sameer paused in the hallway to try and regain his composure.

"Are you alright, my jaan?" I whispered and placed a hand on his chest. The thud of his heart against my palm sounded as loud as the whoosh of blood in my own head.

He took my hand and kissed it. "I've been wanting to say that for so many years. I didn't think I'd ever get a chance."

"Your hand is cold," I whispered.

"Yes. But I'm alright now." He pulled himself upright into his handsome figure and threaded his fingers through mine. "I'm so glad you're here," he said as we walked back to the kitchen.

"Dad is on his way," he announced with a smile when we were back at the table. "He was taking a nap."

Durgaben got up to make more tea.

"I'll have some too, please," I said, hoping the strong tea would help calm my jitters from having witnessed the father-son encounter.

"So, Riya," I began. "What do you say we go shopping this weekend?"

Her eyes brightened. "Where?"

I smiled at Sameer. "We can start at the snooty mall."

"Yes, sure. That's what I am earning for, so my sister and my girlfriend can spend it all on clothes and shoes."

"Don't stereotype us, Sameer," Riya chided. "We're going to shop for books and art supplies, right, Tara?"

She winked.

We laughed. Aunty's face had relaxed now. I looked at her and smiled. She patted my hand. "And don't brag because Tara earns too," she added proudly.

"Wow, now the three of you gang up on me!" Sameer threw up his hands theatrically, but our eyes were on the figure behind him. His father walked up to us and smiled, his eyes red and swollen.

"Riya," he said with a smile. She looked around the table for cues on how to react to him. Sameer got up and stood behind her chair.

"Riya," he said, gently holding her shoulders. "This is Dad. Our Dad."

She burst into tears. "You can hug him if you want." He bent down and whispered in her ear. But she didn't budge. She just kept crying.

Her father moved toward her and placed a light hand on her shoulder. Suddenly, she jumped up, as if his touch was the validation she was waiting for, and fell into his arms. They both wept uninhibitedly. Then we all cried a little. Behind those tears, I saw the smiles waiting to shine through like the rainbow after a storm.

After a light, animated dinner, we retired for the night. I was hesitant to join Sameer in his room and coyly asked his mother if I could use the same room as last time.

She gave me a mischievous smile. "Whatever works for you," she said before proceeding to help Riya settle in.

They had prepared a beautiful, large room on the second floor for her, overlooking the backyard. We helped her unpack and organize her clothes in the closet. I asked her to make a list of personal care items she would need so we could buy them on our weekend shopping spree. After making sure she had settled in comfortably, Sameer and I retired to his room.

"I should really spend the night in the other room, for the sake of appearances, at least."

"Who's judging?" he asked with a frown. "My parents know we're banging. Durgaben and Riya don't care."

"OMG, that's so crude and vulgar."

"Oh yeah?" He pulled me closer, his arms around my waist. "I thought you liked crude and vulgar in bed."

"Stop it, Sameer," I said, pushing him away as he tickled me.

He stopped and kissed my cheek. He held me from behind and exhaled against my neck, a feeling I had come to cherish in the past few weeks. It relaxed me.

"You heard what happened. You know most of it now," he began. "Remember when I told you Dad had incurred massive debts. He had used that money to set up his alternate life. A house, a lifestyle, the baby. He couldn't use the money he had because it could be traced, and Mom would notice it was gone. What he hadn't predicted was his removal from the CEO position. He hoped to repay the debts slowly, with small amounts. If he had been diligent, he could actually have pulled off the whole 'two families, two lives' thing. But he was so enamored with his new life that he began forsaking his duties at the company. It was humiliating to find out that your father was living with another woman barely a decade older than you. Then to find out that he had fathered a child with her! I was furious. I called her every bad name in the language. I called Riya a bastard. Illegitimate."

I could hear his voice choke a little. I placed my hand on his.

"No child is illegitimate," I said softly. He squeezed my hand.

"I hate myself for what I did. I was so angry. We had lost everything. Ma still doesn't know that Dad was ready to quit our family for his new one. I told him he could go live with them and figure out his own life. He had nothing—no assets, no savings. Or he could come with us, and I'd make sure Sangita and Riya would never want for anything. I used the leverage of the money he had invested in my mother's and my name to blackmail him into giving them a secure life. When I asked him to choose between love and money, he chose money. He drinks to forget, and the only thing that kept him going all these years was thinking of ways to ruin me."

My heart breaking, I turned to face him.

"He told me he orchestrated my surprise engagement to Aarti

because he knew I was in love with you, and he didn't want to see me happy. He wanted to see me in a loveless marriage like the one he thinks he's in. He claims I took away his love, so he tried to take away mine."

"Sameer, why did your mom stay? Why didn't she leave?"

"She didn't want to be the wife whose husband left her for a younger woman. He was rightfully hers, not Sangita's, she said. But somewhere, I suspect, she still loves him. Some part of him, at least. I don't understand it, but I did what I thought was right for her at the time."

I cupped his cheeks. "It's all in the past. We're here now. All we can do is make a better, more loving future for Riya. For everyone, right?"

He kissed my hand. "I couldn't have done it without you, Tara. No one else would've supported me and loved me after learning all this."

"You don't know that," I said. "You don't know how people will behave unless they're put in that situation."

"You always look on the bright side of things, don't you? Always looking for the good in people."

I smiled.

"If you didn't, you probably wouldn't have seen the tiny bit of good in me when we met. There wasn't much there—"

I shut him up with a kiss. That night, it felt thrilling and rebellious to have sex under his parents' roof.

EPILOGUE

TARA

Two Years Later

$\mathcal{I}$ stood in the living room in front of an easel, trying to capture the Dallas skyline against a brilliant orange-red-pink sky, when multiple devices began ringing and buzzing in the condo. Annoyed, I answered my phone first.

It was Dr. Hadden, asking after my health. She had become a friend since I moved to Dallas, but I still couldn't bring myself to call her Sylvia. I kept the conversation brief when I saw my mother calling from India on my tablet's video app. I swiped it open while Sameer's cell continued ringing.

"Hi, Aai," I said, as my mother's dewy morning face appeared on the screen. "Let me call you back in a few minutes. I'm finishing up a painting."

"Bara." She smiled and hung up, and my phone rang again.

It was my agent calling about another gallery that wanted to showcase my work. Meanwhile, Sameer's phone kept ringing incessantly.

"Sameer!" I called out in frustration as I ended that call. "Answer your phone."

I picked up my brush and palette and returned to the canvas as a wet Sameer came rushing out, a towel around his waist.

"You're dripping all over the house. Why don't you carry your phone in with you?" I cried with an angry frown.

He hugged me with his wet body and tousled his hair to spray water on me, infuriating me further. I was eight months pregnant, and I don't know if it was the hormones or just his annoying habits that ticked me off at that moment.

He looked at the screen and rolled his eyes before swiping it open to put it on speaker. It was Riya.

"Hey, bro, I'm calling for Tara. She's not answering her phone."

"Hey sweetheart," I said with the brush in my right hand and the palette in my left as Sameer held the phone near me. "I was on another call. What's up?"

"Why are you still calling her Tara?" Sameer interjected. "We've been married for almost two years now. Call her Bhabhi." He winked at me, knowing it would annoy her.

"Ugh, bro, that's so passé! Tara is too young for me to call her Bhabhi," she argued.

"Bhabhi is a relationship. It has nothing to do with age."

"Bro, please, can I talk to her?"

"And what's with this bro business? Where are you picking up this language?"

"Seriously, dude?" she screamed.

Sameer frowned. "Did you just call me dude?"

"Ignore him, Riya. Tell me why you called."

"I'm going dancing with friends, and I need new clothes. Will you take me shopping?"

"You're going dancing where?" Sameer demanded. "And with whom?"

"Ugh, Tara, can you please take me off the speaker? I can't talk to him like this."

I smiled, put my brush down, and took the phone from his hand. We talked for a bit and decided to meet up for a quick shopping trip on Saturday, followed by lunch somewhere.

"Do you know how much I love you?" Sameer asked when I handed him his phone. He touched the scar on my left eyebrow and dropped a kiss on it.

"I do." I smiled and picked up the brush again, looking out at the horizon. I had lost the picture I was planning to paint, but another silhouette had taken shape.

"The picture has changed," I said. "It's even more beautiful now."

Sameer placed his hands on my belly, and we stood together, watching the day's last light paint dark purple and red hues above the lights of the city.

THE END

ACKNOWLEDGMENTS

First things first, if it weren't for my friend Dr. Amanda Lewis-Nang'ea, I wouldn't have considered taking up writing as a full-time occupation. Some years ago, during one of our afternoon tea chats in the beautiful Carlisle, she casually mentioned that if she could, she would spend all her days writing. Two years later, I was presented with another chance to do what I love, and I found Amanda's words echoing in my heart. I haven't looked back since.

In the same spirit, I want to thank my first Ph.D. adviser, Professor Thomas Pantham, who taught me *how* to write. His wise, pithy advice to write in short, clear, crisp sentences has stayed with me through my academic career and my fiction writing journey. His training has certainly made me a better thinker.

This work represents an amalgamation of blessings. The first among them are my beautiful parents, Smita and Sanjiv, who let me read to my heart's content and never stopped me from becoming who I wanted to be. They value my opinion, cherish my intellect, brag about my accomplishments, yet somehow manage to keep me humble. Great job, Mumma and Daddy! I love you more than I can put down in words.

It takes great fortune to have people in your inner circle with whom you can share the raw first draft of your work without fear of being judged. Dr. Himika Nangia, Dr. Skylar Bre'z, and Dr. J. Brendan Shaw are three such friends in my life. Three brilliant minds who hold me up while providing crucial feedback on my work. Thank you for always being in my corner. And to Dipti Mahesh and Aditi Kalra for helping me craft the book blurb. Your honesty and love is something I can always count on.

My book wouldn't be in this shape without the help of two great editors, Dionne McCullough and Sherri Shackleford. I was fortunate to have my work end up on their desks. Their insightful comments and suggestions not only helped polish my writing but made this debut novel more sophisticated in tone and content. I also thank Zuchal Rosyidin for the gorgeous cover art, and Steve Kuhn for getting the interior design to perfection.

Writing might be a solitary endeavor, but a social being like me needs the cocoon of friendship at the end the day. I take this opportunity to thank all my friends in India, Dallas, and elsewhere in the U.S. for keeping me sane. I have basked in your love, and grown. And to my sister, Deepa, with whom I still joke, gossip, and giggle, thank you for keeping me young.

True love, they say, is hard to come by, a true partner even harder. But my faith in romance and love is reinstated every single day by Vaibhav, my lover, husband, partner, critic. You remain the standard against which I measure the male leads of my novels. They have to be at least as good-looking as you, and just as kind, generous, and sensible—a true partner material for my strong-headed heroines. I want to thank you for being all this to me, and more.

This note would not be complete without a mention of Aadi, the kind boy who proudly declared his mom a writer when she only had a rough first draft on her computer. You make me laugh and fall in love with my life every day. I wouldn't be here without you cheering me on. Here's hoping someday I get to write a foreword to your novel. Keep writing and inspiring me.

ABOUT THE AUTHOR

Varsha Chitnis is an award-winning author of heartfelt, angsty romance.

Born in Mumbai, Varsha grew up in the beautiful city of Baroda. Through her Ph.Ds. in Political Science and Women's, Gender, and Sexuality Studies, and a fulfilling teaching career, she has remained a storyteller at heart. She loves writing about South Asian characters and their multifaceted lives. Her work combines romance with high drama and sizzling heat. Her debut novel won the *Indieverse Award for Best Romance*.

Varsha enjoys baking a little more than she should. She loves jewelry, and is seldom spotted without her big, oversized earrings, and her trademark bright lipstick. She has lived in several places in the U.S. and currently calls California her home.

You can find out more about her writing at
varshachitnis.com.

BOOKS BY VARSHA CHITNIS

The Art of Taking Second Chances
The Rules of Playing with Fire
The Ex Factor

WRITING AS VARSHA C.
Un/Bound